# MARY GEORGE
## OF ALLNORTHOVER

# Mary
# George of
# Allnorthover

L A V I N I A  G R E E N L A W

*Houghton Mifflin Company*

Boston   New York

2001

Visit our Web site: www.houghtonmifflinbooks.com.

Library of Congress Cataloging-in-Publication Data

Greenlaw, Lavinia, date.
    Mary George of Allnorthover / Lavinia Greenlaw.
        p.    cm.
    ISBN 0-618-09523-3
    1. Teenage girls—Fiction.   2. Inheritance and succession—
Fiction.   3. Courtship—Fiction.   4. England—Fiction.
I. Title.
PR6057.R375 M3    2001
823'.914—dc21                              2001016913

Book design by Anne Chalmers
Typeface: Electra

Printed in the United States of America
QUM 10 9 8 7 6 5 4 3 2 1

For my daughter,
GEORGIA,
turning thirteen

The death of earth is
to become water, and
the death of water to
become air, and of air,
fire, and the reverse.
—Heraclitus

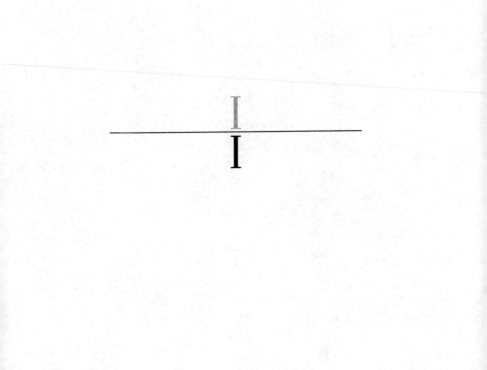

I

ON 28TH JUNE 197–, Mary George of Allnorthover was seen to walk on water. It has to be said that the only witness was Tom Hepple, who was mad and had been away from the village for ten years until he turned up that very day, shouting. Mary had always been thought of as a peculiar child, but not one to seek attention. She had neither grace nor mystery and could not have wanted to become Tom Hepple's angel, especially not the restoring angel he was looking for.

The house that Mary George woke up in was not one she knew. It was part of a straggle of Victorian cottages leading down to the station in Crouchness, built quickly from cheap brick that had now vitrified. The walls resisted hammers and drills, shed plaster, spat out nails and picture hooks. The rooms were low and dark. The front door led, in two steps, to a squat staircase at the top of which were two bedrooms Mary never saw. She had slept in a corner of the living room, which was sallow and square.

The night before had been someone's party. There were half a dozen people on the floor around her, including the boy who had been holding her hand as he closed his eyes. The others lay at odd angles, not touching, bent to whatever space they had found between the slippery three-piece suite, upon which nobody had attempted to rest, and the smoked-glass coffee table. Where the shaggy carpet had been scorched, its nylon thread was gluey and fused. The floor was scattered with crumpled cans and plastic cups half full of dog ends and vinegary dregs. There was a bowl of cornflakes someone must have thought they wanted.

Mary sat up and reached into the bag she had used for a pillow. The right lens of her glasses was cracked, but she put them on anyway and moved towards the boy. He lay on his front, sweating gently inside what might have been his grandfather's pinstripe suit. Mary crouched over him, her left eye squinting behind the one good lens. He had pulled up his right leg and stretched his right arm forward. As if swimming or flying, she thought. Mary studied the bones of his wrist and ankle, exposed by the too-short suit. His long fingers had a delicacy at odds with their large, rough knuckles.

The boy's hair was thick and wavy, both dark and fair. It was brown where it was shaved high at the back of his neck and blond in the matted fringe that obscured most of his face. He was flushed and open-mouthed. Mary concentrated hard and, steadying her glasses with one hand, moved the other towards his cracked lips. In the sour still air of the room, the rush of his breath startled her. She lost her balance and fell back, knocking over a tower of beer cans. Their clatter was surprisingly dull, and Mary had stuffed her glasses in her pocket and left before anyone else had properly opened their eyes.

Crouchness sat on the point of the estuary where clay gave way to mud. It was the first or last stop on the London line, a town built on fishing and coastal trade, now propped up by light industry—packaging, canning, and printing. The clapboard sail lofts perched on stilts along the shore were empty, too high to live in and too draughty to use as stores. The locals had been expert sailors in these shallow waters. They had known how to navigate the narrow passages between the sandbars that riddled the low-lying east coast. They had hauled in so much herring, some had been barrelled, salted, and exported to Russia. In the summer they had crewed on yachts, their local knowledge keeping the gentry from getting stranded. They had earned enough to buy their own homes.

There were boats still, a handful of dinghies owned by local lawyers and doctors, a couple of dredgers and a lightship that had become obsolete five years ago and was left moored in the docks, a heavy-bottomed ark slumped in the mud at low tide.

Mary walked down to the shore and out along a path on top of the dike. The ground here was neither earth nor mud but something in between, greasy, compacted, and dark. It was five o'clock in the morning, bright and warm in a tired, dusty way, like the end of a hot day rather than the beginning. Soon this heat would concentrate itself once again and people would get out of bed to open windows that were already open.

Mary had slept in all her clothes: a heavy ink-blue twenty-year-old dress and a stringy dark-red cardigan she had knitted out of synthetic mohair on the biggest needles she could find. It had no buttons and so she habitually clutched its edges together in her fist. She pulled the cardigan off and stuffed it in her bag, an army-surplus knapsack with a slipping strap. It came loose and banged around her knees as she walked. Her feet sweltered in heavy boots. She tried wearing her glasses again, but seeing the cracked path and wilted grass made her feel even hotter, so she put them away. Squinting back inland, Mary could not tell the creeks and the banks apart, they ran in and out of one another so and nothing shone in a way that suggested water. The town was a blur of grey, like a model waiting to be painted. It had long been stripped of its colour by salt and the winds that blew in "straight from Siberia," as everyone said, not wanting to think such icy cold could be local.

The mud gave off a stink of burning tyres, ammonia, diesel, and harshly treated sewage, nothing natural. What life there was, was amorphous, useless: lugworms and silted shrimp. Farther up where the coast broadened out into the sea and the edge of dry land was definable, there were lobsters, samphire, and crab. Boats put out to sea and did battle with Icelandic fishermen over cod. That was where people went to open their lungs. Crouchness had the only kind of sea air Mary really knew and she tried hard not to breathe it.

It was almost six o'clock. Mary turned back towards the town, hoping for the milk train. When she got to the top of the station road, she found she didn't want to pass the house where the party had been. The boy might have woken. They had been sitting together on the floor talking. Each time their eyes met it was harder and for longer, and then there had been a few vague kisses during which his hand moved to stroke her cheek, then dropped to her thigh, and they had both stopped and looked down. He stared, as if the hand on this strange girl's skirt were nothing to do with him. Mary stared, too, wondering if she should move it, and if so, where to? By the time she had got up the courage to hold his hand, he had fallen asleep, and she stared at their hands until her eyes closed, too.

There was a row of allotments on the embankment through which Mary could reach the railway track and then the station. She climbed over the gate and collected peas and raspberries, stuffing some in her mouth and some in her pockets. They tasted like steel wool. She wandered along the narrow mown strips that separated each plot. Clipped borders, raked earth, intricate constructions of bamboo, netting, and tags were maintained by gardeners unwilling to alter their routine according to the failure of their enterprise— blown courgette plants, yellow lettuces, tightly curled buds that had been scorched before they could open. Mary caught her leg on a tap hidden in a clump of grass. She rinsed off the blood, cupped her hands under the trickle of water, and drank. It was tepid and tasted of lead, as if it had been tinned years ago.

At the track, mindful of the live rail, Mary put on her glasses. Nothing suggested electricity. At least seeing made her feel she could hear, so she would know if a fast train was going to swoop round the bend, blaring out of silence without warning, to catch her as it had caught the child whose bicycle had got stuck or the boy who had fallen while spray-painting a bridge or the woman who had just lain down. But who were they? No one she'd met had ever known them. They were just good stories. Mary crept over the lines.

The ticket office was closed. The guards' room and toilets had been padlocked and abandoned. There was a waiting room with a door jammed only just open. Its one high window was locked, broken, and brown, as if someone had taken the stale chocolate from the vending machine and smeared it all over the glass. There were timetables, but it was too dim to read them, and there was no bulb in the fitting that dangled from the ceiling.

A goods train came through with two passenger carriages attached. Three people got out, the heavy doors slamming behind them with a lethargic clunk. Mary climbed on board. The luggage rack above her sagged like an old string vest, the walls of the carriage were waxy and peeling, and the seat smelt of cardboard and milk. This is like travelling in the back of a cupboard, she thought. She tugged at the window till it gave an inch, then fell asleep.

The train turned back on itself, inland along the estuary with its cargo from the industrial estate of Crouchness: bundles of angling magazines, promotional packs for a new car, dog biscuits, gift jars of sea salt, and printed T-shirts. All this had been brought to the town as paper, ink, bonemeal, cotton, minerals, bottles, and labels. It came with instructions, was put together and sent back again; nothing was made or remained in Crouchness, let alone thought of there. This was the milk train, but it carried no milk, which was delivered by tanker. Sacks of post were still thrown on and off at stations near main sorting offices, but most of that, too, now travelled by road. So there were fewer trains each year and the rolling stock was left to seize up on the sidings, to struggle through these slow, pernickety journeys, stopping at empty platforms and once in a while, at dawn on a Saturday morning, bringing a girl like Mary nearer to home.

Once out of the marshes, the train continued its stop-and-start journey through the inland towns. The flatness of this country was suited to the new large-scale arable farming. Trees had been felled, hedgerows pulled up, ditches filled, footpaths shaved away. A single field could be all there was in sight. The only interruptions were those forced by the twisting lanes, the untidy hamlets and scattered woods. Around here, things had always been small-scale, local, instinctive. To the north, the land was even flatter. There were long stretches of Roman road, few trees, and even fewer houses. The farming was better there.

As the land had been opened and pared away, the old buildings of the landowners once again dominated the view: extravagant brick chimneys and wooden belfreys embellished manor houses, farms and churches that had been poised to be seen and to be able to see for miles. In a place like this, though, distance was more vertical than horizontal. Nothing could look important under such huge skies.

The guard made his way down the train. He was sure that someone had got on and that they would not have a ticket. He opened the sliding door, sauntered through, and stood in front of the sleeping girl, rocking on his heels like a policeman savouring a trivial caution. He paused for a moment, wondering which excuse she would try: the dropped ticket, the lost purse, passing herself off as foreign or dumb. Or asleep? Was that it? Those ones usually overdid it, though, giving themselves away with little touches like snoring or a dropped book. This girl was hunched in the corner of her seat, her head propped on her knees, her hands in fists clenched in her skirt. She looked like someone waiting for a bomb to drop; so much unlike anyone sleeping that the guard was inclined to believe she really was. He shook his head at this small, bony creature dressed up in clothes that were too big and too tatty, and those ridiculous boots. She would trip over everything. She had a slapdash boy's haircut and a furious face. He was about to laugh, cough, and wake her up, but had left it too long. He could not think what to do, so turned round and crept away.

Mary woke up as the train pulled into Ingfield, from where she could walk the three miles home. She followed a string of pylons to the reservoir, along unsigned footpaths shaved to ridges. Withered stalks scratched at her legs. The earth was going to be changed by this drought for ever. The deep clay that had sealed these parts in the wake of a glacier thousands of years ago was now brittle and fractured. Powdery topsoil lay across the surface like dust. When the weather finally broke, it would be blown or washed away.

There was a point where this landscape buckled on a chalk seam and rose and fell in a ridge. Mary climbed and found herself looking down onto the conifers that shielded the water. From up here, she could see the bleached concrete rim that ran along that side of the reservoir's basin. The water was hard to get to. A chain-link fence ran around most of the perimeter and there were just two gates—one for those with fishing or sailing permits and one for the Water Board. At the point closest to the road, there was a path leading to a viewing platform. The noticeboard on the platform offered a key to the birds that could be seen there: cormorants, herring gulls, herons, and Canada geese—seabirds, migratory birds, making do. There was a list of statistics, too, that explained how many cubic metres of water served how many businesses and homes, how much earth had been moved and concrete poured, and how many trees had been planted.

Mary remembered her father coming on a visit when she was ten. It was March, around her birthday. Her mother, Stella, had taken her to Ingfield to meet him. Matthew had arrived with a thermos and a pair of binoculars, and reminded her that a year earlier she had declared herself interested in birds. He drove her out to the reservoir, where they stood in silence on the viewing platform in the searing wind, fumbling the binoculars between them with deadened fingers. To break the silence, Matthew pretended to have seen a heron. When this didn't excite Mary, he spotted a kingfisher, then a hummingbird. "Look! Look!" he had implored, but she wouldn't join in, wouldn't pretend, and had refused to take the binoculars from him.

Tom Hepple held his breath, but still his heart would not slow. He tried not to gulp air as his arms curled and his hands went dead. He leant hard back against the tree, wanting to feel his spine, to know he had bones and could stay standing and would not break. His heart was beating so fast it had to burst, it would be a relief if it burst. When it seemed it might, there was a hollow pause followed by erratic threes and fours, not a light palpitating skitter now but slow hard thumps, like bubbles rising in something solid, a knot surfacing in a piece of wood. This was worse than anything.

He had known about the water and had come back knowing what he would see: no Goose Farm, no Easter Bank, no home. Tom knew, too, that there would be concrete, fences, fir trees, and a bowl of water that stopped the eye in its tracks. These were places where you traced a slope up and over but not down, because a bowl of water stopped you, cut across your vision, and, even when there was no reflection, turned you hard back on yourself. Reservoirs never became part of things. The eye told you first and then the land. You could walk, as Tom had just done, to the water, and look, there were fish and waterfowl, and the trees grew happily over the edge, but it didn't make sense. Least of all here, where the world was flat and the dip below Ingfield Rise had been a place to get out from under the sky.

Tom was scared. If he could just find the house, know where it was. He crouched down and pushed his hands into the earth, wanting to feel the full force of the world push back and steady him, but last year's leaves and pine needles were loose dust. He felt the bubbles escape his chest and press into every part of his body. He tried to hold harder to the earth. I will float away, he thought, as each wave of panic left him with less and less sense of himself. I do not work, I am not flesh, I am light and air exploding.

And although Tom believed this, he settled slowly back into himself, his hands were his hands again and his heart forgotten. He decided to try once more. The hard light hurt his eyes as he emerged from the dullness of the trees. He concentrated, turning his head from right to left until he could be sure that there was the Ridge and Temple Grove marking the edge of Factory Field. He followed the land down without thinking and fixed his gaze on the point where the house should be, just past the fishing jetty, only five yards or so out now that the water level was so low. He walked towards it, bumping and stumbling but looking neither away nor down. It was no good, there was nothing to fix on, just the inscrutable dazzle of sun on water. The harder he stared, the more it kept shifting and shimmering and pushing him away. Tom reached the jetty and made for the shadows beneath it.

As well as being shortsighted, Mary had no sense of direction. More accurately, she had a strong sense of counter-direction and would set off across country absolutely sure of herself, walking miles the wrong way. On the way home with her best friend, Billy Eyre, she would argue fiercely about which path to take, which corner of a field the stile would be in, that the road they wanted lay just beyond it. She was always wrong, and Billy would put up a fight but secretly encourage her, enjoying the angry surprise on her face and the sulky calm that followed. He would go as far out of their way as she led him.

This morning Mary was tired, and although it was only eight o'clock, the sky was not easy to look up into. She had walked for a mile without going wrong, as if not thinking about it kept her from losing her way. Beyond the reservoir was Temple Grove, which gave out onto the Verges, which would in turn lead her home. The simplest thing to do was to walk round the water. It might be cooler, too. Mary made her way through the trees and found what was called the Other Gate, not the locked entrance to which licensed anglers had a key but a panel of the fence a little farther along that had been expertly loosened and replaced. Even those with keys found it easier to reach the jetty this way, especially now that the lock on the real gate had grown so stiff. Mary heaved the panel a little to one side and slipped through.

The drought forced things open, and they gave up whatever was once liquid inside them: the parched trees smelt of resin, the fence of solder, and the jetty of creosote. The reservoir, though, had withdrawn into itself. Mary took off her boots, walked to the end of the jetty, and sat down on the edge, but it was no good, her feet could not reach the water. She walked along to a clump of trees.

Mary and Billy used to climb out along a low bough here. He would watch her take off her shoes and glasses and walk swiftly to the end, only to have to come back, take him by the hand, and inch him along. Mary tried to explain how she could make herself light and steady by not looking, by insisting that there could be no wrong step, what it was to keep moving, not knowing when she had left the bank and was out over the water. Billy had tried once, without success, to get her to do it with her glasses on.

A girl had appeared in the tree over the house. She was standing up straight on the low bough, her arms spread wide. In quick, small steps she reached the end. Tom's eyes followed her, went past, and looked down and there was something, a shadow, like the darkening colour of a sudden change of depth. As Tom stared, the shadow took on shape, and then it wasn't shadow but a house, lingering like a deep-sea creature uncertainly beneath the surface. Its slate roof glittered for a moment and was gone, but the girl was still there, not in the tree now but farther out, where the roof had been, on the water.

A pale thing with cropped hair; a child in an old blue dress that might have been his mother's. She was somehow in suspension, utterly concentrated but also on the verge of slipping away. Tom started to walk towards her, terrified he would make her disappear. Don't move, he begged her silently, not till I get there and see where you are. But then he was crying and could not see, and the sun shifted, enlarged, glared, and somehow he had closed his eyes, and when he opened them he was by the tree and there was a barefooted girl but she was beside him.

"You frightened me." She leaned a little towards him, squinted, and frowned. "Oh! I'm sorry, I didn't recognise you." He didn't look up. "Are you in pain? Have you hurt your eyes?"

"Are you from here?" His voice was an uncertain roar. He had spoken to no one for days.

"Oh! I'm afraid . . . I thought you were someone . . . I'm sorry!" Embarrassed, and a little frightened, Mary turned and half walked, half ran to the jetty.

Tom could not move and did not know what to ask, but just as she disappeared he realised: "I know you!"

Mary, pushing on her glasses and throwing her boots over her shoulder, scrambled up through the trees and squeezed through the Other Gate. She heard another croaking shout as the loose panel fell to the ground with a clatter and twang, like tired percussion. She ran up the track, her bag banging against her knees, one hand pushing her glasses back up her nose. She stopped to shove her feet into her boots. There was no sign of him following, but Mary cut across Factory Field. Her panic was so great that she felt her body drag, as if the corn were as tall as it should have been and she was having to fight her way through slapping waves. She stumbled over the stile and down into the road.

As soon as Mary turned the first corner, she began to calm down. Her cheeks stung, each gulp of air caught like chaff in her throat, and she could run no farther. It was the reservoir that had panicked her, she decided, its artificial plantations and still water, not that man who looked so worried and ill. Her mother would have held his hand and talked to him in her cool, soothing way. Mary knew what that felt like: like being rescued not by an angel but by a statue of an angel, and folded in marble wings; and she had mistaken the man for someone she had thought of as a statue, too, when she was a child, a church saint or an effigy on a tomb.

Mary skirted Temple Grove, a copse of spindly, tangled hazel, ash, and willow: useful, adaptable, flexible trees that had been part of a parcel of land given to the Knights Templar after the first Crusade. The Knights learnt Euclidean geometry from the Arabic and applied it to the building of their barns. While their wattle-and-daub farmhouses had lurched, buckled, and been pulled down, these barns, with their perfectly balanced angles, were still standing. Nothing so regular had been built until the new houses after the last war, tessellated arrangements that had everything to do with numbers.

The Knights had prospered for a hundred years in austerity and chastity before the parish turned on them, when the Crusades failed, with accusations of idolatry, homosexuality, and child murder. There was still a whiff of that six-hundred-year-old scandal about the place. Saplings struggled through nettles and brambles, only to give up before they emerged from the shadows. The wood was dark and difficult to find a way into. Those who wanted to walk their dogs, pick blackberries or bluebells, or tire out their children, went out through the other end of Allnorthover and into the Setts, a solid wildwood of oak, chestnut, and beech with wide paths and clearings, National Trust signs, and bamboo and rhododendrons that made it seem like nothing more than an overgrown garden.

Temple Grove was where you went to build a den, try your first cigarette, and, later, to drink cider round a fire, smoke dope, and scare each other with stories about the Man in the Van and his goats, or about the day someone found a makeshift altar here, three bales of straw, a black candle, and a chicken's foot. Billy and Mary had done these things and had heard all the stories. Neither of them knew who was supposed to have found the altar, but they believed it. Once, they had found a full set of women's clothing, including bra and knickers, next to three old sofa cushions. The cushions had been ripped open and scorched.

At some recent critical point, Temple Grove had become too small to hold secrets. It lost a little more of itself each year as the farmers pushed the fields harder against it. Children went in knowing they could be out in under a minute, that they could always be heard and could hear their friends calling from the road or the field. Ingfield Dip was full of water, the grove was half gone, mile after mile of hedgerow was being uprooted, and clusters of new houses were springing up all around, with new windows from which to be seen. Where was there to go now, not to be visible?

There were people living right next to the grove now, too. The

Strouds had sold off land for a caravan site called Temple Park that the villagers preferred to think didn't really exist. But like the hospital, the courts, or the Social Security office, most people had a connection with the place at some time or other: a friend or relative needing a cheap rent or placed there by the Council. The village was growing older as the old lived longer and the young moved away. Like the two cemeteries, the almshouses were full. A senile widower, a pregnant daughter, all those who might have been cast out or taken in, or sent to an institution, another town, another country, found themselves here. They lived quietly and came to the village as little as possible, mostly to get the prescriptions that helped them sleep, walk, or breathe.

The caravans were set at odd and irregular angles, as if to suggest some spontaneous arrangement or natural development. Packed close together, they were turned away from each other as much as possible, and were painted in unobtrusive shades of pale green, beige, and grey that matched the worn grass, gravel, and cement that defined each plot. The caravan dwellers took on this drabness and were recognised by it. They made cramped, effortful gestures and their skin had a greenish tinge, as if they brought with them the light of their evenings squeezed close to their televisions.

When the heatwave started, they began to leave their doors open all night. Then they took to unclipping their tubular aluminium folding tables and chairs and taking them outside. They began to have their meals outdoors, first in the evenings and then at breakfast, too. They neither disturbed nor joined each other. Couples sat down as usual to talk about the children, the bills, a holiday, an illness, or the weather. They would remain, only yards apart, within the privacy of their small square of grass. The heat opened the pores of their skin; sweat made them conscious of their breasts, bellies, and thighs; their clothes were tight or heavy. The secrets, confessions, and ultimatums that might have surfaced got stuck. No marriages were saved or broken. By the end of June, the tables were making way each evening for mattresses, Lilos, and camp beds, but

15

only after dark. At dawn, everyone crept indoors to dress with the guilt and pleasure they might have got from staying out all night unexpectedly.

Mary crept along the paved road that wound from one end of the site to the other. She passed a couple folding up their camp beds and a young mother gathering sheets, her naked baby fast asleep on a pillow beside her. If they were taken aback by Mary's presence, she didn't notice. She probably didn't even see them. Mary's glasses were the smallest, least obtrusive she could find, but still they weighed upon her heavily. There was too much, anyway, between her and the world, without those thick lenses. They corrected her vision, but she could not feel what she could see. So Mary tended to keep her head down and imagine.

Beyond Temple Park was a small breaker's yard, the size of a meadow in which a family might keep a pony. It was just a worn-out patch of oil-stained earth, now dried and cracked and hardened by the heat. There were always a few cars dumped along the back hedge, mostly those that were too big, too small, or too gimmicky, a Humber perhaps or a Robin Reliant. Some were picked away, scavenged for spare parts; others rusted and sank into the ground. The yard belonged to Fred Spence, a compact and taciturn man who lived with his wife in one of the smallest, oldest caravans in Temple Park. He kept a filthy truck parked in the yard and drove away in it early each morning. Fred was often gone all day, but rarely brought anything back. Mostly he dealt in incidental scrap—guttering, a trailer, a gate, pipes.

Fred Spence's wife spent her days cleaning, and when her home was done, she'd scrub and polish the outside of his "office," a tiny outhouse with a single window. She was not allowed inside, nor were Fred's customers. On the rare occasions that money changed hands in the yard, Fred entered his office and opened the window to receive it. Dorothy Spence was not allowed to touch the truck either.

In those long days of fierce light, Dorothy Spence could not stop thinking about glass and, in particular, windows. It had become too hot to keep cleaning her home, so she worked on the outside, preferring the parts that gave her a glimpse in. Mary George met her at the yard gate. She barely recognised the woman she saw on the bus into town with her line of lipstick and bright hat and gloves. To Mary, without these accessories, Dorothy Spence had no mouth or hair or hands.

"You're the George girl? I thought you were your brother."

"I have no brother."

"Sometimes you look like him."

"Can I help you carry those?"

Dorothy Spence took a step back. "Thank you." She shook her head, scrutinising Mary, before adding, "You need a good wash, my girl," and was satisfied when the child did not protest. She walked carefully away, a bucket of dusters, brushes, and cleaning fluid in either hand. Mary watched her begin to polish the windscreen of a crumpled Ford Cortina.

Mary's pale face was lit with pink across her cheeks and nose, a livid colour that looked not like sunburn but like some internal heat. Her fringe fell limply into her eyes, and so, to keep it off her face, she took a red scarf patterned with dark gold flowers out of her bag, tied it round her head, and set out to walk the last mile home. The makeshift turban made her both majestic and menial, a boy king or a kitchen maid. Her clothes looked accidental, borrowed or found, all of them ill-fitting and far too heavy.

The Verges had ten clear yards of mown grass on either side. In the days when roads like this were a favoured route for merchants, robbers and highwaymen lurked among woods and between villages. A statute was passed, decreeing that all trees and bushes be pulled up so that they would have nowhere to hide. Now this sudden width had a vertiginous effect on drivers who had crept out of the traffic snarl of Camptown, or had been driving under the limit through All-northover on a speed-trap day. The widening landscape encouraged

them, and there were many accidents, as the road was really quite or-
dinarily narrow and its corners particularly nasty, not the gentle
sweeps they appeared at all but full of odd angles that caught you off
guard. The Verges curved slyly back and forth, and then the road
straightened, the banks disappeared, and the village of Allnorthover
began with clusters of small tied cottages set hard on the road. It was
at this point that Mary saw the man again. She had been walking
along the bank, close to the trees, trying to find some shade. He was
standing quite still at the point where everything narrowed again,
facing in the direction of the village.

Mary could not think why he was there. The air prickled
around him, as if he were at war with every muscle and bone in his
body. She felt his pull and disturbance but did not want to know
what it was he wanted. She crossed over the road and walked quickly
past, willing him not to notice her.

Tom had almost reached the village when the road went bad on
him. He felt his legs billow and contract, making contact with the
road more suddenly or later than expected. He had been waiting for
the ground to settle when the girl appeared in front of him. She did
not look back, but Tom sensed that things cleared around her. He
followed her. When he could not catch up with her, he began to
call. Feeling his voice raw and uncertain, he put what strength he
had into making a noise that might reach her but could manage no
more than a string of single sounds.

So it was that the villagers of Allnorthover saw Tom Hepple
come home, walking down the middle of the High Street, looking
more than ever like someone in the grip of a god, only he appeared
to be fixed on Mary George, who was falling over herself in her hurry
to get away. Tom was half singing, half croaking one drawn-out mis-
shapen word after another: "Wait! Stop! Help! Home!"

Mary would not let herself even imagine him. Looking neither
right nor left, she passed the first houses. At the Green, she broke
into a run and pushed open her garden gate. Her mother was just
opening the door when Mary flew past her. Stella was about to follow

her up the stairs when an odd howl came from the Green. She turned back and there was Tom Hepple, just a few feet away. He still looked like the visionary, the genius she had once thought him to be, with blazing eyes and fine bones emphasised by his thinness. He did not look like someone who could have a crude, simple, or mistaken thought. But Stella was ten years older than when she had last seen him, and the difficulty of those years had made her more careful. His face was burnt and lined, and his black curly hair, grey, cropped, and coarse. Stella saw how his elegant fingers ("Musician's fingers!" his mother, Iris, had called them) waved constantly and pointlessly in the air, that his hands could no longer hold or control anything, that his eyes were screwed up with the effort of keeping in focus. She remembered. He was a force, a hurricane, sweeping things up, breaking down doors, sucking people in and under. Stella knew right away what he wanted.

"Tom, my child does not remember you."

"Your child?" Tom's fingers scrabbled and danced as if he were solving an elaborate equation. His voice grew quieter as his mind calmed, able at last to make connections. "I forgave . . . I could come back . . . She showed me!" Tom, who had been staring into the sky all the time he spoke, brought his head slowly down and fixed his gaze on Stella. His voice swelled again: "She walked out on the water! Because I was there! To show me!"

"The house?" It took a moment for Stella to admit to herself that she knew what he was talking about. Then that ten-year-old winter sprang up around her like buildings cutting out the light. She remained silent, as did Tom, whom the past had never ceased to assail and confine in this way.

"Mrs. George!" An exasperated voice was calling to Stella from the bus stop. There was a sound of old brakes being applied too fast, followed by a tentative rumble and then another long screech. A bus was juddering along the High Street, stopping every few yards.

Violet Eley emerged from the shelter. The light found nothing to play on in her pastel clothes, hard white hair, and thickly powdered face. She had seen the mad Hepple brother come stumbling into the village to stop at Stella George's garden gate. To her relief, the bus had appeared on time and she could get away from whatever scene was unfolding. But the bus had begun stopping and starting, and sure enough, there was Stella George's dog, Mim, sitting in front of it in the road. Violet Eley's impatience overcame her distaste. "Mrs. George! This is really too much! I have a train to meet!"

The bus started up quickly, crept forward, and Mim gave chase, barking furiously, darting in front and snapping at the tyres. The bus stopped again and the dog sidled onto the pavement. The driver climbed down from his cab and got as far as putting his hand on Mim's collar. She did not snap or growl but set up such a grating, unbearable howl that the driver let go immediately. Seeing Stella by her gate, he approached, shaking his head.

"Your dog . . . please . . . should be tied up . . ."

Stella kept her eyes on Tom Hepple, who was staring past her now. "Bring the dog here," she said, knowing he couldn't. The bus driver had noticed Tom by now and was full of confusion. "You know how she cries . . ."

"Mrs. George?" Violet Eley pleaded.

People on the bus who were to get off in the village had wandered into the road. One or two tried to move Mim, who yelped as if she had been run over and cut in half. They recoiled, terrified in case anyone had seen them and would think they had inflicted pain on the animal. Those who knew Mim ignored her. Strangers or not, they all came across the Green to where Stella George willed Tom Hepple away from her daughter, and Tom Hepple stared through her walls and windows, and the bus driver and Violet Eley stood as if caught in their spell and miserably rooted to the spot.

"Someone get Christie," Stella managed at last, and the spell was broken. The driver returned to his bus and helped Violet Eley on board. The others faded away. Then Christie Hepple was there. He was as tall as his twin brother but bearded, full-faced, not yet grey, and far more solid. He stood to one side of Tom, as if he were his shadow—one that had more substance than the person who cast it.

Christie put his arm round his brother, talking softly and constantly in his ear until Tom loosened and leant into him, turned, and was taken away. Christie had not even glanced at Stella, who watched them out of sight. Then she walked over to Mim, picked her up in her arms, and carried her home.

Tom had not been staring up at Mary's window as he thought. Her room was at the back of the cottage, overlooking a small garden and endless fields. The old plaster walls bulged between the laths; the wooden floor tilted and creaked, its unpolished grain worn to a shine. There were no shelves, so Mary's books were stacked in precarious towers that she frequently upset or that grew too tall and toppled over. They were mostly her father's. Reading her way through them felt like climbing to his door.

This had been Mary's room all her life and something remained of each of its incarnations. Her only methodical change had been to replace each panel of an alphabet frieze with a face cut from a newspaper or magazine. These were black-and-white pictures of singers, film stars, artists, and writers—anyone Mary liked the look of, so long as their names matched a letter she hadn't covered yet and they were foreign and dead. The panel Mary had painted black ended just below the flowers her father had stencilled, rows of daisies she had insisted upon when, at four, she first went to nursery school and saw other girls and tried being like them for a while.

The sun passed easily through the orange curtains Mary had drawn across the open window and coloured everything in the room that was so black and white. She held up her arms and examined them with pleasure, seeing her pale skin suddenly gold. She drew her hands to her mouth and breathed hard, to remember what it had felt like when she had reached out to the sleeping boy. Mary stretched and curled, feeling ease and pleasure and a lazy excitement, sensations that were all more or less new to her.

That summer, the exchanges and balances of the oil export market went awry. The countries of the Middle East, having been bent to whatever shape the West demanded, consolidated. The price of a barrel of oil changed by the hour, doubling and tripling. At one point the figures on the stock market board trailed a string of numbers like the tail of an ominous comet. Petrol refineries searched the world over for other sources but were still dependent on the rich fields of the Emirates. There were queues at garages, even battles. People walked sanctimoniously or furiously.

Fred Spence's brother, Charlie, had to get up earlier each day. Once a week the man from the company came to fill the well beneath his two petrol pumps. He received a fifth less fuel than usual and was given a price to which he painstakingly altered the plastic push-on numbers on the board on his forecourt. The company sent a letter that explained what the government said. Petrol was to be rationed.

Charlie's bungalow sat behind the garage and he could hear the cars pulling up in a queue before he had got out of bed. As impervious to the heat as he was to the revving engines and tentative then impatient horns, he fried his year-round breakfast. Charlie took his time, stopping to clean his heavy black-framed glasses and to grease back his hair. He was fifty now, and while his florid face had settled in folds and pouches, he persisted in the look he had established during a brief period of interest in such things twenty years before. He sent off for small bottles of unlabelled black liquid by mail order, to dull the grey in his quiff. He wore indestructible synthetic shirts in garish geometric prints that stretched over his sagging breasts and belly. Charlie didn't worry about the petrol crisis but went by the figures and instructions he was given. He felt no joy in his newfound authority either, simply telling angry customers: "The government says . . ."

When the clock reached seven-thirty, he opened his front door. The fetid air of the bungalow, its trapped smells of fried food, cigarettes, sweat, and aftershave, lingered on the forecourt most of the day. Charlie blinked, his only response to the sun. It was a Monday morning and the commuters were there, wanting to be gone in time for the city train. Once Charlie had filled their tanks, they relaxed and said good morning as they turned the key in their ignition. It would occur to those who worked in international banking or on the trading floor that Charlie was, of course, in the same game. They made fraternal, esoteric remarks about indices and monopolies. Charlie was polite: "The government says . . ." He nodded as they accelerated away.

Allnorthover had two bus stops. A brick shelter with wooden seats and a tiled roof sat in a paved square on the edge of the Green near Mary's cottage. There were rarely many people in it, as this was the stop for buses going only to Mortimer Tye, where you could do little more than catch a train. A hundred yards along the High Street, on the opposite side of the road, was the stop where you waited to go into Camptown, where Mary went to school. Here, the Council had recently erected a tin shelter, a single wall with a narrow roof and a plastic ledge on which to sit. It was like an open hinge, already tilting as the paving stones had begun to erupt. The pavement was squeezed between the road and the thrusting hedges of the long front gardens that kept the village's bigger and better houses— square, butter-coloured Georgian villas—out of sight. While the older cottages and shops built on the road had long ago grown dull with dirt from the exhaust fumes of lorries, their windows permanently filmed with dust, the villas gleamed.

The fuel crisis meant that the first three morning services into Camptown were reduced to a single bus that came at eight. Pensioners who usually had to wait till nine o'clock to use their passes were now allowed to travel early, and so, this morning, six elderly members of Allnorthover's First Families—Laceys, Hepples, Kettles, or Strouds—headed the queue. The women wore nylon gloves and lace-knit cardigans over loose floral dresses made from the same material they used to make stretch covers for their chairs. The men dressed in suits that had been so well cared for they were worn to paper, their creases to glass. They wore caps they had had all their adult lives. Married for fifty years or more, couples like the Kettles rarely looked at or spoke to one another but, once in retirement, weren't often seen apart.

Mr. Kettle squinted into the sun at this arrival, a child in old man's clothes, a singlet and baggy flannel trousers, held up by braces and gathered in a wide leather belt. "That a boy or a girl?"

"It's the George one." Mrs. Kettle shifted her weight from hip to hip by way of greeting. Behind the Kettles were some Hepples and Strouds. Spreading themselves just a little, they filled the shelter, taking whatever shade it could afford.

Behind them were the early workers, who usually caught the seven o'clock. They worked the first shift on the industrial estate, making the fruit juice, electrical goods, and sausages for which Camptown was known. The early workers were used to being able to sit apart in a bus that arrived empty. Each took a seat by the window and set down beside them a sandwich box, flask, and bag of clean overalls. They came home together, too, just before the end of the school day, with their overalls back in their bags with their stains: the bright splashes of pig's blood and artificial orange, a whiff of something sweet and rotten or sour and citric. Only men worked in the electronics factory. They smelt of nothing and told their wives that the holes in their sleeves that had been eaten away by hydrochloric acid were cigarette burns.

The early workers stood uneasily in single file while, beyond them, schoolchildren spilled onto the road. The youngest were hot and already bored with pushing each other into hedges or playing chicken with the juggernauts. Two older girls lolled against a fence. Mary tentatively joined them.

"Says you were followed by a loony, Saturday . . ." a Lacey girl began, her doll-face turning sour. She primped her blond curls. "Your type?" Her mouth, already a tight purse like her mother's, clasped in a satisfied grin.

Mary laughed and shook her head, half-heartedly. "Right nutter."

Julie Lacey looked her up and down, unconvinced. "Student

was he?" Then she turned suddenly to a plump girl on her other side. "Says your uncle, June!"

June Hepple swung her lowered head slowly from side to side. "Nothing to do with me . . ."

Mary looked at June's quivering cheeks, her vague brown eyes, her frizzy hair pulled back in a tight ponytail. She didn't know whether she wanted to comfort or shake her. Mary took a book out of her bag and sat down on the kerb to read. Julie Lacey nudged her book with her toe. "There's dirty . . . dogs and that . . ."

The buses were old double-deckers with an exhausted and complicated rumble that everyone living along the High Street could recognise. They rarely bothered to leave their houses to catch one until they heard it coming. Mim began barking long before the eight o'clock pulled up, already half full. The Kettles, Hepples, and Strouds sat downstairs in the two long seats that had been left empty, as if reserved for them. The early workers made for the stairs but were overtaken by a swarm of children and ended up scattered miserably among them. The three girls, all wanting to smoke, went upstairs, too. Julie Lacey cleared a gaggle of younger boys off the front seats with a look.

Tom Hepple had sat up all night, his legs stretched out beyond the end of the child's bed, his face caught in the mirror on the dressing table opposite him. The quilted nylon cover crackled beneath him. He kept his gaze fixed on his reflection, but at the edges of his vision, the rosebuds on the wallpaper throbbed. Above the mirror were shiny posters of musicians and footballers, all eyes and teeth. He had not let Christie turn off the light.

Tom grew tired and could guard against his body no longer. His feet jerked and the fingers of his right hand began to tap rapidly on the bedside table. He became aware of the same acrid breath going in and out of his lungs, getting smaller each time he inhaled. His hand gripped the spindly table, which tipped, its contents slipping to the floor: a china shepherdess, an etched glass, a plastic snowstorm, and a bowl of sequins. Tom got down on his hands and knees. Nothing was broken, but the sequins embedded themselves in the thick strands of the carpet and were too small anyway for his fingers; the shepherdess's head came away in his hands. Tom's chest tightened, his stomach churned, and he felt the pressure of his panic and knew that any minute he would lose control. He rushed into the hall, where identical doors carried flowery ceramic plaques: "Mum and Dad," "Darren and Sean," and "Bathroom." There was one behind him, too: "June." Tom crept into the bathroom. He tried not to make a mess, but he was shaky and all wrong. He rubbed at the wet carpet till the tissue disintegrated and stuck to it.

"Carpet in the bathroom. What would Ma have thought?" Christie stood in the doorway. He lifted Tom to his feet, took the tissue from his hand, and threw it away. "Have a wash and come down. You'll not know where you are yet."

In the kitchen Sophie was filling a kettle. She wrenched the tap on so strongly, water sprayed up over her hands. She banged the kettle down on the hob and tried to strike a match, but it snapped.

"June off to school already?" Christie did not meet her eye.

"Couldn't wait, I reckon. Good job the boys are still over at Mum's." Sophie snapped two more matches. "He's no better, is he?" she continued. "He should've stayed where they know . . . how he is and can help him."

Christie approached and put his hands on her shoulders. She turned abruptly in his arms. "We never could help him, could we?"

He looked into her broad face and saw that its softness had been exhausted. Tom appeared in the doorway. He was trying to smile. Sophie looked past her husband at his brother, the crazy twin who fluttered in and out of their lives, coming close like a moth that must be caught and put out of the window. They would try to hold him and free him, but he would flap out of reach, terrified and bruised by any such contact. Then he would be back, circling them again.

Sophie gestured to a chair, but Tom hovered, uncertain. Her white kitchen and bleached hair dazzled him. She put a mug of tea

in front of him. "It'll have to be black. The milk turned on the step."
His electricity had once seemed like a kind of wild static that confused everything nearby. After ten years of hospitals and halfway
houses, he was still jittery, but his eyes were dull.

"I'll go up for more," Tom gabbled, thinking he wanted to help
and that he wanted to get away. Sophie watched him through the
window. She didn't want him here, and above all, she didn't like to
be reminded that it was because of Tom that she had married
Christie. Sophie had met Tom first, because he had been at the
grammar while she was at the high, before the two schools were
amalgamated. Tom had been beautiful and clever, and she had
taken his trouble for sensitivity and his agitation for great thoughts.
She hadn't had to get too close before realising that he was a very bad
idea—and then there had been Christie. Tom was so away in his
head that he'd barely seemed to notice that something was happening between them, and then that it had changed. She'd felt such a
fool.

You do not have what it takes to be in this world, she thought.
You are a monster.

The bus driver, wanting to be gone from the village before Mim got
loose, revved his engine, but stopped again as Mrs. Kettle yanked the
cord above her head, ringing the bell repeatedly. "Edna isn't here
yet! She's had to collect her dressings." A minute or two passed as
Edna Lacey limped towards the bus stop. She stood there, smiling,
and didn't get on. The bus conductor, a weak-minded, yellow-haired
boy whose mother was a Stroud, hesitated and looked to Mrs. Kettle,
who thought for a moment, then called out, "Are there more to
come, Edna?"

Edna Lacey peered up and down the High Street. "Can't say as
anyone's on the way." She kept looking down the road and made no
move to get on.

"Shall we be off?" Mrs. Kettle asked no one in particular, and
no one felt it their place to reply.

A Triumph came puttering round the bend. Edna Lacey stepped into the road and raised an arm. The car stopped, and as Father Barclay got out to see what she wanted, Edna Lacey opened the passenger door and got in. There were three more villagers in the back of the car already.

Father Barclay stood for a moment between the car and the bus. He smiled and shook his head, as if rehearsing something in a mirror. He rocked on his heels, swung his arms, and clapped his hands. Then he laughed his high, rapid laugh, which began as a bird call and ended as a gunshot.

"Don't let me keep you!" he boomed to the conductor, who was standing on the platform, watching him. "I'll bring up the rear!"

The only people in the village whose petrol wasn't rationed were the two priests, the doctor, and Sergeant Belcher. They never travelled far without being hailed for a lift.

The conductor's face was expressionless and remained so as Mrs. Kettle rang the bell three times on his behalf, the signal that they could set off. The driver waited as Father Swann glided by in his Jaguar, which was also full, then started up the engine and accelerated hard, just as Tom Hepple stepped into the road, stopped in the middle, and put down the pint of milk he was carrying. Although Tom kept moving, the driver was confused by the bottle. He braked late and sharp.

The Kettles, Hepples, and Strouds fell sideways against another heavily but silently. They were too old to be startled and make a noise about it at the same time. The early workers gave hoarse grunts or sighs, perhaps the first sounds of their day. The children shrieked and then immediately began laughing at those whose books had slid from their satchels or whose apples had rolled across the floor to be kicked by whoever could reach them.

Tom had been walking slowly, so as not to be back in Sophie's kitchen too soon. And then there was the bus, the one that he had caught from up by Temple Grove, going to school each day. It was waiting. He didn't have to return to the new road off Back Lane,

Stevas Close, or whatever it was called, and Christie's hard new house. He could go home—but the milk? He could leave it here. They would come to find him and there it would be. The bus was crowded. I know everyone, he thought, there is my grandmother, only she's dead. He got upstairs quickly and saw all the children, boys that were him and Christie, girls that were Sophie. He walked along the aisle as whispered explanations rippled past him. There were three girls across the front seats, and the one on her own in the corner, not turning round, he knew, was her.

"Mary George." He tried hard to say her name softly, but his voice caught and blurted it.

Someone laughed fast and then sucked in their breath. It was quiet for what seemed like a long time, and then the driver was tapping Tom Hepple on the shoulder. "There's no standing on top, sir, come down, take a seat, and we'll be off."

Tom ignored him. "If you could show me again, while the water is falling . . ." Mary had shut her eyes. Julie Lacey was staring at her, not at Tom Hepple like everyone else.

Tom could see the girl was shaking; her back was hunched over and her shoulders raised. He didn't want to frighten her; he must try to explain. "You were just a child, I know that, but it was your father . . ." Why should she be afraid? "Your father could come back . . ."

June Hepple stood. Since the end of childhood, she had moved like someone in heavy clothes underwater, what little she said floating up in small bubbles from her uncertain mouth, and even though she still could not meet her uncle's eye, for once June did not look to Julie Lacey for her cue. "I'll take you back now, Uncle Tom. You don't want to be going anywhere."

June took his arm, and her hand was his mother's hand, and he felt the world settle into place. She led Tom downstairs. The conductor handed her the pint of milk. Things were ordinary and clear again, and Tom could see the children were not him and Christie but what might be their children, and that the old woman looking

29

hard at her folded hands was not his grandmother but his mother's sister, an aged Aunt May. He tried to greet her, but she did not look up. June pulled him gently towards the pavement. "May's deaf sometimes, Uncle Tom. Remember?"

Five minutes silence was all Julie Lacey could manage before she began shifting from side to side, peeling her bare thighs and the damp nylon of her waitress's uniform from the plastic trim of the seat. She tutted and puffed, and fanned herself with one hand. Mary ignored her. "June'll have to watch her uncle don't chop her up into little pieces one night! Mind you, he's not half bad-looking, for a loony, I mean, if you like that sort of thing." She guffawed, but Mary only turned her head farther towards the window, and those children sitting near enough to hear her gasped, not understanding that this was more or less a joke. "You're going to have to be careful, too, Mary George . . . says those Hepples never did forgive your father . . ."

Mary pulled a tobacco pouch and papers from her bag. She slowly teased out the tobacco, laid it on the paper, creased the edge with her nails, and rolled her cigarette. She ran the tip of her tongue along the glued edge and sealed it. Her hands did not shake. Julie had noticed that the children around her were listening eagerly now. "Must have felt bad in the end . . . couldn't face anyone in the end, could he? Face you, does he?" Mary lit her roll-up and closed her eyes.

Julie didn't speak again before she got off at the roundabout on the edge of town. Since leaving school a year before, she had worked at the Amber Grill, the restaurant in the Malibu Motel, built on the site of Barry Spence's old transport café. The eldest Spence brother, Barry had made a deal so mysterious and successful that his greasy spoon with its unofficial bunkhouse was swept away overnight and replaced by a stucco-fronted restaurant with a reception area and a string of pebble-dashed motel rooms. He had a tarmacked car park and a sign with neon palm trees at the entrance to his own sliproad. It was said that Barry's success was due to secrets. The old Amber

Café had been a traditional meeting place for those with unofficial business who thought they would be alone among travellers and strangers. With a sharp eye and careful organisation, Barry had averted many unfortunate meetings. There were councillors, property developers, lawyers, builders, and bankers, husbands and wives who were grateful to him.

Barry loved the constant stream of one-night visitors, the late-night traffic turning off the London road, bringing in people who travelled for a living and saw the world. He thought of England as a wide-open space, crisscrossed by endless motorways and punctuated by places like the Malibu Motel. He thought of America. Barry mugged up on cocktails, turned the Amber Grill into an American diner, and hired burly blondes like Julie Lacey to serve hamburgers topped with pineapple rings to salesmen and lorry drivers who wanted bacon and eggs instead.

The sixth-form common room of Camptown High was the last in a row of prefabs that no one had ever pretended would be temporary. The pupils were allowed a kettle, a record player, and to wear their own clothes. Smoking, although against the rules, was tolerated as long as it was unseen. For this reason, the windows were kept shut and the blinds drawn. There were a dozen low armchairs, arranged in three groups, and a row of desks that were empty and unused. The walls around each group of chairs were covered in posters: psychedelic, sporting, and political. Billy was asleep, stretched across two chairs beneath a lurid album cover of chasms and goblins.

Mary walked over and parted the long hair that covered his face. "Where were you this morning?"

He stretched and sat up, not smiling. "And where were you on Saturday morning?"

Mary sighed. "I went home."

"Without me."

"You had already gone!"

"I got the last train, like we'd planned to."

"You didn't say goodbye."

"You were busy."

Mary stood up, her fists clenched. She and Billy had gone to the party in Crouchness together. She didn't remember seeing much of him there, or noticing when he left.

Billy fiddled with the beads round his neck. "I slept out last night and walked it."

"The state of your feet. You're turning into a satyr!"

Billy smiled and flexed his toes. "Perhaps I am at that." He hadn't worn shoes for weeks and carried a pair of flip-flops to put on if a teacher approached.

"And you stink of patchouli oil, Billy."

"And fresh air . . ."

"Not even fresh air smells of fresh air anymore." Mary had been in the room for five minutes and its atmosphere, soupy and stagnant, was making her sleepy as well. She curled up in another chair and closed her eyes.

When Mary's father, the architect Matthew George, decided to go into partnership with the builder Christie Hepple, undertaking local conversions, he bought the old chapel.

The chapel had been converted from a grain store by the local Baptists. They had replaced the roof, laid a stone floor, and whitewashed the brick and beams. Then their minister, the Reverend Simon Touch, had inherited a gloomy house on the High Street and had built a new chapel in its cavernous basement, complete with an immersion pool. Mary had once gone back there after school with his daughter Hilary, who had promised that she could dip her fingers in the tank. Hilary said people fell into it backwards for God, "so the water runs up their noses." The water in the murky tank looked quite solid and Mary had wondered how anyone managed to sink into it. Whose hands helped them and how did they surface again?

The Baptists had put in a window above their altar, a large triangle of plain glass flush with the roof, under which Matthew worked on a raised platform he'd built along the centre of the building. There were rough stairs at the far end. Mary had liked to creep up and tiptoe along the aisle between the shelves of books, files, and papers, like a library, she said, to the end where the platform broadened to the width of the chapel, level with the foot of the window, and Matthew sat perched on his spindly, rotating stool at his slanted drawing board, pencilling in tiny elegant numerals and angles. Mary would stand behind him at the window, recording her height on each visit by breathing on the glass.

On the ground floor, Christie had kept his tools and machinery. He also had a desk, a trestle table, pushed against one of the small windows that were shuttered and set deep in the wall. Mary would walk solemnly across this space, holding herself straight but looking quickly from side to side at all the sharp edges, the twists, spirals, points, and planes.

Christie let Tom go in ahead of him. "Don't be troubled if it's not right." Even though light pushed through the windows, the interior of the chapel was cool. Tom set down his rucksack and considered the swept floor, bare shelves, trestle table, and stool. "Simple." He smiled.

"It is that." Christie bustled past him to the back, where there was a sink, cupboards, and a Baby Belling two-ring cooker. Matthew had installed all this. He had stayed overnight there sometimes, more so towards the end, locking the door against Stella, whom Christie had found one morning half asleep on the grass outside.

"Cup of tea?" Christie was busy unpacking carrier bags and filling the cupboards with tins of soup, beans, and spaghetti; packets of biscuits, sugar, custard powder, dried milk, and instant mash; bottles of tomato ketchup, malt vinegar, and HP Sauce. Tom had hardly eaten anything, hardly slept either, in the two weeks that he'd been back. "I'll come again first thing. You're to sort out your benefit at the post office and I'll fetch some more groceries." He took as long as he could to put things away, watching over the kettle as it boiled and then leaving the tea to brew till it was bitter and lukewarm and the granules of dried milk floated greasily on its surface. He waited till Tom was nearby before handing him his mug, almost without turning round.

Tom carried his mug and rucksack carefully up the open staircase to where Christie had made up a mattress under the big window. Not having any curtains that would fit, he had taped blue sugar paper over the glass. For Tom, this marine light made the place even cooler. By laying out his clothes, books, papers, pens, and shoes across the floor and along the nearest shelves, he created a rectangle the same size as the space he had lived in on the hospital ward, the same as half the room he'd later shared in the hostel—four by eight paces. June's room had been the wrong shape.

Christie understood that Tom needed to be somewhere familiar. He couldn't be at ease in the new house but needed to be in the village. The chapel was ideal, almost off on its own, nearer than anywhere else to the Dip, but not within sight of the water. Since Matthew had left, Christie had worked for people who had their own offices and drew up their own plans. He hadn't needed the chapel for anything more than a store. It only took a morning to sort out his tools and paints, transfer them to his garden shed, and clean up the outhouse.

There was a filing cabinet of paperwork Matthew had left: old contracts and invoices for barn conversions, extensions, and conservatories; rejected designs in concrete and glass for Havilton New Town; the chalet design they had worked on together for the holiday camp at Crouchness. Christie had also found some of the pamphlets Matthew had designed for Stella's business: beige cards printed with droopy chocolate-brown Art Nouveau script and edged with flowers. She had begun dealing in Victoriana when she came to clear out her parents' home and decided to get rid of the dark, glossy, intricate clutter she had always hated. In doing so, she had discovered a market among London dealers for lace antimacassars, cameo brooches, fur tippets, kid gloves, jet beads, fish knives, and sherry glasses.

When Matthew's great-aunt Alice Spence died in the house she'd lived in for sixty years, Stella made her sons an offer. From there, she'd gone to auctions, placed small ads in local papers, and people had just got in touch. She expanded into forged ironwork that was made to order by the son of Allnorthover's last blacksmith, as the leaflet said—weathervanes, firescreens, and flower-pot stands. When the dairy in the High Street closed down, Stella leased the premises and opened her shop, Hindsight, scrubbing out the abandoned churns and standing them by the door full of corn sheaves and dried flowers. The churns were still there, and now people kept trying to buy them. These days Stella was selling jazzy twenties ceramics, framed prints of adverts from the thirties and forties, and enamelware.

Tom came down, tracing the wiring that was tacked along the side of the stairs. He followed it across the wall to the fusebox and from there to the clutch of switches by the door. He went over to the kitchen and pulled each plug from its socket, for the cooker, the kettle, and the toaster, and put them back in again.

"I've brought you something to keep you busy." Christie waved an arm at a heavy old wireless. "You were the only person that could make that cantankerous old thing behave, so I kept it for you." Tom knelt beside the wireless and ran his hand over the blistered veneer and the dusty cloth that covered the speaker—tiny red and cream diamonds, like material for a dress. The dials had yellowed and their grooves were worn smooth. "I kept this, too." Christie reached into one of the carrier bags and handed Tom a battered tin box. Tom opened it and began sorting through his tools. They were intensely familiar. Either he had always remembered the exact shade of blue paint and the shapes in which it had worn off the wooden handles of his pliers and screwdrivers or they were reminding him of their long existence. The soldering iron weighed exactly in his hand, the cold heavy handle, the hard dullness of its colour, the bitter smell. Solder, fuses, batteries, bulbs, and coils of copper wire all impressed themselves upon him, giving the pleasure of something not thought about for years and then entirely and vividly remembered.

"How . . . therapeutic." It was the first joke Tom had made since coming home.

"You'll be wanting hospital food next!" Christie laughed, encouraged now and sure that his decision to keep Tom close by, to help him set up alone, was right. He was safe in the village, where everyone knew him, and near enough to the water to have to accept it in the end. Christie had explained this to Stella. She was concerned for her daughter, but the girl had just got caught up in Tom's grieving.

Even alone in an old building he'd always known, Tom couldn't sleep. He got up, unplugged everything, plugged it all in again, opened the back of the wireless, and then, looking at its circuitry, felt tired and went to lie down. The thing had leaked memories of times when it had been his head that had buzzed and crackled, as if badly tuned, when it had picked up what appeared to be fragments of different stations: a woman singing a single verse of a song over and over; the Morse code SOS of a sinking ship; a man repeating the same joke: "What did the mouse say when it saw a bat? Look, an angel!"; the thin, high, endless laugh of someone who was exhausted and wanted to stop. His mother had held his head and stroked it in long lines till the noises were gone. She'd called it "ironing out."

When Christie let himself into the chapel the next morning, he found Tom lying on the mattress. He was shaking so badly he couldn't speak. Christie helped him down the stairs and walked him the few hundred yards along the High Street to where Dr. Clough was just opening up for the Saturday-morning emergency surgery. There were half a dozen people waiting already, and they filed into the tiny waiting room where Betty Burgess, the old doctor's wife who still acted as receptionist, took their names. The wooden chairs ranged around all four walls of the room were filled by those waiting. The room was so small that those opposite one another were almost knee to knee. When Dr. Clough called Tom's name first, nobody objected.

Half an hour later, the doctor appeared in the waiting room without Tom and asked Christie to step outside. "I don't have his complete records yet, only a note of what he's supposed to be taking. Why did the hostel let him go?"

"It was up to him, wasn't it?"

Dr. Clough was an elegant figure with a cool manner and hollow good looks. He had arrived in Allnorthover a few months earlier and was already known as Dr. Kill Off.

"He just needs his pills, Doctor. He forgot to bring any back. They always did stop his shakes and help him sleep." Christie couldn't have a brother of his going back into the bin, not again. "We can manage."

Dr. Clough's face was expressionless. "He can have his pills, but you are to see that he takes them, and I won't give him enough of anything to hurt himself. He shouldn't stay alone for the next week. I want to see him here on Monday morning to discuss further treatment. You must be glad that your brother's home, Mr. Hepple, but that doesn't mean it's the best place for him."

Christie flushed, shocked at the doctor's bluntness. Old Dr. Burgess had made every exchange seem like a chat over tea. He had asked after the family, even the dog, and had never said Tom was anything more than "overexcited" while suggesting pills might help as offhandedly as if they were vitamins. And he'd got Tom the best specialist help: an expert in Camptown. When Dr. Burgess retired and the surgery moved from his front room to the old coach house, he had put forward Christie for the conversion. It seemed strange that such a man had recommended this new doctor, but then again, once he'd retired, Dr. Burgess had all but withdrawn from village life, resigning from the Parish Council, threatening not to run his bottle stall at the Fête and barely stopping to greet people in the street. Betty was working out her notice. There was talk of a new life: a boat or a caravan.

Christie followed Dr. Clough back inside to wait with Tom while the doctor unlocked a cupboard in his dispensary and poured two different types of particoloured capsules, brown and blue, red and white, through his pill counter. He scooped them into glass bottles and wrote detailed labels.

"Two of these each morning and two of the others at night. It's all written on the labels, but it might help to, I don't know, think 'red and white: night,' or something like that, to remember." Christie was taken aback. Red sky at night, thought Tom, shepherd's delight.

The doctor continued: "They'll take some days to really help, and in the meantime, you'll feel pretty awful, but try to remember that what you're feeling will pass. Go back and stay with your brother for a bit. Call me anytime." The doctor held out the bottles to Tom, who took them and passed them to Christie, who tried to hand them back.

Camptown had always been a provisional sort of place. It benefited from leading elsewhere, accumulating, by chance, all the historical features expected of an English town. Its name had an ancient derivation from its role as a Roman staging post, halfway between the capital and the more useful and significant Camulodunum on the coast to the north. By the thirteenth century it had acquired a city wall, not as a place worth protecting in itself but as part of the front line against the Danes. The small, orderly grid of Roman streets had been consolidated and extended. As the roads improved, more traffic passed through on its way between London and the coast. These journeyings back and forth rubbed against the town and created a kind of static through which people got stuck. The railway threw out an arm towards it. Manufacturers and merchants trading in wool, wheat, salt, and corn settled on the outskirts, building substantial villas and funding civic works. Camptown broadened and put on weight without gaining character.

Remnants from each era could still be found, leaking through bland new surfaces. The hillock that lay just beyond the fence of the high school's playing fields was a prehistoric burial mound, hemmed in by housing estates. A Roman villa had been excavated by the river, and fragments of its concrete (mixed from stone and lime) and its tesserae had found their way to the British Museum, along with the skeleton of a baby thought to have been a foundation offering to household gods. Newling Hall, the mansion that now housed the art gallery and museum, had a fine Jacobean staircase, carved in the Spanish style. It was regularly hired by film crews who spent days repeating a single scene: the sweeping exit of a woman in a trailing gown or the clanking descent of a cavalier. For safety reasons, the staircase was never polished between hirings. All other floors in the public parts of the building were covered in linoleum.

Holidaymakers sometimes turned off the bypass in search of tea or a bed and were glad of a few sights to make the extra miles worthwhile. There was the small medieval cathedral that made Camptown technically a city, now dwarfed by the new civic hall, for which the derelict Corn Exchange had been demolished. Nobody came to see the cathedral's architecture, although they would make a thorough tour of the building before seeking out the Sheela-na-Gig, one of the few examples to be found in East Anglia. Carved on a pillar in a shadowy corner to one side of the pews, her wildness, her voracious eyes and spurting breasts, her fingers opening her vagina wide between splayed legs were intended to shock parishioners out of temptation. Somehow, she did just this.

Camptown had been damaged by bombs that had missed either London's docks or the coastal defences, or had been jettisoned. The gaps this left in the High Street had now been filled with large commercial premises. The old shopfronts with their ornate masonry, ironwork, and curved glass made way for the flat frames of display windows. The town made room for municipal resources: a multi-storey car park, a library, a theatre, a swimming pool, a bus station, a new hospital. These efficient buildings were oddly cramped and dim inside, with small windows and fussy arrangements of interior walls. They cut across streets which would have been too small to contain them, creating odd alleyways and dead ends. People who'd lived in Camptown all their lives found themselves getting lost and going to the swimming pool to pay a parking fine because these civic façades were all so alike.

Camptown had become awkward and diminished. Its constant, incidental, and halfhearted replanning made it a difficult place to wander about in, but Mary and Billy, who often found themselves with time on their hands, could pass several hours doing just that.

A fortnight after Tom Hepple's return was the last day of term. They left school at four and made their way through the "top end" of Camptown, the point at which the High Street frayed into new roads leading to housing and industrial estates and the multistorey car park. Beyond this were the expensive Edwardian villas with broad curved drives, ivy and wisteria, and long gardens edged with old trees: chestnuts, magnolias, and limes.

There was no shade in the street so they walked slowly and kept stopping. First at a corner shop that would sell them beer, and then at the bus-station newsagent, which was tiny and grim but sold them tobacco and cigarette papers. They came to the park playground. The metal bars of the merry-go-round burned to the touch. A couple of toddlers playing listlessly in the sandpit were hauled away by their mother, and then Mary and Billy had the place to themselves. They kicked off their shoes and sat for a while with their feet in the sand, until Mary noticed all the crisp packets and baked dog turds.

The seesaw was in the shade, so they lay down on either side of its central pivot, more or less balancing each other. Mary drank her beer quickly and drew hard on her cigarette. She gripped both tightly in her hands. Dreamy Billy flopped on the seesaw with one leg trailing to the ground, his long, fair hair spread out behind him, his cheeks the same faint pink as his old T-shirt. His purple corduroy flares were just as faded, and all in all, Billy looked bleached or at least delicately tinted. A roll-up sat loosely between his thumb and forefinger. Mostly, he just let it burn. He had pushed his other thumb into the neck of a bottle of beer and let it dangle.

"Valerie says Christie Hepple brought his brother into the Arms last night." Billy's big sister worked behind the bar of the Hooper's Arms on Allnorthover's High Street. Billy pushed himself up onto his elbows, tipping the seesaw, raising Mary into his line of vision. "What is he to you, anyway?"

"Not to me . . . to my father." Mary tipped her head back. "Come on, you know! The scandal!" She was shouting. She swung her legs round and jumped up. Billy crashed back, but stayed where he was.

Mary came over and knelt beside him, her head close to his but looking the other way. She spoke quietly now. "It's not the truth, you know, Billy. It's just the story. Why should he have stayed after what they said? How could he?" She got up and walked over to climb the slide, which, like everything in the playground, left traces of rust and flakes of old paint on whoever touched it. At the top of the steps, she turned, braced herself on the bars, pushed up and upside-down, her legs straight in the air.

"Do it with your glasses on!" shouted Billy. Mary stayed where she was till her face went crimson and then lowered herself onto the slide. She came to a stop halfway down and stayed there. Billy came over and handed her her beer.

"Are you scared of him?"

There was a long silence before Mary replied: "I don't know . . . I recognised him and then I didn't. I don't remember really, except that he always seemed so gentle, bonkers but gentle. But I feel I'm being sucked in."

"Into what?"

"I hate that fucking village." Mary stood up and ran down the rest of the slide.

It was later that afternoon that Mary saw the boy from the party again. She and Billy had wandered on to Flux Records, a corridor of a shop on the High Street, squeezed between a Wimpy Bar and an estate agent's. Flux Records was lined with deep shelves divided into new and secondhand. Beyond this, the arrangement was subtle, un-alphabetical, and subject to change. The secondhand section began with bargains, the music no one wanted to listen to or even remember listening to. That year, the indulgent and bloated were being thrown out: the last esoteric whisperings of Gong, the bombastic concept albums of Led Zeppelin, the slick disco productions of Donna Summer. Many of these had been bought at full price in the same shop only two years before, and now the manager, Terry Flux, bought back what he had room for, without irony, at a fifth of their original price. To make space for these rejects, the other secondhand records were promoted. Jazz and Psychedelic, Ornette Coleman and The Thirteenth Floor Elevators moved into "Rare Grooves," while the rawest, weirdest experiments of a decade ago, Can and the Velvet Underground, arrived in "Collectables."

Terry Flux believed in cycles, and his system worked. At the front of the new side of the shop, under "Just In," were the same cut-ups, bizarre names, and banner slogans, the same difficult cleverness and anti-finesse to be found among the "Collectables." That summer, no one wanted to listen to anybody famous, so Terry Flux bought records by people he'd never heard of and sold them on their obscurity with such success that the "Just In" shelves were retitled "Punk/New Wave" and other new releases were shuffled along into "Current." Among all the black, white, and red of newsprint-collage covers, there were a few singles in new coloured vinyl—bubblegum pink and cobalt blue packaged in transparent plastic. They were as simple and luminous as children's toys, and the customers, mostly still at school, liked to turn them over and over in their hands.

Billy pushed through to the "Psychedelic" section, oblivious to his difference from the crowd, who wore either black or clashing acid colours, blazers with safety pins and chains, and hair that was at least short, if not shaved or spikey. Mary made her way towards a girl whose blurred outline she thought she recognised, only to find when she got close that it wasn't who she thought it was at all. In her embarrassment, she edged quickly backwards and trod hard on some-one's shoe. She wheeled round to apologise and her head collided with a loud crack with the head of the boy, who had bent down to examine his bruised foot.

"Sorry! Oh, it's you . . ." they said, each other's echoes. The boy stood before her, one hand clasping his nose and his right foot rubbing against his left calf. It's almost the shape he made when asleep! Mary thought, and then panicked: He knows I thought that, he knows I watched him sleeping, he knows I walked into this shop thinking about him. His face, which she had liked very much, seemed impossibly lovely now. He moved his hand and blood trickled from his nose, through his fingers, and dripped down his shirt. Mary opened and closed her mouth, reached into her pocket, fished out a dirty handkerchief, and shoved it into his hand. He nodded and mopped his face, eyes wide with humiliation or pain. It was then that Mary became aware of how airless the shop was, how many people were crammed inside it, and how sweaty they all were. "Air . . ." she managed, before squeezing past him and out the door.

"Mary?" She looked up and there was Terry Flux, small, grey, and middle-aged. "I saw you come in and wanted to catch you," he continued. "I've had something in I thought you'd like. It was selling fast so I held one back, in case." He was holding a new single in a paper bag. Mary didn't bother to ask what it was.

"Thanks, Terry. How much?"

"Call it two quid and see you down at The Stands." He took the notes she offered and went off smiling, an inextricable combination of kindness and business sense.

Just as Billy came out to find her, Mary noticed flecks of Daniel's blood on the tips of her fingers. She made them into an omen, a sign of something, and then put her fingers into her mouth.

By seven o'clock, the hard light had lost its glitter. Camptown faded into flattened perspectives and dull surfaces, making people peer, as if it were already the dusk that wouldn't come for three hours more.

The town's modest brightness had already been smothered by accumulations in the atmosphere that no change of pressure came to release: lead particles from petrol, pale powder sloughed off by the exhausted fields, and trapped acids from the chimneys of the industrial estate. The old brick of the High Street was as grey as the concrete of the new shopping mall. Filmy windows reflected nothing.

A week earlier, fly posters had appeared, not pasted to walls or sellotaped in windows but spiked on railings, wedged between fence posts, blowing across playgrounds and paths in the park. They were the size of a page in a notebook and were scrawled on in thick black felt-tip pen: SUPPORT GRAVITY GRAVITY SUPPORTS U with, in smaller letters underneath, *Fri at 7*. The teenagers from the town and surrounding villages, now making their way into The Stands, needed no further information.

The Stands was a bar tucked under the town's football stadium. The black plastic letters plugged into its white chipboard door said CAMPTOWN FC SOCIAL CLUB, but the football club did its drinking elsewhere. The Stands was the only place in Camptown that would serve underage drinkers. It was a low-ceilinged, windowless, long, narrow room that had a scuffed stage at one end and a bar at the other.

Terry Flux, who moonlighted as a DJ, had set up his coloured lights. He kept a careful eye on the crowd, many of whom appeared to be in the first stages of metamorphosis, with an earring or a safety pin, newly cut and spiked hair, a T-shirt scribbled with swear words and slogans. He reassured them with something familiar but not entirely passé, before surprising them with something new, something they'd want to know, some raw, fast, hard music, so tense and regimented there was nothing to do if you wanted to dance but jump up and down. The girls found this particularly difficult, having grown up on the undulating rhythms of funk and soul. They stopped midsway, interrupted. The dance floor that had been theirs a year ago was now dominated by boys bouncing violently off one another.

The room was soon filled by a crowd that swirled stiffly round between the bar, the stage, the toilets, and the door, some breaking away to dance, drink, kiss, or smoke. Everything was dim, even the music, muffled and distorted by ancient speakers. The drinks were either plastic pint glasses of pale lager or concoctions of something dull and something vivid—cider and blackcurrant, gin and orange, rum and peppermint.

Mary and Billy split up as soon as they were in the door. Billy, indifferent to drink, wove his way through the crowd to stand close to Terry Flux and close enough to a bass speaker to feel it booming through him. Mary inched her way to the bar, waited half an hour, bought three vodkas at once rather than try to go back again, poured them into one glass, rolled a cigarette, and set off towards the stage just as Gravity came on.

Gravity were a Camptown band and their lead singer was a local hero, known as JonJo. JonJo was somewhere in his twenties, which made him several years older than most of the audience. He was skinny and pale. His fine red hair was greased into a lank crest, acne scars broke the surface of his white makeup, and his nipples and ribs stood out beneath the cheap gold Lurex woman's top stretched across his sunken chest. Altogether, he looked like a pantomime version of one of his father's battery hens out on Factory Farm.

JonJo glided through school, with even the teachers turning a blind eye to his lipstick and bangles. In each musical transition he had found a model that required only some minor adjustment to his style, achieved with beads, glasses, frills, a trilby, or a leather waistcoat. He remained himself: flamboyant, effeminate, suave, and lewd but sexless, just as the band's music barely changed, its raw ineptitude and fantastical lyrics somehow always just fitting the bill. Boys acknowledged his glamour but didn't want to look like him, while girls enjoyed his interest and proximity but were undisturbed by desire.

Gravity were so unrehearsed and drunk that their set quickly went to pieces. It sounded as if each member were playing a different song: the drummer was ahead of everyone else; the bass player was locked in a duel with the lead guitarist, both playing faster and more elaborate riffs; and JonJo lurched around the creaking stage, singing more or less to himself. The boys in the front loved it. Then they grew bored and began joining Gravity on stage. One grabbed JonJo's microphone and began singing a Rolling Stones song, "Sweet Virginia." JonJo shouted "Hippie shit!" but danced round him and joined in on backing vocals. This was a song everyone knew. The rest of the band got behind them, more of the boys clambered up on stage, and soon half the room were singing along. Terry Flux smiled. No one would admit to having loved the Stones now, but very few had tried to sell their records back to him. He predicted that within two years early to mid-period Stones would land in "Collectables."

Billy had circled back to Mary, and they leant against each other, laughing and singing in an exaggerated twang. The band fell off stage, and Terry Flux, who had fished around in his boxes and found that very Stones album, "Exile on Main Street," filled the room with "Let It Loose," a wild, tumbling-down song Mary secretly loved. Most of the people in the room stood still and looked at the floor or the ceiling.

Mary was hot and happy, being there with Billy and the song and the room, and then the boy, Daniel, appeared, pushing through the crowd, and they smiled and said nothing, because nothing could be heard, and he put his hands on her shoulders so definitely that she reached up and kissed him before she met his eyes.

Terry Flux rescued his audience by filling the last hour of the evening with hard punk, The Buzzcocks' "Love You More," The Vibrators' "Baby, Baby," the same old love thing but rawer than ever.

When Daniel offered to walk Mary to the bus station, she didn't want to lose the chance to cross town with him by admitting that the last bus had gone. On leaving The Stands, they put their arms around each other, clutching hard, and then walked awkwardly on, perhaps afraid that any adjustment would shatter their strange confidence.

Mary pushed her free hand into her pocket, clutching her glasses, not in case she needed them but as if she thought they might suddenly appear of their own accord. Rather than try to see where they were going, and afraid, in any case, of being seen, she kept her head down. Daniel's hand on her shoulder couldn't keep still but traced her bones as far as he could reach, back and forth and round, from the nape of her neck to her collarbone. It was all she could do to grasp his jacket enough to hold on.

They turned into Camptown High Street, which, though dark, was busy. It was eleven o'clock, closing time, and the six High Street pubs were simultaneously disgorging their customers. Gangs of boys shouted names, football chants, and snatches of songs, and softly punched one another. Older men, as if in bloom with their beer guts, jowls, and burst veins, shook one another's thick hands and tottered off to their cars. There were proud, stiff couples and limp, bored couples; giggling trios of girls who linked arms to hold each other up; and solitary men who went to the same pub for years and sat at the bar, side by side, speaking only to borrow a newspaper or order a drink.

In daytime, people were hemmed onto the pavements of the High Street by heavy traffic. Now they walked in the road in their twos, threes, and fours. The occasional mini-cab or lorry had to slow down and negotiate. The town centre was mostly unlit. There were no neon signs or brilliant shop windows. Even Blazes, the town's nightclub, made do with a carriage lamp over the hand-painted sign in its mews archway. Only the biggest and oldest pub, The Market Place, was lit. Its stout plaster exterior carried a string of bulbs, like beads of sweat, just below its thatch. It was the drinking place of land and money: farmers, bankers, accountants, estate managers, stud owners, gamekeepers.

No one looked ready to go home. Even the few who were not at least a little drunk felt an exaggerated lightness with the relief of the end of the week and the unaccustomed pleasure of warm darkness. It wasn't like being on holiday, because for most people, holidays were not associated with heat. Nor did they have any special holiday clothes. No one was wearing anything bright and it was too hot for the fashionable shades of purple, ochre, yellow, lime, or the bottom-heavy shapes of pear-drop collars, maxi-skirts, and platform boots. Even the farmers and bankers were out in plain white shirtsleeves.

Boys in white T-shirts began to circle and call to girls in white dresses. Daniel in grey and Mary in black kept their silence even when a weeping girl spun into them, stared, laughed, and ran off. Each privately burned with shame when a boy clutching a lamppost vomited just as they passed. There was a couple in a doorway: the girl smoking, her dress unbuttoned; the boy's hands and mouth on her breasts. Someone shouted "You cunt!" and a rush of footsteps was followed by the sound of a windscreen shattering. There was a police car outside Blazes, where two officers were pulling a man up from the gutter, his frilly shirt sprinkled with blood.

Unless summoned, the police kept away from the High Street and concentrated on places like The Stands or the main roads and roundabouts out of town, where they would stop and search whomever they felt like. Billy and Mary were stopped all the time, walking down a lane, driving round on Billy's bike, or hitching a ride home. Mostly, they just had to give their names and addresses and say where they were going. The police were sure a hippie like Billy would have drugs on him, but they never found them, and they were confused by the girl, who didn't look like the hippie's type.

The bus station was a cavernous hangar with fifteen bays. Each had a concrete bench and a plastic frame nailed to the wall where there used to be a timetable, above which were faded indecipherable bus numbers. There was one bus, parked under sprinklers that poured water over its soapy bodywork. Daniel and Mary walked towards it, as if wanting to maintain for as long as possible the fiction that they had come here for Mary to go home. A man in overalls, carrying a large brush, appeared.

"Exempt, see . . ." he said, patting the bus with his brush like an elephant keeper. "Says we have to keep the windows clean, for safety and that." The water gurgled and splashed around their feet. They let go of each other, turned, and walked back out onto the station forecourt.

Now that there was no one singing or shouting or running past, Daniel started talking. How would she get home? Mary thought that if she went out to the Malibu Motel roundabout, she could hitch home from there. They walked along the ring road, Daniel talking in a rush about bands and painters. He was nineteen, an art student at college on the coast. His big sister worked for a gallery in London. He hated provincial life. The country was, in any case, dying, let alone the countryside. And what about Mary? She took the cigarette packet on which he had written his phone number and agreed, quite sincerely, with everything he said.

As soon as they got to the roundabout, a rusting maroon Cadillac emerged from the sliproad and stopped. A window rolled down and Julie Lacey yelled, "Mary George! You hopeless cow! We'll give you a lift, then." Drenched with embarrassment, Mary kissed Daniel's cheek and let Julie pull her into the car. Julie had a pile of papers on her knee and a large calculator in her other hand. Barry Spence was driving, a cigar between his teeth. Now and then he passed a sheet of paper from a heap on the passenger seat back to Julie, who rapidly punched the calculator keys, jotted down numbers, and sighed.

"It's hopeless, Barry. Whichever way I run it, the depreciation of your fixed assets doesn't even dent the profit margin. That's a hell of a bite on your neck, you dirty bitch! What about on-costs, Bal?" Another flurry of pages was thrown into the back.

As they drove out of Camptown onto the heath, a tall figure loomed in the middle of the road and Barry braked hard. He leapt out, half angry, half afraid, while Julie squawked and Mary covered her eyes. It was JonJo. He got into the front, collecting up Barry's papers. "I'll keep hold of these for you, Mr. Spence." He said it so politely, Barry could not take offence.

"I'll drop you at the end of the lane and you can walk to the farm from there."

JonJo's white makeup had faded and run, and his skin beneath was just as pale. "Thank you so much." He lit a cigarette in a plastic tortoiseshell holder and turned to Julie and Mary in the back. "Nice to see you two being friends again." He raised an eyebrow.

"Couldn't leave the blind cow on the road with God knows who, could we?" Julie replied.

"Bitch," Mary mumbled, not looking round but smiling.

"Cow," retorted Julie, also smiling as she continued with her sums.

Barry Spence dropped Mary off on the Green. She hesitated by the gate, as the downstairs lights were still on. She pulled out her glasses and saw Stella at the table, talking to someone who was leaving the room. Then the front door opened and Christie came down the path. He looked at Mary as if he'd never seen her before and hurried past.

Mary wanted to carry the evening unbroken to bed. Above all, she didn't want Stella to see her kissed face. Even in the car, next to Julie, who had barely glanced up from her calculations, Mary had turned away and pushed her head out of the open window. She was sure that anyone who cared to look would notice her swollen mouth, the grainy bruise on her throat, his breath in her breath, the tiny blister gathering just inside the edge of the middle of her upper lip. It's like a flood, she thought, but fire. It comes from inside and out. A bowl of water overturning in a bowl of water.

"Sit down, love," said Stella, before Mary was even in sight. The living room was almost filled by a pine table that her mother kept frighteningly bare. The dresser that ran along one wall and scraped under the beams was crammed with crockery, cutlery, paper, tools, and paints, all ordered so meticulously that the room still looked spacious.

Rather than join her mother, Mary curled up in an undersized armchair by the fireplace. Stella didn't look up. She was bent forward, her head almost on the table but just caught in her hands. Mary stared into the empty grate. There were no ornaments on the mantelpiece, not even a ticking clock. Her mother now seemed neither tall nor still. One of her feet tapped rapidly against the floor.

"You saw Christie was here," Stella began, and the tapping paused, as if those five words had exhausted her, ". . . about Tom." Mary didn't want to hear about Tom, but her mother was talking to her in such an oddly unguarded tone that she waited.

Stella's fair colouring, though now rather vague, was consistent. Her thick hair, her stone-grey eyes and smooth skin made such an even surface that people never asked how she was. Her features were well arranged, locked in place, and certainly not given to grotesqueness. Yet as Mary watched, her mouth twisted, just for a moment, but so extremely that the effect was not only violent but comical. Mary had a sudden vision of her mother spitting out frogs like someone punished for telling lies in a fairy tale.

"I wanted to ask you about the reservoir. All that. Just to be clear."

Mary was shaking. "I didn't do anything on purpose, Mum . . . I didn't know he was there. If I had, I wouldn't have walked . . ."

"No one's blaming you," Stella said, sounding like a teacher intent on a confession. "Tom is agitated. He thinks you . . ."

"He can't think anything!" Mary was shaking and got up to leave, but Stella rose, too, and closed the door.

"To him, to all of us, you are an important part of the picture."

"It's not my picture, though, is it?" Mary had surprised herself and now felt scared.

Stella lost patience. Her head snapped back as her fist smashed down on the table. The bangles on her arm chinked—ridiculously, Mary thought, and as ever felt ashamed of her mother, whose long skirts and dresses, shawls and scarves, beads, feathers, ribbons and lace looked like costumes rather than clothes. At primary school the other children had called her mother a witch. ("A nice witch," Julie had assured her, and it was true that she was kind and helped anyone she could, and the other children adored her.)

"Damn it, Mary! You were not supposed to be there!"

Mary couldn't tell if this was admonition or regret. "I was only walking home," she muttered.

"But you were supposed to be in school!"

"School? What do you mean?" Mary was confused.

Stella gave a hissing sigh. "There's a law in this country that says six-year-olds have to go to school."

"Six-year-olds? What's that to do with me? Mum, it was Saturday morning, right? I cut across from Ingfield, round the water. I didn't know who he was! I didn't even know he was there!"

"Ah." This time Stella's exhalation was hard and sharp, the sound someone might make after running into a wall.

"Don't be angry, Mum, please!" Mary was clutching her cardigan to her with both hands. "I'm not six, I'm seventeen, and all I was doing was walking home and stopping to look at the water."

"When was this?"

"That Saturday he followed me home. When else?" Stella gave a very small nod, which made Mary feel, briefly, like explaining herself. "There's a tree, see, with a branch stretching out over the water. I like to go along it. He saw me there. He said I was near the house."

"And?"

"I walk out along this bough."

"You little fool, you could fall in and drown!"

"But I don't fall. I keep walking."

"And then?"

"And what?"

Stella stood up and Mary stood up to meet her. Neither raised her voice. When Mary said nothing, Stella lowered her eyes and asked almost timidly, "Did you see anything?"

Mary was about to begin but changed her mind. "I had my eyes shut," she whispered, and ran up to her room.

"What did you say?" Stella followed so fast that she filled the doorway before Mary could shut herself in. She spoke so evenly that Mary felt sick. "It's not a joke or a game. Christie's been and Tom is very fragile. What he has been through, what we have all been through. Your father. I just want to go over it again, to get things straight." Mary was shaking her head. "I know you were only six, but you do remember, don't you?" This wasn't really a question and she didn't pause for Mary to answer it. "That's what I'm talking about. Not whatever went on the other day. When you walked out of school, remember? Went to look for your daddy. What you saw in the chapel, remember?"

The village school had still been in the old building then. Mary hadn't liked it because the tables and chairs were so low and the windows so high. The children were divided two school years to each of the two rooms, but tended to sit where they liked. The elderly teachers, Miss Benyon and Mrs. Snape, found it hard to tell the pupils apart, not least because so many were related. Mrs. Snape, who was in with the younger ones, would draw a map and forget what went on it, or fall asleep halfway through a story, and while the other children welcomed these lapses, Mary felt cross. She wanted to know what went where, what happened.

Mrs. Snape was fat, smiling, and vicious. Anger woke her from her slowness—she became fast and precise, cracking heads together or swishing a ruler across the backs of hands or knees. She likes places with lots of small and complicated bones, thought Mary, noting that Mrs. Snape looked as if she had no bones at all.

Mrs. Snape was not fond of clever girls, especially those who dressed oddly and spoke well, like Mary George. You never could tell what the child was thinking. Her head was up in the clouds; she needed pulling back down. That morning, she had had enough of Mary daydreaming, doodling, singing to herself, and still knowing all the answers, so she sent her out into the corridor. Mary relished this sudden out-of-placeness; it made her concentrate. Being alone was always a relief, and the corridor, though chilly, wasn't dark. The front door was hooked back onto the wall and was open all day, so Mary could see the low autumn sun, papery pale and far away but still strong enough to make the scratched varnish on the door gleam.

Mary amused herself deciphering hieroglyphics and making

out treasure maps in the scratches on the door until a draught carried a dying bumblebee in over the step. She watched it stagger in circles on the tiled floor, inches from her feet. She studied its bristling stripes, the worn threads of its legs and bent antennae, and listened to its fading buzz. The other children would have pulled off its wings or taken it outside in a handkerchief to be laid tearfully and ceremoniously under the hedge. Even when it bumped into her shoes, Mary didn't move but only wondered why it seemed to take longer crossing the red tiles than the black, and how such silly little wings could have carried so much. When confronted with something that demanded her attention, she often felt like this—as far away as the sun.

The bee crawled over to the skirting and disappeared. A shadow swung across the doorway and a crate of milk was set down, the free compulsory miniature bottles the children drank each day. The older ones took it in turn to be Milk Monitor, to puncture the foil caps with a knitting needle, push in the straws, and force everyone to drink it. Even in winter the milk was warm, sweet, and cheesy, turning to curd on the tongue. The children spat it out wherever they could, making the spider plants sallow, clouding the goldfish tank, and adding to the rancid stench of the gerbils' cage.

Mary looked out across the playground, a sloping strip of tarmac that ran the length of the school. It was too narrow for any exciting games. Just as you speeded up in British Bulldog or tag, you met the hedge on one side or the wall on the other. It was too easy, in such a confined space, to catch or be caught. It just wasn't interesting.

Mary considered the milk and realised that if she was not in the classroom, she wouldn't have to drink it. The playground gate stood permanently open, grown over by privet. Only the sound of Mrs. Snape's rasping voice held her back, so she blocked her ears, and then it was easy. She didn't want to go along the High Street, because that was the way home and somebody who knew her was sure to see her, so she slipped up Back Lane and into the fields.

It was almost October and the blackberries were at that stage when they were as plump and purple as they would ever be but still sour. Mary followed them, pulling the fruit from their fiddly clumps, trying and spitting, captivated by their colour and baffled by their taste. Eventually, she felt tiny scratches rising on her arms and legs. She stopped and found that she had reached the end of the single field that now ran the length of the back of the village. She began to think about where she might be.

There was a stile ahead, so she clambered over and found herself on the main road. She was out past the first tied cottages, farther away from school and home than she could have imagined. She had lived in Allnorthover all her life and here was a part of it she didn't know at all, at least a part she only ever passed through quickly. What if this were a different village, not her village at all but somewhere else? How could she get back into it if it wasn't hers? A lorry rattled past, too close, its clanking undercarriage and blustering exhaust level with Mary's eyes. The combined force of its size, speed, and noise knocked her off her feet. Mary sat, tearful, on the verge. Then she realised she could see the roof of the chapel, opposite the first cottages, and decided to find her father.

Mary pushed open the door but dared not go in. Matthew was crouched on the floor, doing something with a big piece of paper, chalk, and pencils that reminded Mary of what she ought to be doing right then at school. The piece of paper was a map, or the beginnings of one. It needed names added and some colouring in.

"Are you looking for me?"

"Are you here?" Mary was delighted when she amused her father, even though she rarely understood why.

"And school, Miss Merry Blackberry?" Matthew smiled as he spoke, but Mary could see she'd worried him. He did things carefully and definitely, and had a strong voice that made her feel safe.

"Mrs. Snape put me out so . . . I thought I'd go."

He nodded, accepting the logic of this, and rose to his feet. "And have a feast in the fields by the look of you. Let's get you washed up and I'll take you back. They'll be fretting."

"What country is that?" Mary pointed at the map, stalling for time. She knelt down beside it and Matthew joined her.

"Let's see," he began. "There's a big road." His finger traced a curving line from top to bottom. "Now that there, that little cross on a triangle, what does that remind you of?"

"Church steeple?"

"Good girl! So if that's the church, what's this bit of land along from it?"

Mary studied the long rectangle that began by the steeple and was split by the big road. "It's a Green."

Matthew ran his finger along the row of narrow, different-sized boxes, some missing corners, some with extra corners, that lined the road. Mary caught on: "The High Street." His finger continued to the end of the row, along the road, to a bigger box, on its own. "It's here! It's us!" Matthew lifted his hand and made to get up, but Mary was enjoying her success. She leaned over and put down her forefinger where he had left off. "And this is where the bus goes to Camptown, out through the curvy Verges . . . here's trees . . . it's Temple Grove, isn't it? And Ingfield Dip . . . and you've coloured this bit in, why blue?"

Matthew grasped her waist and swung her into the air, but too quickly, so it hurt. He put her down by the door. "I was seeing what it would be like if we filled the Dip with water," he said, his speech now careful.

"Oh!" Mary was thrilled. "You mean we'd get great big hoses and fill them up with the sea and pour it all out again here?"

"Something like that."

"And then Christie and Tom and Mrs. Iris could live underwater, with fish swimming past their window, and we could dive in and visit them?"

Matthew propelled her down the path. "Something like that."

Stella was still standing in the doorway, still talking: ". . . and when I told you about the plans for the reservoir, you already knew, didn't you?" Mary shook her head. "You've always been good at secrets, haven't you? Like the hospital? No . . . you couldn't quite keep that one in, could you? Oh, sweetheart, you were so little and didn't know, and he thought he could take you about with him and you wouldn't tell, how could you help it, poor duck?" This was worse. Stella came and sat beside Mary and stroked her hair, but able to tell how determinedly Mary had disappeared inside herself, she stopped and moved away. "Just try, please, to remember what happened. It's going to come up, you see, with Tom back and all. You remember Iris, don't you? Remember how she was with your dad?"

---

What Mary couldn't remember was what had made her say it that night, after she'd found her father drawing the map. They had been finishing supper and she had asked Matthew, "Is Christie's mummy your mummy, Daddy, only she's not my gran?"

Stella had laughed, but it hadn't been a happy sound, more as if she'd dropped the plates in her hands and they were bouncing and breaking on the floor. Matthew had picked up his knife and fork again, although the dishes had been cleared. Then Stella was in the kitchen, banging things.

"She's a family friend, sweetheart. Iris was my mother's friend, and after my mother died, she was my friend. Now she's sick in the hospital, I try to comfort and help her."

"What's wrong with her?" Mary remembered how this old woman, in her whiteness and softness, was like snow in winter and fleece in summer, and whose bright eyes had held all colours.

"She has cancer."

Mary thought cancer . . . canker . . . conker . . . and saw a spring cloud shrivel and darken to a hard brown shell. "Will she die?"

"Yes, she will."

"Then how do you help her, Daddy?"

"We talk. We tell each other stories, just like you and me, Mary Fairy."

"And do you brush her hair, like you do mine?"

"Her hair's gone. The medicine . . . you see, her body needs all its strength to get better and hasn't got time to be growing any more hair."

A shell. Smooth and empty. Mary ran to her mother.

The winter that Iris Hepple lay dying was a time of locked cold, in which everything held still. Mary would be woken by Stella climbing the stairs with a paraffin heater, its liquid slopping against its sides. She would bring it into Mary's room and turn the stiff dial that cranked up the wick. She'd strike a match and the room would fill with something warm but so dry it made Mary's eyes sting before she'd opened them. Bundled up in her dressing gown and slippers, she would follow her mother downstairs and crouch by the fire. The coal smoked and changed colour. There would be porridge, and a trip back upstairs again to wash and dress in the damp bathroom, where a single electric bar on the wall gave off a weak glow. Before and after school, it was dark. Even when the snow came and everything was white for weeks on end, it was still dark and her father never seemed to be home. All Mary thought about, though, was trying to get warm.

On Christmas Eve, Mary was woken by shouting. She crept to the top of the stairs and there were her parents in the hallway. She couldn't tell if they were holding on to each other or pushing away. Stella was as tall as Matthew, as broad as he was, and as fair. Even though their faces were close together, they were shouting.

"Why go tomorrow?" Stella's mouth stayed open after she'd finished speaking. Mary could see her teeth.

"Because neither Christie nor Tom will." Matthew looked down and shook his head. Stella put her hand in the hair at the back of his head and tugged, forcing him to raise his face.

"I know Tom can't, he hasn't left the house in years . . . but Christie? Have you really thought about why he doesn't visit his own dying mother?"

"Can't face the state she's in, I don't know . . ."

"Can't face the disappointment when she sees *it's* . . . *not* . . . *you* . . ." And Mary's gentle father had taken his wife's head in his hands and knocked it hard back against the front door, three times, echoing her words.

There was another week without school after Christmas during which Stella went away to London. Matthew and Mary did jigsaw puzzles by the fire in the mornings and went over to the chapel in the afternoons. Mary loved the paper on which he drew his plans, the big squares filled with smaller and fainter squares. Matthew would use a Swiss army knife to whittle his pencil to a fine, long tip. Then he would adjust his right-angled rulers and fill a blank sheet with rooms, doors, roofs, and windows. It was freezing in the chapel, so Matthew brought the paraffin heaters from home, and Mary, who was still too cold to keep still but didn't want to bother him, would scamper between the heaters and his desk, where she would stop to consider his progress and ask to borrow a word: "Axonometric, ax-onometric . . ."

On the second day of Stella's absence, Matthew put Mary in the car and drove into Camptown. For two hours they walked up and down the High Street in the cold, going in and out of shops but not buying anything—no meat from the butcher's, no bread from the baker's, no buttons from the haberdasher's, no chairs from the antiques shop nor buckets from the ironmonger's. Mary enjoyed it all but was puzzled. They walked back to the car but didn't get in. Matthew turned to the big building next to which he had parked.

"I must see a friend, sweetheart." He took her hand and they went into the building and through a number of heavy doors like the one at school, only they swung open and shut so easily, sweeping the rubber floor with a rubber strip, making only the faintest noise, a suck and a sigh. They walked down a very long corridor with the quietest floor Mary had ever come across. There was another set of doors with three chairs to one side. Mary was more properly warm than she had been all winter.

"You'd best wait here," said Matthew, without looking at his daughter. He was gone through the doors before she could respond.

After that, they went to the hospital every day, without bothering with the shops first. Matthew brought her colouring books, even sweets. Mary hated his smell when he tucked her up at night. It was confusing; it made her think of an attic.

One day, Mary got bored with swinging her legs in the corridor. She pushed open the doors and went in. She could see some beds and blue screens arranged like tents. She didn't know where Matthew was, but then she heard his voice coming from a small room at the end and he was singing a song she loved, "My very good friend the milkman says . . ." Mary rushed in smiling to find him but couldn't see him because he wasn't there in the room but there on the bed, curled up with a tiny old woman in his arms, his mouth against the bad egg of her head. She was as brown as a stain. She had tubes coming out of her arms and her bones stuck out everywhere. Her white nightgown was rucked up around the long bones of her thighs, and a flat yellow breast lay nestled in the folds of its open bodice, beneath which Mary thought she could see her father's hand. Machines on either side of the bed bleeped and whispered. Mary screamed.

When they got home, Stella was there. Mary was sent to bed but kept seeing faces without teeth, eyes, or hair in the dark. Stella held and rocked her, and tried to tell her stories, but kept stopping. Mary felt as if she were in the grip of an earthquake. She pretended to be asleep so her mother would leave. Then she sent herself away, in her head, off to a cloud or a cave, where, nonetheless, some words reached her: ". . . sick . . . mother love . . . lover . . ."

Mary had never seen her mother cry, and could not have imagined the ferocity with which she did so now, remembering that winter. She was sitting on the edge of Mary's bed, as upright as ever, staring out Mary's window. She didn't look at her daughter, who, even if she wasn't sleeping, could not be reached. Stella knew Mary wouldn't hear what she said, but she was talking for her own sake. "You saw . . . heard . . . things, and the trouble is now you know and I don't know, do I really? I know he took you to see her. I expect she liked you. She must have done, Matthew's only child . . ." Her body shook violently, as she sobbed but made no sound. "Poor Tom, now he's come back and the trouble is he's found you. Matthew's gone, and now that damned family want you, too . . . His 'angel' is what Christie says he's calling you, as if you can make everything all right for him. I told Christie, I said, That girl can't see beyond the end of her nose! How's she going to find a drowned house! Wasn't it demolished, anyway?"

On this point Stella was uncertain. She had always thought of the reservoir as a concrete bowl beneath which everything had been flattened or removed. "But tell me, tell me again about Daddy and Iris. You don't have to keep their secrets now they've both gone and I want to . . . help you. Don't you miss him? Don't you want to talk to me about that?"

Around 3 a.m., the time that day began again, ahead of itself with birdsong in the blue light, Mary woke from a dream of happiness. She was smiling and her face was wet, and as she opened her eyes, she felt her dream-self disappearing with whatever had happened or been said, and she waited for the dream to come back to her but wasn't able to remember anything about it.

Less than twelve hours after Mary had written her number on Daniel's arm, she was woken by the ringing of the phone. She flailed around for her glasses, only to find them, as she often did, by almost treading on them as she got up. She could hear Stella's voice and thought she had answered, but the phone kept ringing. Mary was about to run downstairs when she heard another voice, a man's, and stopped herself. She was still in last night's clothes. She tugged her T-shirt over her head, but it caught on her glasses, so she had to pull it back, take off her glasses, and start again. She pulled off her trousers and pants, and put her glasses back on as she opened the wardrobe. Then she realised that while Stella was still talking, the phone had stopped.

There she was in the wardrobe mirror, as pale and bony as everyone said, with heavy hair that was no particular colour and that tipped her head forward like the failed balancing act of her wide eyes and narrow chin. She took off her glasses and moved right up to the mirror to scrutinise her face: the circles beneath her eyes made darker by a grainy rim of eyeliner, open pores across her nose and cheeks as if her skin couldn't get enough air, a ragged flush on her face and neck, her dark mouth swollen and cracked. I am so obvious, she thought, then breathed hard on her reflection and went to have a bath.

Stella was knocking on the door as soon as she had locked it. "Mary? I left you my water. It's still warm."

Since the shortage had been announced, people were encouraged to conserve what water they could. The shallow bath Stella had left her had a cloudy sheen, and around the edge was a bubbly, creamy scum. The basin was also half full. As quietly as she could, Mary ran a trickle of cold water into a glass, rubbed a dry flannel against the soap, and, dipping its corner in the glass, washed herself inch by inch.

"Good morning, Mary Mystery!" Lucas greeted her without taking his mouth from the rim of his teacup, so the tea spilt over his lips, staining the white stubble on his chin. Mary smiled but squeezed herself past the other side of the table.

"More tea?" She collected the pot from the table. "Any toast?"

Lucas winced and shook his head. "I wouldn't impose." He smoothed the front of his battered raincoat, which was too small and had no buttons, and under which he appeared to be wearing nothing. He adjusted the string he used as a belt and pushed his hand into a pocket. Just as Mary got to the kitchen, he added, "I have an egg . . . if you wouldn't mind." It was strange to see something so fragile emerge from his filthy coat, in his swollen, arthritic hand.

She took the egg from him and went into the kitchen, where her mother already had not only the kettle but a small pan of water on the boil. Mary put the egg in to cook and after a couple of minutes went back to Lucas. "And would you like a drop more tea with your egg?" He gave a small nod. "And, while you're at it, what about a little toast on the side?"

As they sat down to breakfast together, Lucas took a bite of his heavily buttered toast and mumbled something through his ill-fitting dentures about property.

"What was that?" Mary asked out of politeness more than curiosity.

"I've got property." Lucas had lived for twenty-five years in a shed. "A caravan."

"You're moving into a caravan?"

"Not moving in. I sold it."

"Which caravan?"

"Mrs. Eley, see. She came over and said as how I could live in that caravan she has in her orchard, as how she wanted to put it to good use. To think of it as my home."

"But you don't want to live there?"

"I've got my shed, but I wasn't ungrateful. I met this bloke in the pub who came down and had a look at it and made me an offer on the spot."

Stella had come in from the kitchen now and explained for him. "Lucas was confused. Mrs. Eley was offering him the caravan to live in, not to keep."

Lucas scooped out the remains of his egg with his fingers, slurped his tea, and gave Mary a sidelong smile. "She changed her mind, is all. Now, if you'll excuse me." He heaved himself up and made his way to the downstairs toilet, which he used noisily. Then he left through the front door, without saying goodbye. Lucas's shed was a short distance across the fields behind the house and he liked to visit that way, coming in through the back-garden gate.

Stella pulled on her rubber gloves and went to clean up after him. She came back, shaking her head. "They're trying to ban him from the Arms again. He celebrated his so-called sale last night and upset a few of the new customers. I've got his shirt and trousers here in the wash."

"Not with my stuff?" Mary couldn't help herself. She didn't use the downstairs toilet these days, either. Stella frowned and Mary felt worse, so she continued: "Well, good for him, getting one over on Violet Eley." Mary had never liked that woman and had thought for years that her name was "Eely" and that it suited her sharp face and wriggling voice. "I mean, shouldn't he be in a Council house or something?"

"He'd only try and sell that, too."

"Like his medals?"

"The medals were really his."

"I'm off to the post office, before it shuts." Mary pulled on her boots.

"Don't forget the Fête this afternoon. I'll need quite a lot of help getting everything over from the shop to the church fields." The phone started ringing again and Mary went to answer it, but Stella grabbed her arm. "It's been going all morning. Wrong number."

Ray Cornice would have closed up by the time Mary reached the post office, as it was a minute after half past twelve, only he was busy helping Alf Kettle fill out a fishing permit and couldn't get to the door. In exasperation he had lifted the counter window as high as it would go and had pushed his arms through to point out the words on the form. "Start date doesn't mean today's date but the date you want it to start."

While Alf Kettle chose his date and wrote it in, Ray slipped out from behind the counter and took the door off the latch, closed it firmly, and let down the blind. It was then that Mary realised that the person waiting in front of her and behind Alf Kettle was Tom Hepple. He hadn't turned round as she came in or as Ray closed the door. She couldn't leave now without Tom hearing her, so she waited.

The post office was just the small front room of the Cornices' cottage. Behind the door was a rack of stationery, arranged in brown cardboard boxes: white and manila envelopes, half a dozen aerograms, parcel paper, biros, blotting paper, carbon paper, pencils, sharpeners, bottles and cartridges of ink, sellotape, pots of glue, rubber bands, scissors, and balls of string. Although a small supermarket had recently opened in the village, the post office still sold some "dry goods." Ray Cornice was running down his stocks, but he still displayed a few bags of flour, tins of peas, mushrooms, molasses, and custard powder, Bovril, tomato ketchup, and HP Sauce. On the bottom shelf were worming tablets, flea powder, starch, and bleach. The L-shaped counter was divided between the post office behind a window and the shop. This last part was kept clear except for a pair of scales. Behind it were piles of magazines, boxes of cigarettes, and jars of sweets. There was also toothpaste, shoe polish, and hair oil, and if Ray Cornice couldn't find what you were looking for on the shelves, he would go back to the kitchen and ask his wife, Joan, and if they had what you wanted in the house, they would sell it to you. Stella once brought home a newspaper to find the crossword half done.

Nothing was labelled, displayed, or priced; you had to ask or guess. As a child, Mary would point at one or another of the jars in the dusty gloom and ask for a quarter or two-eighths, and then be astonished when she got outside at the brightness of her sweets, the acid yellow of lemon sherbets, and the glossy orange-red of aniseed twists. It had been the same when Stella made blancmange—the pale granules poured from the sachet into hot milk that thickened and turned so pink that Mary used to call it "cartoon pudding."

Ray Cornice stamped the form and showed Alf where to sign it. "That'll be seventy-five pence."

"What's that, then, when it's at home?"

"Fifteen shillings."

Alf pulled some coins out of his pocket. "Five new pence in a shilling, right?"

"Right."

"Five times fifteen . . ." He picked up the pen attached to the counter by a string and began scribbling on the blotting pad. "Seventy-five pence." He pulled a handful of coins out of his trouser pocket, then put them back again, took out his wallet instead, and gave Ray a pound note.

Ray gave him his change. "There's five bob." Alf tipped his hat and left, with Mary trying to stay hidden by him as he passed, even though Tom didn't turn round. Ray pulled down the window. "What can I do for you, Tom?"

There was a brief conversation that Mary barely heard as she concentrated on staying still and making no noise. Eventually, a page was torn, a book was stamped, and notes were counted and folded. Loose change chinked as it hit the counter, coin by coin. When Ray Cornice stopped counting, Mary turned away and leant into the shelves. She pretended to be looking for something, but though the post office was so small that Tom had to brush past her back as he left, its gloom discouraged anyone from looking round them. He did not appear to have noticed her.

Mary was shaking as she put her savings book on the counter. "I want to take some out, Mr. Cornice, please, five pounds."

He frowned as he flicked through the pages. "You know your signature's nothing like . . ." Mary blushed. She had opened this account five years ago, and the signature at the front of the book was all round loops; the dots over the *i*'s were circles. More recently, she'd been trying to copy her father's italics and had come up with a rather shaky, spiky new version of her name.

"It's almost full, anyway. I'll go out the back and get you a new one. In case you want to use it elsewhere." She was about to thank him, but he had disappeared. When he came back, he was carrying a new blue book and a sheaf of tattered letters, held together with a rubber band. He checked her balance and printed it carefully on the first page of her new book, where she signed her new signature. He counted out five one-pound notes, slipped them inside the book, and handed it to her beneath the window. As she turned to go, he came round the other end of the counter. "There's something else," he said, and held out the letters.

Mary was confused. "Who are they for?" Perhaps he wanted her to deliver them.

Ray Cornice was inscrutable. "I've been meaning to . . . These had to be opened, see, returned to sender, and seeing as how you're . . ."

Mary looked at the first letter. It was addressed to "Iris Hepple, Back House, Ingfield Dip, near Allnorthover." The stamp was in old money. Mary pulled the envelope out and turned it over. It had been slit open and then resealed with tape, Mr. Cornice's official post office tape, Mary supposed.

Not wanting to think about what they said or who they were from, Mary wondered instead how Ray Cornice had come to keep them, remembering how many times she had seen him empty the postbox built into the wall outside, so as to have a sack ready when the van came by.

"Not delivered?" Mary wasn't brave enough to ask her question more directly.

Ray folded his arms, as if to stop Mary handing the letters back. "Look at the postmarks." The letters were dated several months apart in the year when Iris Hepple had first been dead.

"What am I to—?" Mary hesitated. Ray Cornice had taken her into some sort of confidence and then seemed to want to hand it over, entire and unexplained.

"Take them back." Ray stepped round her to clear the greeting cards from the carousel in the window. She stayed there, not knowing what to do, as he went into the back and returned with a basket of damp laundry. "It's past closing," he muttered, his mouth full of clothes pegs. She stuffed the letters in her bag and slipped out, shutting the door on Ray pegging his socks up to dry on the carousel.

The phone was ringing again when Mary got home, and this time she answered it.

"Mary George?"

She recognised his voice and the way he said her name, with a heavy formality. She put the phone down and then, for a moment, felt frightened and ashamed. He was ill. He might only want to ask her something. The phone rang again, and although she couldn't stop herself from picking it up, she still couldn't speak and so put it down once more. The fourth time she replied, "She's not here."

"Mary George?"

"Not here."

There was a silence in which Mary stopped herself saying Sorry or Would you like to leave a message? but Tom Hepple had put the phone down. It didn't ring again.

Half an hour later, Stella came in with her arms full of boxes. "Good job you left the door open," she was saying as she put them down. "In fact, I could do with a hand . . . Mary?" Mary was crouched on the floor by the telephone, her hands over her ears.

"He rang again, didn't he." Stella sat down beside her, not quite touching her. Mim came to lie down on Mary's other side. The dog leant against her, then settled on the floor with her head beneath one paw. Stella looked at them both. "See no evil, hear no evil!" She laughed, then covered her mouth. She could not think what to say next.

It was Mary who began: "When he tried before, what did you say?"

"That you were out, which was true, and then the next time that you couldn't help him, and then, after a while, I went down to the Arms and got Christie."

"Is that why he was here when I got back last night?"

"Yes. Look"—Stella was stroking Mary's hair out of her eyes—"I know you must be scared, but he's not going to hurt you. Christie explained that they've been to see Dr. Clough and Tom's back on his medication and so he should calm down soon. Christie's his only family and is very good to him. He's done up the chapel for when he's well enough to live alone."

"He's staying in the village?"

"He doesn't know anywhere else."

"What about London, can't he go back there?"

"He only went there to get away."

"Why does he want me?"

"He doesn't want you in particular. He wants to be at home." Stella hated the blandness in her voice, but she was sincere. "He's fixed on you because you were there, and then, because you're your father's daughter."

"But Dad was only . . ." Mary felt her mother's body stiffen. "I mean, the reservoir was coming anyway, wasn't it? Mrs. Hepple, she knew that."

"There was compensation."

Mary stood up. "I don't want to hear it."

Stella made herself leave it. "Tom can't have the house back, but he needs to be made to feel at home."

"This village doesn't feel like a home." Mary thought of Allnorthover as a starting point, somewhere she was gradually leaving, each journey getting longer and farther away.

"Not to us, no." Stella remembered arriving twenty years ago with Matthew. Everything they owned had fit in the back of his Mini. Many of their London art-school friends were heading for the country, and Stella, who had lived in the city all her life, had been delighted that they didn't have to land somewhere as strangers. Matthew came from a real place and could take her back there. They even had the cottage that Matthew lived in as a child with his father, Joe. His mother, Elizabeth, had died giving birth to him, so, like Mary, Matthew was an only child. Joe had been one of the Allnorthover Georges, not quite a First Family but rooted thereabouts for several generations. He had worked on Factory Farm back in the days of the Belgian Farmer, whose real name no one could now remember. The Belgian was the one who'd decided to turn Tye Farm into a factory. He'd designed the barns and the chicken crates to go inside them, the feed and water dispensers, as well as the tracks between sheds on which he ran a small locomotive transporting birds and food, sawdust and eggs around the farm. He had a vision of scale and efficiency twenty years before anyone else in the region began to take such notions on. Joseph George was his engineer and manager. It was he who had turned the Belgian's sketches into machines. Joe George had been gifted and careful, but since the death of Elizabeth, he had also been brokenhearted. Matthew crept around him, tried to cheer and comfort him, but could not get near. In the end, they lived in a silence that hardened to the point where no one could stand to be in a room with them. Iris Hepple had been Elizabeth's best friend. She took Matthew just for a few months at first, to give Joe a rest.

Matthew made the cottage his first project, building an extension that added a bathroom upstairs and enlarged the kitchen. He insisted that both these rooms should have huge windows at the back, which he smashed out of the brick. He liked to design windows like these, without panes, so that they looked like empty space. As a child, Mary had found them troubling. To her, they left the cottage unfinished, opened and not closed up again. She liked the old diamond-leaded windows at the front. Stella had hung all the windows, front and back, with muslin curtains, and those at the back of the house were usually kept closed. Matthew painted the interior walls and beams white, stripped and bleached the floorboards and doors, and sank spotlights into the ceilings. Stella bought big pieces of pine furniture with roughly hewn edges and straight lines, and sold off the George family's furniture and ornaments to the dealer who had bought those of her parents. Only Elizabeth's little fireside armchair and old sofa remained, both of which were so frugally stuffed and tightly upholstered that they felt no softer than Stella's wood.

The cottage stood out in a row that was otherwise uniform: net curtains, floral wallpaper, and dark furniture bulging under low ceilings. It didn't fit and it didn't work. Painting it white created no more space and brought in no more light. Its bareness and blankness made it as dull as the dusty, overstuffed places next door. The chains of bells and wind chimes Stella hung indoors and out only added to the icy atmosphere. The large windows at the back faced north and let in hard slabs of sun at odd times of day.

Stella had made a garden that was both exotic and austere. She had dug out the rosebushes, burned the privet topiaries that Joe had clipped into shape, and planted the front with lavender, rosemary, mint, lemon verbena, parsley, and thyme. Each small bed was surrounded by stones she had collected from beaches, which had the kinds of shapes and colours that would have looked enticing before they dried. Honeysuckle was the only decorative element, and it had grown so heavily across the garden fence that the smell of its flowers at this time of year was unbreathably intense. The back garden was filled with rows of beans, potatoes, tomatoes, onions, raspberry canes, and currant bushes. Three fruit trees, apple, pear, and plum, were pinioned to the walls. In addition, Stella grew artichokes, garlic, and salad leaves in a cloche. She also picked up the quinces that fell unwanted from May Hepple's tree next door. To keep the garden going through the drought, Stella recycled all the water she could. There were buckets in the bathroom for the collection of soapy water. The out-pipe of her twin-tub washing machine was used to siphon the grey, sudsy waste water into another. Vegetable water, old tea, everything went in. The garden was surviving, but that year it would produce little.

There was nowhere to sit or lie down in the garden, but Stella didn't mind, because there was the Green. Mary hated this. Nobody sat on the Green. Most people didn't even walk across it. But Stella would lay out a picnic and insist they eat out there in full view. Recently, she had taken to working out there, too, setting up her sewing machine or her pots of glue and paint under an enormous vivid pink, fringed parasol. When she did this, Mary stayed indoors or left by the back gate.

Mary turned to her mother and curled against her. "But I can't help him, can I? And then he'll be cross and want to hurt me."

"Look." Stella pulled Mary away. "I know it's troubling, but he is sick not criminal, and he doesn't hate you. On the contrary, he thinks you're some kind of angel who will guide him home. What did Christie say he said? Something about settling things, putting things in place. Anyway, it was just chance—but for it to have been you of all people he saw there, that was hard."

"Hard? For who?"

"For whom." Stella stood up and began moving the boxes onto the table. She was pulling little ceramic cottages out of tissue-paper bundles, dusting them, and wrapping them up again. "You've always been good at finding things, haven't you?"

"Only other people's." Mary got up and began to repack the little cottages. They bulged like loaves and were crudely painted but identical. Each cottage had two windows, thrown together out of untidy black lines; their doors were lopsided green rectangles with a row of rapidly dotted red flowers on either side; their roofs weren't the crusty colour of thatch but a deep terracotta, and their custardy whitewash looked sunstruck or dirty instead of like sugar or chalk. This was what made them foreign. The people who came into Stella's shop had just begun to go on holidays abroad and were reminded of Spain or the South of France and bought them because they were like the houses they hadn't stayed in or been into but had photographed.

Sophie Hepple came home at midday to find Tom asleep in an armchair. She hadn't wanted to wake him, as he looked so relaxed, so expressionless. She shook him gently and he opened his eyes, but took some time to sit up.

When he came into the kitchen, she laughed: "You look as if you've left part of yourself asleep!" and he smiled vaguely. She gave him two of the blue-and-brown capsules, an extra dose to keep him happy. "Not to worry. All this rest's doing you good."

Yes, thought Tom, but didn't say it. He was finding, day by day, that there was less he needed to try to say and a great deal he could keep to himself. His thoughts were slow and contained. He liked this dead sleep, going to bed early and waking early, back in his niece June's room, where the people in the posters still smiled at him, but from so far away, he smiled back. June had gone to stay with Aunt May till Tom was ready to try the chapel again. Sophie had extended the boys' stay with her mother.

Tom liked being able to sit still and feel nothing of his body. He seldom heard his heart, and his arms and legs felt at ease and worked silently and well. When he went outside, things were bright and defined. The world was well made, as he was, efficient and in place. The great restless pain was still there, in his bones, but it didn't push through him. There was a softening between him and the world, like wool. It was also there between him and his thoughts, but that was good because, as he relaxed, his mind gathered energy and speed. There were things to be done, but now he knew there was time, there were days and weeks left of this dry summer. He could wait and think things through, go carefully and not find himself losing sight of the house again because he did not think to look away from the sun.

"Tom? The phone was off the hook. Did you want to make a call?" Sophie was so kind, so gentle. He shook his head and felt a pleasant sifting.

"I wanted to tell the girl I hadn't meant to . . ." Sophie took his hand. He stared down at her plump brown fingers and her shiny pink nails that looked as if they should hurt but didn't, just brushed against his wrist, causing another sifting, but this time in a rush through his body, like iron filings drawn to a pole. She was so shiny. Her hair was bleached almost silver and her dress was so white. It smelt of almonds, or was that her hair, her skin?

"Don't you worry. Christie had a word."

Tom felt good, like a good man. He raised his other hand and, as lightly as he could manage, stroked Sophie's cheek. "You are kind." She smiled and smiled, and didn't so much let go of his hand as straighten it out and turn it back on him.

. . .

73

"Mrs. George?" Father Barclay appeared in the hallway. "The door was open." He rocked on his heels, nodding and wringing his hands, as if trying to keep warm. His crinkly, receding hair was damp, and his broad farmer's face fell heavily in jowls that spilled over his collar. "I'm portering this morning—ha, ha!—gathering up the goods, not to mention the good people—ha, ha!" He clapped his hands, then kept them clasped. "Ready for the off?" He picked up one of the boxes while Stella, murmuring her thanks, carried out the other. She would walk along later with Mary.

The back of Father Barclay's Triumph was already filled with Edna and Harry Lacey, who were as broad and as lame as each other. Edna carried a large handbag that contained all their medication—the pills for arthritis, high blood pressure, indigestion, and something to help them sleep. Mrs. Eley, driven and bird-like, took exactly the same prescriptions. She knew, because once Betty Burgess had given her the wrong lot and only when she'd finished them and brought the jars back to be refilled had she read the labels. The Laceys were laden with a box of jam and two bags of knitted toys. The boot of Father Barclay's car was propped open to accommodate the legs of a tripod, one of which was broken, and a bag of rusty golf clubs. Beneath them was crammed other bric-a-brac donated for the White Elephant stall Father Barclay ran each year: an ornate gilt-framed mirror that had lost most of its silver, a soup tureen, a set of bone-handled fish knives, a lace shawl, a fox fur—things that had been in families for generations, gathering mildew, moths, and dust, flaking and cracking and falling apart in the homes of those who were too old and tired to look after them, or who had no room or no children who'd want them. These were the things that, ten years ago, Stella had sold in her shop, the things that belonged with the heavy furniture nobody wanted anymore either.

Father Barclay put Stella's boxes on the front seat and set off for the church fields. The Summer Fête was held alternately in the grounds of the two village churches. This year it was the turn of the Catholic church which lay out along Furze Lane, set back on lawns overshadowed by elms. The church itself was plain and functional, but was lent mystery by its gloomy isolation. Its small cemetery was fenced with iron railings and surrounded by tall poplars.

Father Barclay drove carefully, so as not to upset or break anything, but also so as not to miss anyone else who might need a lift. As he turned off the High Street, he saw Tom Hepple walking in the middle of the road in slow, small, regular steps, like someone carrying a warning flag, leading a funeral procession, or painting a line. Father Barclay stopped the car and wound down his window. "I say, Tom, do you need a lift to the Fête?"

Tom kept walking, but turned his head to glance at the full car. "How?" he asked, then added, shaking his head, "I'm going to help." Sophie had set off earlier, and Christie had been gone all morning. When the house was empty, he had felt like a walk and then thought he could be of use. The walk had been going fine, but now, having stopped, he felt very tired, and in a flash, Father Barclay had flitted round to the passenger side, guided Tom into the seat, and placed the boxes on his lap. The Laceys muttered good morning, and then Edna leant forward and put her hand heavily on Tom's shoulder.

"You're back, then. That'd have pleased your mother."

She nudged her husband, who opened and shut his mouth a few times before reaching his hand over to pat Tom, too, saying, "You're all right, my boy." Tom felt stifled and small, and sleepier than ever, but somehow wonderfully cosy, too.

Farther on, they passed Violet Eley backing out of her drive in her Morris Minor. When she saw Father Barclay, she tooted, and he stopped once more and got out. Two trays of pink meringues filled with cream, decorated with glacé cherries, and arranged on paper frills were brought from her car to his and passed back to the Laceys, who held them carefully raised for the rest of the journey. Tom could smell the cream turning sour already.

When Stella and Mary arrived, Tom was unpacking the cottages onto the arts-and-crafts table. He was arranging them in a circle, facing inwards. Mary froze when she saw him, but her mother took her arm. "That's nice of you." With her free hand, she pushed him gently aside. "But we won't need them all out at once." Tom didn't respond, as he was looking at Mary, trying to be still and to smile and not say anything. It was strange, but she didn't look at all like the girl he'd seen by the water. She was wearing dirty glasses with one cracked lens and wouldn't look up.

Tom wandered over to Sophie, who was sitting at a stall of guessing games—How many sweets in the jar? How much does this cake weigh? How many biscuits in the tin? He spent a long time rearranging the prizes and the paper slips on which people would put their estimates. Finally, Sophie sat him down and gave him the money tin and a box of pencils.

Christie had set up a platform over a pool, on which Julie Lacey, in a pink polka-dot bikini, was settling herself. Boys were already queueing to try to kick a football hard and accurately enough to dislodge a loose prop and tip her into the water. Sophie appeared and held out a towel. "You could keep something more on till the actual start. Don't want to get chilly." Julie only stretched and turned her strong brown back. She looked monumental, like a goddess in repose, making the bikini seem even smaller and sillier. Christie kept checking the prop and the boys kept their eyes on the bright blue pool. It was the school's new pool, about fifteen feet across and collapsible. When the school wanted to use it, they had to allow half a day for the hose to fill it, and then it was difficult to get the level right on the playground slope. Christie had got permission from the Parish Council to use the water.

The Fête was opened by a nephew of Violet Eley's, who had starred in a recent television costume drama. He arrived in a cloak and on a horse, made a brief speech, then dismounted to sign autographs for the rest of the afternoon. His name on the posters had attracted more of a crowd than usual. The marquee was crammed with people balancing plates and cups, napkins and knives. Some gave up trying to eat or drink but stayed inside the tent's muggy shade anyway. The trestle tables were piled with donations of Victoria sponges, scones, flapjacks, fruitcakes, chocolate cakes, gingerbread, parkin and fairy cakes. Most of these were made from packet mixes, brightly decorated and overrisen, as sugar was hard to come by, making it difficult to bake from scratch. It had disappeared from the shelves in the supermarkets and there was talk of Caribbean islands hit by tornadoes or revolution, no one was quite sure. Violet Eley's meringues had dribbled and sagged. She had made them with dextrose, bought from the chemist in Mortimer Tye. Stewed, lukewarm tea ran in a tetchy stream from two massive urns. Bottles of milk sweated in crates of melting ice. The cream teas included just three strawberries each. There had been talk of importing them from Spain. Crumbs and cream were ground into the yellow grass. Children pushed their way through, snatching slices of cake and biscuits from the edges of stalls and dropping whatever they couldn't cram into their mouths.

Against the edge of the tent was a line of garden chairs where the older members of the First Families settled themselves, their paper plates arranged on handkerchiefs spread across their knees. The women kept on their hats and their white nylon gloves, but eased their swollen feet out of special-occasion shoes that were ill-fitting but had lasted for years. They didn't notice what they spilt, or the dogs that nuzzled under the canvas to gobble whatever they could reach, or the sparrows that pecked among their feet.

The commuters turned out with their sulky, untidy children, who had Victorian names, hairstyles, and clothes. The adults spent a lot of money, but they talked in shrieks and exclamations and were sloppily dressed. "Come in their gardening clothes," observed Edna Lacey. The current Lady Newling appeared on the arm of Father Swann. She was a surprisingly young blonde who was keen to talk about the stable conversion she and her growing family had moved into in the grounds of the old house.

At one point, the dogs were distracted by a rabbit that staggered out from under the elms. It sat upright but reeling, its eyes curdled and its mouth dripping foam. One of the Stroud grandchildren, a little boy of three who had gone behind the tent to pee, caught sight of it. "Bunny!" he murmured, and started towards it, but the dogs that had been panting, sniffing, licking, and making him laugh stiffened and growled and were on the rabbit in a barking rush. The little Stroud boy was too frightened to scream and just stood and watched as the dogs tore the rabbit to pieces. When he found his mother again, he was smacked for wetting himself.

The men and the teenagers went back again and again to old Dr. Burgess's bottle stall, hoping to win the sherry or even the champagne, but they kept coming away with shampoo or orange squash. Older villagers concentrated on the tombola, where they could fish up tins of salmon and soup. Women bought the arts and crafts, and looked through the White Elephant stall. Children ran about, played their own games in the graveyard, and watched older boys vainly trying to topple Julie Lacey, who had closed her eyes and hidden her face beneath a pink straw hat. The villagers also made a point of going to guess the weight of something, and of welcoming Tom back. He was so angelic-looking, frail, and eager to please that they felt only pity. More than one of the men clapped Christie on the back and mumbled, "Good for you, seeing your brother right." They remembered why he had gone.

Mary had been glancing over at him all afternoon. Not once did she see him look back. When Sophie returned and urged him to have a walk round, Mary watched him circuit the field and saw how the crowd opened up for him to pass, but patted and propelled him, nodding and smiling, setting him on course. She wanted to feel like they did, sympathetic and willing to help.

Father Barclay rang the school bell and announced the Fancy Dress Competition and Dance Display. The crowds moved over to the part of the lawn on which a large rope circle had been laid. The actor was to judge and he came over, looking shiny and tired, and stood politely next to the priest, who had a clipboard and a loudhailer that amplified his high voice into the cluck of a flustered hen. When the crowd had gathered and settled, he announced the Fancy

Dress. There were three fairies, two pirates, a cowboy, and the dance teacher ushered on nine girls dressed in blue tutus, with gold stars attached to their heads. As the others wandered round the ring, prodded and prompted by their parents, the nine stars made a circle in the middle and knelt down. "Europe!" boomed Father Barclay, delighted to have worked it out, and then, anxious to play fair, "What enchanting nymphs! Shoot 'em up, pardner! Yo-ho-ho, and a bottle of rum, what?" At that point, a boy draped in a grey sheet entered the ring. "Oh, and a late entry!" The boy lay down under his sheet, and the other children began tripping over him as Father Barclay continued smoothly, "A thing that goes bump in the night, ha, ha!" One star was crying and trying to leave the ring, but her neighbour held her arm. Another had stood up and was scratching her bottom. Then the boy got up and came over to the priest and said something crossly to him before returning and crawling back under his sheet. "Sorry, folks," came the priest's tight voice. "Young Fred here says he's come, of course, as a puddle! My mistake!" He scribbled something on his clipboard and turned to the actor. After a brief exchange, he announced the winner: "Europe!" and the box of chocolates was handed over to the dance teacher to divide up among the nine girls later.

"Do stay for the Dance Display and the raffle at four! And there's Guess the Weight!" Father Barclay yapped as the audience clapped briefly and wandered off. The cowboy was shooting his cap gun at the priest. Fred stayed where he was, under his sheet.

Mary left the stall and went to find a place to have a cigarette. She had seen Billy making his way towards the cemetery and set off to find him. As she rounded the corner of the church, she bumped into a gaggle of girls she'd been at school with, Julie's friends who'd left after the fifth form, too. They surrounded her, casually, as if they had found her under their feet.

"Oh look! It's the Second Coming!" said Dawn Smith. The others laughed, but Dawn's sister Terri looked baffled.

"What's that, then?"

"Jesus, right?" Dawn rolled her eyes.

Terri looked uncomfortable. "You mean she's holy or something?"

Dawn spluttered, "Her? Holy? Fuck, no. She's just weird, isn't she. Says she walks on water, right? Haven't you heard?"

Terri became alert. "Oh, you mean . . . but that's not true, is it?" She smiled anxiously.

Dawn regarded Mary coldly. "If it was, though, and you could help the poor mad sod, that would only be fair, wouldn't it?" She pushed past, laughing again, followed by Terri and the others, all joining in with Dawn and trying to be the one who laughed the loudest, the one who got the joke, who really got it.

Mary found Billy lying on his great-grandfather's gravestone. He knew which one it was only because his father had told him. The inscription was too badly eroded and covered with moss to read now. He was smoking a joint, which Mary took from his hand. She took a few puffs and handed it back. "Got to go back and help my mum," she said, and left.

The battered prop holding the ledge on which Julie Lacey lay finally gave way and she fell with a long scream into the water. The boys cheered and formed a new queue, and as soon as Julie had clambered back up, she was tipped in again. The fourth time, she slipped, and Christie caught her elbow and said, "That's it, lads. All in a good cause, but enough's enough."

Julie shook her head. She had goose pimples and a bruise on one thigh. Her curls were in knotty clumps and her blue eyeshadow had clouded her cheeks, but the next in the queue was the actor. She took a long time to arrange herself, and when his halfhearted kick tapped against the prop and nothing happened, she gave her biggest shriek and rolled into the water anyway. When she surfaced, wiping her eyes and slicking back her hair, he had already walked away, and the boys, furious and disappointed, put their money back in their pockets. One of them muttered "Slag," as they, too, went away, and another turned round to smile at her and, when she smiled back, spat on the ground. Julie climbed out and lunged at him, but Sophie caught her, wrapped her in a towel, and held her.

The raffle winners were announced by Father Barclay. By now, the crowd was so small that he didn't need a megaphone. He won the flower arrangement and donated it back, so another ticket was drawn and it was given to Joe Kettle. Lucas won a bag of sugar and swapped it with Violet Eley, who'd won the aftershave. He had a swig, but it tasted so awful that he pursued one of the dancing stars who'd got a bottle of sherry and managed to get her to agree to an exchange. Then Father Barclay asked Tom for the winners of Guess the Weight. Sophie had given him a list of the correct answers and he had amused himself by calculating the volume of the jar according to the size and number of sweets, the density of the cake, the layers and shapes of biscuits. From there he imagined the tins filling the church, the cakes piled as high as the steeple, the sweets laid along the High Street, and his mind was agile and quick again, leaping from number to number, gathering, multiplying, holding, and totalling. He proffered the list, but it was scribbled all over with numbers he couldn't remember having written down. He shrugged and shook his head as Father Barclay looked urgently round for Sophie. She wasn't there. She had taken Julie into the vestry to get dressed and drink some tea.

"Any idea, Tom? You were always pretty good with numbers, ha, ha!" Others began to laugh, too, and then realised they might be seen to be laughing at Tom and stopped. It did not matter; everything was muffled by the wool in Tom's head.

Under that wool, Tom worked backwards, pulling down the steeple of cakes, emptying the church of biscuit tins, and picking up all the sweets along the road. He leant against Father Barclay and mumbled, "Cake was three pounds eight ounces. Eighty-three sweets. Thirty-six biscuits." Father Barclay rapped out each number and checked down the lists till he found the nearest winners.

The field was almost empty now. The raffle table and bottle stall were surrounded by crumpled pink tickets. Dr. Burgess was putting away the bottle of champagne, and the women were in the marquee clearing leftovers and the paper cups and plates into bin liners. Lucas was sifting through the full bags with such a delicate and solemn manner that the women offered them to him with deference, as if he were some kind of inspector. Mary hadn't moved again from the arts-and-crafts stall. The dried flowers, ceramic cottages, and straw dollies had sold fastest, then the primary school's donation of leaf collages and Christmas cards. All that was left was a macramé potholder and a couple of crocheted mats.

When Stella went off to help in the marquee, Mary pulled a book from her bag. When she next looked up, there was a girl standing nearby with her back to her, holding up a piece of lace and discussing it with Father Barclay. She was tall and strong, and wore an old chiffon tea dress painted with tiny flowers. She had the loveliest hair Mary had ever seen—long thick red ringlets, film-star hair. Fairy-tale hair, Mary was thinking as the girl turned and smiled, and Mary forgot to smile back because she thought she must be looking at someone else—that long hooked nose and pointed chin, the narrow jaw and eyes, the heavy eyebrows belonged to a different fairy-tale character altogether. The girl was coming over now, tying back her hair with the lace, and Mary, to cover her confusion, pulled off her glasses and began cleaning them on her shirt.

"You're Mary George?" The girl was barefoot and wore a silver ring on one of her long brown toes. Her voice was low and resonant.

"Sorry, I don't remember . . ." Mary began, still polishing her glasses.

"Don't worry, we haven't met. I'm Clara Clough. Have you got a light?" She held out a cigarette while Mary passed her matches to her.

"You're the doctor's daughter?"

"So they say. Want one?" Stella was nowhere to be seen, so Mary accepted. Clara's cigarettes smelt foreign and delicious.

A month earlier, the Cloughs had moved into the Clock House, a Georgian folly built by one of the Newling family at the end of a long drive, just outside the village on the Camptown road. All Mary had heard about them was that Dr. Kill Off was odd but good, that his wife was foreign and even more peculiar, and that they had at least five children and any number of animals. She had liked the sound of them very much indeed.

"You at Camptown High?"

Mary put down her glasses. "For one more year."

Clara settled herself on the edge of the table. "I'm studying painting on the coast."

Mary was startled. "Do you, do you know someone called Daniel, Daniel Mort?"

Clara frowned, which made Mary think she was about to say no, but she said yes, she knew him, of course, had done for years, had lived next door to him before her father's sabbatical year, which they'd spent in Italy with her mother's family.

"I met him at a party, we . . ." Mary wanted Clara to be interested, but she was looking around the field as Mary spoke.

"Sorry, what was that?" She turned back distractedly. "Sorry! I must go and persuade my baby brother to come out from under his puddle." She pulled the lace out of her hair and set off across the grass in enormous strides. Mary couldn't stop watching her, just as Christie, Sophie, Julie, anyone she passed, stared. Clara appeared to take no notice, but once or twice Mary saw someone catch her eye, and she would swing her head away so sharply that her hair flailed out at them, as if she were raising a shield.

After she had gone, Mary went to find Billy. He was floating on his back, fully clothed, in Julie Lacey's pool.

"Come on in," he said. Mary thought about Julie in the pink bikini, Clara's frown, Dawn's joke, Tom Hepple's shuffling circles. She took off her glasses and boots and climbed onto the narrow ridge of the pool. She closed her eyes, walked once round, but did not let herself fall in.

Dr. Clough fiddled with a wooden spatula and swivelled the glass apothecary jar of sweets that he handed out to children after an injection. Tom's right leg was crossed over his left, and his right foot was tapping rapidly in the air. His face quivered and jerked as he spoke, but his fixed stare remained.

The doctor rolled a thin silver fountain pen between his fingers, and then looked down at the new manila envelope in which he had begun Tom Hepple's medical notes. It had Tom's name, Christie's address, Tom's date of birth and NHS number on the front, and contained a single card covered on both sides with the notes he had made at their previous meeting. Beneath it were the notes that had just arrived, forwarded from London, in a bulging, worn-out envelope packed with folded white consultants' letters and flimsy pale-green carbon copies of results and reports. Tom's treatment record covered dozens of cards, and at the back of the London file was clipped another which contained ten years of Dr. Burgess's notes.

Dr. Clough now knew that Tom had been having psychiatric treatment since he was nineteen. He had begun university, and then a breakdown had brought him home. The levels of sedation he'd been given as a young man must have left him barely able to speak. Ten years had followed in which Tom had been prescribed one new drug after another: Valium then Largactil, and once during a crisis in which he was admitted and referred, LSD, at a time when it was being tried out as a treatment for phobias and postnatal depression. The side effects of each drug were noted in Roy Burgess's impatient italic script: lethargy, increased metabolism, anxiety, irregular pulse, nausea, dry mouth, edema, decreased metabolism, morbidity, lack of coordination, arrhythmia, dilated pupils, neuroses, facial tic, narcolepsy, tremors, fits(?). Then there was the correspondence: "Dear Dr. Haight" (the name deleted with a flick of Dr. Burgess's pen and replaced with "Julian"), "I'd be grateful if you could see this troubled but gifted 20-year-old man . . ." Dr. Clough smiled at this; he knew the form. Then the Camptown psychiatrist's eventual letter to London: "Dear Mr. Brooking (a line, and then "Sidney"), I'd be most grateful if you could see this distressed and sensitive 28-year-old man . . ." The record of the Sectioning: Christie's leaden signature committing his brother to hospital care. Then the London notes on psychotherapy, sedatives, antidepressants, ECT, insulin therapy, antipsychotics, behavioural therapy, antidepressants, sedatives, group therapy, analytical therapy, suicide watch, antipsychotics, ECT, voluntary stay.

The doctor held all this knowledge but tried to meet Tom's eyes without it. "Do you think coming back here will do you any good?"

"Dear M," the postcard began. The writing was tiny, disjointed, and precise. "Dinner at CC's on 26th. Would you come? D." The message took up hardly any space. Equally tiny, and far off to the right, the card was addressed to "Mary George of Allnorthover." Who was CC? Mary turned the card over. It was a portrait of a woman, painted entirely in shades of red. She lay on a crimson sofa in a cherry-coloured dress. The wall behind her was a shadowy plum. She looked old-fashioned, powerful, comfortable, and foreign. Her bare arms were somewhere between pink and gold, suggesting skin of a smoothness that, if it changed at all, became darker and stronger. Most of her face and much of her dress were covered by her hair, which was exaggerated and simplified into a solid mass of red-brown, a shade that should have suggested rich earth or old wood but made Mary think more of a precious metal, an element rarely seen and with properties not yet understood.

Clara Clough. And not a party or a pub but "dinner." Mary put the postcard in her father's pipe box, along with the cigarette packet on which Daniel had written his number.

"What's wrong with your eyes?" Stella asked Mary over supper that evening. She kept blinking as if caught by surprise, and her gaze was heavy and direct.

"The lenses."

"You don't have to. We can get your glasses fixed."

"I'll get used to them."

"How long did it take you to get them in?"

"Not long." Mary had been fitted with contact lenses two

months earlier, but had given up trying to get them into her eyes. This was the first time she'd managed to wear them for longer than half an hour, and they felt sharp and pinching. She'd been in front of the bathroom mirror for forty minutes trying not to blink, and then, when she'd got one lens in, had dropped the other and had had to search for it with her one good eye, terrified that it would be scratched or cracked. A second pair would be out of the question.

"Well, don't overdo it." Stella considered her daughter's large, weak eyes, which were a changeable cloudy grey-blue, and wanted to go and find her glasses and put them back on. She'd always hated Mary's glasses. As soon as she had them on her nose, her head tipped forward. She mumbled and didn't hear what was said to her, and still didn't notice anything. Contact lenses had been Stella's idea, but she thought now that Mary looked like a young owl caught in daylight. Her face had no expression, as if it took all her concentration just to keep her eyes open.

"I'll take your glasses into town and get them fixed, anyway. Just in case."

Mary shrugged and finished her food quickly, in silence. As soon as her plate was empty, she jumped up, "Going out for a bit," and hurried off before Stella could respond.

There were two phone boxes in Allnorthover. The one you went to if you didn't mind being seen or overheard was by the crossroads, just along the High Street. It was next to the village's only signpost, whose spindly white arms were embossed with flaking black place-names and numbers of miles that drivers could barely read. Even if they could make this information out, they did not necessarily head off in the right direction. The village boys regularly climbed onto one another's shoulders and turned the signpost like the hands of a clock. The phone box proved useful to travellers who found that their maps or the directions they had been given were at odds with the way in which they were now being pointed.

The other phone box was out past the chapel, on the straight run just before the first curve of the Verges. It was neglected and overgrown, and several of its glass panes had cracked or slipped from their rusting red iron frames. The light was erratic and there was a lingering smell of something like a trapped animal. An injured fox had got caught in there, and Brian Stroud, whose farm was close by, had gone down with a stick and a sack, or so it was said.

Now the door was jammed half open and so nothing shut out the noise of the lorries that thundered past, even at this time in the evening, accelerating out of the Verges and into the straight run of the High Street, close enough to London now to see some point in hurrying. Mary pulled her money out of her pocket. The pennies and halfpence were useless, but among them were four twopences. She recited the number and checked the code for Camptown on the chart, even though she had known it for years. Her eyes ached as the lenses dragged in whatever direction she looked. It was hard to focus on something so close and the light was flickering. She made a pile of her money and dialled the number and then, as it began to ring, slammed the receiver down. She panicked. I haven't remembered it right. There weren't two sevens. And so she set off again, crossed the Green, and slipped into the house. She could hear Stella in the kitchen as she crept upstairs. She took the cigarette packet from the box and checked the number. Although she'd been right all along, this time she took the packet with her.

Back in the phone box, she rang the number again. A woman answered and Mary pushed her first twopence piece against the slot as the pips went, but pressed too hard and dropped it on the floor. As she reached out to grab another coin, she knocked the whole pile over. Leaning down to find them, she could hear the woman's imperious voice shouting, "Press Button B! Press Button B!" and Mary, curious and still given to taking orders, stopped scrabbling around for her money and studied the box. Where was Button B? She even wanted to speak to the woman again, but when she rang back, it was Daniel who answered.

"Your card. I'll come. I'd like to," Mary gabbled.

"Good!" He spoke so lazily that his one word was as long as her seven. "Shall I collect you?"

"No, I'll meet you there. What time should I come?"

"Time?" She heard a hiss or yawn and then realised he was smoking a cigarette. "I don't know. Whatever." She listened more closely. There was music in the background, some kind of jazz, and someone singing, not on the record but in the room, and someone else shouting at them to be quiet. Mary could feel the space of Daniel's house, its age and polish and glow, and she knew that that was what Clara's house would be like, too, full of candles and flowers and people shouting over music.

"Daniel?" The pause in their conversation had gone on too long. "What's Button B?" It was all she could think of to say.

"Button B?"

"In the phone box." A lorry hurtled past as Mary spoke.

"Sorry? Did you say you're in a phone box?"

"Button B? Your mother said to press Button B," Mary tried again.

Daniel laughed. "Don't take any notice of my mother! She's about a hundred and eighty, and she hasn't used a phone box for fifty years!" Someone near Daniel screeched their indignation and he turned away to speak to them. Another three lorries sped by. The pips went and Mary fumbled another coin into the slot, but by the time the line cleared again, he had gone.

It was Saturday night in Allnorthover. At seven o'clock, Ernest Yeo dried the last of the dishes and told his wife he was taking a walk. He set off along the High Street, leaning heavily on his stick. His suit was pressed and his hat was brushed, but his belly spilled out of his shirt. While Mary was laying out her dresses, Ernest Yeo crossed the Green, passed her front door, and made for the bushes that ran along the side of the Perrotts' garden wall. Using his stick to push back nettles and branches, he made his way in among them. Ten minutes later, he emerged and went carefully home.

The bottles in the bushes were Ernest's secret—one he believed nobody shared. Everybody who lived on the Green made a point of not leaving their house at that time on a Saturday.

After dark, the girls who were old enough to go out with their friends in the evening but too young for the pubs or for going into town gathered under the bus shelter on the Green. They smoked one cigarette after another, holding them against their palms and keeping a watch for grown-ups who knew them. They scrutinised one another's erupting bodies, the puppy fat, volatile skin, and growing breasts. They knew the awkward muddle of mortification and pride that caused a girl to wear her loosest clothes, to hunch over or smooth her skirt, and they mocked one another for it. They laughed violently at anything potentially embarrassing, such as Lucas passing on his bicycle, Mrs. Eley carrying a tray of meringues, or someone's sister in Brownie uniform. If any among them tripped over or spilt something, or had a button undone, a love bite, or muck on their shoes, they were turned on avidly by their screeching friends.

They watched for boys, too, who met at the crossroads and hung about kicking the signpost and carving their initials in the phone box, just as some of the girls would scratch a boy's initials into their arm. When the boys got bored, they would strut past the girls, calling and mocking, up the High Street and out along Blind Lane to Cricket Common. Eventually, the braver girls would follow and find the boys out in the middle of the Common, from where they could still see the road but were not easily to be found. Sometimes, someone had beer or cider bought by an older friend or a cocktail of spirits stolen from home, just a little from each bottle, making a kind of cough mixture in a jar. The girls liked these sweet concoctions and drank them too fast. Sometimes they would vomit and weep, or sing. A sober friend might march them up and down, feeding them mints, or a boy might persuade them to take a walk, and he might be worried and hold back their hair while they were sick, or he might push his hand inside their skirt or blouse. If a boy got drunk, he might punch his best friend, or go off and look for something to climb or break, or fall silent, or sleep.

At thirteen, Mary and Billy had spent a few evenings on the Common, excited to be out at night and briefly keen to be part of the gang. They were tolerated because they were known. Mary remembered being kissed once by the youngest of Julie's three big brothers, Martin Lacey. Billy had helped to turn the signpost, but the boy whose shoulders he was on had ducked and run off, and Billy had fallen hard on the ground and winded himself. Sergeant Belcher had picked him up and had chosen to believe his story about a back flip. He hadn't been strong enough to budge the signpost anyway.

While the stack of singles perched on the spindle of her box gramophone dropped one by one onto the turntable, Mary tried on each of her dresses twice. A short, clingy black dress she'd never yet dared wear, a silver-blue cocktail number, her blue print, and her pale-lemon shift.

In the end, she wore the shift, and combed her hair to one side and fixed it with a diamanté clip. She got out her high-heeled sandals, slung them over her shoulder, and set off barefoot, with a small bag for her contact-lens case and mascara. At the front door she met Stella.

"Going somewhere special?" She smiled.

"Clara Clough asked me round."

"Party?"

"Dinner."

"Ah! Dinner!" Stella paused and then said, "Wait a moment," and went into the kitchen. She came back with a bottle of elderberry wine she'd won at the Fête. "You should take something."

Mary blushed. "I know. I mean, thank you." She took the bottle and hurried away.

When she reached the gravel drive that led to the Clock House, Mary pulled on her sandals. They were a pair Stella had thrown out and were too big for Mary, but she loved their delicate apricot-satin bands and the sudden height they gave her. She thought about Clara at the Fête, her long brown legs and how you could see their outline through her chiffon dress. You could see the strong curves of Clara's whole body through that dress. Mary felt like a child in her shift, so straight up and down.

It was half past seven, which had seemed to Mary like the right sort of time to arrive for "dinner." As she approached the house, the crash of her feet on the gravel got louder and louder. By the time she reached the front door, it was so deafening that Mary was surprised no one had rushed out to see what the racket was. She looked for a bell but couldn't find one. The door, in any case, was open. She was about to knock when she noticed a rapid hammering sound. She turned her head towards the noise, slowly, anxious not to unsettle her contact lenses, which still felt tight and heavy. There was a motorbike and she walked over to it, expecting to find someone lying next to it. Nobody was there. Mary looked up and around, unaccustomed to taking in so much and at such a distance. Across a lawn of worn-out grass, there was another motorbike, upside down, a sidecar, and, farther off, a car with its bonnet up and something that looked like a go-kart or a small tractor. Someone had begun to take apart each of these machines. There was a single heap of wheels, and one each of engine parts and bodywork.

Mary looked back at the house and realised that she'd thought it would be beautifully kept and bright white. Three immense cedar trees cut out the light and the house's cement frontage had a dank sheen, like the underside of a stone that had lain for years in forest darkness. The house's embellishments, the parapets with their castellated balustrades, were clogged with moss and weed. The ivy that had crept around the doors and windows had recently been cut back so that the walls of the house were covered with its pallid imprint.

The famous clock tower was supported by crumbling buttresses and wooden joists. When Robert Newling had moved in, he had installed a clock that chimed so loudly it could be heard on the Village Green. He spent most of his time on the Continent and so, rather than disrupt his habits, went by what he believed to be Continental time at home as well. The villagers, who lived by the church bells, were confused to hear different hours being chimed. Robert Newling refused to adapt, and it was only after his death that someone tried to turn the clock back and it had stopped for good.

"You looking for Clara?" A boy of about her age had appeared. His height and thinness were exaggerated by his big head and baggy overalls. He looked like a plant that had grown up in shadows. He had Clara's big nose and black eyes but in a face with such different proportions that their effect was altogether something else. Mary was fascinated. She put out her hand, but his hands were full of tools—a spanner, three screwdrivers, and a hammer. Confused, she lifted her fingers to her face to take off her glasses and then remembered she wasn't wearing them, so she waved in what happened to be the direction of the pile of engine parts. Then she had to think of something to say.

"How do you know what belongs where?"

The boy smiled. "I'm building something new." Mary kept looking as two tortoises ambled out from between the machinery, one slowly chasing the other.

The boy walked past her into the house. *"Clara!"* he roared. There was a distant reply. He turned to Mary. "Sounds like she's in the bath. Come on." Mary followed him across a large hall, tripping over toys and slipping on the parquet floor. A trail of nails and screws fell from the boy's torn pockets. They went upstairs and along a corridor full of piles of books and open boxes in which Mary could see important-looking stone sculptures and porcelain vases alongside toy guns, records, table-tennis racquets, snorkelling masks. They passed a guinea-pig cage on a polished walnut side table that was shoved up against a set of chipped white shelves. The boy pushed open a door, and Mary saw Clara lying in a deep bath, her hair in a knot, a cigarette in one hand.

"Bit early." Clara's mouth snapped momentarily into a smile.

"Don't be a cow," the boy said, and grabbed the bottle from Mary's hand. "She brought you this."

Clara sat up so suddenly that the water crashed against her back and ran down her front. Mary retreated, shocked by Clara's nakedness, her long neck and strong shoulders, her jutting dark nipples and muscular breasts. Mary tried to make sense of the tiny flowers scattered over the peeling wallpaper. The boy put the bottle down on the floor and went behind Mary, opening an airing cupboard. Clara pushed on a tap with her toes and the spurting hot water made more foamy bubbles that rose and spilt over the bath's edge. Mary watched.

"Wait in the garden." Clara sounded more friendly now. "Thanks for the wine. Take it down with you. I won't be long." The water coming from the tap shrank to a dribble, coughed, and stopped.

"Tobias!" she screeched. The boy emerged from the airing cupboard, holding a wrench.

"I've disconnected your supply." Tobias handed the bottle to Mary and steered her away.

"It's round the back." Tobias left Mary where he had found her and returned to his machines. She smashed her way across the gravel, her feet already swelling and aching in Stella's sandals. They tipped her forward as much as her glasses ever had. Thinking about her shoes, she found she could no longer walk in them. One foot lagged behind the other and she fell.

Grateful that nobody had seen, Mary picked herself up and looked for some direction to head in, somewhere she was supposed to be or wait. In front of her was a tall hedge, behind which a number of lights flickered. She skirted the hedge and found that the lights came from candles burning inside a row of pewter lanterns that had been arranged on a trestle table set up on the bottom of an empty swimming pool. The table was covered in a white cloth. There was a pile of white plates and a pile of white bowls and half a dozen glasses. In the middle of the table was a bowl in which floated red, orange, and pink flowers. They were radiant, intricate, hothouse flowers, not garden flowers, and had been crammed into the bowl until they turned in on themselves.

The pool was about seven feet deep. Its dusty tiles were cobalt blue. Mary kicked off her shoes and lowered herself down into it, surprised to feel not a cool smooth floor but the scratchiness of dead leaves, seed husks, and grasses catching between her toes. She waited there, alone, for an hour. She sat first of all in the nearest of the six folding garden chairs and then realised she was at the head of the table and moved on. By the time she heard a car in the drive, she had sat in every chair, opened and shut every lantern, rucked and smoothed the tablecloth, spun the knives by their handles, and rotated the glasses by their stems. Moths battered themselves against the lantern glass. Mary tried to put everything back as she had found it, and when she heard shouts from the front of the house and Clara's hooting call of "Darlings!" she got up and straightened her chair. Too nervous to stand and wait, she climbed out of the pool, slipped on her shoes, and hurried round to the front of the house, in the opposite direction to the one in which she'd come. She reached the drive just in time to catch sight of five—was it?—figures, one unmistakeably Daniel, disappearing round the other side of the house. Mary doubled back on herself and managed to arrive back beside the pool just after everybody else.

"I've been for a walk . . ." Mary began.

"Meet our surprise guest!" Clara laughed. She was wearing what looked like a very beautiful nightdress made of purple silk, with spindly pink velvet straps. Her shoulders now looked delicately bony and deep brown. "Mary George. She's Daniel's surprise, actually. Say hello to your surprise, darling!" She took Daniel by the elbow and pushed him towards Mary.

Mary turned to Clara. "You mean you didn't know I was coming?"

Daniel shook Clara off and smiled at Mary. "Don't worry. She said bring a friend, didn't you, Clara? I didn't realise she'd want to vet them first."

Clara gave a flick of her head and softened. "Don't be stupid, D., Mary and I have met already, haven't we? She's no surprise to me. For God's sake. Jump in, everyone!" And the others, who had stayed out of this exchange, moved towards the pool and climbed in, introducing themselves to Mary. There were two girls, both in short black dresses. The one with the blond bob and an Oriental tattoo was called Julia, and the dark one whose hair was in dozens of tiny plaits, and who had lots of bangles on her right arm, was called something like Dora or Flora, only Mary hadn't taken it in. Nor could she remember which of the tall skinny boys with black curls and white scarves was Ed and which one Paulie.

Clara accepted their bottles of wine and bunches of flowers and lined them up on the pool edge. She turned back to the table. "And where shall I sit?" All the chairs were taken. "Looks like someone forgot I was coming!" She pulled her dress high up over her thighs and her hair flew as she swung herself gracefully up out of the pool and marched into the house shouting, "Eat! We must eat!"

"I'll find another chair." Ed or Paulie made for the swimming-pool steps.

"Clara will need a hand." Julia followed.

The evening was a long and complicated sequence of people following Clara back to the house, fetching and carrying, and lowering food and wine into the pool. Mary moved to get up once, but Daniel's hand on her knee stopped her. She tried to follow a conversation, even to join in, but the swimming pool's odd acoustics blurred words and everyone was talking at the same time. The conversation was loud, fast, and brittle, and veered from one crescendo to another. Daniel sat very close to Mary. He leaned forward and propped himself on one elbow, almost in front of her.

"Where's my plate?" Clara demanded, once all the food was on the table and everyone else had taken the plate she'd offered.

Daniel passed her his. "I'll share Mary's." He gave Clara his glass, too.

Mary was transfixed by Daniel's proximity. Although he was turned away, because he was turned away, his body curved towards her, his back almost touching her shoulder and his propped hand loose and open, as if cupping her face. As she leant forward to pick up her glass, he straightened and her lips met his bare arm. The shock she felt was matched by a jolt in Daniel. He turned suddenly and began to talk to her.

The swimming pool was filling up with everyone's noise and Mary could hardly hear him. Eventually, he just picked up the fork and they took it in turns to eat. Mary couldn't remember exactly what they had. There had been some wet pink beef and a vivid salad of something like beetroot, red cabbage, radishes, tomatoes, and red peppers.

"And now pudding!" Clara announced. She was standing at the head of the table, with the bowl of flowers in her arms. "Mary!" Mary looked at her, confused. "Help yourself!" Clara thrust the bowl towards her.

"Christ, what is this muck!" Ed or Paulie spat their wine onto the floor. Clara looked angry. "I don't serve muck, Paulie sweetie!"

He held up a bottle. "Elderberry? A berry?"

Clara put down the bowl. "Let me see." She snatched up the bottle. "Who brought this?" Her eyes lighted on Mary and she smiled. "A local delicacy?"

"I . . . my mother . . ." Mary began, reaching out to take the bottle from Clara, to put it out of sight.

Daniel caught her hand and held it. He took the wine, poured some into his glass, picked a nasturtium from Clara's bowl, dipped it in the wine, and put it in Mary's mouth. Everyone watched. The drenched flower weighed on her tongue. It had an unexpected sharpness. Mary swallowed it.

Paulie smiled and held out his glass.

Since the Fête, Tom had not stopped counting. The towers of cake and roads of biscuits he'd built while working out who'd won had reawoken the part of his mind that loved numbers. His memory had once had endless room for numbers, and while other parts of his head rested, sleepy and vague beneath the blanket of the coloured capsules, numbers had begun to accumulate again. They would rush at him in elaborate conundrums that he found, to his delight, he could solve. They made beautiful patterns that he could see entire, and twisting threads he could follow all at the same time. Tom amused himself calculating the melting point of a strip of tarmac caught in the sun, or how long it would take for the blistered paint on the chapel door to split and peel. He found some of Matthew's old drawing paper and made intricate geometrical designs on the different-sized squares, without actually drawing anything.

He could remember. He could remember figures, shapes, and sequences. He tested himself. The trees from the chapel out along the Verges: oak, hawthorn, hawthorn, elder, oak, ash, ash, elder, elder, hawthorn. He traced their shapes like a graph, in an unbroken line. How many buttons had there been on Sophie's white dress? Nine. The fourth one down, the one that strained on her belly, had slipped half undone.

Tom had heated a tin of soup. He washed up the saucepan and the bowl, threw away the tin, and wiped the stove. He felt fine, and then he didn't. The tall, thick candles he'd found under the eaves and set to burn on the window ledges and along the shelves helped. They made him think of the chapel as a chapel again, or maybe a lighthouse, out here on the edge of the village, warning and guiding. But the old wooden filing cabinet that Christie had pushed into a corner was worrying him—those three deep drawers tilted and strained, and Tom knew he wouldn't like what was inside them. He decided the cabinet had to be turned round. He leant his body against it and inched it forward a little. He pushed again, hard, and the front edge caught on a ridge in the floor, and the whole thing tipped forward with a crack and a slam. Tom circled it like one animal trying to find a way through the defences of another. He squatted in front of it, squeezed his hands under two corners, and tried to lift it upright, but the brass lock-fitting on the top drawer had broken open and the drawer slid hard against him. While he managed to push the cabinet back up, and it stayed up, the drawer forced him backwards. It landed at his feet. Without rising, he gathered up some of the papers scattered around him. There were letters and photographs, but his head hurt and he was holding them too close to his eyes to be able to see what they were.

When Tom sat up, the things he'd been holding fell from his hands, unnoticed. He looked at the cabinet with its odd empty space, the fallen drawer, the mess, and was frightened. He wanted Christie.

Christie had said, Come to the Arms on a Saturday night, I'll pick you up. But this Saturday he'd been working on the other side of the county and wouldn't be back till late. He might have got back by now, though. Tom set off into the village. It was getting dark and the High Street was empty, or seemed empty, till he noticed shadows and then voices calling softly, whispers and a bray of laughter. Some of the houses he passed were lit and had their windows open. There were more voices, a bored half-formed call, a repetitive imprecation, an angry command, a nervous continuum, the rapid fire of television shows, and the tinkling chatter of guests. All this made him anxious, as it always had done, only now the anxiety was displaced. He felt the wave of panic precisely, but it was no longer at his core. This gave it limits, a shape, a form. He could watch it rise and fall, and survive it.

Christie wasn't in the Arms. The public bar was full of noise and smoke, and Tom almost turned back at the door, but a big man with a red familiar face, a Lacey of almost thirty, clapped him on the back and hauled him into the room. The Lacey was with a number of younger men, all dressed in dazzling blue-white shirts or T-shirts, who filled the middle of the room, surrounding a billiard table. They were in their early twenties, earning but not yet married. They wore the latest heavy watches with dim, digital faces and dropped their chunky, laden key rings on the table as they sat down. Most of them had driven in from other villages and their cars were parked untidily along the Green. The fuel crisis had not affected their journeys. There was always somebody with a siphoning hose and a canister, and more than one villager had found their petrol tank unexpectedly empty. It had happened to Father Barclay twice.

In a little while, these young men would be driving into Camptown, to Blazes, the nightclub, or just on to another pub where there might be a lock-in and they could go on drinking past closing time. Their well-shaven faces were sharply scented. Those with curly hair were relieved by the fashion for a mop of ringlets that made them feel like Continental football players, and the rest styled theirs in tame versions of what was called a "rooster," a pop-star cut with spiky strands on top and long layers over the shoulders and ears. The overall effect was flamboyant, even effeminate, although they would never have seen it in themselves. They didn't think about what suited them or look in the mirror and see spikes or curls. What they saw was, to their relief, a face that fitted in with those of their friends.

Older men, and one or two of their wives, sat at tables or along settles around the edge of the room. It had last been decorated thirty years earlier with cream-and-gold-striped paper that had faded and thinned to greaseproof. Where the plaster had warped, it had bulged and split. The four-foot pike in a glass case over the bar was almost as old and colourless. It was supposed to have been caught in one of the nearby River Mund's deep pools by a great-uncle Kettle who'd been the landlord here, only some claimed he brought it home ready stuffed and framed. Although the hunt drank its stirrup cup outside the King's Head, the Arms had three of its foxes in this bar and several in the saloon. Their desiccated fur didn't polish up like their new glass eyes and had faded to sour orange. Fixed in a staid trot, they looked persistent but down on their luck.

As Tom made his way into the room, people nodded and grinned. Florrie Stroud patted the bench beside her and he sat down. She said something about Iris which he didn't catch, but he smiled. Three pints of bitter were set in front of him.

Tom watched as the Lacey continued his game. When he saw him hesitate over lining up a difficult shot, he rose and studied the table. His mind ran lines between the balls, computed angles. He walked along the side of the table and placed a finger on its edge.

"About here," he said shyly.

The Lacey looked up, frowned, then relaxed. "Says you were always a dab hand, Tom," and he took his shot, bouncing the cue ball off the exact spot Tom suggested and potting the red he wanted. There was a round of muttered approval in the bar, more smiles and nods, and Tom stayed standing, watching the game. He liked the bar, its solidity and crush. He drank his three pints quickly, and when two more appeared, he passed one over to Lucas in the corner.

When the Lacey had finished his game he pulled Tom down into a seat beside him. "Says you've a head for numbers."

Florrie Stroud leaned over. "Iris's boy has the memory of an elephant!"

"That so?" The Lacey smiled. He reached over to the table in front of Lucas and scooped up a dozen dominoes. Lucas mumbled a protest, which the Lacey ignored. "A quid says you can't tell me what these add up to." He slammed them down one after the other and then collected them back up. Tom closed his eyes, keeping his gaze fixed on the white dots on black rectangles, two patterns, two numbers per tile.

"A hundred and two." Tom was sure, but he didn't like this game. Quite suddenly he felt drunk, not pleasantly so but floppy and dizzy.

The Lacey laid the tiles back down on the table, slowly, adding them up as he went along. He shook his head, laughing, grabbed Tom's hand, and slapped the pound note into his palm.

"Drink?" Tom offered back. The Lacey laughed approvingly and threw an arm round Tom's shoulders, yanking him up out of his seat and towards the bar.

"It's on him," he said, handing over the engraved pewter tankard that was kept for him on a ceiling hook. Seeing Tom scan the bar, he spun him round and said, "Another quid says you can't tell me all the shorts and that, along the bar, in the right order."

Tom trembled, and someone called out, "Leave alone, Trevor. And stop throwing your money around!"

There were mumbles of agreement, but Trevor took no notice. He grasped Tom's arms and shook him, like a farmer trying to shake fruit from a tree. "Good game, eh?" All the boredom of Trevor Lacey's life had taught him to find a game and to make people play.

Tom wanted to please. The room slipped, but his mind, that part of it, was still sharp. He nodded, and Trevor turned him round to face the bar again, just for a second or two, and then back. It was there, just behind his eyes: the inverted bottles with their tinted optics: "Beefeater's, Gilbey's, Black Grouse, Jameson's, Naval Rum, Smirnoff, Rémy Martin." Beneath them on the counter the heavy, dark, sweet drinks: "Cherry brandy, advocaat, sherry, crème de menthe"; and then the cordials: "Orange, blackcurrant, lime."

There was a cheer from the men sitting along the bar. Someone tapped Trevor's shoulder and offered him another game of billiards, and he pushed another pound at Tom and turned away.

"Can you remember like that, from far back, like? Not just this minute?" It was someone he didn't recognise, an old man on a stool, drinking from a tankard like Trevor's.

"Some . . . I don't know . . ." Tom felt nervous and thirsty, and even though he knew he'd drunk enough, he was glad when his remaining pint of beer was passed across the room and put in his hand.

The man patted the empty stool beside him and Tom sat down to listen. "I know the place better as it was than I do now." He sounded friendly, but he wasn't smiling. There was a long silence, and the man looked sad. When he spoke again, it was abruptly. "I knew your mother when she was in the dairy. I was delivery boy for Garnett the grocer's, next door."

Tom shook his head vehemently. "Not next door, Garnett's. Opposite."

The man sat back. "What's that? Opposite? Sorry, lad, I remember right as rain. I worked there for years!"

Tom shook his head again. The man looked angry now. He raised his voice, addressing the group sitting playing dominoes with Lucas. "Weren't Garnett's next to the dairy, boys?"

"Was that the butcher's?"

"Don't be daft. The butcher was Maynard's, on the corner."

"Garnett's. Oh yes. Garnett's was right across from the dairy."

"Garnett's!" Florrie Stroud caught the name out of the air. "Right across, that was it."

The name was passed round the room, as some remembered and some didn't, but all agreed that it was opposite the dairy.

The man kept shaking his head. "Well, I never." He crumpled down on his stool again, bent over his drink. Tom didn't notice: the names going round the room had captured him.

"Garnett's, then the hardware, Freans, and the Co-op," and he was back there, thirty years ago, on errands for his mother. "Then the cottages, your cottages, Florrie, with the post office on the end, across Hoop Lane and the smithy."

"That blacksmith! The noise!" Florrie was with him, and Lucas, "Collecting up iron railings in the war," and others, each remembering a part of the village as it had been; all talked at once, to themselves as much as to each other, about characters and shops and horses, romances and scandals and accidents, the Big Freeze and the Spanish Influenza, what chicken used to taste like, and hare and rabbit, and pheasant poached from the estate.

Trevor Lacey swept up his cigarettes and his keys. "Bloody hell! You all make it sound like one of them Saturday matinées!" And so they began to remember the films, *Whisky Galore*, *Brief Encounter*, *The Life and Times of Colonel Blimp*. Trevor and the boys pushed their way out the door, mocking and chuckling. Florrie began to sing.

Every person, place, and drama mentioned, even those he could never have known, rose in Tom's memory, painfully vivid and unreachable. He needed something to concentrate on, to take his mind off it. "Test me! Try me again!" he called, and partly to pass the last hour of the evening, and partly to humour him, they gathered a collection of small objects out of their pockets onto a tray. He was allowed to study them for thirty seconds: first ten things, then twenty, then thirty. Tom remembered every detail, the holes in a button, the initials on a handkerchief, the nick in a pipe. He grew more and more excited, but the drinkers were tired and finding him tiring now. They began to leave. "Test me again!" Tom called after them. Only Lucas and his fellow domino players remained and they had kept out of it, keeping their backs to the fuss and getting on with their game. Tom saw them as his remaining and so most eager audience. He grabbed their dominoes with both hands, but clumsily, so some fell on the floor. He laid the rest out flat on the table, ran his eyes over them once, and turned away.

"Add them up! I tell you, it'll be eighty-two! You'll see!" Hunched with anticipation, his fists clenched and his eyes tight shut to keep the number in his head, Tom heard the click of the tiles being gathered up. Nobody spoke. Chairs were scraped back, and then the door was opened.

Lucas touched him on the arm. "Says you're right, Tom. But there's an end to the evening and folks are too tired to be doing sums."

Tom opened his eyes to find himself alone in the room. John Kettle, the landlord, was ringing the bell in the Saloon and chanting mournfully, "Time please!" Billy's elder sister Valerie came through to the Public to clear glasses and was startled to see Tom still there, staring at nothing.

"You look lost!" She bit her lip. She knew who he was.

Tom brought his gaze to rest on her—a delicate elf. She lifted the side of the bar and walked towards him. She held out her hands and touched his face, and the numbers and names and places subsided. "I'm Valerie Eyre. You wouldn't remember me, but I remember you. I'll walk you back, if you like." She returned to the bar and Tom stared at the space she left behind her, wondering how he had summoned this sprite who looked as if she might break between his hands but also as if she were strong enough to hold anything she wanted to. Eyre: a family of slender, ethereal children came to mind. Could she really remember?

Valerie returned with a heavy bag that she hoisted onto one shoulder. "John will lock up." She took Tom's arm and he followed her carefully.

By the time they reached the chapel, ten minutes at most, Tom dreaded her leaving him. He offered to walk her home, too, but she laughed and shook her head. She looked intently at him and said, "You need to rest. I'll come in the morning, if I may?" Then she slipped away.

Tom's heart was beginning to patter and thud. The voices of those in the bar raced round his head, overlapping and running into one another, beginning in the middle of an anecdote and ending on half a word. He got himself to the outhouse and, as his stomach contracted and released, vomited up in great hawking acid splashes the beer with which the villagers had welcomed him.

Tom laid his head on the stone floor, too weak now to think of numbers or to hold back what lay beneath them. He could not tell if he was dreaming or remembering, but what he could not keep from his mind was Iris's last winter, his last at home, the snow and the talk of water.

On that Christmas morning, Iris Hepple's sister, May, got Father Barclay to drive her into Camptown. On the way, she asked him to stop at Ingfield Dip, to "pick up the boys." May knew that Tom hadn't left the house for years and wouldn't now, even though his mother was dying, and that Christie, for God knows what reason, simply refused to go. But May had an idea that if she turned up with the priest, not asking but simply expecting them to come along, perhaps they would. Father Barclay's tinny Triumph skittered along the icy track and shook to a halt outside the house just as Christie was coming through the door.

Father Barclay leapt out, pulled his seat forward, and gestured Christie into the back. "Well timed, Christie! Season's greetings! Jump in before you freeze!"

Christie muttered something and then caught sight of May. Father Barclay smiled and rocked, banging his arms against his sides and shaking his head at the weather.

Tom appeared behind Christie in the doorway. The priest knew him well. He and Tom had had many discussions about the mind, about good and evil. Tom brought him visions of heaven and hell that were so abstract and intense that Father Barclay had done all he could to remove religious significance from the world for him.

"Tom," he tried now. "Come with me to see your mother today. The roads are empty, no one else will be in town. All's indoors."

Christie moved forward as Tom slipped away back into the house. "He does what he can, Father."

"Ah." Father Barclay clapped his gloved hands and rubbed them together. His sigh plumed in the cold air. He shook his head, shrugged, and opened and shut his mouth with a pop.

Christie looked up at the sky and down at the ground. "No, I won't. Our mother's not to think of us now. She's to think of herself."

"Her days must be long," the priest began, folding his arms.

"I can't think she knows one day from the next anymore. Nor a son from a stranger."

May had had enough. She punched the horn, and the priest, still smiling, waved elaborately and got back into the car.

At the hospital May wanted Iris to know that she'd tried to bring her sons more than she wanted her not to know that they wouldn't come. With some difficulty, she held Iris's hand. Those tiny bones and the papery skin—it was like a reptile's wing.

Iris Hepple felt herself always moving now, travelling through tunnel after tunnel of pain: long, curving, dark holes she was hurled into and had to force her way through as they pressed inwards, and then, when she thought she could not bear it and they would crush her, she was out. Then another one began. Even when she had had her injection, she could not rest. The tunnels still came, although they were light and cool for a time. She did not know it was him, but when Matthew held her, she felt still. Someone was here with her now. She knew because she could feel warmth on her hand and a voice saying, "They won't leave the house."

At this, Iris opened her eyes and said, quite firmly, "Will . . .

will . . ." Then her eyes closed again and she turned her head from side to side, as if trying to shake off the pain. "Sing to me," she whispered. May got up and left.

Iris Hepple died three days into the New Year, when no one was with her. Christie went to the mortuary and the undertaker's. He spoke to Father Barclay about the service and to May about the tea. Tom held Christie's hand as they threw earth onto her coffin. Tom stayed in the graveyard rather than going to the tea.

The day was extraordinarily clear. The snow was packed hard underfoot. People walked in careful steps that left no mark. There was no wind, just a high-pressure stillness in which sound carried far. A single bell was rung before the service and after the burial, and each toll resounded so powerfully that some felt its metal travel through them. Most of the village came to the funeral. Matthew, Stella, and Mary George were among them.

A week later, Christie came to the chapel. "You've to come to Hepworth's for the reading of the will, tomorrow at three." He turned to go almost before finishing his sentence, but in any case, Matthew had not looked up from his plans.

The next evening, Mary found it hard to eat her supper. Her mother was watching her father. What did she think he might do? He wouldn't speak or look up from his plate. Mary got nervous and Stella shouted at her for humming, only Mary hadn't known she was doing it. It occurred to Mary that something had got stuck and that it might be helped if she got out of the way. She took herself off to bed, but the house was so small, she could not help but hear.

"The house?" Her mother's voice flared. A low sound came from her father. Stella continued: "Their home . . ." More low sound, then an explosion, her mother's jagged laugh and a higher, sharper voice than she had heard from her before. "But think of Tom!"

They were in the hall now, and the front door had been opened. Mary crept to the head of the stairs. She could see her father. He was walking out the door, and as he did so, he said, "It means nothing. It's going anyway."

What Tom remembered or dreamt of this was very little. He saw his mother as he'd last seen her, when they'd still tried to manage her at home with the tubes, the nappies and bibs, and the district nurse and Dr. Burgess coming in and out. He'd tried to help but couldn't get it right, and Matthew was always round, like he lived with them again, and Iris would be quiet then, lean her head against his and whisper. Now Tom knew that she must have been telling Matthew of her plans, although Matthew never said a word, just stroked her hand, nodded and cooed in that odd way of his, a noise that could have been a mating call or a warning but that Iris responded to as if it were a lullaby.

Christie couldn't stand to see it, but Tom made himself stay and watch. It was a lesson to him. When she could still shout, his mother had shouted, not exactly at him, but about him, ". . . useless . . . broken . . . stuck . . ." And before she'd had the drugs all the time, there had been moments of nakedness, somewhere between consciousness and sleep, when she had gone on about his being so pointlessly afraid, saying he had to go out into the world, Christie too, not "stay and suck."

"Not like lover boy!" Christie had retorted once, and she had changed colour and withered somehow, right there in front of them. After that she rarely spoke, except in a cool moment after one of Dr. B.'s injections, when she had giggled and slurred out a promise that if she hadn't been sick, she would have gone and got some dynamite and blown them out of the house herself. Sophie, who was bitter at having spent the first eight years of her married life living with Christie's family, had laughed right along with her. "Good for you, Iris, good for you!"

Everything changed when they took her in. Tom had known to stay in the house, that that was where he should be, so she'd know where he was and not worry. It was no time to be leaving, however much good she thought it would do him. Christie had gone to the hospital at first, but he'd come home more angry each time. After his last visit, he'd cleared out Iris's room for June, saying it was ridiculous that he and Sophie were sharing a bedroom with a seven-year-old child, and her six months gone with twins. When Tom had got upset, Christie shouted that the house was going anyway.

The first talk Tom heard of water was from St. John Newling, the local MP. He had come to Allnorthover to open the Brownies' Christmas Bazaar a year before. Somehow, he had threaded his speech with talk of water, of thirsty fields and parched machinery and taps running dry. There had been two consecutive dry summers during which restrictions had been imposed. St. John Newling invoked them, making water into the element of freedom, money, and the future. He warned against the wrong kind of rain.

From then on, Tom noticed talk of water everywhere. In the local paper, parish councillors, farmers, and manufacturers gave warnings. They talked of the land as a thin skin, but they built and dug and grew more each year. St. John Newling had a field of soft fruit under plastic and had sold off several acres outside Camptown for a sports complex, including a swimming pool. There was a new industrial estate and the Council was building houses on the edge of the village. Tom became agitated. From where would they get their water?

Ingfield Dip was a natural basin in which there were three houses, a tenant farm, and a church; fifteen people at most. Nearby, two rivers drew close together, the Mund and the Soley. The rivers were known locally as the Black and White Waters, as the Mund was stained, deep, and slow, and the Soley was shallow and clattered over flint boulders.

There was passing talk of a reservoir, but much of it was contradictory or unbelievable. Tom heard of a plan to run a pipe from the Black Water into an underground holding tank on the Newling Estate, from where the water would be sold in times of drought. Somebody insisted that the White Water was getting shallower each year and that it was already being diverted. There was talk in the pub of filling the Dip, but also of every inhabitant being made a millionaire, so nobody believed it. As the talk thickened Tom began to worry more, but everyone was too busy to bother about it. Iris was sick, and Christie had a young family and his business to take care of.

Perhaps much had gone on that he hadn't noticed that winter. It was white and quiet. The snow-filled Dip was a bowl, so sealed and smooth that Tom could see how the Mund and the Soley might pour into it and how it wouldn't spill a drop. After Iris's funeral, he had walked down to the bottom of the Dip, to the little church that was unused now, except for Father Barclay's monthly service. As it grew dark, the pressure in the atmosphere lifted and it began to snow again. Tom had lain down and looked up into the thick fall, not feeling cold or even wet, except on his face, where the snowflakes caught and melted, gently, without any sting. He forced his eyes to stay open and stared up into the sky, feeling himself buried a long way down. When he had gone back to the house, his hands and face were burning; inside, he was frozen.

What happened next? Christie was reading papers and letters, and walking to the phone box. Men had turned up with measuring tapes and quadrants, sinking rods into the ground and scooping earth into glass test tubes that they corked. Christie didn't explain anything to Tom, but sometimes he gave him a look, as if to say he must know what was happening really and that he, Christie, was only trying to keep the worry from him.

Around the time of the thaw, when the constant, ticking drip of melting ice from under the trees and eaves and windowsills made Tom feel as if he were living under a siege of clocks, Christie had said it: "We've to move."

"But you've refused it, haven't you?"

"Refused what?"

"The compensation."

Christie had laughed. "We'll get none."

"We don't want it, do we, anyway? We've said from the beginning of this talk, we'll not be made to go!" The subject had not been discussed between them.

"I'd not leave for them to fill the Dip with water . . ." Christie began.

Tom grasped him by the shoulders. "We'll stay, won't we?"

Christie would not meet his eyes. "We, Sophie and me and June, we're renting one of the houses in that new close off Back Lane."

"Then I'll stay."

"You can't. It's not ours. Ma left it to Matthew George."

Tom's mind, racing into several possible futures all of which involved staying put, and perhaps some great battle with the authorities, could not absorb this piece of news and so leapt over it. "Then it's still in the family! Matthew's safe hands!"

"He's not blood." Christie shook him off. "As far as I'm concerned, this is your home. You stay if you want to. I'll not help them, but I will help you, as far as I can. Any compensation that's going will be Matthew's now, even though he's only owned the house for five minutes. He may have grown up with us, but he's not blood, and he and Ma, well, you saw how that was. Just don't expect much when there's money in it."

When Mary could wait no longer, she pushed back her chair and stood up. Without looking at Daniel, she made for the pool steps and climbed out. Returning to the cooler air, she did not hear when someone called after her. She stepped through an open French window and into a large, lit, empty room. The house was quiet. She pulled off Stella's shoes but still tipped forwards and knew, regretfully, that she was drunk.

She made her way up the stairs and along the dark corridor to where she remembered there to be a bathroom, feeling her way slowly past the still half-unpacked boxes. When she reached the door, the light was on. She knocked and it opened. It wasn't the bathroom. A boy of about ten, with red curly hair and wearing just a pyjama top, held out his hand. "Freddie," he said. She glanced past him. His room was painted black. There were luminous stars on the ceiling and a large bolt of lightning glowed on one wall. "Would you like to see my rain dance?"

Mary shook his hand. "Mary. No thanks, just the bathroom." Looking crestfallen, Freddie nodded to the right and shut his door.

She blinked out her lenses and, after a couple of fumbles, got them into their case. Coming back through the house was no more difficult now that she couldn't see. At the bottom of the stairs she made out a light and a silhouette. Assuming she was unseen, Mary moved towards the room, which was the kitchen. She squinted at the woman, who she realised must be Clara's mother. Mary moved towards her, getting near enough to make her out properly. She didn't realise that this meant she had entered the room and was standing only a few feet away from Francesca Clough, who wondered what was wrong with this frowning, stumbling girl with screwed-up eyes.

She waited the few moments it took for Mary to collect herself and smile. Francesca nodded and smiled back, but continued laying a long table for breakfast, with what looked like a dozen places. There were at least six boxes of cereal, a huge bowl of fruit, and several pots of jam and honey. Behind her was a heap of dirty saucepans, bowls, knives, and spoons that must have been used in the preparation of Clara's dinner. She finished, looked up, and smiled at Mary, who saw she was beautiful and tired. She was wearing a long, loose, dark dress that looked old and intricately stitched. Her head was framed by a heavy coil of grey, waving hair and her eyes were ringed with dark circles.

Mary faltered. "Thank you . . . for having me, for having us," she managed.

Francesca shrugged and smiled again. "Our pleasure." Her voice was accented and light. She turned away again, but Mary lingered, feeling powerfully drawn to this woman's calm. Mary wanted to stay, to be fed by her, not by Stella or Clara, and not to have to deal with empty swimming pools and edible flowers. Francesca gestured outside. "Please."

Daniel was standing on the gravel path, and as Mary started towards the pool, he stopped her. "Let's not." So they set off across the grass, away into the darkness, at a lazy pace, as if taking a stroll, only they were solemn and tensely aware of each other. As they reached a row of low, knotty trees, Clara's scornful laughter followed them. Mary leaned into the deeper shadows of the tangled branches and broad leaves.

"You want to be gone," Daniel said. It was not a question. To look purposeful, Mary reached back and was surprised to find the trees were not as deep as they seemed, but were espaliered, nailed and spread against a wall like the thin, submitting trees her mother cultivated. These looked as if they'd grown undisturbed for a hundred years. Mary almost said something and then thought Daniel would have noticed or known this already. She raised her arm up under the leaves and found a fruit so full and soft and thin-skinned that it almost burst in her hand. She twisted it off its stem and held it out to Daniel, who smiled and shrugged. Did he not know it either? Mary ran her nail along the purple skin and pulled it back. She held the fruit close to her eyes and studied the red flesh. A fig—something she'd only known dried and chewily sweet. Fresh, it was so beautiful, it had to be far more delicious. She broke it in half and held one piece out to Daniel. He watched her eat and then ate, too. The fig was tasteless, a mouthful of hair and seed. Daniel turned and spat, making Mary blush for both his lack of grace and the disappointment.

They walked quickly away, still following the wall, and came to a toppling brick archway overgrown with heavy-headed roses. They squeezed through and stumbled among long, dry grass. Mary stubbed her bare toes on a stone and picked it up. It was a fallen apple. Thick branches from close-planted apple trees merged above them, making a low canopy beneath which they crouched. They stopped and held one another tightly and blindly, then moved apart.

Mary began to walk backwards. "How far can you see me?"

She was no more than six feet from Daniel when he said, "You're gone."

She ran and crashed into his arms as he let himself fall backwards, pulling her over into the grass.

For a long time Mary lay still on top of him, feeling her pressure against Daniel's body take shape. She kept her head buried in his neck as he stroked her legs, each stroke ending higher, lifting her dress inch by inch. When her dress was round her waist, he grasped her and sat up, pulling her legs round him. Daniel kissed her hard, pushing into her mouth so her head was forced back. She felt herself about to fall again, when he caught hold of her dress and lifted it over her head. Mary had never felt the air on her skin like this. She didn't think about being almost naked in somebody's garden, or even of this boy, almost a stranger still, with her breasts against him. It was too unreal, this sense of freedom that intensified to pleasure as Daniel kissed her, as if his mouth were opening her and letting in light.

He lifted her onto her feet and, kneeling, pulled down her pants. His breath against her thigh created such a hard and fast surge of desire that her body kicked. He stroked her once, very lightly, and she was wet. Daniel murmured something, almost a word, but not quite. Mary was about to ask what he had said when she realised that she couldn't feel him near her anymore. She waited and, when nothing happened, opened her eyes. She looked around and could just make out Daniel doubled over on the grass, as if in pain. Mary picked up her dress and held it against her.

"I'm sorry, did I—" she began. All she had known before had been uncertain: fumblings and directives that overwhelmed any feelings she might have had with bashfulness and a notion of sex as comically lonely. She was shocked now at how her body had taken over, at its obviousness and force. I am too much, she thought.

Daniel eventually spoke: "Not you, me. I couldn't . . . stop."

For a moment Mary didn't understand what he meant, and then she did and wanted to say that it didn't matter, but didn't know how to. She put on her dress and sat down beside him. He turned away and curled up tightly on his side.

Three hours later it was dawn, and Mary and Daniel woke together in the grass. They stood up and Daniel reached out a hand that Mary was about to lean her head into, but he was pulling grass from her hair. She straightened her dress, wiped her mouth, and squinted towards the house.

"Do you want to go in?" Daniel asked.

"Oh no. I'll go home." She didn't want Clara to see her so dishevelled.

They walked round the edge of the lawn, negotiating the heaps of machinery and skirting as much of the gravel drive as they could.

When they reached the road, Mary turned to say goodbye, but Daniel said, "I'll walk you."

They carried on, apart, both made shy by their dirt, sweat, and sour breath. The clean air and blue light made them feel even more shabby. Neither spoke. Then Daniel stopped and almost shouted. "My God! What's that?"

Mary screwed up her eyes, trying to focus the fractured fuzzy outlines of the trees and buildings ahead.

Daniel was walking faster. "Come on, I think it's a fire!"

She stumbled after him, wincing as her bare feet caught on sharp things she couldn't see to avoid, peering and craning. What fire, where? Then she realised he was making for the chapel and that its windows were full of white light.

As her panic rose, Daniel slowed down. "Oh, I see." They were almost at the building now, and as it became clear to Mary, the light shrank and consolidated itself into candle flame. At the same moment, the last darkness slipped from the sky and the flames were reduced to pale flickers.

The door was open and Daniel was going in. Mary stayed behind him, anxious that the place should give no clue as to who lived there, who had once worked there, who she was. Daniel walked from one window to the other, blowing out the candles that had almost, in any case, burnt themselves down. Mary trod in something warm and liquid that oozed between her toes. She gave a small blurted scream, then peered down and realised she had trodden in molten wax, and that there were streams of wax running along the windowsills and down the walls, dripping onto the floor, pooling and congealing. As she drew her foot away, a sticky wad of paper came with it. She pulled it off her skin so fast that some tore.

Daniel hadn't noticed. "What is this place?"

"A workshop, I think." Mary was shaking. What if he was upstairs? What if he heard them and came down? "I want to get home."

She moved towards the door, but Daniel was fascinated. "Why the candles? They look like they belong in a church."

"A chapel." Mary couldn't stand it anymore. She turned and began to walk quickly on into the village.

Daniel ran up behind her. "Sorry. It gave you the creeps, didn't it." His smile was so wide, his body so relaxed, she realised he'd sensed nothing.

"Yes. Something like that." She tried to laugh, but her throat was so constricted that it sounded more like a whimper. He took her hand, but she stopped and stood in front of him. "I'll be fine from here. You go back to Clara's or you'll miss your lift." For a moment he looked confused, even angry; then he smiled again, as widely and easily as before, kissed Mary crisply on the mouth, and walked away.

She tried to watch him, but his outline soon disintegrated, as if there were several of him, walking a little to the left and right of each other, in black suits fading to grey and fair hair dissolving completely.

Mary went to bed but woke again when the church bells began to ring in the looping, cajoling, but lighthearted peals that Father Barclay favoured. The sun was high and strong again. After Stella had left for Mass, Mary ran herself a shallow bath and was startled by the grainy bruise spreading out from one nipple and the delicate graze on her shoulder. The orchard, the swimming pool, Daniel even, seemed part of an overheated dream.

She was drinking tea and still dreaming when Billy arrived. He was carrying two motorcycle helmets. "Sundays are shit," he said, flopping down in the armchair. "Let's go for a ride. I've even got a sidecar now." Mary scribbled a note to her mother, found her newly mended glasses, put her keys and money and a book in her army bag, and followed him out onto the Green.

Mary was used to the motorbike. It was Billy's father's old Norton, black and squat. The sidecar she'd not seen before. It was wooden, varnished, and shaped like a clog. "Billy, I am not riding around in a shoe!"

Billy looked hurt. "But it's beautiful! I saw it in Fred Spence's yard and couldn't resist it!"

Mary considered its absurd little windscreen and flapping plastic hood. "I'm not surprised!" But she was bored and wanted to get out of the village, so she took the helmet he offered her and climbed in.

As Billy kick-started the bike, it gave such an ancient splutter that Mim, who was panting and dozing in a scrap of shade by the front door, leapt up and howled, thinking a bus was about to arrive. Mary got out of the sidecar to reassure her and to shut her in the house. They set off along the High Street, the exhaust belching black smoke, the engine struggling, and the throttle raging, the noisiest, dirtiest thing in a quiet, clean village closed down for a Sunday morning.

As they rode out through the Verges, Mary was getting used to the noise and enjoying the breeze. When Billy turned off towards the reservoir, she tried to shout to him, but he couldn't hear her. He slowed down at the end of the lane and bumped gently along the track, stopping under the pines. They pulled off their helmets and Billy saw how nervous Mary was.

"I saw him this morning, going into Christie's. He didn't look well." Billy shook out his long hair. "So he's not going to be here. This is *our* place, remember?"

She wanted to agree, so she followed him through the Other Gate and out along the rim of the water, to the tree. Billy lay on the bough, leaned back against the tree's trunk, and pulled out a tobacco pouch. He rolled a joint, lit it, and passed it down to Mary, who had stayed on the ground, crouched in the tree's shadow. They smoked in silence, and Mary began to enjoy the peace, the open sky and brilliant water.

"Why do we never swim here, Billy?"

"It's too deep."

"Do you think it's true?"

Billy took so long to respond, she thought he must have fallen asleep. "If you kept going and believed yourself able to . . ." he began.

"I meant the house, not me!" She interrupted him. "Is the house still there? I mean, didn't they just knock everything down? The church and Goose Farm and the houses?"

"You know they say that on a stormy night you can hear the church bells."

"Nonsense!" Mary was angry now. "They wouldn't have left all those buildings in a place they wanted to fill with water!"

"Why not?"

"They'd . . . get in the way?"

Billy snorted. "Of what? The fish?" And the vision of pike swimming in and out of windows and through garden gates made them both laugh, and then they couldn't stop.

When the laughter finally subsided, they sat for a long time just looking out over the water, neither wanting the other to know they were looking for clues. Again and again, Mary traced a line out along the bough onto the water, but there was no change of colour, no shadow or ripple. As soon as her eye let go of the tree, she couldn't make sense of what she was looking at.

. . .

117

Billy and Mary drove on into Camptown, looking for something to eat and drink, something to do. The High Street was empty except for the detritus of Saturday night—crumpled cans, spilt takeaways, pools of vomit, the odd shoe. The only people around walked gingerly through all this, mostly still in their going-out clothes, fragile and awkward and eager to get home. Nobody stopped to look in shop windows at jewellery or washing machines or houses for sale. The precinct was locked away behind an iron grille. The corner shop that would sell them beer had sold its last Sunday paper and closed, and the one in the bus station hadn't opened. Billy took them back out of town, to the Malibu Motel. Outside the Amber Grill, they counted their money and went in.

"Look what the cat dragged in!" Julie Lacey grinned as she marched up to their table. She stroked Billy's head. "A natural blonde and silky smooth! I'm so jealous, Bill!" He wriggled away but pouted and blew her a kiss, which made them all laugh. Julie leaned down to the table and whispered, "Look, have what the fuck you want. Barry's not around. I'll just take a quid."

So Billy and Mary, hungry after smoking the dope, passed the rest of the afternoon eating burgers in fluffy white rolls stuffed with sliced dill pickles, bacon, tomato sauce, and melting squares of cheese, and handfuls of skinny, sodden chips. They drank pink, yellow, and brown milk shakes that all tasted the same and came piled with rosettes of soapy cream topped with hundreds-and-thousands and a paper parasol. When they left, achingly full, they walked out into the glare of the sun, arm in arm, each holding a tiny parasol over the other's head.

When they reached the bike, Mary said, "Will you wait? I want to phone my dad." She walked off down the sliproad to the phone box by the roundabout rather than go back inside and risk having to explain herself to Julie.

Mary reversed the charges. Matthew agreed to pay and they were connected. "Mary, sweetheart, what's happened?"

"Nothing. I just . . ." She thought of him in his house by the sea.

Could she really hear waves and gulls? He did sound far away.

"Well, it's lovely to hear from you. I didn't know . . ." Mary waited, but he didn't finish the sentence. When had they last met? Easter? She had gone down to the coast, and he had taken her to the Royal Hotel and given her a glass of champagne and smoked-salmon sandwiches, and had insisted that she try an oyster.

"Can I see you?" She found herself shaking, almost crying, and Matthew must have heard something of this in her voice, because his voice changed, becoming more definite and serious.

"Whenever you want, darling."

"Now?"

"Now?"

"Now. I'm not at home, you know. I'm outside the Malibu Motel."

"Mary, I—"

It rose up in her. "Come now, Daddy. Come now!" She sobbed and couldn't hear what he said next. She put the phone down.

Billy saw her leave the phone box and revved up the bike, but when Mary reached him, she explained she wasn't coming back now, that she was waiting for her father. She knew it would take an hour for him to drive there, so she went into the Amber Grill's toilets, washed her face, and tried to smooth her hair. She felt sick and excited, and sorry that she was wearing this ripped T-shirt and tatty skirt. There was time for a cigarette, and time to sit in the shade of the back of the building, keeping the sliproad in sight. After an hour, Mary walked to the roundabout and then she walked back. Two cars came up behind her, but she wouldn't turn round. For another hour, she walked back and forth. She sat in the grass and wouldn't look at the road directly or at her watch. He would see her. He would call to her.

At last a car slowed. It wasn't Matthew but Stella, who left her rusty orange Mini in the middle of the road with the door open and strode across the grass to Mary. "That bastard!" she spat.

When Stella was angry with Matthew, Mary felt she was angry

with her. So when Stella threw herself down on the ground and held her hard, Mary felt as though she were being attacked. "Get off, Mum!" Mary pulled herself free.

"He's not coming."

"He said he was."

"He's not."

"He's not coming?"

"A misunderstanding, he said. He has a deadline, he said, so couldn't possibly come. He said you'd probably realise and turn up on the bus, but I wasn't going to leave you waiting around!"

Mary still felt Stella was angry with her, and she was also cross with herself. She went over the conversation with her father. He hadn't actually said he'd come; she hadn't really listened. She was stupid. It was her fault. He would have come if he could have, but he couldn't, and she should have let him say so.

Stella helped her up and they walked back to the car. As they drove home, Mary felt the silliness of the little car and how cramped it made them. She was incredibly tired.

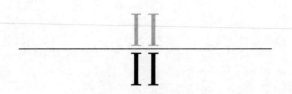

II

It took several months for Matthew George to leave his family. He did it in stages. After he inherited the Hepples' house, he spent longer days away on site visits or at work in the chapel. Christie continued to work with him and Tom continued to live in the Dip. Letters came to the chapel originally addressed to "The Occupier, Back House, Ingfield Dip," which Tom had scribbled on and redirected to "The Owner of." After a while, Matthew opened them and filled in and returned the forms, and then they began to be addressed to him directly.

At Easter, he took Mary and Stella away for a few days on the coast. Each afternoon they had walked along an endless, exposed beach, and the more Mary delayed them by picking up a shell, or by getting sand in her shoe, the faster he hurried away. Mary watched him getting smaller and disappearing, something she found hard to believe when she thought of it later, as her eyes had grown so weak since then. On the first afternoon, Stella had hurried after him, calling out and pulling Mary along and snapping at her if she couldn't keep up. The next day, when Matthew disappeared again, she had sat down and suggested they build a sandcastle with such intense enthusiasm that Mary took it as an order and obeyed. From then on, they separated from Matthew almost as soon as they reached the beach.

When they returned home, everything that had gradually been changing became suddenly different. Matthew didn't unpack his suitcase but left it by the front door. There were times when he didn't speak for days on end, and then one evening he would start pacing around the room, picking things up and putting them down, running a finger along the mantelpiece, a windowsill or tabletop, walking into the kitchen and back, and when Stella was so agitated that she could do nothing but wait for him to start, he would begin. "What did you make me put those big windows in for?"

"I didn't, you . . ."

Matthew stood back in outrage. "God, Stella, you are unbelievable! You insisted!"

"I didn't, it was your . . ."

"Don't quibble! Why do you do this? Why do you always blame other people for your decisions!" This would go on for hours, with Matthew attacking Stella for the white walls, or the garden, or their coming back to live in the village in the first place. When he ran out of surroundings to complain about, he began on her. Why did she always look so miserable? He'd given her a home and she had her own business. Her hair was too long, too girlish for her age, and who did she think she was wearing those pathetic ribbons and beads. Why did she always look at him like that? Like what? As if he'd caused her some terrible injury. Why was she so fucking indignant? She'd taken over his childhood home and was forcing him to find somewhere else. Otherwise, he'd have nowhere. She'd made him take the Hepple house. Want, want, want. Grab, grab, grab. Greedy, heaving cow. He had to go out, he couldn't stand her fat, righteous face anymore, and when Mary came rushing downstairs, weeping and clinging to his legs, he pushed her away because he couldn't stand her terror, either.

He said nothing about his work, so it was from May that Stella heard he was involved in the plans for the reservoir. Everybody in the village knew, but no one said anything to him directly. They watched Tom in the Dip, Christie in his new home, and Matthew up at the chapel. They heard the shouting and they knew that official letters were being sent. They waited.

That summer, Stella and Mary went to London. Mary liked being fussed over by Stella's friends, and being taken on rides on buses and in a boat down the Thames. She was pleased to see her mother looking lively and happy again. Matthew came to get them in the orange Mini. Mary curled up in the back trying not to think about the lorries overtaking them, so much larger, heavier, and faster that they could roll over their little car and not even notice. It was getting dark when Matthew pulled onto the hard shoulder.

"I need a piss," he said as he got out. Mary was startled by his language. When Stella got out as well, Mary clambered into the front and followed her. They had stopped beside some open waste-land, riddled with paths and patches of scrub. When Matthew reached the first clump of bushes he didn't stop. He was walking away again, and when Mary realised this, she began to follow, calling "Daddy, wait! Daddy, stop!" as she stumbled through tufts of grass, brambles, and rabbit holes. She was falling and hurting herself over and over, and nobody stopped her. The last time she picked herself up, it had got much darker and she couldn't see Matthew anymore. She looked back and could only just make out Stella in the deepening haze. Mary made her way back to the car. Stella turned towards the traffic and Mary waited beside her and then screamed as her mother threw herself forward into the road.

A police car swerved, braked, and pulled in. Two officers got out, fixing the straps of their helmets under their chins. "You could have got hurt there, missis," one began, shaking his head, as his fingers fiddled with the helmet's buckle.

Stella was finding it hard to speak, her voice veering from high to low, loud to quiet, rushing and catching. "I had to stop you, had to, my, her father, walked away, over there, you see he didn't want her house but now he's got it, and he won't let go because she, can you find him, can you find him now, can you take us home?"

Mary remembered making herself stay very still because Stella was so frightened, something she had never seen before. She also remembered having to wait a long time. Clouds pressed down through the dark. The policemen wrote in their notebooks and talked on a radio. A van came, and another man got out with two big dogs that had chains round their necks attached to thick leather leads. The man was wearing shiny black gloves and was waving a dazzling torch around. The dogs terrified Mary. Then she realised they were going to hunt her father and she wanted to stop them, but everything was beyond her now. She couldn't remember anything else Stella said or did, or how they got home.

Three days later, Matthew reappeared when she was doing a puzzle on the table. He helped her for a while and then said that there were some pieces missing and there was no point in trying to put any more of it together. Mary got upset, saying they were there, just mixed up with her other puzzles. He left again, but she looked through and found them, and put the completed picture out for Matthew to see. He didn't come back that night, at least not before Stella had made her go to bed. When she came down in the morning, Stella had cleared the puzzle away.

After that, Matthew spent most nights at the chapel. Once or twice Mary woke to hear someone coming in or out of the front door, but it was Stella, and Mary was shaken to realise that she had been left alone in the house as she slept. Stella said little to Mary these days. She played with her, fed her, and got her to school, but Mary knew she was miles away.

By Halloween, the reservoir was becoming visible. Huts were being replaced by brick buildings; huge machinery, pipes, and pumps were installed; there were channels and tunnels, ridges of concrete, and the growing raw wall of the dam. All of this would disappear again behind trees, under earth and water, like secrets.

The compulsory purchase orders arrived. All the explanations and warnings that had preceded them did nothing to reduce the shock. Bill Bennett out at Goose Farm received his and had a stroke the next day. He was in Camptown General, the whole left side of his body crumpled and limp, and whatever anyone remembered of a man who'd been drunk and furious and purple-faced half his life, they nonetheless put the blame on the order. Over the winter, others in the Dip moved out, although the money they were offered was not enough for a new home. Some moved into Allnorthover and others to Ingfield, absorbed by the neighbours they had in any case known for years, but adrift in their new Council houses packed together on new roads. Some liked these houses because they were light, warm, and neat, but others felt exposed. Living in the Dip had meant a view from the window of grass and trees that rose up above your house to the faraway sky.

Apart from Bill Bennett, the people of the Dip were shy and dutiful. They didn't question the judgement of authority nor could they imagine what it meant for their homes and land. The idea of the Mund and the Soley turning and pouring a torrent of black and white water into the Dip was so apocalyptic as to be unreal. They moved out, not quite realising that they were doing so.

Mary had got used to the idea that Matthew was at the chapel. She had one parent at a time now—her mother in the mornings and at night, and her father when he appeared at the school gate or took her off somewhere at the weekend. On Guy Fawkes Night, he turned up in a new car and drove her to Camptown Park for the fireworks. When he took her home, he said good night on the doorstep and drove away so fast that she worried that he would shoot past the chapel and have to turn back. It was then that Stella explained that he had bought a house on the coast. He came once a week, always collecting her from somewhere outside the village, till the reservoir was finished, and then he joined an architects' practice in London. He refused to speak to Stella, to answer her letters or return her calls. Sometimes he remembered Christmas and Mary's birthday, and sometimes he didn't. There were times when he phoned her every other day, and then weeks of silence. A postcard would arrive from a foreign city.

One morning Stella took Mary to Mortimer Tye station, and as the new commuter train from the coast sped through, she held the child high in the air. They were close to the tracks and Mary felt the noise of the train through her body, a deep vibration, as if her blood were separating. Stella looked at Mary's terrified face, running with tears, and held her tightly, saying, "Sorry, sorry, I wish, I can't, I only wanted, sorry, sorry." They both cried on the drive back to All-northover and Stella kept Mary out of school. The next day, they were back at the station again and Mary pulled away when she heard the train coming, but Stella held on to her hand. She had a large yellow umbrella with her this time, and as the train came through, she opened and raised it above them both. "He can't not see us now."

The yellow umbrella haunted Mary's dreams. They had gone back to the station every week, all through that winter. She tried to remember seeing her father's face in a train window once, but decided she must have imagined it. Later, she heard her parents argue about money and the cottage and Matthew going away, but neither of them ever mentioned those vigils. For years the umbrella was kept under the bench in the hall and Mary measured herself against it. When she grew old enough to be able to go out alone after dark, and to carry it and not be afraid, she took it over to the Common, where a bonfire was being built for another Guy Fawkes Night, and pushed it deep into the pile of broken chairs and bits of fence, boxes, and branches. It had disappeared that night in the spitting yellow flames.

The heatwave continued into August and held the village under constant pressure. The boredom of the summer holidays was concentrated by the monotony of equally hot days and nights. The dark made little difference to children who could not settle in their airless rooms and then could not rest in the bright day but ran around, red-eyed and hectic. Games became more dangerous. The little ones chose higher trees to climb and higher walls to jump from. They built fires in the woods because the grass and twigs were so dry they crackled underfoot and fire suggested itself. They moved on from salting slugs to throwing stones at chickens and tying up cats. The older ones were bored with the bus stop, the signpost, and the trips with no money into Camptown, where they just walked up and down the precinct and the High Street, and then got the bus back home again. The boys took their air rifles into the fields and shot rabbits that were riddled with myxomatosis and dying anyway, or tiny birds that made a pathetic handful of feather and bone. Dissatisfied, they took potshots at farmers and walkers, and someone lost an eye. The girls tried on one another's clothes and lay around stewing in bedrooms with shut curtains, reading one another's diaries in the pink light, plucking eyebrows, borrowing one another's makeup, and betraying secrets.

Kevin Lacey was twenty and was four years into his printing apprenticeship. He had saved up enough now to buy his own car. He would cram in five of his friends and speed off down the lanes, thrilled to be so suddenly and easily away from the village. They would find a pub that would serve them, and maybe meet some girls and squeeze them into the car, too, then set off again, Kevin half-drunk and a bit scared, but proud and ready to go faster than anyone would expect him to, skidding round corners, racing blind across junctions, making the girls sitting on boys' laps in the back lurch, shriek, and beg him to slow down. The best bit was the straight stretch that ran all along one side of the reservoir. You could get some speed up there.

If they made it to Camptown, there would be gaggles of other teenagers as bored, drunk, and ready for anything as they were. Some of the boys waved broken bottles around. They might come across hippies or arty student types, whom they mocked. Skinheads, Teds, and bikers they stayed away from.

Mary slept most mornings and was awake much of the night. She read books and listened to records. In the evening she watched television if she could get decent reception on their battered old black-and-white portable set. The aerial had been broken a long time ago and replaced with an extruded wire coat hanger. Allnorthover was on the cusp of broadcasting regions, so London-based channels clashed with local eastern ones. Sometimes Mary could get both, sometimes neither.

Or she met Billy. The less there was to do, the more they focused their attention. They could spend hours lying on their backs in the church fields, "watching the earth revolve." When the evening finally grew dim, swallows circled and dived to feed on the gnats. Billy and Mary would count them and compete to be the first to spot a bat, then the lowest-flying bat. The bats and swallows might briefly be in the air together, the bats slewing past at abrupt angles, bouncing around in their sonar net; the birds repeating and repeating their circles. Billy and Mary could use up more time later, arguing over whether it was better to be a bat or a swallow, the merits of flight, and who had the most insect bites. Then there would be bursts of childish energy during which they would take over Billy's mother's big kitchen and experiment, trying to make things they'd never known to be made at home, such as coconut ice and butterscotch sauce. They would eat these sticky messes in front of the television, and if it was too early in the day for there to be anything on, they would watch the test card and argue over which one of them looked more like the girl beaming out from its centre. Billy usually won, on the basis of his long blond hair.

Daniel had sent another card, this time from Italy. He was on holiday there with his family and wouldn't be back for three weeks. Mary did not see or hear from Clara, although something made her half expect to. Stella was at the shop all day, selling pine spice shelves, bunches of dried flowers, and jars of salt to people on their way home from the sea.

Perhaps because she was so bored, Mary got out the bundle of letters Ray Cornice had given her. She hadn't forgotten about them but rather had been avoiding them. She was not surprised, now, that just holding them made her hands shake. Mary recognised the typeface. It was that of the machine she had in her room now. The one that had been downstairs in Matthew's study. The characters were clenched and narrow, with slab serifs, and printed themselves unevenly apart, making the words look unsettled on the page. The *i* was slightly raised and the *s* clogged almost into an *o*.

There were five letters. They had been slit open along one side (Ray Cornice or some post office official looking for a return address?) and then taped shut, like a trap opened and reset without being sprung. Mary held the first one up to the light. The envelope was thick manila. She turned the letter round and round, over and over, wanting to solve the mystery without having to open it.

If Matthew had written to Iris after her death, what would he have had to say? Would it be about her sons? The house? The reservoir? There was so much that Mary couldn't remember. How the Dip had been before was beyond her. Her memory reached back and then stopped. Her father's leaving was a muddle of fragments and she could only just remember Tom Hepple and when he had left, but the idea of his being forced out of his home made her think of a snail being torn from its shell, a tortoise prised open, something vulnerable and raw.

These letters might help. Her father might have told Iris why he had left, why he sold the house and made Tom go, too. "Just ask him," Billy had said, exasperated, when Mary had tried to explain. "Ask anyone." But it wasn't as simple as that. There were other things Mary remembered, like the hospital visits and seeing her father lying on the bed with that withered old woman in his arms. How could she ask him?

As Mary considered all this, her feelings about the letters began to change. They were not bombs about to go off but something precious and secret, something of her father's that she had been trusted with. She would show her father that she was grown-up, sensitive, and discreet. She took the letters downstairs and put them in a larger envelope, sealed it without adding a note, addressed it to him, and took it straight to the post office, where Ray Cornice weighed it, tore the right stamps out of his book, took her money, and said nothing except "Good morning" and "Thank you."

. . .

131

On Saturdays, Mary helped Stella in the shop. It never went well. Stella told Mary to dust everything and then hovered close by, worrying that she would knock a pot over or break a handle or scratch a veneer. If the phone rang while she was serving someone, she would let Mary answer it, then interrupt and instruct Mary on what to say, until nobody could follow the conversation, and then she'd grab the phone and leave Mary to deal with the customer, who smiled pityingly at her.

One day May Hepple came into the shop and asked Mary if she could help out in her hairdressing salon. Mary was surprised. Stella had talked several people in the village into giving her work and it had always gone wrong. She had tried babysitting for the Baskin triplets but could not keep up with their trail of clothes, food, and toys. Melanie Baskin had quizzed her on her secondhand clothes, thinking that she was forced to wear them by Stella. She felt shabby in the Baskins' new home. She'd tried a paper round but got in a muddle and delivered the papers at random, which led to refreshing arguments between neighbours who'd undergone equal and opposite changes of view.

May was looking for someone to help out over the summer as Tracey, the shampoo girl, had gone off to a pop festival and had not come back. She thought Mary was quiet enough but not as hopelessly shy as June. She was bright and spoke well. Mary agreed to start on the following Monday.

May Hepple's salon was tucked in between the newsagent's and the King's Head, in the square. It wasn't a square with buildings round the outside and space in the middle but the opposite. The buildings backed onto one another, facing four ways, skirted by the High Street and three lanes. The Head was where the gentry drank, old and new. Its whitewashed walls were three feet thick. May's salon huddled alongside, a converted cottage with a sign in Art Nouveau script, *Marie's*, and a woman's pert profile in silhouette. May had refused to let her girls put a sign in the window saying *Unisex*.

The first morning Mary was to sweep up and make tea. The

salon was the two front rooms of the cottage knocked together. Its pink paint was flaking in the damp corners of the low ceiling and peeling from the beams. The linoleum floor's geometric design of thin lines of lavender, cream, and beige was now puddled with grey. The little windows were covered with frothy net curtains, and their deep sills were lined with framed photographs of royalty and hairdressing models cut from magazines. The reception desk was a compact wicker affair, behind which May positioned herself like the captain of a cramped and rickety vessel. She had everything in reach—the appointments book, the telephone, the saucer of boiled sweets, the jar of pencils, the hand mirror, and the clothes brush. The tight silk rosebuds in a pewter vase were so old they had yellowed like teeth. She thought of her salon as a feminine and relaxing place, but unlike Mary, who'd never been inside before, May had long stopped noticing the noise and the smell. Three vast hairdryers droned over customers trying to enjoy themselves and read magazines while their heads ached from the drag of curlers, the boring in their ears, and the scorching air. The atmosphere had a sour-sweet, eggy tang made up of ammonia from dyeing and perming solutions and sugary droplets of hairspray. Underneath this was more than a hint of decay. The cottage was damp, the customers mostly geriatric, the plumbing leaked. Everyone who worked there wore perfume, talc, and deodorant, and took little breath-freshening pills, thickening the air with synthetic scents of lily of the valley, Parma violet, lilac, and mint.

May's girls, Jeanette, Felicity, and Suze, had calloused and tough hands, as if they worked outdoors. They were used to it all, used to May and one another. They worked well in the small space, moving neatly past one another and never getting in the way. Their conversation was as choreographed as their movements. Mary interrupted their sequences. She hovered, trying to be in the right place, but jogged Suze's elbow as she passed her the pink rubber perm curlers, which then spilt from their tray onto the floor and wriggled through Mary's fingers as she tried to pick them up. She knocked against Felicity's ankles when sweeping up hair and slopped tea as she carried it from the cubicle kitchen. They would reprimand her, not raising their voices, just tightening the cooing tone in which they chatted to their customers.

Jeanette was tall and tanned and wore short, sleeveless dresses with a gold chain belt hooked round her skinny hips. She had a cap of brown hair, cut into points on either side of her face and tinted every week so that it looked glossy and hard and, in sunlight, had an iridescent gleam. Her long fingers, which Mary would watch raking and fiddling with thin grey hair, were stained with nicotine. She had a deep, dry voice and a bossy, offhand manner that her customers loved. Suze was also tall, but fair and round. Her skin was apricot-coloured from regular sessions on a sunbed, but slack and dull like that of the fruit starting to rot. She had a big smile and a swaying arc of brittle, back-combed hair. It was Felicity who taught Mary how to shampoo. Mary thought she was more like a PE mistress than a hair-dresser—compact, brisk, and plain. Felicity had an unfussy cut, the kind that women came in and asked for after they started having children.

After a couple of days, Mary was allowed to shampoo a cus-tomer. It was a Mrs. Baker, from the caravan site, someone Mary was grateful to realise she did not know. Mary placed a towel round her shoulders and folded a smaller one under her neck. Mrs. Baker set-tled her head back, shut her eyes, and smiled. Mary fiddled with the taps, running the water from the showerhead over her hands, mut-tering about getting the temperature just right. Mrs. Baker clucked and smiled, settled herself some more, and waited. Mary spread her left hand across the top of the woman's forehead as she had been shown, to protect her face from the spray. She was taken aback to re-alise that she had never touched old hair before. It was crisp and light and felt as if it might come away in her hand. And as she began to run the water over Mrs. Baker's scalp, it did seem as if her hair dis-solved as the colourless strands were quickly soaked and plastered themselves to her scalp. Then Mrs. Baker, who had looked to Mary like any other powdered, wrinkled, grey little old lady when she came in, began to look monstrous. Her opened-out, upside-down face came alive. Her pulled-back hair revealed a line where her foundation ended in a tidemark. Mary imagined peeling it off like a mask. Her face powder caught in the down on her cheeks and in the thicker hairs that had coarsened to whiskers on her chin. Her thin mouth had puckered and collapsed, and her orange-pink lipstick, the sort of colour children use when painting skin, had sunk into the hard lines that hemmed her mouth. Mary saw the tiny knot of veins throbbing at her temple and the thick corded veins among the crumpled skin of her neck. She poured out the shampoo and tried to concentrate on massaging it into Mrs. Baker's hair. The old woman groaned dreamily and muttered, "Lovely," and Mary thought, Nobody ever touches her, this must be the only time she's touched, and tried to stop hating what she was doing. Although she did not admit it to herself, Mary would see all the customers like that from then on, as old people who were not so much decaying as drying up, silting up, withering into dust, sand, and stone. Because of this, it shocked her when her lowered face was caught in their warm breath, or if they burped or farted, as some of them did either unconsciously or in pained submission to their loosening bodies.

The kitchen was reached through a small room in which the hairdressers took their breaks. When they were free at the same time, they stayed back there, squeezed together, drinking coffee, smoking, and talking. This afternoon there were no customers and May was out, but they stayed in the back room. It was too small a space to sit down in, so it was like being in a lift where people had got stuck together and felt compelled to talk. Mary was there, too, taking up as little space as she could. The cooing voices of the salon were released in hisses, splutters, and shrieks, as they grabbed one another and doubled up to stop the noise they made from carrying. Jeanette was avid, hawk-like, pouncing on the beginning of a confession or piece of gossip. She was also generous with her own revelations: "So Father Barclay stood there talking to my tits!" "I laughed so hard

135

when Malcolm couldn't get it up, I wet myself!" Suze would offer herself up, too: "I've got the itch. Can't get rid of it. Been to see that Dr. Kill Off twice." Felicity was still quieter than the others, but more violent: "Better get down the clap clinic before you scratch it off!" and they would gasp and giggle some more.

Mary breathed their smoke and tried to laugh at the right moments. She was fascinated. It was like the changing rooms at school, where someone was always patrolling, looking for something to mock, only here she was safe, not picked on but overlooked. Then Suze said something about Sophie Hepple. "Gagging for it!" Jeanette smirked. "That Christie goes home at closing time each night, full of beer. Brewer's droop, I'll be bound!"

"Perhaps she's getting it from the loony! If you didn't know he was cracked, I mean you might, mightn't you, with looks like that?" It was Felicity who said it. They all looked at Mary.

"Says he has a thing about you," Jeanette began. Mary wished she was by the door and could slip away. Jeanette's voice softened. "Don't let him bother you, love. He's always been cracked, that one, but he's no harm, really. Take no notice."

"No more walking on water, heh?" Felicity was smiling as she said it, but, again, nobody laughed. The end of Jeanette's cigarette sizzled as she dropped it into her cold tea.

Suze began, awkwardly, "I mean, it's like May says, right? If he knew it were all nonsense, if the girl told him straight . . ." Jeanette's eyebrows shot up and Felicity gave a small, rapid shake of her head. Mary began to move through them, to the door. Suze stopped her with a hand on her arm and continued: "Don't get me wrong, love. Says you're a good girl, but it's like they say, Tom's never been right in the head, but he can be put straight. You could just say—"

Mary pulled herself free. She grabbed the broom and made for the salon, overhearing Jeanette mutter, "And what if she did, Suze?"

The three women appeared in the salon. They followed Mary round, cleaning brushes and collecting up towels, curlers, and pins—jobs that Mary was supposed to do.

"Don't worry, love!" Suze tilted her head and gave a pouting, apologetic smile. "The place is full of odd ones, always has been. That boy's nothing to be troubled about. I've known him donkey's years!"

"After all," Jeanette said, "there's my Uncle Bob. Too scared to so much as pick up a kitten since he left the Special Services! Thinks he'll break anything he touches!"

"Wasn't Dr. Burgess called in to get him sent off to hospital last Christmas?"

"Yeah. Sectioned, he was. Stayed there till Easter, but doing fine at home, on the medication. Aunt Em's the man of the house now!"

"Not so much of a man as Dot Grieves!" Felicity put in, picking up the thread. "I've begun to think her old man's clothes suit her!"

"Now, he was a case as well," Suze remembered. "Haunted, he was, by his time in Japan. Dot used to find him curled up in a ball in the field behind the house. I thought she'd be relieved when he was gone!"

"The old ones aren't ever what you think, are they?" Jeanette sounded proud. "Mind you, our lot had some crackers, didn't it, Suze?" They'd been at secondary school together. "Remember Hilary Thropton Smith?"

"Hilary Thropton Smith!" sang Suze. "The posh girl who married that Indian chap!"

"She turned up once, with the baby," Jeanette recalled. "Parents wouldn't let them inside the door."

"Says the baby was a lovely little thing."

"Oo, and what about Lady Kay?"

"I remember that!" said Felicity. "That was all over the papers!"

"She was in our class!" Suze and Jeanette chorused, and Jeanette went on: "You'd never have thought she had it in her. So quiet and dull, with those kneesocks and that violin. She must have been having us all on even then!"

Mary was curious. "What did she do?"

"You never heard of Lady Kay?" said Suze. "Kay d'Arcy, actually. Sounds posh, but her father were only a hand on Factory Farm. She went down to London, called herself Lady, even managed to get it on her chequebook and that. Worked for a politician and took him for thousands. Went to prison, didn't she?"

"And there was her sister, Beverley. Poor old Beverley."

"Wasn't it to do with her glands?" asked Felicity. "That court case made the papers, too."

"What happened?" asked Mary.

"Let's just say it wasn't her glands and that butcher should have been locked up," Jeanette explained tartly.

"She died, you see," simpered Suze.

The names they conjured up were almost familiar, but Mary had never been told these stories. She had heard these people mentioned in a telegraphic shorthand passed between grown-ups, with raised eyebrows and knowing sidelong looks. Hearing such garish dramas was like seeing the village coloured in, made foreign and more unknowable than ever.

Jeanette caught Mary looking in the mirror and leapt behind her: "Don't move!" Mary did what she was told. "What would you care for today?" Jeanette trilled in her best salon voice. Mary frowned as Jeanette reached for the wigs arranged on polystyrene heads with the same profile as that on the sign outside.

She pushed the blond one onto Mary's head, and they all laughed, even Mary, who could not now be cross. "I look like a sick sheep!" she managed, and they roared. She blushed, pleased to have entertained them. Then the red wig went on. "A shy carrot!" Mary was enjoying herself. Lastly, Jeanette turned her into a brunette, and Mary forgot to make a joke as she saw herself with this incongruous but wonderful thick, shiny hair.

"Deep . . . dark," Suze ventured, and the others gathered round Mary, taking off her glasses, pulling the wig a little from side to side, fluffing out and smoothing the hair.

Jeanette regarded the pale, skinny girl in her old-fashioned shift dress. "We could make something of you." She grinned.

"Oo! Would you let us?" Suze was excited. "There's no one in the rest of the afternoon and Madam M.'s pushed off." Felicity was smiling, too.

Mary was charmed. "Okay." They wrapped her in a gown and led her to the sink.

While Jeanette washed her hair, Suze announced she would give her a French manicure. Mary closed her eyes and enjoyed the rush of more water than Stella would ever let her use at home, where they had no showerhead for the bath, just a tin mug with which to wet and rinse. Suze pulled over her little manicure trolley, laid a tissue on a velvet cushion, and arranged Mary's hand upon it. She separated her fingers with puffs of cotton wool and rubbed cream that smelt of almonds into them, murmuring about her "lovely soft skin, so elastic . . ." Mary's hands grew long and light, just as Jeanette's brisk massage of her scalp was easing her head. When her hair had been washed, they moved her in front of a mirror. Suze followed with her trolley and began to file and dab. Jeanette combed her hair through and Felicity came over with a colour chart.

The three hairdressers considered their options expertly: "Just a rinse, give her a bit of colour, but subtle."

"She wants something to make it a bit more definite, but she's a pink not an olive, so watch the aubergine end of things."

"Autumnal, rather than winter, don't you think? Something woody with a bit of warmth to it? A touch of sun?" They weighed up Copper Beech ("too light"), Walnut Gold ("too orange"), and decided on Midnight Chestnut ("subtle but deep"). Mary wanted to say, "Black. Just dye it black," but when she squinted at the square of Midnight Chestnut, it looked as good as black to her. While Felicity swabbed the purple dye onto her head, Suze continued with her nails. First, she put little paper crescents on her fingertips and applied the "bottom coat of natural." Then the strips came off and the bare rims of the nails were painted white. Then a "top coat of clear." Mary held a finished hand up to her face. Her nails looked like an image of naturalness—shiny pink and white. She rather liked it. Her scalp began to itch and burn, but she didn't want to say anything to spoil all this, and before long, Felicity announced it was time to rinse the dye off. When she was returned to the mirror, Mary asked for her glasses, but they said no, she should wait and then get the "full effect."

Jeanette put out her cigarette and took up her scissors. She stood to one side of the mirror, scrutinising Mary's face. "Girls, I've been thinking Mary Quant or Audrey . . ." Suze clapped and squealed. Felicity nodded hard. Mary tried to watch, but although her hair looked darker and more substantial now, even at this short distance it began to blur. When Jeanette had finished, Mary went to get up, but they pushed her back down. "Patience! Patience! We've to do your face yet." Felicity plucked her eyebrows and coloured them with pencil. Suze applied foundation with a wet sponge and then painted Mary's eyelids and mouth with tiny flicks of various brushes, in several colours. "It's ever so subtle," she reassured her. Three coats of mascara followed and a dusting of powder and rouge. They told her to close her eyes and stood her up. Felicity handed her her glasses.

At closing time, they all spilled out of the salon together, laughing and patting Mary's hair. She loved them, loved being surrounded by them, and waved them off as they got into Felicity's car. None of them lived in the village. Suze had grown up there but married an accountant who caught the Mortimer Tye commuter train, so they lived there. Jeanette was divorced and was saving up to buy herself a studio flat in Camptown. For now she was back with her parents, in a tied cottage on the Ingfield Road. Felicity was from Mortimer Over, two train stops down towards Crouchness.

"Mary?" It was Clara. She was bronzer than ever, her hair more firey. She had scraped it back and secured it in a messy knot with what looked like skewers. The ends, which sprung away in all directions, had been bleached blond by the sun. She had on a black T-shirt with a studded hem and tight black jeans. "I only knew it was you from the dress," she laughed. "Been and had your hair done?"

"No, I . . ." Mary pulled off her glasses and rubbed at her face. "I work there, see. They just wanted someone to . . ." She ran a hand through her hair, trying to mess it up a bit, but it fell back into its sleek new shape. "Have you been away?"

"Italy. *Famiglia*. You know . . ." Clara was looking away now. "Christ, this summer is dragging, and with Paulie away with his car, it's almost impossible to get into town."

"The buses are going back to normal this week."

"I meant London." There was a pause. "Anyway," Clara continued, and there was another pause before she asked, "what's this about a Harvest Festival Disco? Any good?"

Mary copied her droll tone. "It's hopeless. Cheesy music, mums and dads, orange squash and lemonade."

"Are you going?"

"Never miss it."

"Good! It'll be a laugh. By the way, Daniel's back as well. Has he been in touch?"

"Yes." Mary thought of the card, then realised Clara might mean since his return. "I mean not since . . . Since your dinner . . . he has, I mean." All this time she had been facing into the light, and already she could feel her makeup clot and run. "I've got to go, good to see you, bye."

Mary hurried past the Head and round onto the Green. Once home, she stood back from her bedroom mirror, still wearing her glasses. The effect was good. She felt more definite. Then she took off her glasses and moved closer. Her skin was a matte biscuit colour. Her bottom lip had been enlarged by a brownish line that ran round and up to her Cupid's bow, which was exaggerated into two high points. Inside the line, her lips were coated with a beige pink and finished with gloss that made her look as if she had dipped her mouth in icing that hadn't dried yet. Mary leant forward and kissed the mirror, and was surprised by the print she made. She quite liked her eyes. The pale lids and black lines were not so different from what she did, anyway. It was just that Suze had wanted to make her pretty and, as she said, "open them up," whereas what Mary wanted was to look artistic.

When she had scrubbed the makeup off, her hair looked harsh against her sore, pink face. It was shockingly smooth and flat. "Washes out," Felicity had promised. So Mary got her radio and turned it on loud to cover the noise of running water, and managed to wash her hair four times before Stella knocked on the door.

After Mary had been working at the salon for two weeks, Tracey the shampoo girl came back from her festival. May Hepple and her girls had become fond of Mary, but she had never managed to get the hang of things. There were always spills, missed heaps of hair, forgotten towels, and a customer complaining of soap in her eyes. They patted Mary, clucked, and shook their heads, but were glad to see Tracey back. Mary was kept on as Saturday girl.

"You a hairdresser now?" Lucas asked her the next morning over breakfast.

"On Saturdays."

"Could you give us a trim, then?" Stella came in with his egg.

"I don't cut hair, I only wash it."

"Just a trim?"

Mary knew what her mother would expect of her. It was only more old hair. It would be like straightening a hem. "Okay." Stella was smiling at her, but she wouldn't look up. "I'll fetch some scissors when you've eaten."

Stella found a towel before she went to open the shop, and Lucas sat back with it tucked like a bib around his shoulders and under his chin. His hair was so lank, the grooves made by Mary's comb stayed visible. The acrid whiff of his skin reminded her of the salon. She thought of May's girls. "Been away this summer?" she chirruped.

Lucas chuckled. "Well, I've been to the water."

"The coast?"

"No, the Dip." Mary began to comb and snip. Lucas went on:

"There's fellows out there'll let me have a fish from their buckets."

"You cook fish in the shed?"

"On my bonfire. Wrap it in newspaper, and into the embers. Old army trick." Scurfy flakes and yellow-grey clumps of hair fell on his shoulders. "Water's right down, you know . . ."

"Low?"

"Low as I've known it."

"Can you see anything?"

Lucas cackled. "Well, still a lot of water, that's for sure!"

"I mean, the buildings—"

"Saw Tom Hepple out there, you know. Writing and measuring, he was. Boy needs to leave well alone."

"Is it still there?"

"The Hepple place, you mean?" Mary's hand shook so much, she held her scissors and comb away from his head. Lucas snorted. "Funny business, that. Old Iris hated the place, you know, hated being stuck out there!"

"But I thought—"

"And those boys, all grown up and not moving on. Drove the woman mad!"

"But my dad—"

"She was good to him, wasn't she? He was like a son, after all. And he was the one who did go, off to university on a scholarship, and a year early. By God, old Iris was proud!"

"But the house—"

"Nasty old place, that. If I were those boys I'd have been glad to see the back of it—pokey, mouldering, miserable pile."

"But the money?"

Lucas shifted in his chair and lowered his head, even though Mary was behind him. "That were up to your dad, weren't it? Between him and them. No one else's business."

"Are you just saying that?"

"I just said it, didn't I!" and he chuckled till tears leaked from his clotted, rheumy eyes. Mary quickly trimmed the last strands at

143

the nape of his neck. He left still wearing the towel, and she let him. She put the scissors in the sink and the comb in the bin. She swept the floor and washed her hands.

Two mornings later, just after Lucas had finished breakfast and gone, in the back and out the front as usual, there was a knock on the door. Stella answered it. Mary was still asleep upstairs.

"Mrs. George?" It was a small man, already sticky in his shiny grey suit. A vest showed through his white nylon shirt. He had a folder under his arm. He put out his hand and grinned, showing small, pointed, stained teeth.

A survey, Stella thought. He wants an opinion or a donation or the promise of a vote. "Ms. Lupton, actually." She didn't take his hand.

The man spat out a brisk "Ha!" and a spot of his saliva landed on Stella's cheek. His breath smelt of cabbage, milk, and baked beans. She wiped her face and stepped backwards. He moved towards her. "Mzzzz Lupton? Your maiden name? But once Mrs. George?"

"What is it you want?"

He looked covertly and obviously from side to side, then opened the file and showed her the top page. "Shall we discuss it indoors?"

"By all means." Stella's voice was flat as she led him through and closed the door.

When Mary was woken by her mother's shouting, she thought for a moment she was a child again, and half asleep, she did what she had done then, crept to the top of the stairs and listened.

"He gives me absolutely nothing!" There was someone else there, murmuring. The door flew open and a man stumbled into the hall. Stella pushed papers into his hands. "Take your damned file and go see him in his smart new seaside home! If he's not there, you can always catch him in the offices of his smart new London practice!" More murmuring. "Yes, he did leave years ago and I do have my own business, but it is going down. You want to see the books again? You people have been through them already! And what the hell do you mean turning up at this time of the morning? Are you spying on me? What the hell for?"

The man's voice was getting stronger: "Reason to believe . . . cohabitation . . . seen leaving your home three consecutive mornings . . ."

"Lucas!" Stella screamed. "You think I'm living with a tramp?"

"Three consecutive mornings constitutes—"

"Get out!" Mary hid behind the banisters but caught a glimpse of Stella yanking open the front door and throwing the file out onto the Green. "Take your government filth and get out!" The man scuttled out the door. Stella followed and Mary rushed into her mother's room and was at the window in time to see May Hepple hurry away from her gate, and a ripple of withdrawing shadows, and windows and doors being closed all round the Green.

"Did you think to ask me? Did you think to ask my neighbours?" Stella screeched as the man stumbled about, picking up spilt papers. "Ask them now!" There was no movement among the doors and windows, and around the noise that Stella was making, the Green held an unusual silence. "You say there's no shame in coming to you for help!" she shouted at the man, who was hurrying towards his car. "Ask anyone about me!" She scanned the houses.

Mary watched the man drive away and her mother turn and turn on the spot, her fists raised and her hair all over her face. She was still wearing the purple kaftan she used as a dressing gown. Her feet were bare, and Mary could see the chain of bells round her left ankle. Mary went back to bed and stayed there till she had heard her mother come indoors and leave again for the shop. It was only then that their neighbours began to come out of their houses again.

Now that it was full of water, people thought of the Dip as a bowl, but it had never been that shape. It was a crooked valley that had come about through pressure and fissure. Its sides were steep in

145

some parts and, in others, almost level. The valley floor had been broad and flat around Goose Farm, but narrowed almost to a point behind the church. In between, it curved and swelled and shrank again. Iris Hepple's house had been built on a shelf, high up one side of the valley, behind which the ground rose so steeply that it had been left wild. To reach the house, you had to take the lane into the Dip and then make your way up the track. Her boys had hung a knotted rope from the long branch of the oak that Mary now walked out on and had swung themselves down, crash-landing in the bracken.

In the chapel Tom Hepple went over and over the arc of that swing, trying to remember how deep and how wide it had been, and how far you had to scrabble up the bank from behind the house to get back to the tree. He drew a line out from the bank and another up from the house, and tried to think himself back to his boyhood scale of things. He thought about floating, jumping, and flying (had she been on the water or in the air?). He drew diagrams and made calculations on the backs of bits of paper that had spilled from the filing cabinet. Some had got stuck together when those candles had burned right down and dripped everywhere. Among them were some photographs he'd tried to separate, only they had torn. He found one of a little girl with plaits, in a woolly hat. A stream of wax had run across her face. He levered it off as carefully as he could, but a whole strip of the picture came away. Nonetheless, Tom liked the old-fashioned tones of the unstable colours, how her thick red coat had taken on a blue sheen like plums, and how the snow had yellowed to fleece. He set the picture on a shelf. On one clump of paper, a puddle of wax had dried with a strange shape in the middle of it, almost like a footprint. Tom put that on the shelf as well.

An alarm clock went off. It was the big old enamel one from home that shook as it hammered at its two bells. Tom reset the clock, rewound the alarm, and put it back far enough away for him not to hear its solid tick. He went to the sink, counted out the capsules, and took them with some water. He needed to drink a lot to feel they had really gone down, and then they left him thirsty. He went back to his work, but could get no further with his sums. There was too much to check. He pushed some paper and pencils into his pockets and set off for the Dip.

The narrow pavement ran out just after the phone box. From then on, Tom walked on the lumpy strip of wilted grass that bordered the hedgerow. The sky was changing, though the weather stayed the same. High grey clouds were beginning to churn overhead. Too insubstantial to be storm clouds, they were more like steam accumulating under a low kitchen ceiling. The atmosphere was becoming dimmer and closer, making it easier to see and more difficult to breathe. Tom looked for shade to walk in, but there was none. He felt a constant itch in his throat and a swelling of his tongue that made him swallow and swallow and drink all day—water, tea, soup, coffee, water. He felt like the man in the myth condemned to insatiable hunger, who finally ate himself. What helped was a couple of pints with Christie in the Arms. He knew not to overdo it now, and Christie kept an eye on him. Tom liked the ease he felt at the end of those evenings, the slow walk back to the chapel, the long satisfying piss in the outhouse, two glasses of water, a few of those capsules, and the certainty of sleep. Then there were the evenings when Valerie offered to walk him home.

As he reached the Verges, Tom could feel sweat flooding his chest and back. His shirt clung to his armpits and his face ran with wet. He raised his hands to wipe it, and the idea burst into his mind that his face was coming away; it was melting. At this, Tom stopped and crouched down. He held his breath and concentrated on the thought of the capsules he had just taken, pushing their cool magic into his veins. He gave himself a sum to do, calculating body weight, temperature, absorption, and circulation. When he had all the numbers in place, he felt better and continued on till he turned off by Temple Grove.

The reservoir looked dull under the new sky. Tom walked away from the jetty, in the opposite direction to the house, to where the bank was shallow and he could clamber down to the water's edge.

Sweat prickled his eyes and his chest ached, but he would neither drink nor swim nor wash himself. He cupped his hands and dipped them in, surprised by how a surface that looked so opaque could give way so readily. He studied the water, looking for clues, but it ran through his fingers, painfully clear.

Even though it was what had brought him here, Tom couldn't face walking along to the tree to take more measurements. He was exhausted. The overcast sky had left him with no sense of time, and he was surprised to realise how late it must be, that the grey was turning purple already.

When Tom reached the Verges, he was walking in near-darkness, which would have been all right, but the road was confusing just here. He had to stick to the edge of it, more so because the long drop back from the road to the bushes darkened and dissolved any farther edges.

If a driver didn't bother to dim the car's headlamps, he was swept away by each passing wave of light. He crossed the road so as not to walk into the oncoming traffic and found it better when the light came from behind him. He walked faster, hoping Christie might pass and pick him up and offer him a pint at the Arms. Tom followed the edge of the road by feel alone. There was no painted line or curb, rise or fall, just a point where the tarmac ended and the grass began.

The car was parked just off the road. Tom would have to pass close by. He had not seen it till he was almost upon it, as although there was someone inside, there was no light or noise and the car itself was stripped down to a grey-green like camouflage. The bushes behind it were deep and tall. The road was empty and Tom set off into it, as far away as he could get from the car while still feeling safe. He could hear the erratic rumble and chug of the Camptown bus as it rounded the bend towards him. The weak yellow beams of its lights were already visible, but he knew the bus was slow and there was time to get past the car and step back onto the grass again. Then, somehow, there were more lights, faster and brighter than those of the bus, coming from nowhere, from the wrong place. He heard a loud, dull noise and a crack, and felt himself stopped in his tracks by a wall that doubled him over and shovelled him sideways. There were other noises, some big, some small: screaming, tearing, and crunching, and a shredding, a crackle, an intense hum like a tuning fork, a sigh and a gurgle, but these sounds were far away. That was all.

Stella and Christie met in one of the long corridors of Camptown Hospital.

"I gave Shirley Lacey a lift," Stella began. "Kevin's not able to say much yet, but she likes to be there."

"Does he know about his mates?"

"No. They're waiting. How's Tom?"

Christie shrugged. "His leg was a clean break—it'll mend. Otherwise it's just cuts and bruises."

"And shock?"

"I suppose so, but he didn't come off worst, did he?"

"No, but still . . . I mean, it'll set him back a bit."

"He'll pull through. What were those boys playing at?"

"I believe it's called Chicken."

"God, yes. We all played that one, didn't we? But on our bikes, going along walls or down the Dip, not overtaking bloody buses on a blind corner in someone else's car."

"Was anyone in the bus hurt?"

"Just cuts and bruises. One or two of the old ones were near done in by the shock. They all had to get off, see, and those lads were half hanging out of the wreck—blood everywhere. They'd swerved away from Tom, straight in front of the bus."

"Who was driving?"

"The Hotchkiss boy; he was only fifteen. Kevin was in the back."

"And Tom? What was he doing?"

Christie's face set. "Walking home. That's allowed, isn't it?"

"I didn't mean to suggest . . ." Stella faltered and reached out a placating hand.

"That's how it is, isn't it?" Stella had never seen him look so angry. "There's a loony wandering all over the road, so it has to be his fault, right? Not just a man minding his own business, walking home. If he's a bit cracked, it has to be him that forced those boys onto the right and stood in front of them laughing, yes? Surprised he wasn't wandering about naked and all?" Stella didn't know what to say. "Don't worry, Mrs. George. My brother's back in the hospital now, where people like you think he belongs!" He marched off.

Stella couldn't stand to be thought of like that. She rushed after Christie and caught his arm. "No! No!" She realised she was shouting and lowered her voice. "I know Tom, remember? I think what you're doing, trying to keep him where he belongs, is . . . right! I've explained to Mary how it is, with the water and seeing her. She's almost grown up now and she understands. No one wants him back in one of those, those . . . prisons of the mind. Oh no!" She shook her head earnestly.

Christie was puzzled. Prisons of the what? He patted her hand and left.

Stella continued to wait, knowing that Kevin was just the same and Shirley Lacey would be just as she had been these last few days: angry, frightened, overjoyed he wasn't dead, and ashamed of her luck.

When Shirley appeared, she was with a man Stella recognised. If there had been a corner or even a cupboard nearby, she would have hidden from him.

"Mrs. George," Shirley began in her tidied-up voice. The man, whose face had been lowered and softened in sympathy, looked up and gave a thin but toothy smile. Stella gave a flick of her head, which he acknowledged with a jerky nod.

"How's Kevin?" Stella asked, avid in her nervousness.

"Same." Shirley was exhausted. "This is Mr. Sedge. He was there. He's a witness. He's a lawyer, too, wants to help, says we can get special aid."

"A lawyer?" Stella's surprise was too obvious.

"Yes. Well, if you'll excuse me, I'll just make myself comfortable for the journey." Shirley Lacey hurried off.

"A lawyer?" Stella stepped back, away from that familiar, rotten breath.

"Not currently attached to a firm, you understand, Ms. Lupton." Tough-looking strings of saliva hung across his open mouth. "Between practices, you might say."

"So they took you on as a government snoop?"

He didn't rise to her. "Temporary and part-time. I am here to aid Mrs. Lacey, in a professional capacity."

"And as a witness, Shirley said."

"That's right."

"It was your car, wasn't it, parked by the road?"

"It was."

"Oh my God."

"Notorious black spot." The Adam's apple in his puckered and ill-shaven throat bobbed urgently.

"And why were you there?"

"Notorious black spot," he repeated.

There was a long silence as Stella made sense of what he'd said. "You creep!" As she put it together, she moved towards Frank Sedge, who backed into the wall. "You were waiting for an accident to happen, weren't you?"

"Well, I—" he spluttered, and pressed himself harder against the wall.

"Did you have your business card? Did you leave it in the pocket of that dead boy's shirt? Or does everyone have to have been there three consecutive nights!"

"Sorry to keep you!" Shirley called, as she reappeared in the corridor. Stella strode off to meet her and steered her so firmly and quickly the other way that Shirley only had the chance to give her lawyer the briefest of waves.

. . .

"What would settle you?" Father Barclay asked, after a long silence. It was the end of visiting time. Through the curtains drawn round Tom's bed he could hear the nurse who wheeled round a trolley each evening doling out a mug of pale cocoa made with homogenised milk and a couple of musty biscuits to each of the patients, who were doing what they could to bring on sleep.

Tom smiled. "Not cocoa." The nurse trundled past without slowing.

"Does it really help, being back in the village?" Father Barclay felt at ease in Tom's company, not agonised by the shyness that compelled him to manic heartiness when he had to play the village priest. Here was someone he knew and understood, and perhaps could help.

"I shouldn't think so . . . really. But the idea . . . of it."

"You mean how it was?"

"No, no. It were always tight and there was . . . ever trouble. I mean what I might have found it to be . . . for me." Father Barclay waited, and eventually, Tom went on. "You grew up . . . in the city, didn't you, Harry?"

"In a boys' home."

"You said. They put the homeless in a home." They both laughed. "Says you look like a farmer!"

"They do." The priest blushed. "Who knows? It might be in my blood."

"So why come to a village? Because your . . . face fits?" They laughed again. Then Tom shook his head. "That matters, though, doesn't it?"

Father Barclay nodded. "You're right. I was drawn to Allnorthover because it seemed that everything belonged, and had belonged for centuries. People don't lock their doors. They know and help each other. There are old houses and old families. I liked the notion of unbroken lines, of things that stay in place."

"And what if your face fits but you don't?" Tom enquired. "When you belong to it, the place holds you so tight, you might not notice how it squeezes."

"If it's like that for you, why come back?"

Tom looked along the high narrow bed, across the cage that protected his plaster cast from the pressure of his blankets. The pain of his leg left the rest of him clear. He had never felt so clear. "You know, Harry. There are things . . . out of place. I did nothing to put them right back then. If I can settle it, it won't hurt to . . . be held here."

"Tom. There's things out of our hands. You have to let go and move on." He knew he was sounding soothing now.

Tom frowned. "How can you let go of something that's out of your hands?" (That blinding light and, somewhere in it, the girl and her gift of walking out onto the water to show him where.)

The priest chuckled, leaned forward, and hugged him awkwardly. "I've missed you, my friend!"

Tom lay awake, enjoying their conversation long after Father Barclay had gone. He would soon be home. He was getting to know the girl through where she went and when. At the right moment, he would catch her. And there was much to do before the first frost.

"Dear D," wrote Mary, gauging the scale of her writing to an imagined square far smaller than the size of the card itself. "The Harvest Festival Disco on the 20th? Clara thinks it might be a laugh. M." She paused and then followed her initial with the rest of her name. The disco was three weeks away. Perhaps she should wait a few days till school started and she was in Camptown and might bump into him anyway. If she waited, he might phone. She found his address in the telephone directory and copied it out. She thought of how it might arrive stamped by the sorting office — "Remember Your Post Code," and of how that might obliterate part or all of her message, something crucial like a name or a date. Should she try to find out his post code? She remembered how he had addressed her as "Mary George of Allnorthover" and left the card as it was. The picture on the front was of a sculpture of a blue tree. It had a frothy top, a spindly fluid trunk, and a puddle of roots at the bottom. The shadow it cast on the white wall behind it was like the neck of a full jug from which a trickle of liquid poured. Mary had seen this sculpture at an exhibition once when she was small and had been so captivated by the foreign shade of blue that Stella had bought her the card.

Beside her on her desk were two rejected versions of her note. One was a picture of a woman in white, carrying a man on her shoulders. They were floating over a green river and they were smiling. His right hand covered her right eye, and in his left was a raised glass of red wine. His head had slipped to one side and looked as if it were about to be carried off by the winged woman in purple who was swooping past. "Dear Daniel," this card read. "What a summer!!! I've been washing half the village's hair, hearing all sorts of scandal, and praying for rain. How about the Harvest Festival Disco? I was talking to Clara and SHE said it should be an absolute hoot!! Believe me, it is *surreal*. It's on the 20th, so let me know what you think. Love from Mary." There was a cross, a kiss, after her name. It was another card Mary had had for years, but only now did she notice that the woman in white's dress was slashed at the front, a purple-stockinged leg was exposed, and her low-cut bodice was falling off one breast. The third card was a photograph that reminded Mary of somewhere she had been to, marshes near the coast. It was of a narrow boardwalk disappearing into rushes. On the horizon, at the other end of the path, was the silhouette of a house. It had one tall chimney, like a periscope. On the back of this one Mary had written: "Après la récolte, la danse. The Harvest Festival Disco on the 20th? An experience." No names, initials, "dear," or "love." The French was something she'd read somewhere. She had to look up "récolte," "harvest," to check the direction of the accent. Perhaps she'd made it up. Mary put all three cards back in a drawer.

When June Hepple found out that Tom was going to be coming to stay again, she put away her ornaments, packed a bag, and went back to her Great-aunt May's. The twins, Darren and Sean, were home and Sophie was busy getting them new shorts, shirts, blazers, and shoes, haircuts and pencils. She didn't mind June being out of the way.

154

If people tried to ask June about her mad uncle, she had nothing to say, because she didn't see him, she wasn't there. May liked her company and approved of Christie keeping Tom with him. The chapel was not a place to live.

Sophie kept the bottles of capsules lined up on the kitchen counter, along with the painkillers and antibiotics the hospital had prescribed. Each morning Christie helped Tom into the bathroom and then downstairs. He spent the day in the big armchair, his broken leg in its cast, as rigid as the rest of him was limp. Sophie bustled around, feeling the need to go in and check on him frequently.

Although Sophie left the windows open, little air came through the nylon lace curtains. The high-backed armchair had been in the old house, but Sophie had given it a smooth new cover, and once Tom had sunk into it, it was impossible for him to get up again. If he needed to use the downstairs toilet when Christie was out, Sophie had to help him up. She did this by taking his wrists rather than his hands, pulling him quickly onto his feet, and then, as he straightened, faltered, and leant towards her, she would slip a crutch under each of his elbows and hurry off. But Sophie never really hurried. She was always careful, made-up and dressed up. Tom liked to see how she placed herself in a room, how she leaned back on her high heels, and how her hips rolled from side to side. Whenever she walked away, he watched her.

Outside, all day, Darren and Sean kicked a ball against the side of the house. They took it in turns to try and keep the ball in the air, so it hammered against the wall in long volleys. Then there would be a disappointed shout, silence, and the hammering would start again.

"Let's go in on the bike!"

"Billy, I am not turning up at school in your bloody shoe!"

"You don't have to. I'll leave it behind. Just ride pillion."

It was the day before the beginning of term. Billy and Mary were sitting in the Catholic cemetery, smoking dope. It was still hot, but the sky had begun to move. One minute the poplars cast tall shadows, and the next, the light was even again.

Billy, as usual, was lounging on his great-grandfather's grave. "It's our last year, our last start. We might as well do it in style," he persisted.

"I just want to get on with things now," Mary tried to explain. "No fuss."

"Worried your boyfriend will see you?" Billy didn't usually tease her and she didn't like it.

"Fuck off. Anyway, who said he's my boyfriend?"

"Excuse me! First Crouchness, then a little al fresco do in the doctor's pool?"

"What do you know about that?"

"Little bird . . ." he chanted.

"Christ, you're beginning to sound just like Julie!"

Billy sat up. "It's a small world."

"If you're going to talk in clichés, Billy, I'm going home." He looked unperturbed, but followed Mary as she stomped out of the cemetery.

"Forget about tomorrow, then. Let's just go for a ride now. No one will see you in the sidecar, anyway." He knew how much Mary liked to get away from the village. She shrugged and continued marching, but Billy saw her clenched fists relax, and then, when she reached the bike parked on the road, she clambered ungraciously in.

As they passed the chapel, the rear wheel of the motorbike hit a pothole where the heat-cracked road had erupted. Billy rode on for a minute or two, until he could no longer ignore the violent hobbling of the burst tyre. He pulled over at the end of the Clock House drive. As he was taking off his helmet, they could hear someone running towards them along the gravel. Mary thought it might be Clara, and tugged with one hand at the chin strap of her helmet and at her glasses with the other. The strap was frayed and its buckle stiff, and her glasses were held fast. As the figure approached from behind, she could not bear to turn round and be seen. There was nothing for it but to sink as low as she could in the sidecar and to hope whoever it was would pass.

"Tobias, man!" Billy was waving his arms, flapping the extravagantly flared sleeves of his T-shirt like semaphore flags.

"Recognised the engine, Bill, then I heard you had a limp. Must've hit that crater back by the chapel." Mary was baffled but also pleased to hear Tobias's voice again and its accompanying clatter of tools as he squatted down by the bike. But although she was on the other side of the machine, in plain view, she wouldn't turn her head.

The two boys knelt beside the wheel, probing and testing, and then Tobias stood up and stretched, casting his shadow across Mary's back. She shivered. "Wheel it up to the lawn and we'll find a spare. You can leave the sidecar here." He leant across the bike to uncouple it. Mary felt a jolt. She wanted to face them after all, even just so that she could take the helmet and her glasses off, but by this time, it seemed less embarrassing to stay put. She didn't see Billy frown and open his mouth to speak to her, or Tobias smile and put his finger to his lips. Mary listened as they pushed the bike up the drive. She was too confused to notice that the slow crunch of the motorbike's wheels had given way to something faster and stronger. When she realised that there was a car coming down from the house, she tried not only to remove the helmet and take off her glasses but also to climb out. She managed to get herself free while yanking at the helmet, the strap of which abruptly gave way. Her loosened glasses tipped forwards, so she dropped the helmet and lurched to grab them, lost her balance, and fell sprawling as the car braked hard and stopped, its nearest front wheel just inches from Mary's outstretched hand.

"Darling!" Clara leapt from the passenger door and helped Mary up. Mary was shaking, but more out of humiliation than shock or pain.

Paulie came sheepishly forward from the driver's side. "Sorry, sweetheart." A flush was spreading messily over his throat and up into his cheeks. "You came from nowhere." He held out his hands in a wide shrug.

Clara, her arm still clamped round Mary's shoulder, tittered.

"Not quite nowhere." She pointed at the sidecar. Paulie snorted, held his breath, saw Mary smile, and then giggled, and Mary began laughing, too, laughing and crying and shaking, and all the time feeling Clara's strong arm round her.

"You need a drink," Clara pronounced, and pushed Mary into the car.

Mary decided not to ask where they were going and was relieved that Paulie didn't stop at one of the High Street pubs, where she knew no one would serve her. The car continued out along the Mortimer Tye road and stopped instead at The Crown, the last pub inside the parish boundary. Although this meant that it officially belonged to the village, few thought of it as such. The Crown, with its carvery and banqueting hall, was for occasions.

They sat in the garden and drank gin-and-tonics, while the clouds quickened and moved over them, making Mary pull off her cardigan, only to put it back on again a minute later. Her trousers were ripped across one knee (but so were Clara's black jeans), and one shin and both hands were grazed. Mary was happy. She listened to Paulie and Clara's languid chat and turned from one to the other, fascinated by how they were both—Clara with her witch's face and Paulie, so smooth and bland—so attractive. Mary felt sleepy and talkative at once, and began to join in. She told them about Hilary Thropton Smith's racist parents and Kay d'Arcy's scam. She described the tramp who came for breakfast, bringing his egg, and who sold a caravan that didn't belong to him. They were laughing, and she was pleased and thinking up other stories when Clara yelled, "Over here!"

It was Daniel, Julia, and Ed. Mary squinted up at Daniel as he approached, forgetting to smile because of not being able to see that he was smiling at her, which made him hesitate and sit away from her, next to Paulie. Mary leant back in her chair and was grateful that Clara talked on, about Italy and the term ahead.

"How's your summer been?" Daniel leant forward and Paulie leant back.

"Oh, sort of boring and sort of lively . . . you know . . ." She stared down into the glass clutched in her hands.

"Mary's been telling us fabulous stories about the village!" Paulie said.

"Really?" Daniel sounded interested or piqued—Mary couldn't tell.

Then Clara got up and Paulie, Julia, and Ed, too. They all sang their goodbyes, blew kisses, and left.

A bell rang in the pub. "Another drink? That'll be last orders. It's almost half past two." While Daniel was gone, Mary moved into Paulie's chair. Sitting next to him made everything easier. They lit cigarettes and spun out their drinks, managing to talk a little but mostly happy just to sit together. Daniel took her hand and stood up. "Looks like we'll have to walk back across the fields."

"Fine. I'll just . . ." Mary rushed off to the toilet, a converted stable that ran along the side of the pub. She peered into the speckled mirror, unlit by the dangling bare bulb, and tried to animate herself, stretching her lips, baring her teeth, flicking her hair, and wrinkling her nose. Then she went back out to meet Daniel with the wide smile she'd practised still fixed on her face.

"Are you all right?" he said. Mary faltered and nodded. "It's just you looked for a moment as if you'd seen a ghost!" This made her laugh. Daniel took her arm and led her over a stile and onto the footpath back to Allnorthover.

"Do you know the way?" she spluttered, still giggling and now beginning to hiccup.

He could see the spire of Allnorthover's first church. "It's obvious, isn't it!"

By midafternoon the sky was harsh and clear. The light that had in just a few dull days been forgotten returned. Lying in a hollow in the meadow behind the church fields, Mary woke feeling not just burnt but scorched, like paper hit by a beam concentrated through a magnifying glass. Daniel was kneeling beside her. When they had lain down, the world had been revolving in jerky repeated lurches. She didn't remember going to sleep, just waking up full of heat, her eyes swollen and her stomach both churning and empty. Her shirt was open. Mary did not move as Daniel leaned forward, kissed her mouth, and undid the last two buttons. He pulled down her bra straps, carefully, as if arranging her, then ran a finger between her breasts and licked it.

"Salt." He smiled, but Mary, now conscious of the sweat that had collected on her chest as she slept, made to get up. He leant down to meet her. Unable to push back and raise them both, Mary pulled his head hard against her instead.

He tugged himself free. "Let me look at you."

"No!" She hadn't meant to shout. The sun would exaggerate her pallor and emphasise every pimple and freckle and hair. She could see the tracery of veins along her arm. "It's too bright." She yanked at the straps of her bra and rolled onto her front.

Daniel laid her shirt across her. "Put this back on, then. You'll burn." As she dressed, he turned away. They got to their feet, Mary stiff and blinking.

"How long did I sleep?"

"A couple of hours."

"You, too?"

"On and off."

"Why didn't you wake me?"

"I wanted to look at you."

Mary was silent: to say the wrong thing or anything that assumed anything could shatter this precarious intimacy. She didn't want to ask Daniel how he had come to be in The Crown, nor to question Clara's peculiar kindness. It might not be luck or fate but something altogether ordinary and nothing to do with her that had brought him here. They walked in silence past the church and round the Common till they met the far end of the High Street, where Mary led Daniel to the bus stop. Daniel drew Mary to him, but she stiffened.

"Don't look; then nobody will see you." He held her head against his chest, and she believed him and gave in completely as he kissed and stroked her hair and said, "You're a strange and lovely creature, Mary George."

The bus arrived, just ahead of Mim. The old dog almost fell over herself in her attempt to make it stop before it chose to. When she heard Mary's sharp call, she wobbled, confused, sat down, and whimpered.

"Mimosa!" Mary repeated sternly. "Don't come the hit-and-run with me, my girl!" The dog slunk towards her. When Mary had her by the collar, she realised Daniel was waiting to say goodbye and had one foot already on the platform of the bus. She started towards him, but Mim, thinking she was being forced to submit to her enemy, would not budge. Mary knew if she let go of her collar, the dog would follow and taunt the bus all the way out to the Verges. She tried again, and this time Mim ungraciously followed.

Daniel leaned down and kissed Mary. Mim hung back, panting noisily and baring her raddled tongue and brown teeth in a smelly yawn. Daniel looked at the dog ("Good night . . . Mimosa!") and then back at Mary as the bus conductor pointedly rang the bell three times and the bus juddered into life.

"A strange and lovely creature," Mary heard Daniel say again, but softly, so perhaps not really, as, once more, he disappeared quickly and easily out of sight.

At the end of the first week of term, Mary received a note from her father: "Dear Mary, I will be in Camptown next Tuesday afternoon and was wondering if we could meet for tea after school? Say, 4.30 in C & L's? If not poss, leave a message for me at home. Love, Daddy." She was so anxious and excited that she went for a walk, something she did these days only to get somewhere. It was early evening. As she got towards the end of Low Lane, she could see orderly plumes of smoke rising from the harvested fields where the farmers were burning stubble. Mary was drawn by the odd tameness of these fires, how the farmers decided on lines and the flames obeyed. The cropped straw glowed orange and charred black. There would be a glimmer of fire well into the night.

Mary walked along a track to one side of a field where the fire was still high. The earthy autumnal smell of burning made her wish for cold. Then the wind turned sharply, almost at right angles, as if it had bounced off Temple Grove, and the smoke had Mary surrounded. She couldn't breathe. A second later, it was blown back.

Charlemeyne & Lere's was Camptown's snobby, dowdy, and only department store. The tearoom was on the top, third floor. The ground floor was crammed with departments that prided themselves on the variety of their stock and the expertise of their assistants: haberdashery, millinery, stationery, hosiery, jewellery, and perfumery. Expert at judging customers, none of these slight men and formidable women bothered to offer Mary any help, and they prickled when she ran her hand absentmindedly along a shelf of ribbons, riffled a heap of vellum, or stroked a jar of feathers. She scurried into the lift, pulled the concertina door shut, and pressed the button. Chains clanked and cables sighed.

On the third floor, Mary made her way through lingerie, electrical goods, and soft furnishings, towards the corner roped off with swagged gold cord, where a counter was staffed by a waitress. There were ten tables covered in glassy beige cotton that passed for linen at a distance and fell in awkward folds to the floor. Peach-coloured napkins, starched and pressed into pleats, were fanned out in plastic clips. Each table held a laminated menu, a bowl of sugar lumps with tongs, and another filled with sachets of salad cream, mustard, and tomato sauce.

Mary could tell from the set of her father's back that he was not happy and realised how much she'd been hoping for from this meeting.

"God!" He jumped, turned, and quickly smiled. "You gave me a shock, creeping up on me like that!" He looked well, though.

"Sorry, Dad!" She leant down and kissed his cheek. "I didn't mean to. You looked like you didn't want to be disturbed."

"Never mind, never mind." He waved a hand impatiently across the table. "Sit down, dear. What'll you have? A milk shake? Would you like that?"

The waitress loomed. Mary addressed her directly: "A cup of coffee, please."

"Filter or instant?"

"Filter, please." It was what Matthew had just had brought to him. The water was still seeping through the grounds in the paper cushion in its plastic ring, into the cup.

They looked at each other, and then around the empty room.

"How's school?" He patted his jacket pockets and brought out a box of matches and a case. She waited for him to light his cigarillo, only to be overwhelmed by the familiarity of its smell.

"It's my last year."

"Is it now?" He'd been caught out. "Of course it is!"

Mary's coffee arrived and dripped. It was weak, sour, and luke-warm, but she drank it religiously, in tiny mouthfuls. They talked about school ("Okay, you know, they're piling it on, at least we can wear what we like, within reason") and work ("Red tape, preservation orders, international competitions"). Matthew leaned back and puffed. Mary was as impressed as ever by his air of authority, but she thought she saw his hands shake.

"How's your mother?" he asked suddenly, his head veering closer.

"Okay, I think."

"Wary Mary!" he chanted and, pleased with himself, relaxed again.

She screwed up her eyes to stop the tears coming. Matthew was busy rummaging in his leather satchel. He had something in his hand but kept it by his side, grinned, and shook his head. "You don't have to protect her, sweetheart. After all, you clearly know now how . . . impossible she became back there for a while. It must have been

163

a shock finding out like that, and you were right to, how shall I put it, let me know, but if we are going to help her, you'll have to be straight. It's no betrayal, love."

Mary stared. "I don't understand," she said.

Matthew put an envelope on the table. It was addressed to him, in Mary's writing—the package of letters to Iris Hepple.

It took some time for Mary to make any kind of sense of it. "You mean they're not from you?"

Matthew's face hardened and his hand flew into the air and, just as quickly, fell again. "Did you seriously, for one moment, imagine they were?"

"But I haven't, I didn't look . . ." This was bad, all wrong, really wrong, and Mary couldn't work out why.

Matthew continued: "There's so much you don't know and, to be frank, that you don't need to know, sweetie. Iris took me in and brought me up. I wasn't going to be put off by a bit of blood, shit, and vomit." Mary shuddered and her father smiled. "They couldn't take it, you see. Couldn't think of that kind of closeness as being anything other than . . . nor could they do the other right thing and go and get on with their lives." Then, more to himself, "Hung around like watchdogs, terrified I'd—how did good old Father B. put it?—'replace them in her heart.' Replace them in her house turned out to be more like it!"

He laughed drily, ground out his cigarillo in the glass ashtray, looked at his watch, and rose. "It's nice to see you, but I have to say, I am most disappointed." He turned to the waitress, gave her a charming smile, which was met with a blank sneer, and left a pound note on the table before ruffling Mary's hair a little too fiercely and hurrying out.

Mary felt sick. She stuffed the envelope into her bag, ran out of the tearoom and straight into the "Powder Room," where Dorothy Spence was sitting by the door arranging a shelf of air freshener and disinfectant beside a delicately flowered saucer in which she had placed a small card neatly printed with the words "Thank you." Still sobbing, Mary rushed out back past her. Mrs. Spence, unmade-up

164

and unnoticed by Mary, regarded the swinging door. "Thank you." She was still rehearsing it. "Thank you."

Once the reservoir had been filled, the machinery driven away, the builders' huts taken down, the signs put up, and the fence completed, the villagers stopped coming to look. Those who had lived in the Dip kept away, and later, those who had watched remembered it differently. No one recalled the roar and gush they had expected. "A great pipe, like a hose filling a pool for days on end, weeks even." "It was like a seeping, a slow leak, a muddy puddle getting a bit bigger every day." "So fast, you blinked and you missed it, and then it seemed natural." "So slow, it seemed natural by the end." "It took a month," "a year," "ages." "The buildings? That falling-down church and that farm stuck in the Middle Ages? Says it even had a moat! Fat lot of good that did it in the end!" A delighted, strenuous wheeze.

It was same with Matthew, his absence seeping and rising and finally levelling. "Didn't he stay up at the chapel after that wife of his got so difficult? The man had work in the city, on the coast. He has a place out there now, doesn't he?" "Matthew George, the architect? Joe's son. He grew up here. Doing very well for himself. Nice car. One child, a girl; looks nothing like either of them."

Tom Hepple's departure was not a story that people wanted to be close to, let alone part of. Papers had changed hands and so, then, had the house. It wasn't right, but it was the law. He had no right to stay, not anymore, and the place was going anyway. The boy had no need to disappear completely. There was help close at hand, housing and the hospital, and family, plenty of that.

Tom remembered the day Matthew finally came to tell him himself. Otherwise, he'd have never believed it. On the wish of his mother and the say of his oldest friend, his home slipped away, like Iris herself, not quite gone but out of reach. He'd felt his skin break then, an unbearable lack of edges. Nothing helped, only going and staying far away, in any opposite place that would have him. The police had traced him and told Christie which hospital he was in, but also that the doctors felt that, for now, he was best left alone. So for the next ten years that was what Christie had done, for Tom's own good—left him alone. (The days and nights of it. The dreams and voices and determinations, the fearful hopes, the fears.)

Stella was cutting out something at the table. Everything was laid neatly around her: large pointed and small rounded scissors, and pinking shears; the sewing machine that had belonged to her mother, so ancient it didn't even have a treadle, let alone a plug; a tin of needles, another of pins; tape, ribbon, stiffener, and facing; buttons, a box of cotton reels, and another of wool. To untidy Mary this looked like instruments laid out for an operation.

There was safety in her mother's preoccupation, and right now, she wanted her mother. She offered to make them both a cup of tea, and Stella, pleased and surprised, accepted. Mary laid it all out on a tray and poured milk from a bottle into a jug.

"What are you making?" Mary asked, as she poured the tea carefully through the strainer, for which she had thought to provide a saucer. Stella didn't even do that when they had company.

"A dress for Billy's dad."

Mary giggled. "They've roped you in for the Christmas panto again?"

"You know our Violet . . ."

"I've never dared call her Violet!" Old Eely. "She looks down on us, Mum. Why help her out?"

"I don't mind. And it's Morris I'm helping right now, isn't it?" She held up the voluminous pink dress to which she'd been adding a frill. "Just his colour, no?"

Mary wanted to hug her. I love you, she thought, watching her mother sew and snip, making instant choices from everything laid out around her. Tonight her mother's face didn't look plain. Her scarves and beads were softness on a body in which every last bone was strong. She's made from girders, Mary thought gladly.

"You're back late," Stella remarked.

"I met Dad. For coffee. He asked me to."

"Well, that was nice."

"Not really . . ." (Wary Mary.)

"Oh, I'm sorry." Stella said it so diffidently that Mary found, for the first time, she wanted to tell her mother everything.

"Oh, Mum. I did such a terrible thing. I didn't mean to, I thought they were Dad's, I'm sorry, I didn't know. You'd every right . . ."

Stella looked at her, baffled. "Slow down, love. What terrible thing?"

"The letters. I got given them by Mr. Cornice, to give back!"

"What letters?"

"Your letters! I thought they were Dad's. I didn't look, I mean, I know letters are private and I thought they were Dad's!"

"What letters?"

Mary pulled the envelope from her bag and handed it over. Stella studied the five identically typed addresses and the postmarks.

"Where did you say you got these?"

"Mr. Cornice. He said they were to be given back to you."

"To me?"

"Well, he said to be given back." Mary shook as she reminded herself of why she was doing this, not to hurt her mother as she had her father, just to say she knew and that it was all right.

Stella picked one up. "Have you read them?"

Mary shook her head and watched as Stella turned the letter over. It had been opened. "I didn't look, really. I just sent them straight to Dad. I thought they were his."

Stella wasn't listening. She read the page of dense type that Mary could only just make out through the translucent paper. "What does it say?"

Stella crumpled the letter back into the envelope and snatched up the other four. "You thought I wrote that?" Her face was mottled and she was breathing deeply.

"Not me, Dad. He said—"

"He said what?"

Mary felt as if someone had hold of her and was turning her very quickly in one direction and then the other, back and forth. "He didn't say, I mean he realised you must have—"

"Must have what? Written this?"

"Written what? Mum, I told you. I haven't looked."

"Don't give me that!" Stella snapped. "You believed every word he said, didn't you! That I would do something like that! What was the tea for? Felt sorry for your mad old ma, did you?"

Mary tried. "There's nothing wrong with wanting to express your feelings, even to someone who's dead."

"Well! What a wise little woman you're growing up to be! I tell you what, listen to your father. He'll teach you how to look after yourself!"

"Mum, I'm not on his, anyone's, side."

Stella wasn't listening. "Why have you always behaved like some little ambassador? You're not the United Nations, remember? You're Airy Mary! Isn't that what they called you at school? Not the girl who walks on water but the girl who walks into walls!"

Mary was pleading, "Stop it now! Stop it now!" but when her mother did stop, suddenly shocked by herself, Mary still couldn't stand it. Next came the super-soft voice, the cooing, the outstretched arms. "I didn't mean it, honey, I was just . . ."

Stella came round and Mary moved away, and so they circled the table until Mary made a break for the door, then changed her mind and turned, and for the first time in her life shouted at her mother, "Now do you see why I thought it was you?" She made a grab for the letters, but Stella got to them first.

"If they're not yours, you can't keep them," Mary faltered.

"You've grown quite a tongue, haven't you?" Stella slumped and looked exhausted. She turned away. "Just go to bed, why don't you?"

The Village Hall where the Harvest Festival Disco was to be held was out along Low Lane. It was a flimsy building set on brick piers and squashed between a pitched roof and an excessive number of broad front steps. All the village halls Mary had been to looked like this. They must come as a kit, she thought, or arrive ready-made on the back of a long truck, the way houses did in America. The hall accommodated most village groups. It was used for jumble sales, fêtes, play groups, coffee mornings, and pensioners' clubs. The Cubs and Brownies met there, as did the Parish Council and the Women's Institute. It acted as classroom, church, or shop, and the conversations that were held there about money, families, and health were an extension of those heard in Allnorthover's surgery, pubs, kitchens, and front rooms. The hall could be as dim as the post office or as brightly lit as the school. It adjusted itself to the formal murmur of councillors at their single long table as well as it did to the shrieks of toddlers with their rushing about and toys. The floor was polished every week with a machine, and so the place smelt of cedar with undertones of old food, old clothes, baking, and sweat. The windows were not often opened, and their aluminium frames had warped and set. There was a small kitchen with a serving hatch, an enormous tea urn, and cupboards full of the same cheap crockery and glasses that were used in the school.

Jumble sales were tricky, as no one wanted to buy their neighbours' cast-offs. They would pick something up and carry it round the hall till they could pay someone they barely knew. Mary had always loved jumble sales and hadn't thought about wearing second-hand clothes till Dawn stopped her in the corridor at school once, when she was twelve. "Julie says she saw you get that tat at a jumble sale!" Mary had found a fashionable, if rather worn-out, black smock coat edged with brocade.

"That's right, Saturday." Mary was perplexed. Stella had always bought things at charity shops and jumble sales, and didn't hesitate to say so.

Dawn looked taken aback—as far as Mary could tell beneath her back-combed hair and her chalk-white eyelids. Even Mrs. Rike had given up scrubbing Dawn's face and taking acetone to her frosted fingernails. "Wouldn't catch me wearing someone else's rags. My mum wouldn't let me out the house in that!" She strutted away with her gang. Only later, at home, did Mary begin to see what had happened, and it was as if she had just cracked a code that everybody else had long understood. Doing so brought something the opposite to relief. In those adolescent years she had felt herself wrenched slowly out of her head and into the world, made to think and worry about things she'd never noticed before. She put on her glasses and looked in the mirror. The coat was a cheap version of what had been modish that last autumn. One pocket was torn, the cuffs were thread-bare, the brocade faded and coming apart.

The Harvest Festival Disco was organised by a subcommittee of the committees for the Church Restoration Fund, the Young Farmers, the Sunday school, and the Ingfield Youth Club, together with rep-resentatives of the Rotary Club, the Licensed Victuallers' Associa-tion, and the Small Tradesmen's Alliance. The Restoration Fund supported both churches, as well as one in Ingfield. They split the proceeds with the Youth Club, whereas the other groups organised donations from their contacts as a show of power and goodwill: cheap printing, window space for posters, books of tickets, and a wholesale deal on beer, crisps, and soft drinks. WI members and the women of other churchgoing families sent along cakes and sand-wiches with their children. Several teenagers turned up early, skulk-ing along the lane, trying to hide a tray covered with a teacloth or doily which they would shove into the hands of the nearest person at the hall before hurrying off to make a second entrance with their friends.

Terry Flux had DJ'ed for this disco for so long that he'd seen some of the teenagers disappear and come back as early arrivals, en-gaged or married, and now serious, dignified, and careful with their money. He started the evening with jaunty, familiar tunes that would encourage the girls gathered in threes and fours around the walls to begin swaying and nudging one another to join in. Then a bit of rock 'n' roll that got the older ones tapping their feet—"Rock Around the Clock" and "Runaround Sue." Somebody's parents stepped halfway towards the middle of the room to jitterbug, the woman blushing and letting herself be led by the man, who was good and proud of it. He kept his head down and concentrated on his flourishes.

The dancing spread. The eleven- and twelve-year-olds, allowed to accompany their parents for the first hour or so of the evening, began with giggling imitations of the grown-ups. The girls, in versions of their older sisters' outfits, rushed from one corner to the next, watching everything avidly. The boys stuck close to the kitchen hatch, clubbing together for another fizzy drink and grabbing handfuls of crisps and cake when no one was looking. As the rock 'n' rollers began to falter, Terry played novelty songs, "The Laughing Gnome" and "Lily the Pink," which brought some of the younger ones into the middle of the room, parading, gesticulating, and singing along. The adults queued up to buy plastic glasses of white wine or lemonade, or beer poured from a big tin with two holes punched in the top. The women gathered up chairs and arranged them in circles, balancing their drinks and cigarette packets on their knees, while the men leaned against the walls.

The room began to get properly dark by eight-thirty. The children were taken home, and most of the older adults left, too. More and more teenagers arrived from the surrounding farms and villages, and soon the hall was full. Most people there were between the ages of fourteen and twenty-four, but even if they lived next door to or had known each other all their lives, under Terry Flux's coloured lights and revolving mirror balls, they were abashed.

Terry Flux wanted to bring the crowd together, so he started with the girls and some hard funk that would have them united on the floor. Earth, Wind & Fire's "Saturday Nite" brought them forwards, gesticulating and singing along, punctuating the staccato blasts of brass with jutting hips or jabbing fingers. Each cluster of girls threw down their clutch bags or shoulder bags, nestled their drinks among them, and formed a tight ring. They danced to please themselves and to entertain one another, giggling and clowning, and very simply happy. To break open the circles, Terry Flux switched to ska — "Johnny Reggae," something with a straight enough beat for the boys to start moving to, and then, faster, "Al Capone," the screeching, squealing brakes that announced the song, the warning: "Al Capone's gun don't argue!" bringing gangster imitations and echoes from the boys and yelps of recognition from the girls as they worked themselves into a long line down the room and set about a dance somewhere between tribal and country, right over left foot, back and forth, left over right, back and forth again, but only half a skip each way, all stomping their feet on the wooden floor, then a jump and a quarter turn, landing heavily together on their platform shoes. Their hips and bellies were undulating, but their upper bodies and raised arms were stiff. Terry led them into something slower but just as punchy, "Me and Baby Brother," to which they adapted the same dance, three heavy sways, then the jump and turn to punctuate the chorus: "Me and baby brother" — SLAM! 1—2—3—SLAM! In the middle of the row was Julie Lacey in a glittery halter top and slithery pencil skirt, big curls and high stiletto heels, hardly dancing at all, just making small mocking gestures that captivated everyone watching her. At the near end, June Hepple followed the others by watching the feet of a neighbour, caught her long skirt on the heels of her clogs, flung her arms out, and never quite managed to get in time. By the door was Mary George, swaying a little. Terry could see her mouthing the words of the song and noticed her look along the line, smiling but resisting, and then turn back to the people she had arrived with, the art-school lot. Mary looked neater than usual, more sophisticated, in a short black dress and high heels. She had smoothed back her hair and made it look particularly glossy and dark. She set off across the hall, glancing anxiously back at her friends, only to be reeled in by Julie, who shoved her into the line. Mary, for all her shyness, loved to dance and knew these steps from the time, only three years earlier, when she had tried to hang around with Julie at Youth Club discos and on Saturday nights.

After a couple more crashing dances, during which Billy, already drunk, whirled into the line and was half swaying, half being held up by June, Terry cooled things down with a slow punk number that had the familiarity of a reggae beat—"Police and Thieves" by The Clash. Then he sped it all up again, differently this time, bringing in the boys and the art-school lot. He found a song that counted as New Wave, but that still gave the girls already on the floor a rhythm they could dance to—Blondie—and before anyone could go and sit down again, he ran it straight into Disco Tex and the Sex-O-Lettes and "Get Dancin'": hard enough and camp enough to count as ironic. It worked—the art students were rolling their eyes and raising their eyebrows at one another, but they stayed on their feet. The girls carried on bumping and grinding, oblivious. A few songs later, everyone was looking red-faced and frayed, and the local boys were spending longer outside. Someone out there was selling the cans of cider they had brought into the hall inside their jackets and poured it into the plastic cups in which they'd bought their squash. Terry Flux lowered the lights and began the slow dancing with a number that had a long and subtle enough intro to give them all a chance to decide what to do.

As the first bars of The Chi-Lites' "Have You Seen Her?" filled the room, the girls were quick to disperse and make themselves busy, not looking or waiting. Mary wandered over to where Daniel, Clara, and Paulie were sitting, deep in conversation. Each of them had their hands in the air, a drink in one and a cigarette in the other. Mary hesitated, not knowing how to find a way in. She was about to tap Daniel on the arm when somebody caught her shoulder.

"Mary, my love!" It was Martin Lacey, and even though Mary knew now that he was not her type, she still felt the attraction that had led to her long adolescent crush on Julie's brother. He wrapped Mary in his arms and moved her forcefully into the centre of the floor. Martin was confident and he danced well. Nothing could detract from his good looks, not his tight white cap-sleeved T-shirt with the cigarette packet tucked into one sleeve, or his streaked jeans, his sprayed hair, or the citrus and soap smell of his aftershave. As he twirled her round, Mary tried to catch a glimpse of her friends each time they came into view. Once, she saw Daniel and Clara looking towards her, smiling or laughing. Then Paulie and Clara were dancing next to her. Clara had her eyes shut, her head flung back, and her long arms reaching straight into the air on either side of Paulie's neck; her odd profile quite lovely, her clasped fingers exaggerated by their black-painted nails. Paulie's face was impassive as he stared rigidly past Clara's shoulder, but he was transformed by his dancing, which was so elegant that it made him appear mysterious and sexual, unlike his everyday self.

Mary was so fascinated by this that she forgot to look for Daniel, and then the record finished and she saw he was standing alone, looking awkward with his long black raincoat still belted and buttoned up, lighting another French cigarette and staring, not at her, but at Paulie's hand on Clara's bottom. She, too, was wearing a black dress and it ended not above the knee, like Mary's, but high on her thigh, just meeting the top of her fishnet stockings. Her loose hair was cut at the front so that sprays of ringlets framed and almost hid her face. As the next song started, Chicago's "If You Leave Me Now," Martin turned from Mary without a word and started towards Clara, who smiled and reached out a hand but moved past him. Mary saw Martin tense and swerve away, and Daniel stub out his cigarette and come forward. Confused, Mary turned slowly round on the spot and was relieved when Paulie appeared ("Dance, sweetheart?") and drew her lightly to him with one hand, the other holding his cigarette away to one side. He did dance beautifully, but he kept his head turned towards his cigarette. Again, as they revolved, Mary tried to watch Daniel and saw, as if in a series of photographs illustrating how to do something step by step, Clara undoing the belt of Daniel's coat, then the buttons, and then shucking it off his shoulders and letting it drop. He looked entranced as she wrapped his arms round her waist and began to dance. The song ended, Paulie and Mary drifted apart, but Clara kept hold of Daniel till the music began again.

Terry Flux had his eye on the girls who'd had nothing to do for the last half hour and gave them a fast-paced dance number, an excuse for some energetic shaking and twirling—more Blondie, "X Offender." Clara broke away into a scything, sinuous dance of her own. For a while, Daniel tried clumsily to mirror Clara and stay with her, but he soon got lost, and when he looked to her with a pleading smile, she shrugged and turned her back on him and found herself opposite Martin Lacey, who caught her by the hand and easily matched her. Mary went and sat down, where she was joined by Daniel, who had been to the bar and come back with four glasses of orange squash. He reached a hand into a black velvet bag— Clara's—and produced a bottle of vodka, with which he topped up each glass. He handed one to Mary: "Cheers." The music was too loud to talk over, so they watched the dancers: Clara with Martin Lacey, Paulie absorbed and on his own but attracting a small crowd, and Julie at the centre of her gang.

Daniel leaned over and said something in Mary's ear.

"What? I couldn't hear you!"

This time he shouted: "I said look at those old hippies over there!" He pointed, and she saw he meant Billy and June, who had slung their arms round each other and were executing an unsteady cancan at the back of the hall. They were laughing and staggering, and Mary knew that, another time, she would have joined them. She blushed.

Clara broke away from Martin in the middle of a song and dashed over. She threw herself into a chair next to Mary and took a gulp from a glass. "Thank you, darling," she gasped. "I'm worn out! That boy's quite something, isn't he, Mary? An old flame?"

"No!" She was horrified. "He's just . . . we only . . . ." but Clara wasn't listening.

"Quite a freak show, isn't it?" Her voice, always loud, carried over the music. "That yokel wanted to take me out the back for some 'cider'! Oooh, look at Hippie Corner! And that fat tart with the frizzy perm. She's falling out of her tinsel top!" Mary pretended not to hear.

Paulie joined them. "God, this is a dump!" He looked livid. "I went for a piss and there were these animals in there who went all shrieky and limp-wristed when they saw me. One tried to grab my earring!"

"Jealous, darling." Clara shrugged.

"And then he groped my balls!"

"They're all dying to grope you, really," Clara drawled. "What did they say when you got your cock out?"

"You've got to be fucking kidding. I went outside instead!" They were both laughing. "Let's go." Paulie stood up.

"But it's just getting interesting!" Clara tugged at his sleeve. "I'll find you a nice girl to pursue. There's a fabulous blonde . . ." They set off across the floor together.

Mary had sat through this saying nothing and concentrating on her drink. She was shaking as Daniel turned her head gently towards him. "They don't mean it."

"They're such fucking snobs!" Mary was furious. "And anyway, Julie's hair isn't permed, it's natural!"

"I expect your friends can give as good as they get."

"They're not my friends!"

"Then why are you . . ."

"I mean, Oh, for God's sake!" Mary was shocked to find she was crying. She rushed off to the toilet, where she found both Clara and Julie in front of the mirror.

"Mary! Come here, you daft baggage! Your eyeliner's all over the place!" Julie saw her first and began rummaging in her handbag.

"Here, I've got a tissue." Clara dipped it under a running tap and wiped hard at Mary's eyes.

"My lens!" The one in her left eye had slipped. The two girls huddled round, tipping her head back and forth.

"Oh my God, it's halfway round your eyeball," Julie murmured.

"Let me see." Clara pulled Mary's head back towards her. "Oh yes, there it is. Yuck! Your eye's going all bloodshot!"

Mary shook them off and squinted into the mirror. She coaxed the lens into place, then stood back and took in her red face, limp hair, and the smears beneath her eyes. "I look a state!"

Clara and Julie considered her and then set to work. Clara held her wrists under the cold tap to cool her down while Julie fussed at her hair, back-combing and twiddling strands which she then set with hairspray. They turned her round and cleaned her face with Julie's cold cream and another of Clara's tissues. Then Julie patted on some powder, and Clara relined her eyes. They both produced lipsticks, and Mary took them both, smudging Julie's shiny pink over Clara's red. Last of all, Clara produced a vial of perfume and used her little finger to dot a drop behind Mary's ears. Mary sniffed and muttered thank you, then went back into the hall. Julie and Clara returned to the mirror in silence, finished what they were doing, and left one after the other, not having exchanged a word.

The room was beginning to empty, and those who remained were all drunk. Terry Flux turned down the lights, a kindness to the couples who'd found themselves a corner. Terry had his eye on Billy and June, who were sitting on the floor, smoking a joint, something June had never done before. June could drink anyone under the table and remain as prim and sober as ever. She felt different now, though, elated and unsteady.

June's hair was long and straight and centre-parted, just like Billy's, only hers was dark and coarse. Until this summer, she had dressed to oppose Sophie, her feminine mother, choosing heavy fabrics and staid cuts and colours. If she added anything fashionable, it was to pacify Julie and the gang. Then with Tom coming back and her having to live at Aunt May's, and being in Camptown after school while Julie was still busy at work, she'd begun to choose for herself. And what June found she liked was what the shop assistants called "peasant" or "ethnic." She had an embroidered cheesecloth smock and a maxi skirt with little mirrors sewn round the hem. She pulled her hair forward from behind her ears, across her face, and dabbed what Julie called her "pulse points" with patchouli oil. Tonight Billy had called her hair "wild" and said she looked like "Janis."

Terry Flux put on the Moody Blues' "Nights in White Satin," and sure enough, Billy pulled June up onto her feet and they slumped against each other and inched round. Paulie had persuaded Julie to dance, and found he was enjoying himself at last. "God, you smell wonderful!" he sighed into her hair, meaning it. Julie sniggered and put her hand on his bottom.

Although Daniel had been holding and kissing her since she had sat back down, Mary couldn't get rid of her uneasiness. She kept wanting to look over at Paulie or Clara, or Billy and June, Julie, even Martin. When Daniel got up to go to the toilet, she escaped outside and then felt unable to go back in. There were too many different people all in the same place and Daniel—to be drawn so powerfully to someone she barely knew, to whom she found it difficult to speak and whose friends were so glamorous and awful—it was all too confusing to bear.

Her heart was racing and her skin prickled in the damp, electrified air. She concentrated on slowing her breath and held her hands to her cheeks in an effort to cool them.

At last, the pressure that had weakened over the last few days gave way and the sky broke with a splintering of thunder. A strange warm wind gusted through the trees, and Mary drew back along the side of the hall. She heard the doors open. It was Daniel. She could see his face caught in the light and was shocked again that she could have a boyfriend, if he was her boyfriend, who was so lovely. It frightened her. Everything he made her feel frightened her.

There was another slam of thunder as he disappeared back inside. I love your voice, I love your face, Mary whispered into her fists. The place shook as those who remained stamped and sang. Terry Flux had decided to enjoy himself and finished the evening with a wild combination of his favourite punk, jazz, reggae, glam rock, and funk. Mary crept along a ledge and looked in and saw Daniel with Clara, but not very clearly, as the window was dirty and the hall half-dark. They were dancing together again and Daniel looked more animated than she ever felt he was when he was with her. Clara reached up and smoothed his hair, or ran her fingers through it; she stroked his cheek; she whispered in his ear, or was it a kiss? Mary's tired eyes strained to make sense of the flickering scene. Watching them, she felt pain fill her chest and cramp her gut. Uncontrollable tears were coming to her eyes again, as the thunder returned with such endless deep thuds and slams that Mary thought buildings were falling down. There was going to be a storm and Mary was not about to go back inside when the weather matched her feelings so exactly. She turned away from the window, closed her eyes, and lifted her head, but the rain didn't come.

Terry played the final track, cutting the volume for the chorus as he had done at the end of every disco he'd DJ'ed, and leaving the drunken, overwound girls and boys to bellow, "And it's hi ho silver lining . . ." Then they knew it was time to go home.

People came drifting out of the hall, stumbling and shouting. Somebody was arguing, and someone else managed only a few steps before being sick. Mary wanted to get home quickly, before Daniel appeared.

"Mary, are you all right?" It was Billy, carrying two crash helmets.

Mary was overjoyed. "Thank God, Billy. Take me home!" She grabbed one of the helmets. "Where's the bike?"

Billy hesitated. "Just behind you, farther up the alley, but I was . . ."

June Hepple appeared from behind him and gave Mary a firm smile. "Well, I'll be getting off!" She turned to go, but Billy caught her arm.

Mary was still trying not to cry. "Yeah, good night, June, see you. Come on, Billy! We've got to go now! I need to!" Billy turned towards June, who shook her head and slipped away. He followed Mary to the bike.

"So, where to?" he asked flatly.

Mary gabbled, "Well, not back into the village, or we'll meet them, and not home, so away, Billy, I don't know, but quick!" There was another roll of thunder and the first blanching sheet of lightning, in which Billy caught the look on Mary's face.

"Get on, then." He turned the bike on the gravel, revving it noisily and reaching the road just as Clara, Paulie, and Daniel emerged from the hall. They had waited for Mary and were looking for her now, but in the wrong direction. Cheers greeted each blast of thunder. They climbed into Paulie's car and drove slowly away as Mary clutched onto Billy and cried into his back.

Billy struggled to steer the bike through the web of narrow lanes that spread like capillaries, meeting and diverging, going everywhere you might want to go from Allnorthover, only indirectly. He didn't decide on a route; that wasn't the point. He was enjoying the ride, the jumpy lightning and the quickening thunder; he wanted to think. He liked the challenge of the hairpin bends, sudden gradients, abrupt dips and double curves; the humpback bridge which he could meet at just the right speed to propel his bike into the air. There was no one else on the road. It was midnight, so the drivers who fell out of the pubs and into their cars at closing time had had their hour to get home, and they were the only ones who chose the lanes, for the same reasons Billy did.

Rain fell. A few heavy drops streaked Billy's visor, and he heard Mary shout, and looked back and saw she had raised one arm and felt it, too. From those first drops, the rain intensified and came down as suddenly as floodwater bursting through a swollen ceiling. Billy pushed back his visor, but the rain still blinded him. Just as he started up the humpback bridge, and out of habit, accelerated, he thought to slow down and confused himself. A fork of lightning struck a nearby field, illuminating the already charred earth. There was a hiss like the flaring of a huge match. The air screamed in Billy's ears, only it was Mary screaming as the bike flung them sideways and skidded away beneath them.

The storm was right above them—the rain, thunder, and lightning together—so that although Billy and Mary were too drunk and floppy to have been badly hurt, they did not get up but huddled in the long yellow grass where they had landed. This was where Billy's father, Morris, found them, after Billy had not come home and someone mentioned him going off on his bike, and he'd met Stella George soaked through, halfway to the hall, looking for her girl.

"Two fledglings drowned in the nest" was how Morris later described them. Mary didn't remember screaming, only falling and landing and finding it altogether natural to cling onto Billy, giggle, and sleep.

The rain continued through Sunday and into Sunday night, and on Monday morning the village woke to a world it couldn't remember. It was too late in the year for the rain to revive anything. Instead, it laid things bare. Leaves that had turned were pelted and blown free. Precarious heavy-headed flowers, chrysanthemums and pansies, became waterlogged and collapsed, snapping their undernourished stems. The Green gave way to mud. All the warmth was washed out of the brick, stone, whitewash, tile, timber, and thatch. The rain needled its way in, exposing new leaks and cracks. Gutters babbled and choked while clogged drains belched up ammoniac pools. Damp spored behind the heat-cracked paint of window frames. The fields had dried out so deeply that even the newly turned earth was too dry to hold much water. Topsoil ran off the land in urinous streams.

People hobbled along slick pavements. Drivers braked late, swerved along the lanes, blinding themselves with the spray of puddles that spread from one hedgerow to the other, like sheets. Dr. Clough was kept busy treating flare-ups of rheumatism and arthritis. His morning-round visits to the dying and the newly born were prolonged.

Mary George had stayed awake for most of the night, for the pleasure of listening to the rain. By six o'clock she was too tired to sleep, so she got dressed and crept downstairs, planning tea and toast over a book before school. She could hear Stella in the kitchen, though, so continued out through the front door.

The morning astonished her. The rain had just stopped, and the sun was still a low pink light that suffused the wet houses with a foreign rosiness and made leafless branches shine. Mary strode out along the High Street, sure she would make it at least halfway to school before a bus came. She was wearing her boots and one of her father's jerseys over flannel trousers. For once, the weather suited her.

By the time she passed the chapel, the sun had risen but had not dried anything yet, so the world just glittered more brightly. Mary was walking round a flooded corner glazed in white light when she met Tom Hepple. He was leaning delicately on his stick. "Good morning," he murmured. He was dressed in wool and tweed, all of which looked damp.

Mary nodded, then added, "I mean, good morning."

"It's a fine light."

"It is." It occurred to Mary that they could have been any two villagers and they would have had the same conversation, and she smiled. Tom said nothing but smiled back. She wondered. He looked fine, just frail as Billy said Valerie had said.

Mary felt grown up. "I was sorry to hear about the—your—accident."

Tom shook his head, as anyone would. If he could just keep the girl here, persuade her, take her. Her pale skin glowed so that he wanted to reach out and touch her, knowing his fingers would go right through her, because at moments like this she wasn't the silly girl everyone said she was but his angel, all light. His hand began to reach out, but a sleepless night, no food, and all those pretty capsules restrained him.

His head dropped. "It's only my leg and it'll . . . mend, but . . . Kevin Lacey's still in there being put together with metal . . . pins, and as for . . . the Hotchkiss boy, a terrible . . . waste." His broken phrases were charming. Mary made herself smile widely and said a firm goodbye before setting back off for school. A tiny thought, that she was safe because he couldn't chase her with that leg, flitted through her mind. The clean adult feeling of a moment ago collapsed and Mary started to argue with herself in an effort to shore it up. By the time she reached Temple Grove, she had Tom Hepple back as just needy, not very well, and practically a relative.

Dorothy Spence from the scrapyard was at the Temple Park bus stop, wearing a see-through raincoat and hat, the kind that folded away into your bag. She had a blue overall on over her dress and Mary deduced that she must now have a cleaning job in Camptown. Mary was curious but said nothing. Mrs. Spence did not appear to recognise her. The summer was over and people had other things to talk about now.

By the time Tom reached the chapel, he was trembling. The morning's observations were scribbled on bits of paper he'd stuffed into his pockets. Each detail and statistic Tom had noted had a glint of significance that he knew, from experience, could evaporate. He had to transfer the information to his book right away or things would not connect and the whole thing would slip through his fingers. He fumbled the red ledger open and began to write. This book had fallen out of the broken filing cabinet. Tom had torn out the few pages that had been used and had adapted the double-entry columns to his system of "Submergence" and "Disturbance." Among the scraps from which he was now copying, he found the smashed glasses that he'd picked up at the end of the Clock House drive. They had been lying like a broken bird with one wing adrift and the other folded. The crazed lenses were almost intact. He put them up on the shelf, next to the torn photo and the puddle of wax.

Tom had been at the reservoir for an hour before sunrise, finding it easier to try and make sense of things in the cool half-dark before the water took on reflections. He was sure it was rising already, after just two days' rain, and so his calculations would have to be revised. He had limped the two miles home, his head bubbling with numbers. Meeting the girl like that had been a piece of luck. She was still nervous, but he'd managed not to upset her, mostly because he was tired and muzzy. She'd been trying so hard to disguise herself, to look like any other daffy young girl, clutching the sleeves of her jersey as they swallowed her hands. Only he'd heard about her and Billy Eyre, and how she'd come off his bike in the storm and landed without a scratch. She was so light.

Tom lay down on his back and tried to sleep. His leg ached. He had thought too much about the girl and had lost some of his ideas. He warmed himself with the memory of afternoons in Sophie's airtight living room: the unintended scent that seeped from beneath her arms as she reached out to raise him, and the intended scent of peach and vanilla that he caught from the burnt and feathering skin just above and between her breasts. Tom pushed his hand into his trousers, shut his eyes, and tried to think of Valerie Eyre's cropped head and rosy mouth, but what came to mind was peach, and then vanilla, then burst buttons on a tight white dress, wet with a new stain.

Stella caught her hip on the corner of the table, making herself lurch and sending Lucas's toast sliding from the plate. She knelt down and scrabbled it up in her apron. "I'll make fresh." She shook her head at Lucas's protest. She came back and snatched the egg as he took it from his pocket, but he didn't quite let go in time and they smashed it between them. Mary was shocked to see her mother tearful and frantic. Stella ran to find a cloth and began to dab at Lucas's filthy coat while he tried to calm her. "Mrs. G., it's just an egg."

"We've got half a dozen in the fridge, Mum. I'll put another one on. An egg's not going to do any harm."

"Eggs used to be used in paint, to make it shine. My coat'll shine!" Lucas mumbled through his toast. "And my mum used to paint egg white on the little one's bottom if it got sore. Kept the you-know-what out. So my coat's going to be waterproof, too!" Stella gave up wiping. She hurried back into the kitchen, and Mary followed.

"Mum," she began, feeling irritated and responsible. "Like he said, it's just an egg. Who cares?"

Stella swung round and Mary flinched as she saw a tremor run through her face, a knot that caught in her forehead, creased her eyes, and dragged at her mouth. Mary stepped back as her mother reached out, but all she did was stroke Mary's cheek. Mary wanted to tell her to get off but wasn't brave enough, so she made sounds instead of words and shook her away. When Morris had delivered her home in the storm after the disco, Stella had been standing out in the rain on the Green and had held out her arms, but Mary slipped through them and went upstairs to run a hot bath. Since their conversation about the letters, Mary had not wanted to hear her mother say another word.

Now Stella was gulping and snivelling. "Mary, love, you know it wasn't me. I'd never, however desperate, have done something like that." She looked so pitiful that Mary was appalled. Then in a different, more familiar voice: "Your father has a tendency to, what do they say, displace . . ."

"Fuck it!" The words shot out of Mary's mouth. "Fuck your jargon and fuck you!"

"As I was saying—" Stella tried to continue.

Mary turned in the doorway. "And fuck Dad, too, fuck the reservoir and the house and fuck those fucking letters!" She barged past Lucas. "And you, always playing the wise old fucking fool, fuck you, too!" She slammed the front door so hard a bowl jumped from the sideboard and shattered on the floor. Lucas shook his head admiringly and settled down to his tea.

"Do you want to do something on Sunday?" The line fizzed and buzzed.

"Sunday? Yes, all right, fine, I'd love to." He'd rung. Mary bit her lip to stop herself spoiling it.

"Anything you'd like to see?"

"The sea? Why not?"

"The what?"

"Like you said, the sea."

"I said the sea?"

"I thought. Oh, never mind."

"But would you like that?"

Mary couldn't bear to ask Daniel what he meant, so she said "Yes" and arranged to meet him at midday at Camptown Station. When she put the phone down, the buzz was still in her ear.

He was wearing his big raincoat and a tall felt hat that he referred to as "my grandpa's homburg." Mary had never known a boy to have so many accessories. As well as the hat, Daniel had a silk scarf, leather gloves, sunglasses, a fob watch in his waistcoat pocket, and a flat pewter flask of whisky inside his coat. When she remarked on any of these things, Daniel explained that the object in question had belonged to his grandfather or had been found in a junk shop or flea market, and that it was "thirties." Even the oval tortoiseshell sunglasses were thirties.

Camptown Station was built on a viaduct and there was a long climb up to either platform. Mary headed for the ticket office, but Daniel caught her arm and steered her past the stationmaster, who was standing in the dim hallway at the foot of the stairs. "No need to pay."

The stationmaster touched his cap. "Good morning!"

Daniel replied so charmingly, adding, "And which side for the sea?" that the stationmaster called him "sir," and gave a small bow as he gestured through the foot tunnel to the other staircase.

You could go straight through to Lodenum or change onto the other line at Procklewell for Crouchness or Thende. Mary wanted to ask where they were going, but her anticipation of going anywhere alone with Daniel made her so happy and anxious that she held her breath.

They got on the first train that came in, which was going only as far as Procklewell. There, they caught a stopping train to Thende. They were getting into a closed carriage when Mary missed her footing on the worn wooden step and slipped, grazing her shin. Daniel picked her up and lifted her into the carriage, while she blushed and muttered something about being able to manage.

186

It was like having a room to themselves. There was no corridor; the carriage itself was like a short corridor, with two facing banquettes that would seat four or five people each, and a door at either end. Daniel sprawled on one of the seats and Mary lay down on the other.

"What do you feel?" he asked as the train waddled and swung out of the station.

Mary wondered if this was a test or just a game. "With my hands, the cloth on the seat, like bristles." She dragged her fingers across it, against the nap, and there was a small explosion of dust that made her sneeze. "Under my back, the springs—spirals, I think—and clumps of stuffing. Horsehair?"

"Princess!" Daniel teased, but Mary frowned. He reached over and stroked her shin, circling the graze. "So pale . . ." Her coat was open and her blue dress rucked up round her knees. She raised herself and looked down at the shocking white gap in the torn black tights that made her skinny legs look even thinner as they disappeared into her big boots. Daniel pushed his finger under the hole, tracing broader and broader circles. "What do you feel now?"

The train pulled into a station. "I hope no one—"

"Shhh . . ." Then Daniel was lying on top of her and putting a finger to her mouth. "Be quiet. People will think this carriage is empty and then they won't get in."

"Don't you mean they'll get in because it looks empty?" She felt his belt buckle press hard into her hip. "Ssshhh . . ." His mouth made a full round O as he hushed and kissed her.

The last time Mary had been to Thende was with Julie, when they were fourteen. They had gone to the Roller Disco in the dilapidated dance hall on the front. They were both good at skating and circled the rink at some speed, chatting and giggling. The rink was an old wooden dance floor, still dotted with slim columns that had once held extravagant arrangements of flowers. Mary and Julie had invented a game of hooking an arm round these columns and spinning off in the opposite direction, against the general flow. They annoyed the best skaters, who were practising their fancy steps and turns in the centre, and alarmed the beginners teetering round in twos and threes with their arms linked, which meant that if one of them wavered, they all fell down. For some reason, the rest of Julie's gang hadn't come on this trip. Mary couldn't remember any other occasion when they had done something alone together. They had had a good time, but they never did it again.

It was Mary who knew how to get from the station to the sea. A strong wind had taken hold of the town and caught them as she led Daniel over the footbridge. Mary's fringe was flattened over her eyes, and Daniel's homburg was lifted in a gust and thrown down on the tracks, where it rolled under a departing train. He hurried off down the steps and waited till the train had gone in order to retrieve it, but the hat had disappeared. He came back up onto the bridge, his face screwed up against the wind, his shoulders hunched and his collar turned up. Mary was about to make a joke of it (Julie would have been squawking with laughter) but saw his irritation and hesitated. They made their way down the ramp that curved round the multistorey car park and through the shopping precinct. Here the wind had concentrated and channelled itself into walls of air that came slamming through the wide walkways, ripping off more hats and tossing, rattling, and loosening anything it could get in its grip—signs, posters, tiles, sweet wrappers, squashed cans, plastic bags.

Daniel and Mary continued across the hotel car park and the dual carriageway, through the municipal gardens, and into the fun fair. The seafront was closing down for the winter. The lights were out. There was one man in charge of the three rides that remained open. He was huddled in a booth, smoking and reading a paper, and came out when he saw them, scowling expectantly and halfheartedly jingling the change in the sack bag that hung from his waist. (Julie would have flirted with him and got them a free ride and made the whole thing fun.) He had a thin, sunken face over which hung a lank crest of greased curls. Twenty years ago he would have been king of the waltzer boys, astounding the girls as he posed casually on the rippling floor of the ride, spinning their carriages as they shrieked and clung together and tried to keep singing along to "Runaround Sue." When he found the girl he wanted, he would lean in close, whisper, and catch her, a different one every night. The posh ones had been particularly easy. He met them at closing time and took them down under the pier, rain or shine. They lay on his chest afterwards, captivated by the pattering of his heart, which he let them think was due to them and not to the long lines of sulphate he snorted just before cranking up the waltzer each night.

Mary hesitated, Daniel looked away, and the wind prodded at the carriages on the Ferris wheel, making them swing and clank.

"Oh, a ghost train!" Mary had only just noticed it.

"Come on, then!" Daniel sprung into action.

The man sidled his cigarette to one corner of his mouth and spoke out of the other: "That'll be two bob apiece." He took their money and shouted, "Wayne! Two for the train!"

A chubby boy's face blinked out from behind the crumbling entrance, an arch caked with papier-mâché, painted black and studded with crumbling rubber Halloween masks. "Shall I wait for it to fill up a bit?"

The man jerked his lip in a sneer, and the last half-inch of his cigarette toppled to the ground. "Don't be fucking daft!" He turned his back on Daniel and Mary and returned to his booth, grumbling and blowing on his hands.

The ghost train trundled into a tunnel that smelt of stale hot dogs mixed with the tang of fried onions and pickled shellfish. As they rounded the first corner, Daniel and Mary could hear Wayne and half-see his shadow keeping up with them on the other side of the papier-mâché wall. He desperately wound something which gave a wild mechanical whoop. Then a spotlight came on, revealing an elongated and flattened ghost painted on the tunnel roof. They moved slowly through a curtain of shredded black rubber, while Wayne waved things about that cackled and hissed. A red bulb lit up the inside of a plastic skull, and Wayne squirted water through a cobwebby mesh. There were more ghosts and skeletons and dangling rubber creepy-crawlies.

When Wayne appeared to let them out of their carriage at the end, he was purple-cheeked and exhausted and looked upset. Neither Mary nor Daniel had moved or made a sound during the ride. They thanked him and turned round to find the man from the booth observing them balefully.

"Something else?" he called out.

"I don't think . . . I mean thanks, and we, you know . . ." Mary faltered.

"Have you got a hall of mirrors?" Daniel asked.

"The Hall of Mirrors is shut."

"That's a pity." Daniel took Mary's arm.

"Two bob each!" he called after them.

"What for?" Daniel countered.

"The Hall of Mirrors." They started back towards him. "Only, if I'm to get the keys and all, you may as well see the Crooked House." They looked at each other and nodded. "And that'll be another two bob. Each."

The man took a padlock off a plywood door and ushered Mary and Daniel through into the dark. He fumbled on the ground and flicked a number of switches. With each switch, another part of the room was lit, and the darkness filled up with mirrors that came closer and closer until they had Mary and Daniel surrounded. "Off you go, then." The man gave Mary a nudge and she looked down to see a strip of carpet, a kind of path. She took Daniel's hand and led him towards the first mirror, only to find that it wasn't one, just a frame, beyond which was a real one. They stepped through and went right up to the glass and traced their reflections as if they couldn't see at all and were trying to make out a shape. There were no reflections to either side, so Mary decided to turn left and bumped hard up against blank glass. They turned a corner to the right, and now there were reflections on every side, bounced back and forth like a trapped echo and then frittering away, getting infinitely smaller. It took a long time to find a way through the maze, as each step became more tentative, and although they could see, it was only their hands that told them which way to go. They came out looking as shaken and impressed as Wayne might have hoped they would be after their train ride.

The man noticed the swelling on Mary's cheekbone and looked proud. "That's shopfront glass, that is, near enough unbreakable." He had already taken the padlock off the Crooked House and turned on its lights, but these were only strings of small bulbs that drooped along the walls. After the multiple brightnesses of the Hall of Mirrors, it took some time for their eyes to adjust. Mary liked this best of all. It was like being at sea, or how she imagined it would be to be at sea. The staircase forced them to stumble and stretch as if it were rolling over high waves. The tilted floors threw them from one side to another. There was a mirror that made you tall and thin, one that made you short and fat, and another, the best, in which your body was bent wildly out of shape into a drawn-out serpentine S.

Afterwards, they walked along the pier. It looked solid and straight from a distance, when in fact it had given way in places to the sea. A smashed strut dragged one side downwards; a missing plank left a sudden gap underfoot through which you could see slack, colourless waves jostling around slimy foundations. Thende Pier was, famously, the longest in Europe. There was a train that ran along it, but only in summer. It took forty-five minutes to walk to the end, and when you got there, there was nothing much to see or do, just a flat view in which you might make out the smudge of a freighter, ferry, trawler, or aeroplane. There was a penny arcade, and a bandstand that was rarely used now, except by sheltering seagulls and fishermen wanting to eat their sandwiches out of the rain.

The wind hurtled inland. Mary's head ached with cold, her eyes and nose ran, and she pulled the sleeves of her jersey over her hands and buried them in the deep pockets of her coat. It was a leather flying coat that had belonged to one of Matthew's uncles, so seasoned and worn that it draped softly around little Mary and rumpled on the toes of her boots. Daniel kept one arm round her and clutched the collar of his coat with the other.

They reached the end of the pier, where they crouched on the wet bandstand step and huddled together. Mary tipped her head against Daniel's chest and listened to the wind rattle a loose pane in the arcade window. A door slammed shut, then flew open again. The wires that anchored the bandstand's awning in summer were singing.

Clara came into the salon the next Saturday. She marched up to Mary, who was trying to keep in order the three sizes of perm curlers and the tissue squares she was alternately handing to Felicity. "You and D. weren't at The Stands last night."

"No, we went for a drink." Mary almost went on to apologise, but Clara was rearranging her fringe in the mirror, leaning over Felicity's customer's head. Felicity raised an eyebrow and continued her work.

"Come over later?"

Mary stopped herself from asking why. "Sure, I finish at three."

"See you then." Clara stalked out.

"Lovely hair your friend's got," Suze murmured dreamily. "Really, really lovely."

"Looked brittle to me," Felicity snapped. "Come on, Mary, concentrate. You're not taking tea with Little Miss Whatsername yet, you know."

"Madame Whatsername," put in Jeanette, striking a pose that was just like Clara's haughty slouch.

"Mademoiselle, actually," Mary dared. Felicity raised another eyebrow.

As Mary started down the Clock House drive, it began to rain hard. The tall trees that met over her head dripped heavily. The house looked even more dank and the front lawn had been churned to mud around Tobias's heaps of machinery. Mary was shivering as Clara let her in. They passed the kitchen, where Mary glimpsed Tobias sitting at the table with Billy. She was going to stop and say hello, she was certainly curious, but Clara swept on down the corridor. They came to another set of stairs, narrower and plainer than the ones that led up from the hall with their elegantly curved banister.

Clara's big bedroom was a mess. Clothes spilt off the brass bed and out of cupboards onto the floor, a tangle of orange, pink, red, purple, and black. Mary trailed her hand through one heap and found a feather boa, something studded, silk, and then fur, which wriggled and mewed and revealed itself to be a spitting Persian cat, a white and fluffy creature missing half an ear and most of one back leg. The cat limped out, ignoring Clara's call: "Lucretia! You old bruiser! She was only making friends! Sorry, Mary. She loves a spat!"

Clara's dressing table had a gilt-framed vanity mirror, a smaller oval mirror on a stand, and three hand mirrors of different sizes. A powder compact stood open, and it, too, had a dusty mirror. Scattered among this were lipsticks, perfumes, mascara wands, and cakes of eyeshadow, all left open or undone.

"Where are your paints?" There were no pictures on the walls, just another, full-length, mirror.

"In my studio." Clara drew out the word into a long pout.

"At college?"

"I have a studio here, too, in one of the attics." It was the first time Mary had thought of Clara as a painter, perhaps because today she was wearing splattered dungarees and her hands were filthy.

There were three cups next to the bed and another three on the floor. Mary peered into the one nearest her, and at its bottom was a curdy blue mould. The record player, a sleek chrome stereo with enormous speakers, was surrounded by records, empty record sleeves, and full ashtrays. Mary picked out a cover. "Oh, you've got this! I love this!"

"What's that?" Clara was rolling a joint. She glanced at the cover. "Oh, I think that's one of Tobias's. In fact, they're probably all his, you know, he just passes them on." Mary remembered Tobias turning off the water.

Clara put on the record Mary had found and settled back beside her against the bed, so close that their shoulders and elbows were touching. "So . . ." Clara drawled. She flexed her toes and inhaled hard, then blew out smoke through her nose, the way Matthew had when Mary had wanted him to be a dragon when she was a child. Clara passed the joint to Mary. "Julie Lacey."

Clara said her name as a statement, but Mary knew it was a prompt. She tried to say two things at once. "She's very bright, a bit tacky, a good laugh, and can be a complete bitch but means well."

"Are you two friends?"

"Sometimes. Why?"

"Her brother."

"Kevin? He's getting pins in his leg after the—"

"No, no, no! The older one!"

"Trevor?" Mary passed the joint back. She was enjoying herself. Clara winced. "Trevor?"

"Well, he's the eldest. Runs some kind of business: reproduction furniture, I think he calls it. He must be pushing thirty now."

"He didn't look that old at the disco!"

"The disco? Trev wouldn't be seen dead at any village disco!"

"Then it wasn't him who . . ." She looked directly at Mary, who leant her head back and shut her eyes. For some time neither of them spoke, then Clara stubbed out the end of the joint. "You're quite a story around here, aren't you?" Mary gave no response. "Something to do with that lovely man I see walking up and down all the time, limping up and down since those yobs almost bumped him off!" She sniffed. "Something to do with your father, isn't it? Did he try to bump off the lovely lunatic as well?" She was laughing rather messily. "Doesn't he tell everyone you walked on water or something, and something to do with his old house? It's positively gothic!" She slung an arm round Mary's shoulders.

Mary shifted forward. "He doesn't tell 'everyone' anything. As far as I know, he keeps himself to himself."

"In a place like this, you don't have to tell anyone anything. They tell each other." Clara wiped her eyes and nose on her sleeve, and was fumbling around for her dope, papers, and cigarettes when the loud clackety-clack of a football rattle came from downstairs. Clara stood up. "That's Mama calling us for tea."

The kitchen table was covered with plates of cakes and biscuits, cheese, chopped white cabbage, sliced oranges, and seeds and nuts Mary couldn't put names to. The whole Clough family was there, except little Freddie: the doctor, the doctor's wife, Clara, Tobias, Juliette, and Bobo. Mary couldn't put them in any obvious order. Tobias was taller than Clara; fourteen-year-old Juliette's spectacles gave her great poise (Mary wished she'd chosen heavy frames like hers); and Bobo was a beaming bun of a boy whose plump cheeks made him look younger than Freddie, an angular and serious-faced child of eight, three years his brother's junior. Clara was the boss, Tobias the mender, Juliette the brains, Freddie the wise child, and eleven-year-old Bobo, everyone's doll.

Billy was ensconced between Tobias and Juliette, sifting through the biscuit tin, wondering where to start. Francesca Clough, pouring tea, waved Mary towards the table, where she took a chair. It gave way beneath her, folding and collapsing. She landed hard on her bottom and found herself holding an armrest in the air and looking up into mildly concerned faces.

Billy was shaking his head in admiration. "Good one, George."

Freddie appeared through the door that gave onto the garden, wearing a dripping mackintosh and sou'wester. "If I'd known you wanted to sit in my chair," he said slowly and clearly, "I'd have explained. You need to approach it from a certain angle, you see, and not disturb the string."

Mary nodded seriously. Clara threw a chocolate biscuit fast, hard, and accurately at Freddie's head. "Don't be a creep, *bambino*. He refused to let Ma replace that chair when she got these others. No one else knows how to deal with it. Come by me." She nudged Juliette, who sighed and rose.

The next half hour was a whirl of eating, talking, teasing, and argument. Everyone chattered at once, getting their conversations so confused that Tobias would find his question about the relative merits of different stroke engines answered by Juliette's retort to Clara's insistence that it was still radical to wear black. "But it's such old hat, so Left Bank!" (Clara, not getting it: "You mean left wing, Jules.")

Dr. Clough joined in with a dry aside ("Jules should know, being named after La Greco") and caught hold of his fluttering wife as she jumped up to boil another kettle, fetch more fruit, or open more biscuits. "Francesca darling, sit and drink your tea."

Suddenly everyone was getting up. Dr. Clough returned to the surgery and the children dispersed, leaving their arguments in midair. Only Mary said thank you to Francesca Clough, and nobody stayed to help her clear up.

This time Clara led Mary towards the other stairs and along the corridor to Tobias's room. Late-afternoon sun exposed the house as more neglected than it had seemed the night of the swimming-pool dinner. Mary ran her finger through the dust on a side table and across a mirror. The parquet floor was dull, and the rugs were thin and torn (but real, thought Mary, lived with and passed down!).

Clara didn't knock. Tobias was bent over another large record player, the workings of which had been added to and exposed. Billy was stretched out on the floor among heaps of tools, lighting a joint. "Just in time!" Clara flung herself on the bed.

"Smoke your own." Tobias didn't bother to turn round. Clara dangled her hand over the side of the bed, and Billy passed her the joint. Tobias relented, turned round, and gestured to Mary, still hovering in the doorway. "Sit down. Listen to this." Clara passed her the joint, and Mary, already lightheaded from what she'd smoked earlier, took a deep drag. Tobias lowered the needle onto the record and settled himself on the floor. "Concentrate," he said, and they did. The music began with a sparse melody, then broadened with a lilting bass, a full horn section, and tantalising fragments of voice, the whole spinning itself out and out, and bursting into wild overembellishments. It went on and on building up, and took as long to die down. By the time the last whoops and twiddles faded, Mary was lying back against the wall, her eyes closed, smiling at the sheer, ridiculous delight of it.

"Wow . . ." Billy exhaled.

"Earth, Wind & Fire," Mary murmured. She waited for Clara to make some cutting remark, but it didn't come. All they heard from her was a deep snore. Tobias played a Bob Dylan duet with Johnny Cash, then Joe Cocker, The Cars, Can, and the Velvet Underground's endless "Sister Ray." In that white room with the rain coming down, all this sounded wonderful to Mary, both for being familiar and for being heard as if for the first time.

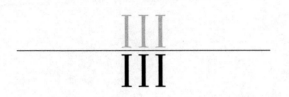

III

IN OCTOBER, as the first days of real cold arrived, the village returned to loving the insides of its houses. People put eiderdowns and counterpanes back on their beds, rooted out hot-water bottles, and hugged the dry warmth of the kitchen. They had afternoon tea in front of a coal, gas, or electric fire. Clothes now had to be dried indoors, on a wooden horse.

Petrol was unrationed but three times as expensive as it had been at the start of the year. People would grumble and skimp, and then get used to it. Now the villagers hoarded candles, matches, paraffin, and oil. Talk of power cuts spread—something else that Allnorthover was used to. Overhead lines were regularly blown down by winter gales so strong they could uproot the hollow oaks marooned in the enlarged fields. One of these old trees had caught in the lines as it fell and had crashed to the ground in a haze of sparks. Telegraph poles lurched in the unsettled earth. Only the pylons, which crested the view like steel models of a more efficient kind of tree, remained unmoved. Every house that could afford them had lamps and torches laid within sight and reach.

Valerie Eyre was worried about Tom. He hadn't been into the Arms for a week, nor had she seen him walking out of the village in the mornings, or nipping into the post office, or coming up Back Lane from Christie's. After three days of waking to a frost, she packed her father's old kitbag with clothes and food and set off for the chapel.

It was freezing. Bitter air gusted below the door, lifting drifts of paper. Odd sheets flapped against the wall and fell back. There were two large paraffin heaters, each of which Valerie weighed in her hands. They were full but cold.

The sink was clogged. There was a bottle of milk on the hob of the Baby Belling and a tin kettle on one shelf of the open fridge. Valerie lugged the kitbag upstairs.

Tom was dead. For a moment, Valerie really thought it. He was curled up and turned away against the covered window, and may well just have been asleep. It was the stiffness of his body, its absolute stillness, something she'd never seen in him before, that convinced her. She didn't scream or run or rush towards him. She carried on as if he *were* asleep, laid the kitbag down, and crept nearer.

It took time to turn him onto his back. She warmed his face and hands, blowing and rubbing as he stared at her out of dull yellow eyes. His skin was yellow, too, bristled and pimply, and his breath was rotten-sweet. Catarrh had crusted around his nose. His clothes were musty and his burning cheeks were stained deep red. Valerie went downstairs, boiled a kettle, and carried up a cup of tea, a basin, and a cloth. She washed his face, dabbing gently. He sipped the tea. She heaved one of the paraffin heaters upstairs and lit it. She fetched a clean basin of water and continued to wash him, his neck, ears, feet, and hands, drying each part of him roughly and thoroughly with a towel she took from her bag. Tom smiled but winced as a scab in the corner of his mouth cracked and dribbled blood.

Valerie pulled off his shirt and washed his chest, stopping for each bout of his scraping cough. She dressed him in her father's vest, flannel shirt, and oiled-wool jersey. She briskly took off his trousers and underpants, swabbed up and down and between his legs, then put him in the bottoms of a pair of her father's warmest pyjamas. Tom was as tall as Morris, but not nearly as broad, so the clothes accentuated his thinness. No skin, all bones. Valerie wrapped him in her mother's quilt and propped him up against the wall. Then she filled her hot-water bottle and heated a jar of her homemade soup, which she held to his mouth, waiting out the time it took for him to swallow every drop.

Christie got his coat. "I'll go straight up and fetch him back."

"He won't want that," Valerie replied. She heard the rustle of Sophie as she came out into the hall to see who their visitor was. "He needs to get on with it, on his own, but someone should be keeping an eye." Her voice shook. "I mean, three days?"

"It's not been that long!" Christie turned to his wife. "You've been looking in on him, haven't you?"

"Me?" Sophie was indignant. "I never . . . I mean, you were up there all the time, weren't you, you said . . ."

"I said nothing! I've got work to do!"

"Exactly. You said nothing!" Sophie snapped. She nodded at Valerie and walked away.

Christie stroked his beard and shook his head. "Looks like there's been a bit of a misunderstanding."

"A dangerous one," Valerie said.

Christie raised his voice. "Now, don't go saying that! You've nothing to learn me about my own brother!"

Valerie could see that Christie was as upset as she was. "Come on, let's get back to him. You go straight up and I'll go home for some painkillers to bring his temperature down."

"He ought to come back here."

"It's all right. I'll stay with him and bring him down to the surgery in the morning. He'll need antibiotics."

"Says you're a nurse now."

"In training." She had recently applied. "Perhaps you could fix up the chapel so as to make it a bit warmer?"

Christie hurried with her up the lane, puffing so hard that his face was almost obscured by his condensing breath. "He won't be needing hospital, will he? That wouldn't be right for him, would it? We can look after him here, can't we?"

"Of course." Valerie saved her breath. She had never met anyone as delicate and special as Tom. She couldn't wait to get back to him.

Billy and Mary were starving. They rushed into Billy's kitchen and fell upon a tray of flapjacks cooling on a windowsill.

"Valerie's such a good cook!" Billy spoke through a mouthful.

As Valerie came in, Mary exclaimed, "These are delicious!"

"And not for you," Valerie retorted. Mary reddened and dropped her slice onto her plate. Valerie relented. "Go ahead. It's just I wanted to take them up to—"

"Tom Hepple," Billy groaned. He, too, put his flapjack down.

Mary followed the line of the white Formica surfaces, their kidney-shaped curve around the breakfast bar, and then out past the split-level cooker to the huge new fridge. The marbled vinyl floor tiles shone. This was the smartest room in Billy's house, and the cupboards were always exorbitantly full, although Billy's mother, Linda, hated cooking. She held down three part-time jobs and was chronically tired. She hated having to think of things for her family to eat when she herself never felt hungry, but she wanted them to eat well.

At twenty, Valerie was the eldest and had grown up looking after Billy and Little Andrea, as she was still called, though she was now fifteen and taller than all of them, except her dad. Andrea had won a scholarship to ballet school, then in the next year had grown four inches. A transfer had been negotiated to a performing-arts college, where she boarded during the week. "Musicals, panto, and tap!" she groaned. "Everyone wants to be a Bunny Girl, and even the teachers seem to think *Swan* bloody *Lake* is just an ice routine." Andrea had taken up smoking ("All dancers smoke!"). When her family suggested she come home, she insisted she was happy. She had, at least, got out of the sticks. Valerie baked more than ever and sent parcels.

"Tom Hepple has had a bad dose of flu," Valerie explained. "It surprises me that kids like you condemn someone for having been ill."

Mary started. "We don't condemn him! It's not his fault he has flu!"

Valerie and Billy both laughed. "No, you dolt," Billy teased. "She means that you shouldn't mind that he's 'ill.' You know, 'off colour,' but *not* nuts, raving, barking enough to chase you round the water and down the High Street! You're not supposed to mind that!"

"Lay off!" Valerie lost her temper. "Of course Mary must have been scared; who wouldn't be? But doesn't it occur to either of you that the man has something to be upset about?" Mary blanched. "I'm sorry, Mary, but—"

"You don't understand," Mary managed stiffly. "Tom Hepple was always ill."

"Yeah, and how would you know different, Val, being all of ten at the time?" put in Billy.

"He talks to me," Valerie said, but it wasn't true.

"About wanting Mary to fish up his house?" Billy sneered.

"Don't be stupid. Of course he knows she can't do that!"

"Then what's he think she can do for him?"

"Nothing. I don't know. I mean, he hasn't . . ." Valerie switched her attention to Mary. "Look. Like everyone, I've heard he called you his angel or something, said you could put things back, but is he pursuing you?"

Mary thought about the meeting on the road. "No, not—"

"He said she walked on water!" Billy cut in.

"Maybe he was describing what he saw, the way he saw it, but he must know that's not actually what happened. He's hardly been going round yelling about it since."

"For God's sake!" Billy shouted. "You're jealous that he's fixed on my Mary!"

"*Your* Mary?" Valerie had been so surprised at hearing Billy raise his voice that she had nearly missed it.

"*Your* Tom?"

She made for the door, calling without turning round, "*Your* June?"

Mary pushed the piece of flapjack around her plate, making circles in the crumbs. Billy shook his head and sighed, nodded, and drummed his fingers. Mary had never seen him so agitated.

"What did she mean?" she asked at last.

"Do I really have to spell it out?"

"No . . . about June. What did she mean?"

Daniel met her outside school. "Come home with me."

What would the hundred-and-eighty-year-old mother think? At least she was dressed okay, all in black with a white shirt, a raincoat, and a beret. ("You look like you ought to be in a convent," Billy had greeted her as he got on the bus that morning. "That's rich coming from Jesus himself!" she'd retorted.) She tried to walk beside Daniel as if she did so every day.

He let them in with a big key that turned comfortably in the lock. A dark hall gave way to a long dining room, beyond which a garden went on farther than Mary could make out. A deep tick resounded through the house, though Mary couldn't see the grandfather clock she imagined. Daniel steered her into the living room, and she held her breath and began to smile, but there was no one in there. The furniture was ill-matched, heavy, and worn. To Mary, nothing looked like less than an heirloom. There was plenty of dark wood, but it was fashioned in clean foreign lines that made it appear unfamiliar and so good. The colours of the Oriental embroidered cushions, the velvet chaise longue, and the purples, reds, oranges, pinks, greens, and blues submerged in the stitched rug were unlike any others. Mary thought of her own pale home and its unseasoned pine that even after all these years had not aged.

Daniel reappeared, holding a bottle of wine and two glasses. "Come on." She followed him up two flights of stairs, glimpsing mirrors and paintings but no sign of anyone else being at home. They clambered up a steep flight of steps that led to an attic scattered with paints and canvases. An easel stood at the far end and a mattress lay under a dormer window. Daniel pulled Mary down and poured them both some wine. He pushed a cassette into a machine by the bed and the small room filled with hectic jazz.

"Do you like this?" Daniel asked, and she was touched to realise he might be anxious.

"That high saxophone . . ." Mary tried.

"The soprano?" She knew that.

"Yes. It sounds like a bird that's got caught behind a window." Daniel looked mystified, but Mary pushed on: "And the low one, spiralling down and then up again."

"The tenor?" She knew that, too.

"It's a . . . it's a fighter plane with its tail on fire!" Why say that? She knew she sounded like a child.

Daniel began fiddling with a jar of brushes. Mary felt uneasy and drank her glass of wine in one gulp. She fumbled for her cigarettes.

"Before you light up," Daniel began. Getting to his feet and crouching under the low roof, he moved away and turned his back. She waited but he said nothing further. As ever, she thought any confusion was her fault. "I'm cold." It was something to say.

"I won't be long." He pinned up a piece of paper and picked out some charcoal. "Close your eyes."

"Yes."

"Good. Now that scar on your forehead, a crescent moon, is it not?"

She could hear him drawing. "I can't remember." She ran a finger over the tiny ridge and into the dip.

"You were how old?"

"I don't remember; four, I think. I fell and hit my head on the grate."

"The three moles to the side of your throat, a belt of stars?" Mary fingered her throat. A belt of stars!

"The feather on your head."

"The feather?"

"Just below your crown. The patch where your hair doesn't grow."

"Oh, that!" He'd noticed that! "I was eight, I think. I'd been trying to stand on Julie's shoulders." She remembered the shaved patch of skull, its strange blankness around the raised, forking wound and the tiny stitches; of course, a feather.

"Your left wrist. Suicide?"

"No!" She laughed. "The side of a hot iron."

"You were?"

"Twelve." She was getting good at this.

"The sword on your belly."

Mary ran her hand across her stomach. "Appendicitis. Fourteen." Two weeks in bed and a visit from her father.

Daniel stopped drawing. "Anything else?" he asked.

Mary didn't want to open her eyes. She stretched her hand down. "My right thigh."

"Inner or outer?"

"Inner. Halfway above my knee. An island."

"When?"

"Before I was born."

"Which island?"

"Oh, somewhere almost even-sided. Greenland, perhaps." He continued to draw.

"And a river across my left foot. I jumped from a swing onto glass. Ten." She raised her leg and traced the rippling thinness across all those little bones, wishing she had more to offer.

The tape had ended and Daniel came over to put another in the machine. He leant over her and kissed her, and then lay down. His hands slid under her shirt and round her waist, his fingers tracing a circle, round and round. "The sword?"

She propped herself up, undid her trousers, and lowered them just enough for him to be able to see her scar. He kissed it.

"Greenland?"

Mary was trembling, but she pushed her trousers down and then off. She raised one knee and put his hand on her thigh. He stroked her birthmark, but as his fingers moved beneath her pants, she pulled his hand back. "I'm . . ."

"Ah." He nodded, sprang up, and went over to the easel. Mary sat up and saw her constellation—feather, moon and stars, sword, island and river; and now, just below the sword but more towards the centre, a tiny red flame.

Daniel lay down again, holding her hard against him. She kept lifting her head to look across at the picture.

"You like it? It's not finished. I need your landscape next."

She rolled on top of him. "You've made them into something for me—not just accidents."

"The myth of Mary George!" He held her for a long time and then looked at his watch. "Ma will be home soon. Will you have supper?"

Too much, too much. "I'd better go." She jumped up and rushed down the three flights of stairs, with Daniel asking her again to stay and eat, reassuring her, and then offering to walk her to the bus station.

As they set off up the road, Mary saw a large old car go past, one with the fine low form of an ocean liner, driven by a woman with silver hair. She tooted and waved. Daniel waved back while Mary tried to hide behind him.

By the end of October, school had become just a place Mary was leaving. The teachers were neither frightening nor charismatic now. If Mary had to knock at the staff-room door, she no longer shook at the thought of Mrs. Rike being the one who opened it, sallow, hunched, and pugnacious, looming up through a fug of smoke. Mrs. Rike had been the reason Mary spent a year begging to be let off school. She would put the thermometer on a radiator or pour a bucket of water down the toilet or scratch at her chest—I've got a fever, I've been sick, a rash. Mrs. Rike locked the first years in cupboards till they were hysterical and refused permission for them to go to the toilet, so that they wet themselves. She would keep a class lined up in the corridor till no one twitched or breathed, homing in on the ones the other children most admired or ostracised. They would be interrogated, slapped when they tried to respond ("But, ma'am . . ." "Don't talk back!"), humiliated, slapped again, and only let go when they cried. Mrs. Rike's dinner duty consisted of stopping anyone emptying anything into the slops bucket and sitting them down in front of their leftovers for the entire afternoon if necessary.

Mary remembered the gristle she had pushed down her sock when Mrs. Rike leant out of the window to have a cigarette. Once home, she had vomited anyway.

Now the pupils could eat more or less what they wanted of the grey roast beef, tinned burgers, mince, and luncheon-meat fritters; the glasses of green jelly topped with a stiff peak of artificial cream, dry treacle tart, and tepid custard with a rubbery skin. All his school life Billy had gone into one end of the canteen and come out of the other with a plate of grated cheese. He'd persuaded his mother to write to the school about his "dietary restrictions." Mrs. Rike hated him almost as much as she hated Mary, and measured his hair weekly with a ruler until the skinheads caught her attention and her determination shifted from cutting to growing.

For Mary, school was now a small place of which she occupied a small part. She studied English, Latin, and French and so had just three teachers. In class, the pupils sat around chatting in groups of half a dozen or so, and the teachers spoke quietly and without authority. People still fell asleep or failed to turn up, but no one misbehaved. Mary liked the work and her books, but understood all this to be just a prelude to something that would begin next year. Her English teacher, Miss Anna Starr, had been lending Mary her own books and offering to read her stories and poems. Miss Starr was always thoroughly made-up, her face powdered, her lips pale and finely outlined. She wore fashionable but elegant clothes and said as little as possible. If a class became rowdy, she spoke more and more quietly until she had recovered everyone's attention. Her coolness could give way to a blast of warmth that was prized by her pupils for being so rarely received.

Mr. Travers was in the geography department and had been given the new role of careers adviser. All of the upper sixth had to visit him. Mary sat in his office, scanning the posters: a nurse holding out a tray of medicine, like a waiter presenting a meal; a smiling young white woman pumping a well in an African village as if she were doing a folk dance; a man in a white coat frowning at a machine; an eager dentist; and several shots of students in gowns and mortarboards, with no longer fashionable haircuts and shoes.

"Your father was an architect, you say?" Mr. Travers looked nervously at Mary.

"Is an architect, actually, sir."

"Of course. And you?"

"I'm not. I mean, I don't think that it's my thing."

"Of course. And what might be your thing?"

Mary surveyed the walls. "Do you have any pictures of colleges in London?"

"I can lend you some prospectuses." He jumped up and pulled a number of alphabetically labelled cardboard boxes off a shelf.

Mary watched the pile grow in front of her as he sorted the brochures like a gambler shuffling and dealing a pack of cards. "Do they have pictures?"

"I expect so. But you'll want to know more than what a place looks like, won't you?"

"Yes. I mean, what do the people look like, what are they like?"

Mr. Travers stopped. "What people?" He gave her a university application form to practise filling in.

Autumn was the busiest time in the village economy, even this year. People washed jars and dusted off preserving pans. They gathered windfalls or picked fruit in the hedgerows and from their gardens. Jars of plum jam and green-tomato chutney were left on doorsteps. Marrows that had managed to bloat in spite of the drought were hoarded for the Horticultural Society Show or forced onto neighbours who cooked them the only way they knew how: boiled well and served with diluted tomato ketchup.

Buckets of wormy, blighted apples were left outside garden gates for people to help themselves. There were cobnuts, hazelnuts, blackberries, elderberries, rose hips, sloes, and haws. Stella heaved what Mary called her "cauldron" onto the stove, and for days on end, the kitchen was filled with chopping, bubbling, and dripping. Everyone used the same ingredients, but the result was their own. Stella made jellies that were strained, skimmed clean of any cloudiness, and barely sweet. Her chutneys were firey and smooth, and her sloppy jam had a raw fruitiness that came, again, from skimping on sugar. Mary liked to help with the chopping and stirring, but she kept out of the way when the time came for Stella to judge a setting point. She would tip a little into a saucer and blow on it, and took great trouble to get it right, but didn't bother soaking the labels off the jars and loathed the frilly paper disks others used for covers. Stella's gifts to her neighbours were often redirected, sometimes more than once.

People who would do no more than greet Tom in the street, and who would never cross the threshold of the chapel in order to see him, left jars and baskets on his doorstep. He lined up the jams and jellies on the windowsills and watched the light struggle through them. The apples, plums, and pears looked pretty, and he did not notice them rot.

One Saturday, at Stella's insistence, Mary took in jars for May and her girls in the salon. They thanked her politely. After closing, when Mary stayed behind to clear up, she found one jar under a chair and another dropped into the dirty towel basket. She left them where they were and was still blushing when the door opened with its ding-donging bell and flutter of curtain.

It was Billy. "Are you done?"

"I'm still here. An appointment, sir?"

He didn't laugh. "Since you're offering . . ."

"What?" Mary yelped.

"I was thinking of a bit of a change."

"What?"

"Oh, stop it. I want a haircut. What's wrong with that?"

"It's just you've never—I mean, have you had one before?"

Billy tutted and pushed past her. He slouched low in one of the chairs and put his feet up on the counter. "Just get on with it, George."

"Me?"

"Stop being so bloody astonished. You work here, so you can cut hair."

"I can't."

"Doesn't matter. Cut mine."

"A trim?" She picked up Jeanette's scissors and slipped them out of their vinyl sheath, relishing their sharpness and the specialised curve of their handles.

"No. A real cut."

"I'll have to wash it."

"But then you won't be able to see what you're doing! I'll wash it later."

"Sit up, then. I can't get at your hair as it is." Billy sat up straight, but didn't look into the mirror.

Mary cut round, taking off a couple of inches. "That do?"

Billy didn't even look up. "More off. A lot more."

She cut again, and now it sat on his shoulders in a limp bob. This time, Billy looked. "God, George, that's somewhat terrible. Can't you do, watchamacallit, layers?" Mary studied Jeanette's scissors and tried to remember how they travelled slowly and vertically at a sharp angle to the head, cutting as the hair slipped through the comb.

"Of course."

"Well, do them, then. But not soft. You know, hard."

Mary thought of the boys that hung around in Flux Records. "Sort of like spikes?"

"Yeah. Might as well."

She felt more sure now that she had got the idea. May had gone off on a Rotary Club outing and her girls were doing some early Christmas shopping in the precinct in Havilton New Town. The light was already weakening. No one would disturb them.

Mary took her time. She didn't find the combing part as easy as it looked, but Billy wasn't to know. She experimented with speed and angles, pretending to snip. When she finally found the courage to start cutting, she was surprised to discover that if she kept going, the hair fell in smooth, even fronds. She started with the front right side, working backwards from Billy's face, although she knew that the girls always started at the back, clipping the front hair up out of the way.

"Hold on a minute." Billy leaned forward. "Let's have a smoke."

"Here?"

"I could cope better with the pictures if we did."

Mary agreed. It might help. She sat down in the next chair and waited while Billy rolled a joint. It did help. When she returned to her cutting, she snipped confidently and then spent long minutes contemplating the effect. Each time, she decided that she needed to make it shorter. Eventually, she declared the right side of his head done. Billy studied the ragged wisps he was left with ("spikes"), and was about to pronounce his verdict when the lights went out.

The dark was so concentrated that Billy and Mary could not see their hands in front of their faces, let alone one another. Mary tried to take charge, fumbling around on her hands and knees, finding sockets in the skirting board, flicking switches, plugging and unplugging, but nothing worked.

"It must be a power cut, Billy. Let's go back to mine and I'll find a lantern or a torch or something and finish it."

"I am not walking through the village like this." Billy was adamant.

Mary laughed. "What better moment?"

"It might only last a few minutes. Let's wait."

So they settled down in the dark, crouched close together on the floor, hand in hand, too uneasy to sit apart. Neither spoke for a while, and when they did, it was in whispers.

"What's the time?" Mary was agitated.

"God knows. Why?"

"I'm supposed to be, you know, going out."

"Going out?" Billy echoed sarcastically.

"You know . . ."

"You mean going out of here? Or the village? The country? The universe, perhaps?"

"Stop being so childish, Billy! I'm meeting my—a friend. For a drink. That's all."

"Oh. Him."

"What's the matter with him?"

Billy shuffled about, restlessly. "George, he's perfectly okay, but really, I mean . . ."

"What? You mean what?"

"He's not really, you know, serious. Not your type."

"My type? What the fuck is my type, Eyre?"

"I don't mean . . . you know, I mean he's a bit pretentious."

"Because he doesn't wear orange flares or drive around attached to a clog?"

Billy tried to swipe her but missed. "No! Don't be silly."

"You're the one being silly. Fucking stupid, more like!"

Billy flinched. "Look, George. That gang, the doctor's daughter and that arty lot. They're only killing time, passing through. They're snobs, you know? People like us are just passing phases. They find us 'amusing.' They'll be off in London next year—"

"So will I."

"London? You never said."

"Where else? And anyway, who is this 'us'? You think Tobias is just amusing himself with you, too?"

"No! That's—he's not like that."

"And how would you know?"

"It's obvious, isn't it?"

Mary moved away so Billy had no sense of her. "No, it's not. But what is obvious is that you think I've been taken in and you haven't."

Billy considered this. "Yes," he said eventually. "That's right, I do."

Mary kicked out and caught a stand of perm curlers that toppled silently to the floor. She heard their almost inaudible scurry across the linoleum and began feeling around for them, but soon gave up. She had begun to think of them as malevolent creatures.

Billy spoke when she went quiet. "Where've you got to, George?" He heard a shuffle, a rattle and clink. "George?" The door flew open with a crashing ding-dong and there was a shock of cool, wet air. Billy got up and made towards it. When he was outside, he pulled his jersey over his face as Mary locked up.

"Finish it at yours?" he asked timidly. The village was so dark that the Green and Mary's cottage might as well have been on the other side of the world.

"Sorry," Mary retorted. "No scissors." She slipped away. Billy flailed around, not realising that she had gone, then heard her bump against a car, stumble over the kerb, and collide with her garden gate. He heard Mim's bark and saw the small light of a lantern swing out through the opening front door, and the darkness swing back as the door shut again.

On Sunday morning before church, May Hepple waited until she saw Lucas leave through the front gate, and then went and knocked on Stella George's door. She had just been to check the salon after the power cut and had found all the lights on and hair and curlers all over the floor. Mary should have finished and locked up before dark. Stella tutted and soothed, but she couldn't really help. Mary had said she was staying with a friend and hadn't got back yet. Stella offered May a cup of tea and let her talk.

"So you've still got June?" Stella tried to change the subject.

"Oh yes. Tom's settled in the chapel now, but Christie's twins are a growing handful."

"How old are the boys now?"

"Ten. The spitting image of Tom and Christie at that age."

"Really?" Stella thought they were fairer, more open-faced, nothing like.

"Yes. Darren is big, stubborn. Little Sean, well, he's quick, good at numbers, but not, we hope, too sensitive."

"You say Tom's settled now? That's good."

"We're doing what we can to make him cosy. Christie's set up some heaters and I've dug out some old curtains. That Valerie Eyre girl has got quite friendly with him and she's a nurse."

"Really? I didn't know."

"Yes, and always ready to help. Unlike our Sophie . . ."

"Sophie?" Stella remembered the sweet-featured girl that the Hepple brothers had seemed to court together. How at ease Tom had been in her company, and then how from one day to the next things had changed and she'd looked stung. There was a rapid wedding, June arrived, and they all disappeared into the Dip; or so it seemed, as Sophie rarely managed to get into the village once Iris became ill. June was seven before the twins were expected, as if Sophie had waited until she knew for sure that after those creeping years of sickness, Iris was dying at last. Stella refused the complicity she was being offered, in which she would be expected to make some lazy, vicious judgement of someone she barely knew. "Sophie has done a lot of looking after."

"You mean Iris?"

"And Tom."

"But she won't go up to the chapel!" May burst out. "She cooks things for him but sends one of the boys! And it's me that'll have to go in and give the place a once-over, if I can persuade Tom I won't disturb his studies."

"What's he studying?"

May thought for a bit. "Just . . . studies. Piles and piles of studies."

June was in the kitchen making tea when someone knocked on the back door. It was Billy, wearing a knitted tea cosy on his head.

"New hat?"

"Couldn't find a hat. Quick, let me in. I'm freezing. I've been waiting ages for the old dear to go." He sat down at the scrubbed linoleum table folded against the wall and pulled off the tea cosy to reveal his hair: one side still long, the other hacked into short, uneven clumps.

June gasped. "Who did that to you?"

"Doesn't matter. Can you finish it?"

June reached out and separated some of the flattened wisps. "You've got bald patches."

"What!" His hands flew to his head. "What the fuck am I going to do?"

June tried to be decisive. "Shave it all off."

Billy's face brightened. "Would you?"

"If you like." May was going from church to a golf-club luncheon and wouldn't be back till late afternoon. "Come on."

They went upstairs and Billy sat on the toilet with a salon towel round his shoulders. June produced a packet of pink-handled disposable razors. "Ladyshave?" Billy groaned. "Do they work? On real hair, I mean."

June was too mortified to answer. She found some of May's scissors in a drawer and quickly cut away as much hair as she could. When Billy's head was nothing but tufts, she let him feel it. He tried to get up and look in the mirror, but June pushed him back down. He closed his eyes as, trembling, June ran her hand over his scalp, trying to find more hair to cut. Billy's face was emerging not only from behind his sheet of hair but also from behind its adolescent softness. He was falling into place. June looked and looked.

She lifted a razor and made a tiny scrape. Billy winced. "Shouldn't you use foam or soap or something?"

"Oh. Sorry. And hot water to open the pores." She leaned over the bath and turned the hot tap full on. Within seconds, the small room was full of steam. June wet a flannel and held it against Billy's head. She lathered some soap and began, working slowly and stopping to rinse the razor under the basin tap, which she left to run as well.

At first she tried short hesitant lines, wincing at the idea of the delicate skin beneath it. Billy, too, was tense and hunched. But as June grew more concentrated, she passed the blade over his head in firm sweeps, progressing methodically from one side to the other and going over each part in the opposite way. She traced and retraced the shape of his head, its dips and curves and crown, and felt it told her all she needed to know about him. Billy breathed in the steam and, with it, the scent of June as she turned this way and that and caught against him.

All the things that happened next happened together. June put the razor down and wiped Billy's head, and then was stroking it and could not stop. Billy raised his hands, wanting to feel, too, then grasped her fingers and pulled her down. The forgotten bath over-flowed and Billy plunged in his arm to pull out the plug. June knelt down to mop the floor, and when they stood up, she caught at the drenched sleeve of his jersey and he wriggled out of it. The steam had condensed and settled on the mirror, the walls and window, and Billy's fine hair was everywhere. June felt it prickle on her hands and face. The bath was half empty when Billy put the plug back in. June turned off the running basin tap. She went to open the window, but Billy stopped her. He pointed at the wet patches on her jeans and she undid them. She tried to brush hair from the neck of his T-shirt, and he slipped that off, too. The bones of his thin body were as clear as those of his face, his skin a pale brown she would never have imag-ined. Then they were naked and stepping one after the other into the bath, where Billy leant back against June, mesmerised by her full dark softness as she whispered against his naked head and let her hand follow his to his cock, and they made him come, together.

The first frosts that had brought Valerie Eyre to the chapel were also the reason Tom had become so ill. He had had to start digging before the ground hardened, but he mustn't be seen, so had gone only at night, fetching his spade from behind a poplar and trying to loosen the earth in a way that he could disguise. It was a neglected corner, where some small disturbance would not be noticed. Even though he wasn't really ready, hadn't got everything in place, and still needed to persuade the girl to go with him, he felt wonderful to have started at last. So he had dug for hours while the hurricane lamp he'd carried guttered and burnt out. Then he had to wait for first light, to make sure he had left everything looking all right. When he got back to the chapel, his cramped hands could hardly open the door.

The next night he decided to stay indoors, but still couldn't sleep. He bundled up May's old curtains into a long, thin shape which he weighed in his arms. He tried dropping it from the upstairs gallery to the ground floor and made notes on how it fell. But all that wasn't much use unless he had everything right about the water.

On the third cold day he had got up and dressed, and had begun to make tea, but then felt tired and went upstairs for a sleep.

Valerie came twice a day now and may, or may not, have stayed the night. She tidied up a bit, changing the sheets and cleaning around the sink and cooker, but he wouldn't let her touch anything—not the streams of wax, the heaps of rubbish, the up-ended filing cabinet, or the chaos of paper. Christie came every other day, to refill the paraffin heaters and to hang blankets that made Tom feel as if he were living in a series of tents. He had an electric bar fire that May had brought over, and often someone—Valerie, May, or Sophie— sent a hot meal. There were talks with Father Barclay and the odd drink with Christie. May said Sophie complained that her husband was out almost every night, but no one saw him in the Arms more often than a Wednesday and Friday.

One afternoon, Valerie watched Tom moving sheets of paper and making notes and, as she knew better than to ask him what he was doing, found a compromise. "What's missing?"

He looked intently at her. "What's missing is the girl, what she saw, where it was."

"You mean Mary George?"

"I do."

"You think she really—"

"I don't know, but it might help to see her do it again."

Valerie thought quickly. Whether or not Mary gave him what he wanted if she tried, she was taken care of, out of the picture. "Would you like me to have a word?"

Anything, Tom thought, anything. "Would you?"

"It might help. I know her a bit. She's often at ours with Billy."

"Would you?" He thought of everything falling into place, as easily as this, and a rare smile lit his face. What he was smiling about was a vision far back in his mind, but it was Valerie who caught and hoarded it—a smile for her.

The power cuts came regularly now, so when the lights went out as Mary sat alone in the kitchen writing an essay one evening, she wasn't afraid. Stella was out somewhere, in the shop, she had said, doing the books. Mary went to the dresser and fumbled around for candles and matches: once she had got some light, she could find the lanterns. The matchbox gave a weak rattle as she picked it up, and as she pushed it open, the last match fell to the floor. After ten minutes on her hands and knees, Mary gave up looking for it and made her way upstairs to Stella's room, where she might find a torch. In the top drawer of Stella's desk she could make out pens and pencils, scraps of ribbon or material, business cards, paper clips, pebbles. The next drawer was full of paper. The last, deep drawer was untidy. Mary pulled out files but also handkerchiefs, perfume bottles, jewellery boxes, and finally a torch. She switched it on and shone it across the last thing she'd pulled out from above it, an envelope. Her fingers had recognised it already by its weight, shape, and wornness. Mary shook the letters out and was taken aback once more by the familiarity of the typeface.

> The house you were so eager to get rid of is empty now. Ready to go under like you. I wish you'd died in time to be buried down there. Your precious church, making a show of yourself as a christian woman, bitch. They're going to seal off the graveyard with concrete, I heard, to stop those old bones floating up to the surface!! If I had my way you'd be sealed off with them, *rotting* under concrete and water. No one would visit your grave then, would they? Even where they've put you now, I'll never come and see you. I'll be too busy looking after the people you SMASHED . . .

Everything's ready. The whole village has been invited to the pumping station to have it explained. They got someone to come to the hall and give a talk about the wildlife the water will attract. No one says a word about what's been drowned. AND DO YOU KNOW I DON'T GIVE A FUCK ANYMORE, JUST WANT IT DONE AND OVER!! You're nothing now, him too, ALL POWERFUL ONCE WEREN'T YOU NOW NOTHING!!!

Today I watched the first water pour into the Dip and I wished you still stuck indoors like you were, wetting yourself in your armchair, stinking and rotting and dying while everyone ran round doing your bidding. Queen Bee. Only this time no one would be there. The water would slosh about your twisted old feet, your claws, you HAG, and rise up your skinny legs, wash away your nappy and your stick and your blanket, and you'd be screaming for him, that old woman's dried-up scream, and he wouldn't come and save you. The water would suck the clothes off you and who would want your saggy old body now? Not him. He's COUNTING HIS MONEY . . .

You're gone under now. The house too, but no one with it. You forced everyone out, so desperate to please him. What about TOM? He's out of his skin, in agony, can't settle. You forced him out, you bitch. DID YOU THINK IT WOULD MAKE HIM BETTER? We'll all have to prop him up, for you, because of what you've done. He could have managed. You gave us years of HELL, your fancies and games. Kept the golden boy twisted round your little finger, so you thought. He's not here weeping over your grave though is he? No one goes. Weeds already, no flowers, and it's really dark there in that corner. He has fucked off to God knows where but you are paying for it. You are nothing but a vain, evil old woman and I wish you were stuck down there, not dead but DROWNING SLOWLY FOREVER SCREAMING AND SCREAMING AS THE WATER FILLS AND BURSTS YOUR LUNGS NEVER ENDING NEVER . . .

You KNEW he wouldn't be able to cope. That boy's been passed from pillar to post, stuffed with drugs and electricity and NOW HE'S GONE TOO. Is that what you wanted? Thought you'd force him into the real world and smash up a marriage while you were at it? Both your favourites gone now, see, they don't give a fuck about you, do they? Just me, left to cope as usual. You thought you knew what was best for us all, didn't you, when it was just an old woman's SICK FANTASY. You'd been stuck looking after a broken man for too long and wanted some fun, didn't you? Thought you could interest the architect in your wrinkled old sack? I know, I remember and you forget. You were a mother to him and that's all he was looking for, a mother (and a mother's money of course but not her juiceless cunt!!). Couldn't fix Tom so you'd damn well fix the rest of us. Well guess what, the water's full up now, settled. Like it's always been there. You're forgotten. Like me. OVERLOOKED.

Mary had swept the torch across each letter. She left them on the floor, took the torch into her room, packed a bag, and left. She stopped at the phone box, piled up her twopences, and rang Daniel's number. He answered and she burst into tears.

"Thank God! Oh, Daniel! It's just so awful!"

"What's happened?"

"I read the letters! Her letters!" Mary blurted and sobbed.

Daniel hesitated. "What letters? What's happened?" Mary realised that there had been music playing in the background and that it had just been turned off. She knew the room now, as she had stayed at the house twice, sleeping up in the attic with her picture. Daniel slipped downstairs to his bed before morning. His mother, Helen, made scented tea in a big pot and didn't bother to strain it. His father smoked a pipe in his "library." There was an old Great Dane called Thor and a sister, Rebecca, who phoned from London, where she worked in a gallery. Invitations to the private views she arranged were on the mantelpiece, stark abstracts among the curlicued, engraved "At Home" and "Drinks" cards addressed to

Professor and Mrs. Reinhardt Mort. Daniel's double-barrelled! Mary had thought excitedly until she realised Reinhardt was his father— Ray, as he had introduced himself.

"My mother's letters!"

"To whom? What's the big deal?"

"She's dead!"

"Your mother?"

"No, Iris Hepple. She died, and then Daddy went, too, and Mum got so angry. I didn't know, she must be sick or something, she says they . . ."

"Iris who?"

"Tom's mother. Daddy's mother, sort of, but then my mum says . . . Oh, Daniel, please!"

"Tom?"

After all, she had told him nothing. But the idea, now, of explaining the whole story left her exhausted. She put down the phone.

Valerie answered the door. "Billy's out. What's happened?" She steered Mary into the kitchen, made her a cup of tea, and put a plate of flapjacks on the counter.

"I can't stand it anymore!" Mary whimpered.

"Boyfriend trouble?"

For a moment Mary was indignant. "No!" Then she collapsed again. "The reservoir, my parents, what they did, what they think I did. I didn't know anything, I just heard and saw, and I bloody well wish I hadn't! How would you feel if your father went round stealing houses and your witch of a mother tormented the dead!"

Valerie was fascinated, but knew that whatever truth lay behind all this, it wouldn't be so colourful or so simple. She put her hand on Mary's. "Look. I think I can help." She meant it, and not just because of Tom. "There is one part of all this you can put a stop to."

Halloween was the last ritual that the children of the village grew out of. They gave up Cubs and Brownies, carol singing and sponsored skips, Youth Club and collecting for charity, but they still enjoyed the plastic fangs and fake blood of Trick or Treating. At dusk, the young ones would rush around, stumbling over their cloaks, bothered by their makeup or too-tight masks. They were given biscuits and apples, sometimes toffee or boiled sweets, and made their threat so timidly that those who answered the door smiled and knelt down to compliment them on their frightening appearance. When the older children went round, there were some who wouldn't open the door. A few of the boys carried eggs and flour but weren't quite brave enough to throw them at anyone except their friends, and at the houses of one or two perpetual and uncomplaining enemies.

This year Halloween fell on a Friday, and Mary was to meet Daniel and go to the Odeon, where Flux Promotions was staging a Halloween Horror Show with Mystery Guests. On Monday evening Mary considered her clothes. Black, she decided, was what really suited her. She was burning candles, practising lining her eyes, and playing Velvet Underground songs, the clanking "Venus in Furs," "All Tomorrow's Parties," and "Femme Fatale." Mary had read about kabuki theatre and had bought some white face powder and red lipstick. She had that little dress of Stella's that she'd worn to the Harvest Festival Disco, but it had got torn when she and Billy came off the bike. Then she remembered the boys in Flux Records and their safety pins. The dress had a jagged tear from waist to hem. Mary rifled through Stella's sewing box and began to pin the tear together, loosely, unevenly. She pulled on some tights, remembered Clara's fishnet stockings (Where on earth did you buy something like that?), and dragged her nails along her shins, making tentative ladders. It would be cold and Mary didn't want to be waiting at the bus stop in next to nothing (Clara wouldn't care). What else? Her holey cardigan was the wrong colour. She could ask Stella, but she was out, stocktaking or something.

Mary knew there were bags of Matthew's clothes in the landing cupboard. She pulled out a couple and began to empty them in her room. She picked up a shirt and held it against her. It was familiar — its pattern, texture, and shape, the frayed cuffs and floppy collar, and above all, its smell of tobacco and ink. Mary rummaged some more and found several old jackets that might even have been her grandfather's and looked thirties, just what she wanted, and some more shirts that were wonderfully too big but all the wrong colours, hippie shades of yellow and brown.

At lunchtime on Tuesday, Mary went down into Camptown from school and bought several tins of black dye. Once she had done that, she could not wait, so skipped her afternoon lessons and caught an early bus home, hoping that Stella would be at the shop. The house was empty and so Mary set to work. She gathered up the shirts and her cardigan, and then decided that while she was at it, she might as well dye a couple of other tops, too. She made up the dye in Stella's "cauldron." The instructions were folded tightly beneath the cellophane on each tin. Mary thought she had read them, but when she looked again, they mentioned salt, pounds of it. She dashed out to the post office and cleared the remaining packets from Mr. Cornice's dry-goods shelves. It was just enough.

When Stella got home that evening, the acrid smell of the dye had filled the hall. She followed it into the kitchen and found the sink and her preserving pan full of murky water. Several stained wooden spoons were scattered on the floor and the tiles behind the Aga were filmed with what looked like soot. The back door was open and a trail of dark splashes led through it. She found Mary pinning clothes to the washing line in the dark. The spoons were stood in a jug of diluted bleach. Mary was still scrubbing the floor at midnight.

On Wednesday, Mary only pretended to go to school. The dye had got under her nails and had splashed grimy shadows on her neck and arms. She hung around the Common and, when the coast was clear, slipped home the back way, knowing Stella wouldn't have bothered locking the back door. The clothes hung drably in the damp air. They weren't the pure black she had imagined but were blotched and streaked. Her cardigan was shrunken and matted. Nothing had dried. Mary gathered them up and carried them indoors, where she arranged them on a clotheshorse in front of the Aga and waited for them to be dry enough to put away.

On Thursday evening Mary leafed through her pile of old foreign novels with black covers, picking out the wintry ones about grand passions conducted through notes and glances, tuberculosis, long coach journeys, duty, and death. She made up her face differently, not attempting to even out her features but exaggerating them instead. She drew right round her wide eyes and whited out her pale face. She loaded her eyelashes with mascara, plucked her eyebrows to a thin line, pencilled them black, and painted her big mouth bright red. She back-combed her hair and set it in twisted strands with the last of Stella's hairspray, which was too expensive to give the rock-hard effect she wanted.

Late afternoon on Friday was misty and damp. Mary put on her dress and tights and chose her big boots (not like Clara) over high heels. She pulled on her shrunken cardigan and was pleased to see that it looked just right. Her hair and face were just as she wanted them, too. Billy had agreed to lend her his leather jacket, graciously setting aside her old gibes about him looking like a rocker. Mary was about to set off when she caught sight of a group of girls in fancy dress, crossing the Green and heading for the Camptown bus stop. Dawn was among them. Mary slipped back into the house and set off the garden way, thinking that if she hurried along the path and across the Common, she could get to the stop just beyond the chapel and get on after them, staying downstairs and hopefully out of sight.

As she began to cross the Common, the air was thickening to fog. It caught among the surrounding trees and bushes and billowed inwards to where the cricket pitch had been reseeded and fenced off. Mary breathed the strange fullness of this condensed air, its wet iron taste on the tongue. She felt strong.

When she reached what she thought was the middle, she looked around for the fence skirting the pitch and realised that she could make out the swings and benches and that she was in fact almost at the Common's northern edge. Unnerved, she decided to keep going in a straight line and to get back onto the road. As she drew near the benches, the fog cleared a little and she could make out someone there. Mary screwed up her eyes and peered. She moved a little nearer. A girl, a woman, was sitting on the bench with her head thrown back, eyes shut, her mouth caught somewhere between a smile and a yawn. Her face was framed with blond curls. Someone, a man, was crouched in front of her, his dark head half buried. Mary misunderstood and was about to shout and run forward when the man raised his head and Mary saw cropped dark hair she recognised. Then he turned a little towards her and she saw that she had been wrong, or at least half wrong: this man's wet face was full and bearded.

The Odeon in Camptown High Street had a crumbling stucco façade and an interior of warped veneer and sticky red plush velvet. The manager wore a braided jacket that he was now bursting out of, and the two elderly box-office staff doubled as usherettes, selling ice cream and soft drinks in the interval. After the B-movie, these old women would stand trembling in the aisles as the audience rushed to lighten the load of the trays slung round their chests: tubs of strawberry, chocolate, or vanilla that had less taste than the wooden spatulas with which they were eaten; nuts and raisins coated in stale chocolate; and wobbly cartons of overflavoured bright orange squash. After the main feature, the projectionist played the national anthem and people stood up immediately but did not stay. By the end of the tune, the place was empty and the Ice Cream Ladies would start to tidy up.

As business was slack, the manager had begun to put on events. When Terry Flux approached him, he was wary, remembering the mods, rockers, and Teddy Boys of not so long before. There were still battles at Thende and Crouchness during Bank Holiday weekends—razor blades, cycle chains, Stanley knives. On the other hand, Terry Flux was something of an old friend and offered his assurance and a fair deposit against damages, in addition to the rather high fee.

Even an hour before the show began, it looked as if Terry Flux was going to make more than his money back. Teenagers arrived from all over the county and beyond. They came in from the coast and even from London, drawn by the excitement of a kind of music that had already made its way out of the city and was bubbling up through bedrooms and garages out in the sticks. For the first time, urban boys and girls wished themselves provincial, hopelessly cut off and with an easily shockable audience on hand. Their clothes shops and clubs didn't matter. There were only one or two decent gigs in London, and the bands that had got that far were already being sucked into the machine. What they wanted was what Terry Flux could provide: a string of shambolic unknowns whose acne and rotten teeth were natural. They wanted the pigeon-chested, pale, spotty boy who sneered and gargled into the microphone and the three girls wearing ripped white school shirts and skirts made from dustbin liners, especially the fat one with braces on her teeth and a studded dog collar round her neck.

In the packed hall Mary clung to Daniel's hand and tried to be nonchalant about what was happening. Where had all these kids come from? And the bands? The only one she recognised was Gravity, although Terry Flux introduced them as Spit, and JonJo had bleached his hair and drawn it out into long spikes that were tipped with pink (cochineal, Mary reckoned). JonJo shouted a lot and whipped up his band to play faster. Everyone played all the time, and the more distortion they got from Terry Flux's weary PA, the better. Because they were playing so fast, each song lasted about ninety seconds instead of the more usual five minutes. The audience loved them, and jumped up and down on the flip-up seats till their ancient springs gave way. The manager had stayed at home, but the Ice Cream Ladies were in the projection room, cut off from the music and wondering what was going on and when the right moment would be to offer their wares. At the end of the evening, out of overpowering habit, they lined up at the doors to wish everyone good night. Almost all returned their greeting.

There were others who had come to Camptown that night: the bored young men who by closing time had had enough beer and heard enough talk about the punks, students, and queers trashing the

Odeon. They gathered in the High Street, drawn by the cacophony coming from inside the cinema. The first one that came out had a half-shaved head and chains from ear to nose. The bored young men looked at one another, ground their right fists in their left palms, and smiled. The first boy they got was a green-haired Londoner who heard their taunts and spat. He disappeared under four of them while his girlfriend pummelled the backs of his attackers, tried to drag them off, and screamed for help till one swung round and punched her in the face. Another boy came up and tried to intervene. He was turned on by more locals, who chased him into an alley, where he was kicked unconscious. The audience were still spilling out of the doors, saying good night to the Ice Cream Ladies, and walking straight into the fight.

A police car's lazy siren wound down as it pulled up in the road. The punched girl leapt at the car, hammering on the window. The two officers took in the scene, locked their doors, and stared straight ahead. They had radioed for backup on the way and had colleagues from the riot squad on call. Everyone had been talking about this punk do for weeks. They had been looking forward to it.

Tense men in helmets and body protectors ripped the identifying numbers from their lapels. Their Black Marias were parked in a side street and they fanned out, sealing off the area as they approached. The first people they confronted were frightened teenagers trying to get home, but from behind a visor, one looked as unsavoury as the next. Silently, the officers formed a wall and pushed the audience back towards the fight. Anyone who refused to move was shoved in the chest till they were provoked into shouting abuse or trying to force their way through. Then they were passed back behind the line and dealt with. There was a sound of plate glass breaking as someone threw a bin against a shop window. The boy who did it later said in court that he had been trying to make the police get out of their car and help the injured. This didn't wash with the magistrates.

The riot squad was made up of policemen who worked in small

market towns in one of the country's quietest counties. They had trained for this and knew that among these youngsters who looked still wet behind the ears were anarchists from the city, foul-mouthed, drug-ridden, and dangerous. They would not want to come here again. Among the shouts and snarls, kicks and punches, there was suddenly a long, high cry and someone shouted, "He's got a knife, for fuck's sake, a knife!" Then everything was still and quiet for a moment, and Terry Flux appeared on the steps, having ushered the Ice Cream Ladies back indoors. "I've called an ambulance," he said, and walked towards the boy who was kneeling on the ground, slumped forward as blood flooded his bare back. Terry Flux pulled off his own shirt and held it against him. The riot squad were busy corralling the audience up against a wall. Their batons cracked against heads, chests, legs, and arms. Several people were crying.

Daniel and Mary were among the last to leave and were caught almost at the cinema doors. "I don't understand!" Mary shouted in Daniel's ear as he clutched her. "It's just a gig! Why are the police dressed up like that? Who's fighting?" Daniel began pulling her sideways, trying to reach the edge of the crowd. When they got there, Mary caught sight of JonJo in the middle of a fray and Trevor Lacey pulling someone off him, shouting "Not him, mate! I know him!" before turning round to kick someone else's head.

Daniel pulled Mary round a corner, where they bumped straight into three of the riot-squad officers. "Please help!" Mary began. "There's a terrible fight going on, someone's been stabbed and no one can get home!" The officers laughed and began prodding Mary and Daniel with their batons, forcing them to walk backwards and rejoin the crowd.

An ambulance appeared behind them, and as the paramedics jumped out, the police changed demeanour and called "This way lads!" and trotted off, swinging their batons.

Daniel yanked Mary round the corner again, but now she was too angry to want to leave. "The bastards! We should complain! Take them to court! Those cowards in the car, too!"

Daniel put his arm round her and held her so tightly that she had to stop speaking. "Forget it. Let's get home while we can."

Mary wrenched herself away. "But that boy! I saw the blood, Daniel. He might die! And what about those others getting kicked to death! It might have been us!"

"Yes, but it wasn't, was it?"

She tried to calm down and do what he said, forget it. He was sounding bored already.

Daniel sat Mary in the living room, put on the television, and went to make some tea. His parents were in bed. They watched a Marx Brothers film, A *Night at the Opera*, and Mary waited for Daniel to talk about the evening: the bands, the atmosphere, the weird police dressed up like baddies from a twenty-first-century space war. Daniel was glued to the film, laughing at every wisecrack and reciting many of them simultaneously. Then the film started repeating itself, the same scenes and gags and helter-skelter sequences, and Mary became agitated.

"Isn't this wrong? Haven't we already seen this?"

"That's the point!" Daniel snapped. But as the repetitions accumulated, his attention began to sag, and when the credits rolled, the announcer apologised for one reel of the film having been played twice. Mary was cautious enough not to say anything. Daniel switched off the television and took her up to the attic. Lying naked beside him, the stunned unreality Mary felt gave way to panic, and that in turn took her back to what he couldn't help her with. As he stroked her, she began to shake and cry. He kissed her face and hushed her, but stopped when she didn't calm down. "Come on. It wasn't that bad." Mary tried, but even though she was weeping now, the pressure did not ease. Instead, it seemed to grow, as if there were more bad things piled up inside her than she had been even vaguely aware of.

"Settle down. My parents will hear." Mary shook her head, sat up, and pulled on her clothes. "What are you doing now?" She grabbed her bag and Billy's leather jacket and hurried down the stairs. Daniel caught up with her at the front door. "What is it with you? Always on the verge of some bloody great eruption, always disappearing, always scared or sad or furious or what?" He looked angry, but reached out with both hands and held her face. She kissed the corner of his mouth and ran.

"Will you come and get me?"

"I thought you were staying at your friend's." Stella sounded half asleep.

"I was, Mum. But I really want to come home. Please?" Mary hated herself for this when Stella pulled up half an hour later in the orange Mini, wearing a kaftan and shawl, and driving in bare feet. On the way back, Stella didn't ask any questions, but she noticed Mary was wearing her old dress and tried to remember when she had last worn it, when she had been a shape to wear it, and what it had meant to her to wear it. A little black dress. The child appeared to have cut it to shreds and pinned it back together.

Mary took out her lenses over a handkerchief on her lap and fingered them into their case. She remembered to keep it with her now, ever since Daniel's mother had almost washed the egg cups she had borrowed. She started to cry again and was grateful to Stella for pretending not to notice. She felt pleased to see her mother, in spite of everything and not just for the lift, and this confused and surprised her.

Five days later, the village gathered on the Common for Guy Fawkes Night. The fog of Halloween had been blown away by a wind that brought with it a gale. Christie had stopped off before work, a local barn conversion, to check on the tarpaulin that he and the rest of the Bonfire Committee had used to cover the wood. A heavy rope was laced through holes punched in its hem, which was also weighed down with bricks, but the thing still looked as if, without one more adjustment, it would topple at any moment, never mind let in rain. They had managed to gather up quite a number of floorboards and offcuts to burn. There were wooden crates, a couple of railway sleepers, even the old plough that had been getting in the way in Stroud's yard for years. Christie had got hold of some oak panelling that had been stripped out of another conversion and had pulled several pairs of shutters out of the site's skip. Others had brought along unwieldy rocking chairs, settles and claw-footed tables, bedframes and chests of drawers. There were also things in the heap that contained asbestos, foam, and plastic, even glass, but if no one minded the smell and a bit of black smoke, they would add to the fun as they sizzled and exploded.

By evening the wind had worn down to gusts that flung intermittent bursts of rain across the Common. The fire was lit in one of the lulls and glutted with paraffin, so that by the next downpour the flames were strong enough not to be quenched. The Refreshments Committee had set up in the cricket pavilion, where Stella was persuading Violet Eley to let the baked potatoes char as they would if cooked in the embers of the fire. One of the commuters had set up a barbecue grill on the pavilion's verandah and was trying to take charge of the sausages. His wife was getting in Violet's way at the stove, pouring bottles of red wine into a big pan along with spices, sliced oranges, and hot water.

Billy and June climbed on top of the pavilion and huddled together under Billy's big cycling cape. June tried not to keep stroking the soft silver stubble on Billy's head. He waved to Tobias, who arrived with both of his little brothers on the back of his bike. Tobias sized up the fire. Christie was frantically splurging paraffin onto one side of it as the wind threw a burst of rain against it and the flames petered out. Tobias slipped round to the opposite side and began opening up the fire, creating channels for air that would draw the flames towards the most flammable materials, forcing them to catch. He pulled out and discarded a fibreglass seat and three ripped, scorched, and mouldy cushions.

Billy pointed out the rest of the Cloughs to June as they arrived under colourful umbrellas: the doctor with his wife on his arm in a flared fur coat that swung like a bell; Juliette, the brainy one, whose heavy-framed glasses Billy privately thought made her look rather sexy; and Clara, with some man in tow. She looked different, but it was hard to tell whether this was because she was swaddled in a big old tweed coat that obviously belonged to her friend or because her face had lost its restless avidity.

Tom had arrived with Father Barclay and was hanging back in the shadows, near Tobias. He had been hoping to enjoy the fireworks, but then he saw the heap of smouldering cushions and remembered where they came from—the treehouse he and Christie had built behind the house in the Dip. What were they doing turning up now? Where had they been all this time? He tried not to think about it, tried concentrating on the fire and Christie's proud face as the flames grew and consolidated, but the cushions were bothering him.

As soon as the first fireworks exploded, Mim whimpered and scuttled up the stairs. She jumped onto Mary's bed and settled down beside her.

"Poor old thing. You never liked them, did you?" Mary gratefully pulled the dog against her. The room was dark, cold, and silent, making each explosion acutely noisy and bright. Mary had meant to go to the Common—she always had—but was feeling weak and tearful again, and panicked at the prospect of having to deal with any of her friends. Daniel hadn't rung and it had been five days. Even curled up in bed, Mary felt so heavy that she was surprised she didn't sink into the earth. Mim whined and licked the tears on Mary's cheek, which made her cry even more.

"You awake?" Mary was lying facing the wall and only turned over now because she didn't recognise the voice. It was the evening after Guy Fawkes and she was still in bed and beginning to feel grimy. Stella had not been able to persuade her to eat, but brought up a posset every few hours, Mary's favourite childhood drink of hot milk, honey, and cinnamon. Mary's eyes were swollen with crying and sleep, and she blinked as this visitor turned on the bedside light. A tall silhouette fell across the bed and climbed the wall, where it flared into shadow. It took a moment for Mary to put the two things together: the scattered mess of her room and Clara. Mary leaned forward and felt around for her glasses. Clara passed them over and sat on the very edge of the bed. She was wearing her paint-splashed dungarees with a ragged guernsey over the top, and had thrown down a big tweed coat on the floor. Her hair was scraped back in a complicated knot.

"I met your ma at the fireworks last night. She said you weren't too well." She almost yawned it.

"My *mother*?"

"Yes," Clara replied. Then added warmly, "She's really nice, isn't she? And so stylish!"

"My *mother*?" They both giggled.

Clara stayed for two hours, chattering about college and the village, parties and clothes. She hadn't been at the Halloween gig and wanted to hear all about it. She also had something she wanted to tell.

"Weren't the village fireworks a bit of a bore?" Mary wondered. "I mean, you could've gone into town . . ." London.

Clara licked her lips and patted her hair. "No, no, it was great. I mean, T. came along."

"T.?" Mary was tired, but Clara's wide grin made her sit up and pay attention.

"Torquil Cholmondeley, actually. But everyone calls him T."

"Choll-mond-olay? Oh, you mean Chumley."

"No, it's spelt C-H-O-L-M-O-N . . ." Clara looked nervous.

"Yes, I know. Chumley."

"*Chum*ley?" Clara repeated weakly. Mary nodded. "Oh Christ, darling! I sat through Sunday lunch calling his mother Mrs. Choll-mond-olay! No one said a thing except his father, the swine, who kept calling me Miss *Klowg* and I thought he'd just misheard or something." Mary was rocking with laughter, and Clara soon recovered herself and scowled. "Fucking English!"

"But you're half-English."

Clara shrugged. "Yes, but you're all so inbred, the gene's recessive. I'm far more Italian, and I have lived there half my life! It's infectious, you see. Even Papa's quite Italian, and he only married into it."

"But I thought you grew up in Camptown, next door to Daniel?"

"Daniel? Did I say that? We rented the house next door for a year or two, after America. Anyway," she curled up at the foot of the bed, "I was telling you about T."

Torquil Cholmondeley was not a painter or a pop star or even a Londoner. He was more or less local, the son of a farmer, a landowner really, and T. wanted to farm, too, "but small scale, without chemicals, rare kinds of vegetables and extinct breeds."

Mary didn't know what to say. "How did you meet him?"

"Painting."

"So he paints?"

"No! I was painting—on his land." Mary realised she had never seen a picture by Clara, had never thought to ask, so she asked now. Clara pulled a small watercolour pad from her dungarees bib pocket and tossed it into Mary's lap. The sketches were tiny landscapes: liquid but precisely stratified, two-thirds firey sky. Mary was astounded.

"When do you paint?"

"Every day."

"These?"

"I like the early-winter light, so I walk till I find the right sky." Clara sounded offhand, even embarrassed.

Mary put the pad down and crumpled into herself. "You work every day."

Clara shrugged. "Sure."

"I don't even know what work I want to do," Mary said, "and I'm bloody well going to cry again! I can't bloody stop!"

237

Clara leant forward and patted her. When Mary was quiet again, she asked, "Shall I ring Dan? Let him know you're not too well?"

"What for?"

"What do you mean what for?"

"He's not been in touch. For ages, actually." She had already told Clara about the Odeon, the bands and fights and police, but not about the Marx Brothers or going home. Once she had explained all that, she felt incredibly tired and sidled down under her covers.

Clara waited till she'd settled. "What did he say, then, when you said you had to go?"

"Something about me going inwards or outwards, up or down. Can't remember exactly, but he sounded pissed off." She was speaking into her blankets.

"What would you think if he was always running out on you like that?"

"What do you mean, 'always'?"

"After the party in Crouchness where you met, after my dinner, the Harvest Festival Disco, Halloween . . ."

Mary was startled. "How do you know about Crouchness?"

"He told me, silly!"

"He told you?"

"He talks about you all the time!"

"He does? But I thought . . ."

"Thought what?"

"You and he?"

Clara looked astonished. "Me and D.? God, no! I mean, he's like a brother or something!"

"But you danced . . . and kissed . . . I saw you!"

"Mary George. You may have seen me trying to teach him to dance or trying to get you to pay the poor sod some attention and whispering a few hints in his ear, but I never went so far as to kiss him!"

"To get me to pay him attention?"

"The poor boy doesn't know if he's coming or going! You're so cool and mysterious! So *distrait*!"

By the time Clara left, Mary was tingling with excitement, delighted at how wrong she had been. Clara wrapped herself in T.'s big coat and walked home, trying to convince herself that it was all right, what she'd said was basically true, her part of it anyway, and Daniel was very taken with little Mary, he'd just about said as much.

Tom kept his fortnightly appointment at the surgery, but arrived an hour early and couldn't sit still. He paced the waiting room, three steps one way, three steps back, till Betty Burgess nudged her trainee replacement, Melanie Pannessey, and muttered to her to watch. Betty came out via the dispensary and offered Mr. Hepple the blue chair in the hall. She spoke to him loudly enough for the doctor to hear from behind the closed door of his room. When his present consultation ended, Dr. Clough was prepared. He invited Tom straight in. He listened as Tom talked rapidly and continuously for twenty minutes. Not a single sentence connected with the one that preceded or followed it. Tom's eyes were bloodshot and dilated. He licked his lips and chewed his tongue as he spoke.

"How are you finding your medication?"

Tom broke off in the middle of a word. "Doctor Clough, Doctor Kill Off!" He laughed. "Kill off they're killing me Doctor Off!"

The doctor realised that he wasn't taking his pills properly. "Aren't you tired, Tom?"

He began to nod and couldn't stop. "So much to do" emerged from the middle of his next mumblings.

"I could arrange a rest." The nodding became shaking. "If you wanted to, you know, talk to someone who could help you feel better, make sure you took care of yourself."

"Family" came out from between almost chattering teeth.

"Sometimes family is the problem, not the solution." Dr. Clough's bluntness was soothing, and Tom was able, briefly, to concentrate.

239

"Just put things in place, then if I feel bad maybe you're right maybe go somewhere for a little rest."

The doctor was surprised and pleased. "How long will you need, Tom? To put things in place, I mean."

"Rain's supposed to clear after Remembrance Sunday, say the end of next week?"

Dr. Clough stood up. He could hear the orchestrated coughing and tutting from the waiting room as he opened his door. "Come and see me then. Speak to Betty, I mean Melanie, and she'll write an appointment down for you."

"Thank you Doctor I'll be off Doctor Off Clough Doctor . . ." Tom went on following this string of words while Betty dictated his appointment to Melanie, who wrote it on a card and handed it over, and he continued to follow it all the way back to the chapel.

Mary had gone back to school, but much of the rest of the time she spent at home. Billy went in every day on his bike now and often gave June a lift, as if to spite her. She didn't want to see him anyway. He made her feel childish.

Mary didn't want to talk to anyone; it was just too tiring. Each afternoon she ran to get the first bus home so that there would be no chance of bumping into Daniel. Once or twice she had longed for him to be waiting at the gates like he had that time, but mostly she felt so feeble and awful, she dreaded being seen. She was always cold, even though there had been no frost for weeks. She ate her supper, did her homework, and got into bed. She hardly read at all now, and the sight of those Russian novels with their thick black spines, the poetry books with their jazzy graphic covers, the sight of anything she had read and knew and loved was exhausting. She dug out some older books, *Tintin*, *Asterix*, and *Babar*, and was comforted by her name carefully inscribed on each flyleaf in leaden, wonky script. She had written both *R*'s backwards and thought now that it looked rather stylish; she might try it out again. Sometimes she listened to records, but music didn't work anymore either, it left her cold. Once, her mother had come in to tell her that her father was on the phone, but she went on pretending to be asleep.

One Sunday morning Stella went off with two poppies in the lapels of her purple maxi coat, one white and one red. She bustled in to pull back Mary's curtains and wake her up. Mary could smell real coffee, something they hardly ever had.

"There's a bit of a special breakfast for you downstairs. Don't let it get cold. I'd better be off to start helping the ancients get to church. It's the Armistice Parade, remember?"

The coffee smelt delicious. Mary went down and poured herself a cup from the enamelled pot on the stove and found two croissants on top of the oven. They had things like this only for birthdays and Christmas. Then she remembered. It was Stella's birthday.

Each year, the Armistice Parade got smaller and its pace slowed. Harry Marten led the procession of veterans with his bandsman's drum, and the beat they marched to had slowed, too. Ever since Mary could remember, Remembrance Sunday had been a dull day just like this, when the traffic stopped and the only sign of life was this handful of tottering shrunken old men, straightbacked and tight-faced, with ribbons and medals pinned to the breast of their black coats and worn as if they were the only colour in these men's lives. Behind them came the congregations of the two churches and the chapel, hushed and cold. The men gathered at the war memorial and several laid wreaths. The three ministers lined up and each said a prayer. Harry Marten beat his drum to settle the crowd and to count them into the minute's silence. As he stopped, the drumming continued, and he looked down at his hands, startled to think they had carried on without him and even more surprised to realise that although they hadn't, the beat persisted, like a delayed echo.

Mary, wrapped in a blanket and watching from her mother's window, saw what was coming before anyone out on the Green did: another procession. This time, the marchers were dressed in white. Their leader also had a drum, and they, too, walked at a stiff and measured pace. The drummer was wearing a fox mask and there were others, dogs and cats and monkeys. There were banners, too, and Mary screwed up her eyes and made out the animals on them, rivetted into wired metal skullcaps, clamped in cages, scarred, amputated, and full of pipes and tubes. Mary realised that they must be marching on the research centre out past the Setts.

The gaggle around the war memorial jostled and nudged one another. Questions went round followed by explanations, and a second later, the decision was circulated to stay put. The veterans were still standing to attention as Eric Mower had forgotten to play reveille on his trumpet, with which he signalled the end of the minute's silence. He was staring at the marchers in white, who were almost upon them now. The congregations drew close together, some holding on to their neighbours, children shielded between arms and legs. The drummer in white reached them and stopped. The entire white procession stopped, too, and waited in silence as the drummer counted off a minute on his watch and then raised his sticks and began his beat again. During that minute, most of the congregation could not resist casting a quick look at the marchers. They saw their banners and were sickened and outraged.

Mary watched the drummer in white lead the procession towards the massed congregations, and saw how easily they parted to let the protesters pass through in single file. Separated out like this, each person in white became distinct, and Mary recognised the tall, skinny drummer with the shock of blond hair as JonJo, and among the others was the crop-haired and ambling Billy, clumping June, even Clara, her thick plait bound in a white silk scarf. Everyone she knew! As the last marchers passed through the crowd, Mary saw they were carrying a bucket and that all along the High Street was a dribbled line of red paint. She traced its path through the congregations, a thin line like a border just glimpsed before Eric Mower began to quaver on his trumpet and the two halves of the crowd shut like an eye.

. . .

Mary was so angry at being left out that she got dressed, tore up and ate the croissants, gulped the coffee, and marched off towards the research centre. It was a place she had never liked to pass on foot because of the dogs, Alsatians with an enormous bark, who hurled themselves against the high fence in a casual frenzy that gave passersby an idea of what they were capable of. Without the dogs, everyone would forget the centre was there. They rarely saw anyone go in and out of the double-gated drive with its shaded sentry box, and the lights inside the shielded compound were always kept at the same level of dimness.

The centre was tucked beyond the postcard end of the village: the C of E church with its sunny white spire, Mary's old school, which was now a house, the almshouses and their knot garden, the village pump, horse trough, and milestone. If you turned off down Hive Lane instead of continuing along the High Street out towards Mortimer Tye, you came first to Brock Hall, derelict, overgrown, and earmarked for "development." Mary remembered sneaking into the grounds with Billy and Julie and a gang of other children from school. There had been a jungle of rhododendrons and enormous beds of dead plants. There had been so little glass left in the greenhouses that no one had had the heart to break what remained.

Hive Lane was a dark tunnel grown over by hedgerows and trees, but when Mary turned into it that morning, it was crammed with white. She saw JonJo's skinny back and blond hair and almost tapped him on the shoulder, then thought, Not him; why should he have thought to tell her? She looked for Billy. The crowd was milling and people talked among themselves until someone established a chant or call and echo, which they took up and repeated till they grew bored. The guard dogs sat rigidly behind the fence, impassive but alert. There was no sign of anyone inside. Mary pushed her way rudely through the crowd, too cross to care. She saw someone like Billy in a cat mask talking to someone in a puppy mask, who might be June. Mary stomped up to them and pulled Billy round. "How come I didn't get to hear about this?"

It wasn't Billy but a girl that Mary had never seen before. She had forgotten about Billy's hair. She said sorry, rather grumpily, and moved off, still searching. In the end, it was Billy, a cat, who found her, and he was with June, who was a cat, too. With them were Tobias and Clara (both rats).

"Mary! We didn't think you were up to it!"

"You didn't ask!" Mary was still angry, but chastened by her audience. "You must have all been planning this for months and . . . and it's my village!"

"Sweetie," Clara cooed, throwing an arm round Mary's shoulders. "These people plan nothing that far in advance, because it would get stopped. It's all last minute and word of mouth."

"Well, why didn't any words come out of your mouth?" Mary turned on Billy again, who muttered something about her not having been around.

The drum began to beat, the crowd barked, whined, mewed, and howled, and JonJo scaled a fence post. The dogs leapt up in a scrum, jumping and snapping, but he was too high for them. Two Black Marias skidded to a halt at either end of the lane and turned their sirens on. JonJo waved and screamed "Pigs! Pigs!" and the fence rocked. When Mary saw the men in riot helmets again, she made for the hedgerow, shouting to her friends to follow. They managed to hide among the rhododendron bushes of Brock Hall until the police had gone.

Later, when the protest march was talked about on the bus, in the common room, at pubs and parties, Mary said little. She never felt as if she had quite joined in.

Whatever else Mary let slip, she turned up at the salon on time every Saturday. She needed the five pounds May paid her. The Saturday after the protest march Suze had flu, so Mary was put by the phone and told to cancel her appointments. May said she had "ever such a nice voice" and was getting her to answer the phone more. Mary listened to as much or as little as each disappointed client wanted to tell her, passing on the kindest remarks to Jeanette and Felicity and keeping the most unpleasant to herself. Jeanette wasn't fooled.

"Didn't poor old Suze have that harridan Vi Eley this morning?"

"Yes," Mary said. "Cut and perm."

"Special occasion tomorrow?"

"That's right."

"Always a special occasion with that one. Didn't she complain?"

Mary could still hear Mrs. Eley's waspish remark, "Too many late nights out and about with not enough on, that's what's given her flu!" She demurred, "Oh, you know how she goes on!"

The hairdryer clicked off at that moment, and anything they said now would be heard by Jeanette's boiled-looking client. "Mary, fetch my lady a glass of water, would you?" Her voice was full of warm air.

"Certainly, Jeanette." Mary got just enough of a singsong into her reply for Jeanette to notice and wink. She was in the mood to enjoy the cosiness of the salon and the constant patter of rain across the outside of windows that, inside, dripped with condensation.

The door tinkled as it opened and there was Valerie Eyre. Mary was about to ask if she wanted to make an appointment, but her hair was so short, her appearance so efficient, that Mary hesitated. Valerie spoke first: "Hello. What time do you finish?"

Mary wondered anxiously if she was supposed to know what Valerie was talking about. "Three."

"Could I collect you? The rain's clearing up and I'll have my mum's car."

"Where do you want to take me?" Mary felt stupid. I should know what this is all about, she thought. Have I forgotten something?

Valerie glanced over at Jeanette. Felicity was sorting and piling up magazines as she waited for her next client. Both made a show of not looking up. "You know what I said about putting a stop to it? Remember?" She was almost whispering, and Mary, not wanting more to be said in case it was something she didn't want the others to hear, said yes, of course she remembered. "We could drop by the water, see. All you'd have to do is point it out." Mary shuddered as she realised what was being asked of her, but she felt Valerie's calm and was tired of being so endlessly afraid. This was grown-up life, real life. You kept things to yourself and you faced up to things by yourself. For the next two hours Mary swept, cleaned, folded, washed up, chatted, smiled, and served with all her strength, trying to wear out her unbearable nerves.

Valerie was waiting as Mary locked up. They walked along to the Green together, so that Mary could drop the salon keys through May's letterbox. Mary turned round to walk back to the square, thinking the car must be parked there, but Valerie took her arm. "No. I left it out by the chapel." She did not let go of Mary until they got there.

Tom was crouched in the back seat of the Cortina. He twisted one leg round the other, sat on his hands, and dared not try to speak, as he might not be able to stop. As Valerie drove to the reservoir, she could see in her rearview mirror how his poor head twitched and shook. She parked at the end of the track and Tom rushed ahead to loosen the Other Gate. He nearly let the whole thing drop, but managed to hold it back courteously as Valerie and Mary stepped through. He followed, pleased to feel the soft mulch of earth and leaves under his feet. Two weeks ago, during the cold snap, the ground had begun to harden, but now this warm spell looked like lasting long enough, which was good, except if there was too much rain. He hung back as Valerie had advised him to do and watched the girl, whose footsteps got slower as she neared the tree. Valerie said something to her and then came to him and held his hand. He showed her the heap of stones with which he had marked his vantage point, like a cairn.

At first Tom thought it wasn't right. The girl didn't look right.

She was wearing jeans and a boy's leather jacket, and had gained in substance. What was there about this hard-looking little thing that could float?

Valerie was amused, watching Mary climb awkwardly up onto the bough. This should lay that particular ghost. Mary had worried because everything was still so wet from the rain, but Valerie gripped her shoulders and told her she was doing a good thing, and that all she needed to do was go along a bit and point or something—that would do.

Mary did not like the look of the water. It was a drab grey and she could hear its heavy slop against the concrete bank. She crouched down and slipped her glasses into her pocket. The greasy sheen of the wet bark became a splintered gleam. She put her glasses back on and stood up. In less than three paces she faltered and slipped. It had never seemed high before. She retreated and crouched down again. The rain began, in hard drops that slapped against her face. This was awful. Mary wished she had never pretended not to be scared, or that she was grown up and able to do the right thing. She hadn't, after all, thought of doing this for herself. It was Valerie's conviction, Valerie's big ideas and bossiness, that she had clung to, and Valerie was only, after all, ordinary. It was just that no one else had come up with anything that might make her feel better and she had thought that being brave would.

Mary closed her eyes, took off her glasses, and shoved them back into her shirt pocket—one of Matthew's voluminous old shirts dyed a patchy black now, its tails dropping to her knees, its cuffs trailing out of Billy's jacket sleeves. She stood up. This felt better. She took a step, kept her eyes shut, and sent her mind away into one of Clara's burning watercolour skies. It worked. She kept going and each step grew lighter, the bough beneath it lighter, till the perfect moment came, of oblivion and suspension, of being nothing in nothing, empty and free.

The rain was falling hard now, but Tom didn't notice. This time his mind wasn't woolly with drugs or frayed by panic but quick and clear. He followed the line of the Dip, the line of the girl, and the line of the water, and when he tried to bring them together, it worked—he could follow them beneath the surface, up into the air and out. He made notes on angles, using the girl as a fixed point. Now he did not have to look for clues in the water.

Valerie was cold and uneasy. There was something about Mary George, after all. She was right out there, over the water, and looked as if she could step from the end of the bough and would not fall. She didn't even look where she was going. Valerie saw Tom's excitement and knew he was scribbling something in one of his notebooks, keeping his eyes on the girl. She tried to catch a glimpse of what he was writing, but rain spattered the page. Then the air seemed to buckle and the girl was shaken, doubled over, and jumped or fell.

Tom needed no sleep now. He had such energy and everything was ready at last. He had sent Valerie away after drinking her soup and had gone to finish the digging, even though the rain went on steadily into the night. The deep clay clung to his spade and sucked at his boots. Mud splattered his head and clothes. Just before dawn, he found it, worked it loose and left it. Patience. He hid the new earth, laid across the board and turf, and scattered clumps of dead leaves and weeds over them. The place looked the same as ever—neglected.

Tom wasn't going to let himself get ill again, either. He hurried back through the fields to the chapel, took off his clothes, and wrapped himself in a blanket. He pulled all his papers into a circle under the lightbulb downstairs and gathered his paraffin heaters around it. He lit them all, and the bar fire for good measure. He sat in the middle and got to work.

The next night was perfect, still and clear. The power Tom had felt for the last few days had not subsided. He needed neither sleep nor rest and only ate because a meal arrived for him. He went over his sums once more, stuffed his papers in his pockets, packed a knapsack with a blanket, a hurricane lamp, and tools, and set out at midnight. There was enough of a moon, but not so much of one that he could easily be seen. He loved walking through the village at this time because he would meet almost no one. Only Dot Grieves, who didn't sleep either, or Violet Eley walking her silly little dog. Neither acknowledged him that night, perhaps didn't even see him pass. ("The smell of him!" Violet Eley said later, adding, only to wish that she hadn't, "Like he'd come out of a hole in the ground!" Dot Grieves thought it a peculiarly concentrated smell, like that of a long-locked room when first opened. She offered nothing.) Tom had tried to look unperturbed at each meeting. It was easy for him to hurry on down the lane and to slip off along the path to find her.

God, she was light, so small and light. He could not look at her, only weigh her in his arms and wrap her in his blanket. Even then she was nothing to carry, and not even after he had crossed five fields, splashing along the waterlogged footpaths, half limping on his gammy leg, boots caked in mud, did she feel like much of a burden.

He laid her down by the stones, opened the blanket, and folded the stones in next to her, leaving one out to mark the spot. Then he lit his hurricane lamp, cut off a length of twine with his clasp knife, threaded one of Iris's old darning needles, and sewed the blanket up. He worked slowly, in big jagged stitches. When he was finished, he picked her up, and the stones collected and dragged at the hem. The blanket sack had doubled in weight. It would do.

He left it there and walked to the tree, pulled himself up onto the bough, and shuffled along, sitting, to hang the lamp on the broken stem at the spot from which the girl had fallen. He walked back to the stone and took off his boots. He picked her up and walked along the shore, triangulating and measuring from the stone to the bough to the water. Then he focused on the point where the water darkened and lowered himself in, dragging the sack in the crook of one arm like someone he was trying to save. The water was freezing. Tom swam clumsily out till he felt a change of temperature and depth. He checked the lamp and looked for the stone and was convinced: this was it. The blanket sack pulled under. She wanted to go, so he let her.

Lucas was trying to remember what the Scots called houses that had no chimneys. Black, a black house. It was getting too cold now for a fire outside his shed and so he'd have to fashion some kind of stove inside. He could bash a hole in the roof and stick an old tin through it.

His joints ached and he'd got the shakes. He lay on his mattress and listened to the night. It must be five o'clock by now, as he could hear the first lorries gearing up for their run down the High Street. The milk train trundled through, its rattle abstracted across the fields into a soft but unmistakeable burr. He waited for the shudder of the early workers' bus and then remembered that this was a Sunday.

Lucas planned to be up and making a brew by the first church bells, but he was fixed in a chilly torpor. When a man came stumbling through the door, he reached for his torch and turned it on, then blinked and blinked, unsure of what he was seeing, wondering even if this was a spirit come in from the fields: a man of clay, like they said. The man stood shaking in the middle of the hut, and in the time it took Lucas to haul himself up and think it out, he realised it was Tom.

He was soaked and bruised, and covered in a thin skin of something between earth and water. Lucas turned his torch to one side, but not before he saw that Tom had no boots on, just socks swollen to clods of mud. "Had a bit of an accident, lad?" Tom just gasped. Lucas pulled him down into the small pool of light.

"You'll be needing a blanket." Tom thought of her in her blanket, slipping away, in the right place. Lucas took his old army blanket off his mattress and wrapped it around Tom's shoulders. Then he made his way outside, took a slow difficult piss, and warmed his hands at the still glowing fire. He never let it go out and had piled it high before turning in that night. It was this light that Tom had seen across the fields and had made his way towards.

Behind the shed, under a plastic sheet, Lucas had a pile of kindling and wood that he'd scavenged or been given. It didn't take long to get a blaze going, and when he felt it warming him, Lucas went inside and got Tom. He sat him down on a log and went off to fill his kettle from the trough at the bottom of Stroud's field. He threw in several large pinches of tea, some sugar lumps, and the last half of an open tin of condensed milk, and boiled it up in the kettle together. Later, he'd go up to the yard to help himself to his egg.

Lucas gave Tom his mug and drank tea from a saucer. When the boy had finished, he started talking. "You remember, don't you, the Dip?" Tom's teeth rattled. Lucas nodded. "You knew my mother and me and Christie and our house and the church and the farm like it was yesterday, don't you?"

"Like it was yesterday," Lucas concurred. It was.

"All I've wanted is to put what I could back in place and then in my head it would be in place and I could get a bit of peace. You know that, don't you?"

Lucas had tried to concentrate, but the words came so fast that it was hard to follow what Tom was saying, so he held on to what felt most important. "Yes. Of course. Peace." Yellow was weakening the dark sky.

"I took her back there."

Lucas, who had been nodding vaguely as Tom spoke, stopped at this and wondered: "Took her back?"

"Back."

"Back?"

"Back home. I know now I can't go back, but she could, and that's enough."

"What have you done?" Lucas turned to face him, but Tom stared into the fire.

"She's there now back." When Lucas said nothing, Tom felt safe and able to explain. "You knew us all so you would understand, Lucas, I had to do something, everything was so out of place I couldn't go home, it was all wrong. Christie too so hating her, and I thought if she was at home at least one of us would be in the right place, because she should have been buried there but they put the concrete down and then the water. It's all I want, for her to rest in peace and me too to rest, you understand, don't you?"

"You mean Iris?"

"Iris?"

"You took Iris . . . home?"

"That's right, you understand, I carried my ma so carefully and worked it all out, the right place and how she would go down."

"You took her?"

"She was in the wrong place."

"That was her grave, son."

"But not her place."

The previous night's drink, the cold, the wet, the layers of newspaper and clothes, his aches and pains and deadenings made Lucas feel so far away that it took time for things to sink in. His first thought was, Of course, this is just one of the boy's hallucinations. How could he have dug up a coffin, disturbed a ten-year-old grave without anyone noticing? How could he have carried a body all the way to the water? Then again, when had he, Lucas, ever visited Iris's grave? And he knew that Father Barclay liked to encourage "wilderness." He was trying to persuade the Parish Council to think of the Catholic cemetery as a nature reserve. It was said he wanted to let Stroud put his sheep in there to graze when the grass needed cutting back.

Lucas could sense Tom's great energy and knew he could have dug up his mother's coffin with his bare hands if he'd wanted to and carried her bones all the way to the sea.

Remembering Iris, her sadness and her kindness, stirred something in Lucas. "You can't just go round digging up graves and carrying bodies about! That was your mother!"

Tom flinched. What was he doing? He had held it all so beautifully secret and now it had been given away to Lucas, who knew everything and told everything, who had pretended to understand. "You think I did wrong?" His fists were clenched in his pockets, the left one empty, the right one round his knife.

Lucas saw that the boy was no better. All that talk about him being best off where he belonged was nonsense. He'd been propped up these last six months by people who had no idea what was really going on in his head, family and friends who would not admit they weren't enough. Where to start? "You did wrong," he said.

It was enough. Allnorthover had given its judgement. Not good old Tom for seeing his mother right after all that work and care, but bad Tom, mad Tom. The pounding certainty upon which Tom had depended these last few weeks drained from him. All that was left was the village and its judgement given by this filthy, raddled old man whom no one turned away. Tom couldn't stand the reproach in that sloppy face, those rheumy eyes. Poor Tom. Mad, laughable Tom.

"You think I'm not right . . . in my head . . ." He was speaking hesitantly again.

"You're apt to fix on something, get it all out of shape."

"But my ma. I had to do right by my ma!"

Lucas sighed. "Your mother knew what she was doing. To her, the Dip was a trap."

"She loved it there! We loved it!"

Lucas kicked at the fire, stirring it up, thinking of another pot of tea. Tom needed to be told now. "You did, yes. What I'm trying to say is that you mustn't go on troubling yourself for her sake. Giving away the house to someone who would let it go was her way of—" Lucas was overtaken by a booming, rackety cough that left him spluttering for breath. His yellow tongue waggled in his wide-open toothless mouth as he brought up thick brown phlegm. His eyes streamed.

Tom poured all the disgust he had been made to feel about himself onto this pathetic old man. "How do you know?"

"We were friends, boy. You remember?" Lucas after the war, bright, shaky, moving from job to job but always turning up for Sunday tea. Another cuckoo. Tom was restless, angry now, his energy returning, his left hand tapping against the log on which he sat, his right hand opening and shutting the knife.

"Maybe so but you . . . didn't know her, understand her like I did. That's why I came . . . home from university, why I stayed, she needed me!"

Why couldn't Lucas stop himself? Why did he need to claim Iris now? "You were troubled, lad. It was you as needed her." Then, as if that wasn't enough, because he was angry: "You should have left her where she was! She had a terrible painful death and she was at rest! Not being bundled about the place just to give you a happy ending! You should have gone to her in the hospital when she needed you, not now! She doesn't need you now!"

Tom broke. He couldn't stand those eyes anymore and how wrong they made him feel. He pushed them away, pushed Lucas away with his right hand, in which there was his knife, now open, and it was the blade not his fingers that jabbed and jabbed, taking away the old man's sight.

Valerie had wanted to help Mary indoors, explain her shock to Stella, and make sure she was cared for. "You've had a nasty fall," she insisted, remembering how for one long second it had looked as if the girl was floating not falling, but that must have been when her jacket caught. Mary had almost shouted that she wanted nothing said, no one was to know, to forget it, just forget it. She had leapt out of the car, run indoors, and got into bed.

Mary had no trouble sleeping now. She wanted to stay in bed for ever. It was better than trying to do anything, because things always went wrong, especially when she tried to do what was right and it turned out not to be. Other people seemed to know what was right, and then they didn't.

It had all been so stupid. The tree had been far too slippery, but she hadn't felt able to say anything, to just climb down and say no, not even when the rain grew so heavy. There had been that bare patch, a knot and a stumble, then Billy's jacket catching on a branch and snapping it but breaking her fall, tugging her back and giving her time to reach up and catch hold. Valerie had come running, crawled out along the bough, helped her up, and coaxed her back.

That man had just stayed where he was, and was still smiling as they drove back (Valerie chalk-faced, the bones of her tiny fingers standing out as she grasped the steering wheel, saying "Sorry, sorry, sorry"). Mary was sick of him. He might look like some kind of martyr, but he was just mad. So what if everyone had known him all their lives and he was "Iris's boy"? He was a loony, like Julie said.

Mary's secret wasn't what anyone thought at all, nothing that meant anything, just emptiness. That was what she was looking for now, and she was relieved to be so weak and feverish. It left her mind free to wander and kept everyone else away. Mim spent most of the day lying at her feet like an anchor, not even stirring when the buses came through. It was the only contact Mary wanted. Stella fluttered in and out, saying less and less. Dr. Clough visited on the Monday. He didn't ask her any questions, so she told him things, not about that man and the water, but about fear and helplessness, and crying all the time and getting everything wrong. He didn't make a fuss or say much, which helped.

In her room at the back of the house, with her windows closed and curtains drawn, Mary got a sense of something happening in the village. There was more traffic and noise, more voices and comings and goings on the Green. The tone of the place was different. People kept knocking at the door. Mary heard the doctor insisting to Stella that first she must be left to recover, explanations could come later, something about giving a statement and something about shock. He prescribed tablets for her fever, which Mary liked because they thickened her sleep.

When Mary did wake up, she remembered the way the world had turned over, so she had been half-falling, half-clinging to the bough, looking up into deep water. She'd seen that there was nothing in it, no house or church or farm. It was just empty water. As Valerie hauled her up and steadied her, the sky swung back over her head and it, too, was empty. Nothing was holding Mary in place. She would never walk out over the water again.

Her parents came in together during one half-sleep, or she

dreamt they did. They spoke at the same time, even sounding alike and saying her name, all her names over and over: "Mary, Mary Fairy, Mary Mystery, Miss Mary, Mary Mary Quite Contrary, Merry Mary Blackberry . . ." She could feel the rough chill of her father's hand on her burning arm and her mother's cool fingers raking her hair and, in her drowsiness, felt as if she were flowing in both directions. Later, when she woke and the room was empty, she called for her mother and was going to ask about her father's visit but didn't, in case it hadn't been real.

Julie came, in her waitress's uniform, on the way to her evening shift. She sat Mary up and puffed her pillows, brought in a flannel and washed her face. "You must be filthy, lying about in this heap of blankets all day! Says you've been rotting away since Saturday night! That's two days, you lazy cow!" She had brought sweets—the ones they'd shared as children: milk bottles, black jacks, fruit salads, foamy pink shrimps, and rubbery teeth—and Mary ate them. Julie put on a record, The Supremes, and tried each of Mary's perfumes on herself before choosing one for her patient. She dabbed Mary's wrists and temples with 4711 cologne, because it smelt "healthy and refreshing." She had a tale to tell.

She went into it thinking Mary already knew, then realised, to her horror, that no one had dared tell her. Tom Hepple had dug up his mother's body and sunk her in the Dip, then he'd stabbed Lucas in the eyes. Tom had been found the next morning by Charlie Spooner, one of the hands out on Stroud's farm, dragging Lucas across a flooded field. Charlie had thought Tom was struggling with some animal that was sick or dead. He'd gone over to help and had stopped at the edge of a pool, in the middle of which Tom had stopped, too. Charlie said the morning had been bright and the floodwater like a mirror that Tom was staring down into. He had kept hold of Lucas's sleeve with one hand, and took no notice of the blood leaking from his half-submerged body. Before Charlie could think what to do, Tom saw him, howled, and ran, and Charlie had waded in to drag whatever it was out. Only then did he realise it was human. He knew Lucas by his coat and covered his face as soon as he saw it. He'd run up to Stroud's and rung the police, and Constable Belcher had followed Tom's chaotic tracks out to the Dip. It was said that when he was found he had been almost dead himself, half-drowned and half-buried, halfway into or out of the water.

Julie told Mary all this as plainly as she could, not entirely able to resist its drama. She was astonished that Stella had encouraged her to visit, knowing she was bound to say something, couldn't not.

Somewhere between the hut and the field, Lucas had died. All sorts of people had been asked to make statements.

It was so much for Mary to take in that she started with something easy. "How's Christie taking it?"

Julie flushed. Mary remembered and bit her lip. "How'd I know?" Julie's retort was too quick.

Mary was direct. "I saw you. On the Common. Halloween. Not really saw you, but enough."

Julie was agitated. "What did you see?" Christie raising his wet, buried head; Julie's head thrown back. Mary said nothing. "So, Mary George! Because I'm blond and have got a bit of a mouth on me, you think I'm a slag?"

"No!" And she really didn't. "I didn't know what to think!"

Julie was hurt, but she laughed. "Well, think what the fuck you like, girl. Yeah, he's come after me, says he's in love with me, God knows. He talks and I don't really listen. These days, he just cries." Christie's wet face. "I babysat the twins a lot last year when I was finishing school, and he used to drop me home. The first time he tried it on, I was petrified! I didn't know how to get him to stop without being rude!"

"What about Sophie?"

"What about her? Sophie's great!"

"Well, then?"

"They don't anymore."

Mary said gently, "I should think they do."

Julie shrugged. "Yeah. Reckon they do."

The pause that followed brought back Tom and Lucas. Mary grasped Julie's hand and they sat in silence. Beyond the facts there was nothing that could safely be discussed. The smallest "what if" would open a door from which an avalanche of events, connections, and secrets would fall. It would flatten them all. Instead, Mary absorbed the truth. She was grateful to Julie for being straight with her, so when the next shadow crossed her mind, she offered it up immediately.

"Do you know there were letters? Hate mail or whatever."

"Hate mail? To Tom Hepple, you mean?"

"No, to his mum."

Mary had hidden the letters in her room. She fetched them now and laid each envelope in front of Julie, pointing at the name, address, and date. "See? See?"

Julie frowned. "I don't get it."

"Iris Hepple was dead. That New Year. I checked again on her gravestone." Mary tried to remember the grave in that overgrown corner of the Catholic cemetery as having been disturbed. She couldn't, though; she'd never have noticed.

Julie picked the first letter up and Mary nudged her. "Go on." She watched Julie read all five, her expression changing from embarrassed amusement to shock, pity, and disgust.

"Who would do this?"

"That's the thing, Julie. It was my mum!"

Julie shook her head vigorously. "No! Oh no, not your mum, never in a million years!"

Mary explained about the typewriter, and Julie thought for a bit and then sat up. "Of course! I know who it was! Mary, where was that typewriter kept after your dad did his moonlight flit?"

"It sat around in the chapel and then Mum brought it down here. But it wasn't my dad, you can see that from what's said!"

"When did she bring it here?"

"How would I remember? Some time later . . ."

"How much later?"

"Maybe years later."

Julie asked, "Who really hated Iris Hepple?"

"My mum. She took Dad away from us."

"Maybe so, but do you know who else hated her?" Mary shook her head. Julie whispered it: "Christie."

"How do you know?"

"From Sophie first. We had a chat, see, when she realised what Christie was up to."

"And she told you he hated his mother?"

"Said he hated her, too."

"But you think they still, you know . . ."

"I don't think he hates her. He's bloody awful to her, though."

"Wasn't she angry with you?"

"Just sad, really. Nice, even. Concerned for me, oddly enough."

"She was right to be."

"I know that now, but I thought I knew it all then. I laughed all the way home, but God, I was scared. She thinks she put an end to it. I thought she had, too, but after Tom came back, Christie started coming round me again."

There were several things Mary didn't understand, so she tried to ask about them together. "If he hates Sophie and hated his mother, why is he so mad about you? Won't he end up hating you, too?"

Julie stuck to the least personal point. "Sophie was right about that, you know, it wasn't just her saying it. It comes out when he cries, like when Tom got sick again or was in that crash with our Kevin. I was crying that time, too. Halloween, I mean, when you saw us. I didn't know if Kevin would even walk again, but Christie sort of took over. Anyway, sometimes it was about Iris and . . . well . . . your dad. He's got some bloody weird ideas about them. You know, when there was the first talk of the water, Christie offered to build her a new home, up out of the Dip. She said he was not an architect, or something, and laughed in his face, and he spat in hers, Sophie said."

"Will you stop it, Julie?"

"Oh, I think it'll stop itself now Tom's going to be gone."

"Gone?"

"He'll go to prison or one of those hospital prisons, won't he?"

"And not come back?"

"I shouldn't think so. Anyway, I'll be gone, too."

"Where?"

"I've wasted enough time helping Barry run his business while having to wear this tarty outfit and getting the pay to match."

"Are you going to come back to school?"

"Not a chance! I'm going to get some proper business training, a course in London next year. After that, I want to set up with our Trevor."

"Furniture?"

"Antiques. He's been doing well enough out of his reproduction stuff, but this place is swimming in the real thing! I've persuaded him to start dealing in the proper stuff, to work on some of his contacts."

Mary was exhausted. "I'd better get a bit of rest."

"I'll be off to work," Julie said.

As she was going, Julie prodded the letters and said, "You know, Mary, your mother's a daft bitch for not warning me you didn't know about Lucas and all that. She's weird and moody, and dresses like she should be dancing round under a full moon, but how could you ever have thought she'd do something like this?"

Mary didn't know what to say.

The local reporters banged on front doors, and if no one answered, they went away, whereas those from the national papers, the television and radio, pushed notes through letterboxes and waited. Sophie took the twins to her mother's, saying she'd be back for Christmas. Mary returned to school on the Wednesday, leaving by the garden gate and meeting up in Low Lane with Julie and June and the others. While reporters loitered at the bus stop, Father Barclay and Father

Swann, Dr. Burgess and a retired commuter, a lawyer, ferried the children out of the village and dropped them off at a stop well past the Dip.

Christie gave the police the keys to the chapel and they cordoned it off; Lucas's hut, too. Stark flash photographs of his shed, his stained mattress, the bucket and bin bags, the bloody rags and rat droppings in the corners appeared in the papers, and the village was ashamed that people would think they had let one of their own live like that. No one outside would know that Lucas had insisted. The pictures of Tom, too, snatched headshots of him being led in handcuffs from a car through a door, his bleached-out face and wavering eyes, made it obvious that the man was dangerously disturbed. But they knew him, didn't they?

The journalists circled the field where Charlie Spooner had found them and tried to open the rusted gate in the fence around the reservoir. Both sites were being minutely examined by men in plastic suits.

The day of Lucas's funeral was as bitter and still as that of Iris's had been. Once again, Mary, Stella, and Matthew George were there together. When Mary's father had turned up at the house, Stella hadn't looked surprised. No one in the village batted an eyelid. They said cheerful hellos and patted and pulled him in, just as they had Tom. Mary was amazed to see him so at home in the village, and now walking into church with her and her mum. She could take in nothing of Father Swann's service, nor of the many things said about Lucas's life. Dr. Burgess and Judge Smallbone spoke, as well as one of the dominoes players, someone from the Royal Legion, and more people Mary recognised but couldn't put a name to. They were all people she had grown up among, in a small place where it was possible for paths to cross without trace.

There was a tea in the Village Hall, with Constable Belcher on the door, letting in only those he knew. Afterwards, Matthew said he had to go and Mary walked back to the house with him. He went straight over to his car, gave her a big hug, and asked if she'd like to come for Christmas.

"You know, Dad. Now that it's all, now that he's, I mean, couldn't you . . ." She could hardly form the words "come back."

Matthew bent down, as if she were still a child, and laid his hands on her shoulders. "I didn't leave the village because of Tom Hepple."

"Because of the house, then? The reservoir?"

"No."

Mary turned away before he could tell her more. "I'll see you in the New Year, then, Dad." She walked quickly off. "Around. Whatever."

The next day, the press disappeared and the village began to emerge once more.

On the last day of term, Billy and June approached Mary in the sixth form common room and asked her if she wanted to come down to Terry Flux's Christmas party at The Stands with them that night. Crêpe streamers and paper chains drooped across the prefab's low ceiling, and someone had tried to spray Merry Christmas across the windows in fake snow but had run out of space.

Mary was struck by how alike Billy and June looked now, their expressions and how they dressed and stood. Billy's hair had been shaved again and June's was a nest of plaits and beads. Mary was touched, both by her friends (who were holding hands quite casually) and by their invitation. When June went off to a class, Mary was embarrassed to realise that she was still wearing Billy's leather jacket.

She took it off. "Give it to June."

Billy smiled. "No. Keep it, George. It suits you."

"You're in a generous mood, Eyre! Must be love!"

He threw the jacket back at her. "Fuck off!" Mary caught his smile, his happiness, and was glad for him, although sorry to be losing him and sorry, too, that she hadn't noticed.

. . .

Mary thought all day about whether or not to go to The Stands, and if she should go alone or with Billy and June. What she was trying not to think about was the possibility of bumping into Daniel. It had been weeks now since she had seen him, and although there had been no proper ending, it appeared that they had stopped. She dreamed her way through her classes just as she had as a child and, when the last bell rang, went to the toilets, squeezed some soap into her hair, sprinkled on a little water, and back-combed it. The girls in the salon dyed it regularly now, and she was getting good at messing it up as soon as she got home, using soap or sugar, hairspray, and a fine-toothed metal comb. She could pencil in her eyebrows, line her eyes, and paint her mouth in a matter of minutes, and she carried her compact of white face powder everywhere.

Mary walked out of school into the dark afternoon. She crossed the road and went into the park, then the playground, where she saw some kids, too old for it but younger than she, thirteen or so, lounging on the swings and smoking. Unseen, Mary withdrew and continued down towards the river. She turned up the collar of Billy's jacket and wrapped her scarf round her chin. Her eyes stung in the icy air but did not water, and she was warm enough in her father's long shirt, a pinstriped jumble-sale waistcoat, her mohair cardigan, flannel trousers, and big boots. At the river she sat down on a bench and lit a cigarette.

Camptown wasn't built on the Wene but had grown up beside it. Here at the edge of the park, the river was shallow and sluggish, frothy with chemical waste. Pale reeds grew just taller than the dead grass. The asphalt path that ran from the gate by the school to the gate by the industrial estate crossed over a little bridge here. Several people passed, cycling slowly home, by which Mary supposed the time to be after five o'clock. The lamps that lit the path cast a dingy pink light across the water. Mary considered the flatness of the town, of it being neither one thing nor the other, and wanted more than ever to get out. She didn't feel scared now, or even excited or impatient, just clear.

When she had decided what to do, she walked the long way round, past the bowling green and the boating lake and out onto the bypass link road, where she doubled back on herself, following the broad curve of the Market Road back into town. It was past seven when she arrived outside Daniel's house. He answered the door.

"Are you coming out?" Her voice was muffled behind her scarf.

"Yes." He stepped back into the hall, called out something to his mother, and returned with his coat and a new homburg. Mary took his arm firmly as they crossed town, reaching The Stands in what felt like a matter of minutes. She tried to think of things to say, but nothing that had been happening to her had anything to do with him. Daniel was tentative and treated her carefully.

Her name had not been mentioned in the papers. Valerie had kept her promise not to tell anyone about that afternoon, and it certainly didn't matter now. Even so, Mary had no idea what Daniel knew and didn't know, so she couldn't work out how to be with him.

Terry Flux set aside his planned first few records. The kids literally needed a warm-up; they had been queuing outside for over an hour and could also do with a reminder that school was over. He went straight for punk and decided to push it, to keep the speed up all night.

When The Stands closed at eleven, the audience staggered out, filthy, sweating, exhausted, and excited, and feeling such a sense of camaraderie that they called good night to people they barely knew. Mary and Daniel reached the pavement and stopped. They had been all right inside. Now what?

Billy and June went by smiling and waved as they set off on the bike. Then Clara appeared and put her arms round them both. "Lovely to see you! Well, I'm off!"

She solved it for Mary, who shouted after her, "How are you getting back?" Clara turned and raised her thumb, and Mary said to Daniel, "She can't hitch back alone, I'll go with her, good night!"

Daniel held her. "I'm glad you came round. It was good to see you. I'm sorry about all that, when you were upset and I didn't understand. I don't understand really, but it was lovely . . . to see you." Mary stared into his eyes. He wants me, she thought, and let herself believe it. She still wanted to go home, but wanted to leave him something so he'd know she hadn't meant to disappear again. While he kissed her, she tugged a gold sleeper from her ear and pushed it into his pocket, then ran to catch up with Clara.

They walked up to the Malibu Motel roundabout, Clara chattering on about T., whose coat she was wearing again, about how he wasn't remotely interested in music or clothes. He talked about the weather, and land and water, how one became the other, and what he told her made her want to paint and paint.

They stopped at the first lay-by on the Allnorthover road, close enough to the roundabout to be seen by drivers before they found it too much of a bother to stop.

"So, how is it?" Clara asked with her usual intensity.

"The village?" Mary countered.

"God, no! That's all too awful to think about. I mean you, you and Dan?"

"Nothing." As Mary said it, she knew it. "I mean, it's gone, I think, I don't know."

"Poor you." Clara's face was so at odds with her expressed concern that Mary resisted it. "I'd be surprised if you could feel anything much at all at the moment."

That made sense. She said nothing, still confused by this glamorous, volatile, ugly, mesmerising enemy/friend. She decided to be more careful, and to wait and see what she felt.

They got a lift from a peculiar little man in a stripped-down green car, who pulled out of the Malibu Motel. He said he was a lawyer and had been to a client's drinks party, a local government team. He lived in Camptown but had seen the girls with their thumbs out and felt like a spin. By the time they got to the Verges, he was trying to persuade them to come back into town, to his "studio flat," for a Christmas drink and a bit of fun. He could show them his new "hi-fi."

Mary and Clara sat in the back, too uproariously amused to be frightened as the car slewed across the road. Just before they came into the Verges, it coughed to a stop. "No petrol," the man said flatly.

Clara nudged Mary. "We'll go get you some. We know a place, oh, just over there . . ." and they jumped out and began walking down the road. The man followed and caught Clara by the shoulder, letting his hand slip down onto her breast. She drew back from his milky, beery breath and shouted "Fuck off!" in his face. The girls hurried on and he followed again, baying incoherently.

Mary couldn't stand it. "Come on, let's run!" She could make out a gate, and they scrambled over it. The man was still behind them, and he sounded angry now. "You little tarts! Come back!" They heard him crash into the gate and give a loud grunt as he fell over the other side.

"Fucking creep!" Clara screamed, and she grabbed Mary's hand as they ran out into a ploughed and frozen field. They lost the footpath almost immediately and stumbled on, as best they could, from one gouged furrow to the next, falling and laughing until the road and the man were far behind them and they were nowhere.

Mary was woken up the next morning by Clara's little brother Freddie. "Tea?" He held out a cup. He was wearing a red silk dressing gown that trailed a good yard behind him. Mary was in his bed.

"It was most kind of you to give me your room." She spoke to the child as if he were an old man, as everyone did.

He shrugged, graciously. "Not at all. I gather that when you and Clara arrived home, I was in any case in with my parents. I walk, you see, in my sleep and sometimes I end up there." He turned and left. Mary could hear music coming through the wall from Tobias's room. She leant back against the black wall painted with lightning. She looked up at the ceiling and was startled to see that she had slept beneath an enormous round yellow face, a sun split by a smile.

The snow that fell that week was heavy enough to cover everything. It piled up in drifts against the hedgerows and turned the High Street and the Green into a continuous expanse of white in which every journey from house to house or shop or anywhere was recorded. Walls and fences were blurred by slopes of snow that soaked up what little noise remained when there was no traffic and most people were indoors. The snow joined everything together and lay across every roof.

Mary had meant to go into Camptown on Christmas Eve and meet Daniel for a drink, but the roads were closed. She didn't mind, not even when all there was to do was walk down to the Arms and hope that the landlord would realise that she had to be more or less eighteen by now, would be, in fact, in a couple of months' time. Valerie would serve her. Before going to the pub, she watched a music show on television. The reception was poor and the picture warped and disintegrated, but she could hear it. One of the bands was the trio of girls that Terry Flux had put on at the Odeon. He'd got Mary to buy their record, and there they were on the cover, sticking up their fingers and sneering—just brilliant.

By the time Mary reached the Arms, the public bar was packed, so she hovered in the porch. Someone was playing the piano and people were singing. She caught sight of Billy and June, all four Laceys (Trevor, Julie, Martin, and Kevin, who was still on crutches), Sophie and Christie, and, to her surprise, Stella, wearing a paper hat and duetting with Edna as they sat together on a settle near the fire. Several people caught sight of Mary, smiled, waved, and gestured her over, but she felt, with horror, that everyone there was stuck together and that if she entered the room, she would never leave. There was no space, anyway, not even a gap left by those who were missing—her dad, Lucas, and Tom.

Mary walked down the middle of the High Street. The snow lit the night and opened up the village. For once it seemed spacious. Mary felt as serious, sad, and calm as she had the day Julie told her about how Lucas had died. What could she have done? What could she do?

The police cordon around the chapel had sunk into the snow

that had settled in a high drift against the front of the building, almost reaching the window. A narrow path had been cut to the door and was half filled in again, but Mary managed to make her way along it. She scraped the door open a few inches and squeezed inside. She felt around for the light switch and found it, and a bulb that hung through the floorboards above came on. There was a heap of paper in the middle of the room and Mary felt excited. This must be evidence. There might be clues the police had missed. She wanted to work out her part in it all, or part of the truth at least.

The room had the deep cold of a place left empty for a long time. Mary turned on the bar heater and, when that wasn't enough, turned up the wicks on the paraffin heaters and lit them, too. There was a blanket on the floor that she wrapped around her shoulders.

Midnight Mass in the Catholic church was packed. Judge Smallbone played the organ, just as he did every Sunday, and the choir endeavoured to follow him. Father Barclay loved his congregation and never failed to be moved by the judge's arthritic but dogged performance, or the cracking voices and shambolic descants of the ageing singers. Only half of those there were regular attendees. The others had rolled out of the pubs and stumbled off the last bus, or had torn themselves away from the television. They stood up throughout the service, swaying and blearily singing the carols they half-remembered, their eyes wet with sentimental goodwill. Father Barclay's eyes were wet, too, but he was thinking of Tom Hepple and Lucas, and what the village of Allnorthover might really mean or be. He went into the service as nervous as ever, stuttering and hesitating, losing his place on the page or, when he extemporised, his train of thought. He broke into a sweat and felt his voice disappearing, but got through it somehow and with some sense of how much his congregation loved him back. There was too much incense and not enough wafers for Holy Communion, and the inevitable bleats from the drunks when they got to "Lamb of God." At the Sign of Peace, though, everyone calmed down and solemnly shook hands with their neighbours. Father Barclay wandered the aisle, greeting whomsoever he could and getting so involved in exchanges of good wishes that he almost forgot to go back up to the altar.

Dr. and Mrs. Clough were regular attendees. They arrived just before the service started with their three youngest children, all, except the doctor, in foreign-looking fur coats. Their eldest son, Tobias, arrived late and saw the church was full. He was relieved, having enjoyed the slow walk across the village alone, and turned back immediately.

The pavement edge of the High Street was puddled with footprints, but one person had taken to the middle of the road and walked straight out of the village. Tobias followed the prints.

The papers were a mess, but among those spilling out of the filing cabinet Mary recognised both Matthew's writing and Stella's. She pulled these sheets out first and was dismayed to find they were only old invoices, receipts, records, and accounts. She reached back into the cabinet to see what else there was, but whatever Mary found, she knew about already.

Disappointed, she turned her attention to the heaps in the middle of the floor. The first page she picked up was crammed with numbers, diagrams, and, in several places, what might have been her name. It was hard to tell, as the writing was so small and difficult to read. Every bit of space had been used, and on some sheets the filled page had been turned sideways and new lines added at right angles, like stitches running over and under. The next sheet she picked up had a list of times and places on it and, again, her name. There were long passages that appeared to have been copied from old books. They were legal or historical, about land and property. There were sketches of maps on which she could make out local names, but the shapes were so askew that they could have been foreign countries. Even the puddles of wax on the floor were scratched with figures or letters.

Mary got up and wandered round, peering through the little

windows at the snow and thinking that if this place didn't make her think of that madman, that murderer, it would be a good place to be. The snow would soon swallow it up. She opened and shut the cupboards above the sink, struck by how empty they were, turned the taps on and off, and jumped as the geyser ignited. Then she saw an odd collection of things on a shelf. She picked up the puddle of wax and shuddered as she remembered her foot sinking into the warm pool when she and Daniel had thought the chapel was on fire. There were her old glasses, too, the ones with the cracked lens that had been knocked off at the bottom of the Clock House drive. How had he found them and known they were hers? This was creepy.

Then the photograph. It was one Matthew had taken of her during another winter of snow. She had her hair in plaits and was wearing what she'd called her "cherry best coat." Tom had torn out her eyes. Lucas. Mary's first thought was to run and get Stella, to give her the photo and let her tell the police, but then she thought of how it would put her back at the centre of things when she'd managed, at last, to get to the edge.

She crouched by the bar fire and held the photograph in front of it until the picture blistered and turned black. Then she gathered up the bits of paper with her name on them and began to light them with matches, but this was too slow. She made a little heap, quite carefully, on the floor, and cleared a space around it. She lit the corner of one sheet with a match. It did not catch, so she unscrewed the lid to the well of one of the heaters and splashed a little paraffin onto it. This time when she lit the match there was a whoosh of flame and the heap burned quickly down to cinders. Mary decided to get rid of the filing cabinet stuff, too, all Stella and Matthew's boring old history. The next fire was bigger and burned longer, and while it was still smouldering, she decided to check upstairs.

The window was covered in blue paper, which Mary ripped down, taken aback to see nothing behind it but familiar glass. The bed was tidily made or not slept in, and piles of clothes and books were laid out in lines around it. The shelves that edged the gallery were bare. Disappointed she started back down the stairs.

As she reached the bottom step, she saw that the smouldering pile she had left was now tall flames, and just as she was making herself believe this and working out how to get round it and out, there was a muffled but powerful bang as one of the heaters exploded. The force of it threw Mary back against the wall. The light went out.

Too dazed to move, she was hypnotised by the blinding centre of the fire. It was such a pure light. She did not notice its edges spread, nor would she have cared, but her body was holding her breath, and when it insisted, she gulped for air and choked on scalding smoke. Her body took over and pushed her away from the fire, back up the stairs, unable to think where she was going or what she was going to do. The smoke was crawling up through the floorboards. Mary crouched where she was, quite content to watch this astonishing spectacle, staring at the window at the other end of the gallery, illuminated by the flames below but gradually disappearing behind smoke. For a long time Mary did nothing but wait. Then another explosion rocked the building and threw her forwards and she was moving, then running, jumping, flying.

There were two things that Mary remembered and told no one. The first was the stillness of the moment in which the window billowed and held her, and how it was long enough for her to realise what was happening, so that when the glass exploded and she fell, she wasn't afraid. The second thing was that when she opened her eyes and found herself lying in the snow, there had been someone lying beside her, holding her head in his hands, and this had brought her such peace that despite her shock and pain, she was angry when the village came towards them with all its noise.

# Acknowledgements

The author would like to thank the Harold Hyam Wingate Foundation for the scholarship given to support the writing of this book and the K. Blundell Trust for assistance in the early stages.